# The Short Stories of Aphra Behn

Volume I

Aphra Behn was a prolific and well established writer but facts about her remain scant and difficult to confirm. What can safely be said though is that Aphra Behn is now regarded as a key English playwright and a major figure in Restoration theatre

Aphra was born into the rising tensions to the English Civil War. Obviously a time of much division and difficulty as the King and Parliament, and their respective forces, came ever closer to conflict.

There are claims she was a spy, that she travelled abroad, possibly as far as Surinam.

By 1664 her marriage was over (though by death or separation is not known but presumably the former as it occurred in the year of their marriage) and she now used Mrs Behn as her professional name.

Aphra now moved towards pursuing a more sustainable and substantial career and began work for the King's Company and the Duke's Company players as a scribe.

Previously her only writing had been poetry but now she would become a playwright. Her first, "The Forc'd Marriage", was staged in 1670, followed by "The Amorous Prince" (1671). After her third play, "The Dutch Lover", Aphra had a three year lull in her writing career. Again it is speculated that she went travelling again, possibly once again as a spy.

After this sojourn her writing moves towards comic works, which prove commercially more successful. Her most popular works included "The Rover" and "Love-Letters Between a Nobleman and His Sister" (1684–87).

With her growing reputation Aphra became friends with many of the most notable writers of the day. This is The Age of Dryden and his literary dominance.

From the mid 1680's Aphra's health began to decline.  This was exacerbated by her continual state of debt and descent into poverty.

Aphra Behn died on April 16th 1689, and is buried in the East Cloister of Westminster Abbey. The inscription on her tombstone reads: "Here lies a Proof that Wit can never be Defence enough against Mortality." She was quoted as stating that she had led a "life dedicated to pleasure and poetry."

## Index of Contents

The Adventure of the Black Lady
The Court of the King of Bantam
The Unfortunate Happy Lady: A True History
The Fair Jilt
Oroonoko; or, The Royal Slave
Agnes De Castro
Aphra Behn – A Short Biography
Aphra Behn – A Concise Bibliography

# THE ADVENTURE OF THE BLACK LADY

About the Beginning of last June (as near as I can remember) Bellamora came to Town from Hampshire, and was obliged to lodge the first Night at the same Inn where the Stage-Coach set up. The next Day she took Coach for Covent-Garden, where she thought to find Madam Brightly, a Relation of hers, with whom she design'd to continue for about half a Year undiscover'd, if possible, by her Friends in the Country: and order'd therefore her Trunk, with her Clothes, and most of her Money and Jewels, to be brought after her to Madame Brightly's by a strange Porter, whom she spoke to in the Street as she was taking Coach; being utterly unacquainted with the neat Practices of this fine City. When she came to Bridges-Street, where indeed her Cousin had lodged near three or four Years since, she was strangely surprized that she could not learn anything of her; no, nor so much as meet with anyone that had ever heard of her Cousin's Name: Till, at last, describing Madam Brightly to one of the House-keepers in that Place, he told her, that there was such a kind of Lady, whom he had sometimes seen there about a Year and a half ago; but that he believed she was married and remov'd towards Soho. In this Perplexity she quite forgot her Trunk and Money, &c, and wander'd in her Hackney-Coach all over St. Anne's Parish; inquiring for Madam Brightly, still describing her Person, but in vain; for no Soul could give her any Tale or Tidings of such a Lady. After she had thus fruitlessly rambled, till she, the Coachman, and the very Horses were even tired, by good Fortune for her, she happen'd on a private House, where lived a good, discreet, ancient Gentlewoman, who was fallen to Decay, and forc'd to let Lodgings for the best Part of her Livelihood: From whom she understood, that there was such a kind of Lady, who had lain there somewhat more than a Twelvemonth, being near three Months after she was married; but that she was now gone abroad with the Gentleman her Husband, either to the Play, or to take the fresh Air; and she believ'd would not return till Night. This Discourse of the Good Gentlewoman's so elevated Bellamora's drooping Spirits, that after she had beg'd the liberty of staying there till they came home, she discharg'd the Coachman in all haste, still forgetting her Trunk, and the more valuable Furniture of it.

When they were alone, Bellamora desired she might be permitted the Freedom to send for a Pint of Sack; which, with some little Difficulty, was at last allow'd her. They began then to chat for a matter of half an Hour of things indifferent: and at length the ancient Gentlewoman ask'd the fair Innocent (I must not say foolish) one, of what Country, and what her Name was: to both which she answer'd directly and truly, tho' it might have prov'd not discreetly. She then enquir'd of Bellamora if her Parents were living, and the Occasion of her coming to Town. The fair unthinking Creature reply'd, that her Father and Mother were both dead; and that she had escap'd from her Uncle, under the pretence of making a Visit to a young Lady, her Cousin, who was lately married, and liv'd above twenty Miles from her Uncle's, in the Road to London, and that the Cause of her quitting the Country, was to avoid the hated Importinities of a Gentleman, whose pretended Love to her she fear'd had been her eternal Ruin. At which she wept and sigh'd most extravagantly. The discreet Gentlewoman endeavour'd to comfort her by all the softest and most powerful Arguments in her Capacity; promising her all the friendly Assistance that she could expect from her, during Bellamora's stay in Town: which she did with so much Earnestness, and visible Integrity, that the pretty innocent Creature was going to make her a full and real Discovery of her imaginary insupportable Misfortunes; and (doubtless) had done it, had she not been prevented by the Return of the Lady, whom she hop'd to have found her Cousin Brightly. The Gentleman, her Husband just saw her within Doors, and order'd the Coach to drive to some of his Bottle-Companions; which gave the Women the better Opportunity of entertaining one another, which happen'd to be with some Surprize on all Sides. As the Lady was going up into her Apartment, the Gentlewoman of the House told her there was a young Lady in the Parlour, who came out of the Country that very Day on purpose to visit her: The Lady stept immediately to see who it was, and Bellamora approaching to receive her hop'd-for Cousin, stop'd on the sudden just as she came to her; and sigh'd out aloud, Ah, Madam! I am lost. It is not your Ladyship I seek. No, Madam (return'd the other) I am apt to think you did not intend me this Honour. But you are as welcome to me, as you could be to the dearest of your Acquaintance: Have you forgot me, Madame Bellamora? (continued she.) That Name startled the other: However, it was with a kind of Joy. Alas! Madam, (replied the young one) I now remember that I have been so happy to have seen you; but where and when, my Memory can't tell me. 'Tis indeed some Years since, (return'd the Lady) But of that another time. Mean while, if you are unprovided of a Lodging, I dare undertake, you shall be welcome to this Gentlewoman. The Unfortunate returned her Thanks; and whilst a Chamber was preparing for her, the Lady entertain'd her in her own. About Ten o'Clock they parted, Bellamora being conducted to her Lodging by the Mistress of the House, who then left her to take what Rest she could amidst her so many Misfortunes; returning to the other Lady, who desir'd her to search into the Cause of Bellamora's Retreat to Town.

The next Morning the good Gentlewoman of the House coming up to her, found Bellamora almost drown'd in Tears, which by many kind and sweet Words she at last stopp'd; and asking whence so great Signs of Sorrow should proceed, vow'd a most profound Secrecy if she would discover to her their Occasion; which, after some little Reluctancy, she did, in this manner.

I was courted (said she) above three Years ago, when my Mother was yet living, by one Mr. Fondlove, a Gentleman of good Estate, and true Worth; and one who, I dare believe, did then really love me: He continu'd his Passion for me, with all the earnest and honest Sollicitations imaginable, till some Months before my Mother's Death; who, at that time, was most desirous to see me disposed of in Marriage to another Gentleman, of much better Estate than Mr. Fondlove; but one whose Person and Humour did by no means hit with my Inclinations: And this gave Fondlove the unhappy Advantage over me. For, finding me one Day all alone in my Chamber, and lying on my Bed, in as mournful and wretched a Condition to my then foolish Apprehension, as now I am, he urged his Passion with such Violence, and accursed Success for me, with reiterated Promises of Marriage, whensoever I pleas'd to challenge 'em, which he bound with the most sacred Oaths, and most dreadful Execrations: that partly with my Aversion to the other, and partly with my Inclinations to pity him, I ruin'd my self. Here she relaps'd into a greater Extravagance of Grief than before; which was so extreme that it did not continue long. When therefore she was pretty well come to herself, the antient Gentlewoman ask'd her, why she imagin'd herself ruin'd: To which she answer'd, I am great with Child by him, Madam, and wonder you did not perceive it last Night. Alas! I have not a Month to go: I am asham'd, ruin'd, and damn'd, I fear, for ever lost. Oh! fie, Madam, think not so, (said the other) for the Gentleman may yet prove true, and marry you. Ay, Madam (replied Bellamora) I doubt not that he would marry me; for soon after my Mother's Death, when I came to be at my own Disposal, which happen'd about two Months after, he offer'd, nay most earnestly sollicited me to it, which still he perseveres to do. This is strange! (return'd the other) and it appears to me to be your own Fault, that you are yet miserable. Why did you not, or why will you not consent to your own Happiness? Alas! (cry'd Bellamora) 'tis the only Thing I dread in this World: For, I am certain, he can never love me. Besides, ever since I have abhorr'd the Sight of him: and this is the only Cause that obliges me to forsake my Uncle, and all my Friends and Relations in the Country, hoping in this populous and publick Place to be most private, especially, Madam, in your House, and in your Fidelity and Discretion. Of the last you may assure yourself, Madam, (said the other:) but what Provision have you made for the Reception of the young Stranger that you carry about you? Ah, Madam! (cryd Bellamora) you have brought to my Mind another Misfortune: Then she acquainted her with the suppos'd loss of her Money and Jewels, telling her withall, that she had but three Guineas and some Silver left, and the Rings she wore, in her present possession. The good Gentlewoman of the House told her, she would send to enquire at the Inn where she lay the first

Night she came to Town; for, haply, they might give some Account of the Porter to whom she had entrusted her Trunk; and withal repeated her Promise of all the Help in her Power, and for that time left her much more compos'd than she found her. The good Gentlewoman went directly to the other Lady, her Lodger, to whom she recounted Bellamora's mournful Confession; at which the Lady appear'd mightily concern'd: and at last she told her Landlady, that she would take Care that Bellamora should lie in according to her Quality: For, added she, the Child, it seems, is my own Brother's.

As soon as she had din'd, she went to the Exchange, and bought Child-bed Linen; but desired that Bellamora might not have the least Notice of it: And at her return dispatch'd a Letter to her Brother Fondlove in Hampshire, with an Account of every Particular; which soon brought him up to Town, without satisfying any of his or her Friends with the Reason of his sudden Departure. Mean while, the good Gentlewoman of the House had sent to the Star Inn on Fish-street-Hill, to demand the Trunk, which she rightly suppos'd to have been carried back thither: For by good Luck, it was a Fellow that ply'd thereabouts, who brought it to Bellamora's Lodgings that very Night, but unknown to her. Fondlove no sooner got to London, but he posts to his Sister's Lodgings, where he was advis'd not to be seen of Bellamora till they had work'd farther upon her, which the Landlady began in this manner; she told her that her Things were miscarried, and she fear'd, lost; that she had but a little Money her self, and if the Overseers of the Poor (justly so call'd from their over-looking 'em) should have the least Suspicion of a strange and unmarried Person, who was entertain'd in her House big with Child, and so near her Time as Bellamora was, she should be troubled, if they could not give Security to the Parish of twenty or thirty Pounds, that they should not suffer by her, which she could not; or otherwise she must be sent to the House of Correction, and her Child to a Parish-Nurse. This Discourse, one may imagine, was very dreadful to a Person of her Youth, Beauty, Education, Family and Estate: However, she resolutely protested, that she had rather undergo all this, than be expos'd to the Scorn of her Friends and Relations in the Country. The other told her then, that she must write down to her Uncle a Farewell-Letter, as if she were just going aboard the Pacquet-Boat for Holland, that he might not send to enquire for her in Town, when he should understand she was not at her new-married Cousin's in the Country; which accordingly she did, keeping her self close Prisoner to her Chamber; where she was daily visited by Fondlove's Sister and the Landlady, but by no Soul else, the first dissembling the Knowledge she had of her Misfortunes. Thus she continued for above three Weeks, not a Servant being suffer'd to enter her Chamber, so much as to make her Bed, lest they should take Notice of her great Belly: but for all this Caution, the Secret had taken Wind, by the means of an Attendant of the other Lady below, who had over-heard her speaking of it to her Husband. This soon got out of Doors, and spread abroad, till it reach'd the long Ears of the Wolves of the Parish, who next Day design'd to pay her a Visit: But Fondlove, by good Providence, prevented it; who, the Night before, was usher'd into Bellamora's Chamber by his Sister, his Brother-in-Law, and the Landlady. At the Sight of him she had like to have swoon'd away: but he taking her in his Arms, began again, as he was wont to do, with Tears in his Eyes, to beg that she would marry him ere she was deliver'd; if not for his, nor her own, yet for the Child's Sake, which she hourly expected; that it might not be born out of Wedlock, and so be made uncapable of inheriting either of their Estates; with a great many more pressing Arguments on all Sides: To which at last she consented; and an honest officious Gentleman, whom they had before provided, was call'd up, who made an End of the Dispute: So to Bed they went together that Night; next Day to the Exchange, for several pretty Businesses that Ladies in her Condition want. Whilst they were abroad, came the Vermin of the Parish, (I mean, the Overseers of the Poor, who eat the Bread from 'em) to search for a young Blackhair'd Lady (for so was Bellamora) who was either brought to Bed, or just ready to lie down. The Landlady shew'd 'em all the Rooms in her House, but no such Lady could be found. At last she bethought her self, and led 'em into her Parlour, where she open'd a little Closet-door, and shew'd 'em a black Cat that had just kitten'd: assuring 'em, that she should never trouble the Parish as long as she had Rats or Mice in the House; and so dismiss'd 'em like Loggerheads as they came.

NOTES: The Black Lady.

**Bridges-Street.** Brydges Street lies between Russell Street and Catherine Street. Drury Lane Theatre is at its N.E. corner. It early acquired no very enviable repute, e.g. In the Epilogue to Crowne's Sir Courtly Nice (1685) we have: 'Our Bridges Street is grown a strumpet fair'; and Dryden, in the Epilogue to King Arthur (1691), gave Mrs. Bracegirdle, who entered, her hands full of billets-doux, the following lines to speak:

Here one desires my ladyship to meet  [Pulls out one.
At the kind couch above in Bridges-Street.
Oh sharping knave! that would have - you know what,
For a poor sneaking treat of chocolate.

**Star-Inn on Fish-street-Hill.** Fish Street Hill, or, New Fish Street, runs from Eastcheap to Lower Thames Street, and was the main thoroughfare to old London Bridge, cf. 2 Henry VI, IV, viii: 'Cade. Up Fish Street! down St. Magnus' corner! kill and knock down! throw them into the Thames.'

**The Exchange.** The New Exchange, a kind of bazaar on the South side of the Strand. It was an immensely popular resort, and continued so until the latter years of the reign of Queen Anne. There are innumerable references to its shops, its sempstresses and haberdashers. Thomas Duffet was a milliner here before he took to writing farces, prologues and poems.

## THE COURT OF THE KING OF BANTAM

This Money certainly is a most devilish Thing! I'm sure the Want of it had like to have ruin'd my dear Philibella, in her Love to Valentine Goodland; who was really a pretty deserving Gentleman, Heir to about fifteen hundred Pounds a Year; which, however, did not so much recommend him, as the Sweetness of his Temper, the Comeliness of his Person, and the Excellency of his Parts: In all which Circumstances my obliging Acquaintance equal'd him, unless in the Advantage of their Fortune. Old Sir George Goodland knew of his Son's Passion for Philibella; and tho' he was generous, and of a Humour sufficiently complying, yet he could by no means think it convenient, that his only Son should marry with a young Lady of so slender a Fortune as my Friend, who had not above five hundred Pound, and that the Gift of her Uncle Sir Philip Friendly: tho' her Virtue and Beauty might have deserv'd, and have adorn'd the Throne of an Alexander or a Cæsar.

Sir Philip himself, indeed, was but a younger Brother, tho' of a good Family, and of a generous Education; which, with his Person, Bravery, and Wit, recommended him to his Lady Philadelphia, Widow of Sir Bartholomew Banquier, who left her possess'd of two thousand Pounds per Annum, besides twenty thousand Pounds in Money and Jewels; which oblig'd him to get himself dubb'd, that she might not descend to an inferior Quality. When he was in Town, he liv'd, let me see! in the Strand; or, as near as I can remember, somewhere about Charing-Cross; where first of all Mr. Would-be King, a Gentleman of a large Estate in Houses, Land and Money, of a haughty, extravagant and profuse Humour, very fond of every new Face, had the Misfortune to fall passionately in love with Philibella, who then liv'd with her Uncle.

This Mr. Would-be it seems had often been told, when he was yet a Stripling, either by one of his Nurses, or his own Grandmother, or by some other Gypsy, that he should infallibly be what his Sirname imply'd, a King, by Providence or Chance, ere he dy'd, or never. This glorious Prophecy had so great an Influence on all his Thoughts and Actions, that he distributed and dispers'd his Wealth sometimes so largely, that one would have thought he had undoubtedly been King of some Part of the Indies; to see a Present made to-day of a Diamond Ring, worth two or three hundred Pounds, to Madam Flippant; to-morrow, a large Chest of the finest China to my Lady Fleecewell; and next Day, perhaps, a rich Necklace of large Oriental Pearl, with a Locket to it of Saphires, Emeralds, Rubies, &c., to pretty Miss Ogle-me, for an amorous Glance, for a Smile, and (it may be, tho' but rarely) for the mighty Blessing of one single Kiss. But such were his Largesses, not to reckon his Treats, his Balls, and Serenades besides, tho' at the same time he had marry'd a virtuous Lady, and of good Quality: But her Relation to him (it may be fear'd) made her very disagreeable: For a Man of his Humour and Estate can no more be satisfy'd with one Woman, than with one Dish of Meat; and to say Truth, 'tis something unmodish. However, he might have dy'd a pure Celibate, and altogether unexpert of Women, had his good or bad Hopes only terminated in Sir Philip's Niece. But the brave and haughty Mr. Would-be was not to be baulk'd by Appearances of Virtue, which he thought all Womankind only did affect; besides, he promis'd himself the Victory over any Lady whom he attempted, by the Force of his damn'd Money, tho' her Virtue were ever so real and strict.

With Philibella he found another pretty young Creature, very like her, who had been a quondam Mistress to Sir Philip: He, with young Goodland, was then diverting his Mistress and Niece at a Game at Cards, when Would-be came to visit him; he found 'em very merry, with a Flask or two of Claret before 'em, and Oranges roasting by a large Fire, for it was Christmas-time. The Lady Friendly understanding that this extraordinary Man was with Sir Philip in the Parlour, came in to 'em, to make the number of both Sexes equal, as well as in Hopes to make up a Purse of Guineas toward the Purchase of some new fine Business that she had in her Head, from his accustom'd Design of losing at Play to her. Indeed, she had Part of her Wish, for she got twenty Guineas of him; Philibella ten; and Lucy, Sir Philip's quondam, five: Not but that Would-be intended better Fortune to the young ones, than he did to Sir Philip's Lady; but her Ladyship was utterly unwilling to give him over to their Management, tho' at the last, when they were all tir'd with the Cards, after Would-be had said as many obliging things as his present Genius would give him leave, to Philibella and Lucy, especially to the first, not forgetting his Baisemains to the Lady Friendly, he bid the Knight and Goodland adieu; but with a Promise of repeating his Visit at six a-clock in the Evening on Twelfth-Day, to renew the famous and antient Solemnity of chusing King and Queen; to which Sir Philip before invited him, with a Design yet unknown to you, I hope.

As soon as he was gone, every one made their Remarks on him, but with very little or no Difference in all their Figures of him. In short, all Mankind, had they ever known him, would have universally agreed in this his Character, That he was an Original; since nothing in Humanity was ever so vain, so haughty, so profuse, so fond, and so ridiculously ambitious, as Mr. Would-be King. They laugh'd and talk'd about an Hour longer, and then young Goodland was oblig'd to see Lucy home in his Coach; tho' he had rather have sat up all Night in the same House with Philibella, I fancy, of whom he took but an unwilling Leave; which was visible enough to every one there, since they were all acquainted with his Passion for my fair Friend.

About twelve a-clock on the Day prefix'd, young Goodland came to dine with Sir Philip, whom he found just return'd from Court, in a very good Humour. On the Sight of Valentine, the Knight ran to him, and embracing him, told him, That he had prevented his Wishes, in coming thither before he sent for him, as he had just then design'd. The other return'd, that he therefore hoped he might be of some Service to him, by so happy a Prevention of his intended Kindness. No doubt (reply'd Sir Philip) the Kindness, I hope, will be to us both; I am assur'd it will, if you will act according to my

Measures. I desire no better Prescriptions for my Happiness (return'd Valentine) than what you shall please to set down to me: But is it necessary or convenient that I should know 'em first? It is, (answer'd Sir Philip) let us sit, and you shall understand 'em. I am very sensible (continu'd he) of your sincere and honourable Affection and Pretension to my Niece, who, perhaps, is as dear to me as my own Child could be, had I one; nor am I ignorant how averse Sir George your Father is to your Marriage with her, insomuch that I am confident he would disinherit you immediately upon it, merely for want of a Fortune somewhat proportionable to your Estate: but I have now contrived the Means to add two or three thousand Pounds to the five hundred I have design'd to give with her; I mean, if you marry her, Val, not otherwise; for I will not labour so for any other Man. What inviolable Obligations you put upon me! (cry'd Goodland.) No Return, by way of Compliments, good Val, (said the Knight:) Had I not engag'd to my Wife, before Marriage, that I would not dispose of any part of what she brought me, without her Consent, I would certainly make Philibella's Fortune answerable to your Estate: And besides, my Wife is not yet full eight and twenty, and we may therefore expect Children of our own, which hinders me from proposing any thing more for the Advantage of my Niece. But now to my Instructions; King will be here this Evening without fail, and, at some Time or other to-night, will shew the Haughtiness of his Temper to you, I doubt not, since you are in a manner a Stranger to him: Be sure therefore you seem to quarrel with him before you part, but suffer as much as you can first from his Tongue; for I know he will give you Occasions enough to exercise your passive Valour. I must appear his Friend, and you must retire Home, if you please, for this Night, but let me see you as early as your Convenience will permit to-morrow: my late Friend Lucy must be my Niece too. Observe this, and leave the rest to me. I shall most punctually, and will in all things be directed by you, (said Valentine.) I had forgot to tell you (said Friendly) that I have so order'd matters, that he must be King to-night, and Lucy Queen, by the Lots in the Cake. By all means (return'd Goodland;) it must be Majesty.

Exactly at six a'clock came Wou'd-be in his Coach and six, and found Sir Philip, and his Lady, Goodland, Philibella, and Lucy ready to receive him; Lucy as fine as a Dutchess, and almost as beautiful as she was before her Fall. All things were in ample Order for his Entertainment. They play'd till Supper was serv'd in, which was between eight and nine. The Treat was very seasonable and splendid. Just as the second Course was set on the Table, they were all on a sudden surpriz'd, except Would-be, with a Flourish of Violins, and other Instruments, which proceeded to entertain 'em with the best and newest Airs in the last new Plays, being then in the Year 1683. The Ladies were curious to know to whom they ow'd the chearful part of their Entertainment: On which he call'd out, Hey! Tom Farmer! Ale-worth! Eccles! Hall! and the rest of you! Here's a Health to these Ladies, and all this honourable Company. They bow'd; he drank, and commanded another Glass to be fill'd, into which he put something yet better than the Wine, I mean, ten Guineas: Here, Farmer, (said he then) this for you and your Friends. We humbly thank the honourable Mr. Would-be King. They all return'd, and struck up with more Spriteliness than before. For Gold and Wine, doubtless, are the best Rosin for Musicians.

After Supper they took a hearty Glass or two to the King, Queen, Duke, &c. And then the mighty Cake, teeming with the Fate of this extraordinary Personage, was brought in, the Musicians playing an Overture at the Entrance of the Alimental Oracle; which was then cut and consulted, and the royal Bean and Pea fell to those to whom Sir Philip had design'd 'em. 'Twas then the Knight began a merry Bumper, with three Huzza's, and, Long live King Would-be! to Goodland, who echo'd and pledg'd him, putting the Glass about to the harmonious Attendants; while the Ladies drank their own Quantities among themselves, To his aforesaid Majesty. Then of course you may believe Queen Lucy's Health went merrily round, with the same Ceremony: After which he saluted his Royal Consort, and condescended to do the same Honour to the two other Ladies.

Then they fell a dancing, like Lightning; I mean, they mov'd as swift, and made almost as little Noise; But his Majesty was soon weary of that; for he long'd to be making love both to Philibella and Lucy, who (believe me) that Night might well enough have passed for a Queen.

They fell then to Questions and Commands; to cross Purposes: I think a Thought, what is it like? &c. In all which, his Would-be Majesty took the Opportunity of shewing the Excellency of his Parts, as, How fit he was to govern! How dextrous at mining and countermining! and, How he could reconcile the most contrary and distant Thoughts! The Musick, at last, good as it was, grew troublesome and too loud; which made him dismiss them: And then he began to this effect, addressing himself to Philibella: Madam, had Fortune been just, and were it possible that the World should be govern'd and influenc'd by two Suns, undoubtedly we had all been Subjects to you, from this Night's Chance, as well as to that Lady, who indeed alone can equal you in the Empire of Beauty, which yet you share with her Majesty here present, who only could dispute it with you, and is only superior to you in Title. My Wife is infinitely oblig'd to your Majesty, (interrupted Sir Philip) who in my Opinion, has greater Charms, and more than both of them together. You ought to think so, Sir Philip (returned the new dubb'd King) however you should not liberally have express'd your self, in Opposition and Derogation to Majesty: Let me tell you 'tis a saucy Boldness that thus has loos'd your Tongue! What think you, young Kinsman and Counsellor? (said he to Goodland.) With all Respect due to your sacred Title, (return'd Valentene, rising and bowing) Sir Philip spoke as became a truly affectionate Husband; and it had been Presumption in him, unpardonable, to have seem'd to prefer her Majesty, or that other sweet Lady, in his Thoughts, since your Majesty has been pleas'd to say so much and so particularly of their Merits: 'Twould appear as if he durst lift up his Eyes, with Thoughts too near the Heaven you only would enjoy. And only can deserve, you should have added, (said King, no longer Would-be.) How! may it please your Majesty (cry'd Friendly) both my Nieces! tho' you deserve ten thousand more, and better, would your Majesty enjoy them both? Are they then both your Nieces? (asked Chance's King). Yes, both, Sir (return'd the Knight,) her Majesty's the eldest, and in that Fortune has shewn some Justice. So she has (reply'd the titular Monarch): My Lot is fair (pursu'd he) tho' I can be bless'd but with one.

Let Majesty with Majesty be join'd,
To get and leave a Race of Kings behind.

Come, Madam (continued he, kissing Lucy,) this, as an Earnest of our future Endeavours. I fear (return'd the pretty Queen) your Majesty will forget the unhappy Statira, when you return to the Embraces of your dear and beautiful Roxana. There is none beautiful but you (reply'd the titular King) unless this Lady, to whom I yet could pay my Vows most zealously, were't not that Fortune has thus pre-engaged me. But, Madam (continued he) to shew that still you hold our Royal Favour, and that, next to our Royal Consort, we esteem you, we greet you thus (kissing Philibella;) and as a Signal of our continued Love, wear this rich Diamond: (here he put a Diamond Ring on her Finger, worth three hundred Pounds.) Your Majesty (pursu'd he to Lucy) may please to wear this Necklace, with this Locket of Emeralds. Your Majesty is bounteous as a God! (said Valentine.) Art thou in Want, young Spark? (ask'd the King of Bantam) I'll give thee an Estate shall make thee merit the Mistress of thy Vows, be she who she will. That is my other Niece, Sir, (cry'd Friendly.) How! how! presumptious Youth! How are thy Eyes and Thoughts exalted? ha! To Bliss your Majesty must never hope for, (reply'd Goodland.) How now! thou Creature of the basest Mold! Not hope for what thou dost aspire to! Mock-King; thou canst not, dar'st not, shalt not hope it: (return'd Valentine in a heat.) Hold, Val, (cry'd Sir Philip) you grow warm, forget your Duty to their Majesties, and abuse your Friends, by making us suspected. Good-night, dear Philibella, and my Queen! Madam, I am your Ladyship's Servant (said Goodland:) Farewel, Sir Philip: Adieu, thou Pageant! thou Property-King! I shall see thy Brother on the Stage ere long; but first I'll visit thee: and in the meantime, by way of Return to thy proffer'd Estate, I shall add a real Territory to the rest of thy empty Titles; for from thy Education, barbarous manner of Conversation, and Complexion, I think I may justly proclaim thee, King of Bantam. So, Hail, King that Would-be! Hail thou King of Christmas! All-hail, Wou'd-be King of Bantam, and so he left 'em. They all seem'd amazed, and gaz'd on one another, without speaking a Syllable; 'till Sir Philip broke the Charm, and sigh'd out, Oh, the monstrous Effects of Passion! Say rather, Oh, the foolish Effects of a mean Education! (interrupted his Majesty of Bantam.) For Passions were given us for Use, Reason to govern and direct us in the Use, and Education to cultivate and refine that Reason. But (pursu'd he) for all his Impudence to me, which I shall take a time to correct, I am oblig'd to him, that at last he has found me out a Kingdom to my Title; and if I were Monarch of that Place (believe me, Ladies) I would make you all Princesses and Duchesses; and thou, my old Companion, Friendly, should rule the Roast with me. But these Ladies should be with us there, where we could erect Temples and Altars to 'em; build Golden Palaces of Love, and Castles, in the Air (interrupted her Majesty, Lucy I. smiling.) 'Gad take me (cry'd King Wou'd-be) thou dear Partner of my Greatness, and shalt be, of all my Pleasures! thy pretty satirical Observation has oblig'd me beyond Imitation.' I think your Majesty is got into a Vein of Rhiming to-night, (said Philadelphia.) Ay! Pox of that young insipid Fop, we could else have been as great as an Emperor of China, and as witty as Horace in his Wine; but let him go, like a pragmatical, captious, giddy Fool as he is! I shall take a Time to see him. Nay, Sir, (said Philibella) he has promis'd your Majesty a Visit in our Hearing. Come, Sir, I beg your Majesty to pledge me this Glass to your long and happy Reign; laying aside all Thoughts of ungovern'd Youth: Besides, this Discourse must needs be ungrateful to her Majesty, to whom, I fear, he will be marry'd within this Month! How! (cry'd King and no King) married to my Queen! I must not, cannot suffer it! Pray restrain your self a little, Sir (said Sir Philip) and when once these Ladies have left us, I will discourse your Majesty further about this Business. Well, pray, Sir Philip, (said his Lady) let not your Worship be pleas'd to sit up too long for his Majesty: About five o'Clock I shall expect you; 'tis your old Hour. And yours, Madam, to wake to receive me coming to Bed - Your Ladyship understands me, (return'd Friendly.) You're merry, my Love, you're merry, (cry'd Philadelphia:) Come, Niece, to Bed! to Bed! Ay, (said the Knight) Go, both of you and sleep together, if you can, without the Thoughts of a Lover, or a Husband. His Majesty was pleas'd to wish them a good Repose; and so, with a Kiss, they parted for that time.

Now we're alone (said Sir Philip) let me assure you, Sir, I resent this Affront done to you by Mr. Goodland, almost as highly as you can: and tho' I can't wish that you should take such Satisfaction, as perhaps some other hotter Sparks would; yet let me say, his Miscarriage ought not to go unpunish'd in him. Fear not (reply'd t'other) I shall give him a sharp Lesson. No, Sir (return'd Friendly) I would not have you think of a bloody Revenge; for 'tis that which possibly he designs on you: I know him brave as any Man. However, were it convenient that the Sword should determine betwixt you, you should not want mine: The Affront is partly to me, since done in my House; but I've already laid down safer Measures for us, tho' of more fatal Consequence to him: that is, I've form'd them in my Thoughts. Dismiss your Coach and Equipage, all but one Servant, and I will discourse it to you at large. 'Tis now past Twelve; and if you please, I would invite you to take up as easy a Lodging here, as my House will afford. (Accordingly they were dismiss'd, and he proceeded:) As I hinted to you before, he is in love with my youngest Niece, Philibella; but her Fortune not exceeding five hundred Pound, his Father will assuredly disinherit him, if he marries her: tho' he has given his Consent that he should marry her eldest Sister, whose Father dying ere he knew his Wife was with child of the youngest, left Lucy three thousand Pounds, being as much as he thought convenient to match her handsomly; and accordingly the Nuptials of young Goodland and Lucy are to be celebrated next Easter. They shall not, if I can hinder them (interrupted his offended Majesty.) Never endeavour the Obstruction (said the Knight) for I'll shew you the Way to a dearer Vengeance: Women are Women, your Majesty knows; she may be won to your Embraces before that time, and then you antedate him your Creature. A Cuckold, you mean (cry'd King in Fancy:) O exquisite Revenge! but can you consent that I should attempt it? What is't to me? We live not in Spain, where all the Relations of the Family are oblig'd to vindicate a Whore: No, I would wound him in his most tender Part. But how shall we compass it? (ask'd t'other.) Why thus, throw away three thousand Pounds on the youngest Sister, as a Portion, to make her as happy as she can be in her new Lover, Sir Frederick Flygold, an extravagant young Fop, and wholly given over to Gaming; so, ten to one, but you may retrieve your Money of him, and have the two Sisters at your Devotion. Oh, thou my better Genius than that which was given to me by Heaven at my Birth! What Thanks, what Praises shall I return and sing to thee for this! (cry'd King Conundrum.) No Thanks, no Praises, I beseech your Majesty, since in this I gratify my self. You think I am your Friend? and, you will agree to this? (said Friendly, by way of Question.) Most readily, (returned the Fop King:) Would it were broad Day, that I might send for the Money to my Banker's; for in all my Life, in all my Frolicks, Encounters and Extravagances, I never had one so grateful, and so pleasant as this will be, if you are in earnest, to gratify both my Love and Revenge! That I am in earnest, you will not doubt, when you see with what Application I shall pursue my Design: In the mean Time, My Duty to your Majesty; To our good Success in this Affair. While he drank, t'other return'd, With all my Heart; and pledg'd him. Then Friendly began afresh: Leave the whole Management of this to me; only one thing more I think necessary, that you make a Present of five hundred Guineas to her Majesty, the Bride that must be. By all means (return'd the wealthy King of Bantam;) I had so design'd before. Well, Sir (said Sir Philip) what think you of a set Party or two at Piquet, to pass away a few Hours, till we can sleep? A seasonable and welcome Proposition (returned the King;) but I won't play above twenty Guineas the Game, and forty the Lurch. Agreed (said Friendly;) first call in your Servant; mine is here already. The Slave came in, and they began, with unequal Fortune at first; for the Knight had lost a hundred Guineas to Majesty, which he paid in Specie; and then propos'd fifty Guineas the Game, and a hundred the Lurch. To which t'other consented; and without winning more than three Games, and those not together, made shift to get three thousand two hundred Guineas in debt to Sir Philip; for which Majesty was pleas'd to give him Bond, whether Friendly would or no,

Seal'd and deliver'd in the Presence of,

The Mark of (W.) Will. Watchful.
And, (S) Sim. Slyboots.

A couple of delicate Beagles, their mighty Attendants.

It was then about the Hour that Sir Philip's (and, it may be, other Ladies) began to yawn and stretch; when the Spirits refresh'd, troul'd about, and tickled the Blood with Desires of Action; which made Majesty and Worship think of a Retreat to Bed: where in less than half an Hour, or before ever he cou'd say his Prayers, I'm sure the first fell fast asleep; but the last, perhaps, paid his accustom'd Devotion, ere he begun his Progress to the Shadow of Death. However, he waked earlier than his Cully Majesty, and got up to receive young Goodland, who came according to his Word, with the first Opportunity. Sir Philip receiv'd him with more than usual Joy, tho' not with greater Kindness, and let him know every Syllable and Accident that had pass'd between them till they went to Bed: which you may believe was not a little pleasantly surprizing to Valentine, who began then to have some Assurance of his Happiness with Philibella. His Friend told him, that he must now be reconcil'd to his Mock-Majesty, tho' with some Difficulty; and so taking one hearty Glass a-piece, he left Valentine in the Parlour to carry the ungrateful News of his Visit to him that Morning. King — was in an odd sort of taking, when he heard that Valentine was below; and had been, as Sir Philip inform'd Majesty, at Majesty's Palace, to enquire for him there: But when he told him, that he had already school'd him on his own Behalf, for the Affront done in his House, and that he believ'd he could bring his Majesty off without any loss of present Honour, his Countenance visibly discover'd his past Fear, and present Satisfaction; which was much encreas'd too, when Friendly shewing him his Bond for the Money he won of him at play, let him know, that if he paid three thousand Guineas to Philibella, he would immediately deliver him up his Bond, and not expect the two hundred Guineas overplus. His Majesty of Bantam was then in so good a Humour, that he could have made Love to Sir Philip; nay, I believe he could have kiss'd Valentine, instead of seeming angry. Down they came, and saluted like Gentlemen: But after the Greeting was over, Goodland began to talk something of Affront, Satisfaction, Honour, &c. when immediately Friendly interpos'd, and after a little seeming Uneasiness and Reluctancy, reconcil'd the hot and cholerick Youth to the cold phlegmatick King.

Peace was no sooner proclaim'd, than the King of Bantam took his Rival and late Antagonist with him in his own Coach, not excluding Sir Philip by any means, to Locket's, where they din'd: Thence he would have 'em to Court with him, where he met the Lady Flippant, the Lady Harpy, the Lady Crocodile, Madam Tattlemore, Miss Medler, Mrs. Gingerly, a rich Grocer's Wife, and some others, besides Knights and Gentlemen of as good Humours as the Ladies; all whom he invited to a Ball at his own House, the Night following; his own Lady being then in the Country. Madam Tattlemore, I think was the first he spoke to in Court, and whom first he surpriz'd with the happy News of his Advancement to the Title of King of Bantam. How wondrous hasty was she to be gone, as soon as she heard it! 'Twas not in her Power, because not in her Nature, to stay long enough to take a civil Leave of the Company; but away she flew, big with the empty Title of a fantastick King, proclaiming it to every one of her Acquaintance, as she passed through every Room, till she came to the Presence-Chamber, where she only whisper'd it; but her Whispers made above half the honourable Company quit the Presence of the King of Great-Britain, to go make their Court to his Majesty of Bantam: some cry'd, God bless your Majesty! Some Long live the King of Bantam! Others, All Hail to your Sacred Majesty; In short, he was congratulated on all Sides. Indeed I don't hear that his Majesty King Charles II. ever sent an Ambassador to compliment him; tho' possibly, he saluted him by his Title the first time he saw him afterwards: For, you know, he is a wonderful good-natur'd and well-bred Gentleman.

After he thought the Court of England was universally acquainted with his mighty Honour, he was pleas'd to think fit to retire to his own more private Palace, with Sir Philip and Goodland, whom he entertain'd that Night very handsomly, till about seven o'Clock; when they went together to the Play, which was that Night, A King and no King. His Attendant-Friends could not forbear smiling, to think how aptly the Title of the Play suited his Circumstances. Nor could he choose but take Notice of it behind the Scenes, between Jest and Earnest; telling the Players how kind Fortune had been the Night past, in disposing the Bean to him; and justifying what one of her Prophetesses had foretold some Years since. I shall now no more regard (said he) that old doating Fellow Pythagoras's Saying Abstineto a Fabis, That is, (added he, by way of Construction) Abstain from Beans: for I find the Excellency of 'em in Cakes and Dishes; from the first, they inspire the Soul with mighty Thoughts; and from the last our Bodies receive a strong and wholesom Nourishment. That is, (said a Wag among those sharp Youths, I think 'twas my Friend the Count) these puff you up in Mind, Sir, those in Body. They had some further Discourse among the Nymphs of the Stage, ere they went into the Pit; where Sir Philip spread the News of his Friend's Accession to the Title, tho' not yet to the Throne of Bantam; upon which he was there again complimented on that Occasion. Several of the Ladies and Gentlemen who saluted him, he invited to the next Night's Ball at his Palace.

The Play done, they took each of them a Bottle at the Rose, and parted till Seven the Night following; which came not sooner than desired: for he had taken such Care, that all things were in readiness before Eight, only he was not to expect the Musick till the End of the Play. About Nine, Sir Philip, his Lady, Goodland, Philibella, and Lucy came. Sir Philip return'd him Rabelais, which he had borrow'd of him, wherein the Knight had written, in an old odd sort of a Character, this Prophecy of his own making; with which he surpriz'd the Majesty of Bantam, who vow'd he had never taken Notice of it before; but he said, he perceiv'd it had been long written by the Character; and here it follows, as near as I can remember:

When M. D. C. come L. before,
Three XXX's, two II's and one I. more;
Then KING, tho' now but Name to thee,
Shall both thy Name and Title be.

They had hardly made an End of reading it, ere the whole Company, and more than he had invited, came in, and were receiv'd with a great deal of Formality and Magnificence. Lucy was there attended as his Queen; and Philibella, as the Princess her Sister. They danc'd then till they were weary; and afterwards retired to another large Room, where they found the Tables spread and furnished with all the most seasonable cold Meat; which was succeeded by the choicest Fruits, and the richest Desert of Sweetmeats that Luxury could think on, or at least that this Town could afford. The Wines were all most excellent in their Kind; and their Spirits flew about thro' every Corner of the House: There was scarce a Spark sober in the whole Company, with drinking repeated Glasses to the Health of the King of Bantam, and his Royal Consort, with the Princess Philibella's who sat together under a Royal Canopy of State, his Majesty between the two beautiful Sisters: only Friendly and Goodland wisely manag'd that part of the Engagement where they were concern'd, and preserv'd themselves from the Heat of the Debauch.

Between Three and Four most of them began to draw off, laden with Fruit and Sweetmeats, and rich Favours compos'd of Yellow, Green, Red and White, the Colours of his new Majesty of Bantam. Before Five they were left to themselves; when the Lady Friendly was discompos'd, for want of Sleep, and her usual Cordial, which obliged Sir Philip to wait on her Home, with his two Nieces: But his Majesty would by no means part with Goodland; whom, before Nine that Morning, he made as drunk as a Lord, and by Consequence, one of his Peers; for Majesty was then, indeed, as great as an Emperor: He fancy'd himself Alexander, and young Valentine his Hephestion; and did so be-buss him, that the young Gentleman fear'd he was fallen into the Hands of an Italian. However, by the kind Persuasions of his condescending and dissembling Majesty, he ventur'd to go into Bed with him; where King Would-be fell asleep, hand-over-head: and not long after, Goodland, his new-made Peer, follow'd him to the cool Retreats of Morpheus.

About Three the next Afternoon they both wak'd, as by consent, and called to dress. And after that Business was over, I think they swallow'd each of 'em a Pint of Old-Hock, with a little Sugar, by the way of healing. Their Coaches were got ready in the mean time; but the Peer was forced to accept of the Honour of being carried in his Majesty's to Sir Philip's, whom they found just risen from Dinner, with Philadelphia and his two Nieces. They sat down, and ask'd for something to relish a Glass of Wine, and Sir Philip order'd a cold Chine to be set before 'em, of which they eat about an Ounce a-piece; but they drank more by half, I dare say.

After their little Repast, Friendly call'd the Would-be-Monarch aside, and told him, that he would have him go to the Play that Night, which was The London-Cuckolds; promising to meet him there in less than half an Hour after his Departure: telling him withal, that he would surprize him with a much better Entertainment than the Stage afforded. Majesty took the Hint, imagining, and that rightly, that the Knight had some Intrigue in his Head, for the Promotion of the Commonwealth of Cuckoldom: In order therefore to his Advice, he took his leave about a quarter of an Hour after.

When he was gone, Sir Philip thus bespoke his pretended Niece: Madam, I hope your Majesty will not refuse me the Honour of waiting on you to a Place where you will meet with better Entertainment than your Majesty can expect from the best Comedy in Christendom. Val, (continued he) you must go with us, to secure me against the Jealousy of my Wife. That, indeed (return'd his Lady) is very material; and you are mightily concern'd not to give me Occasion, I must own. You see I am now, (replied he:) But, come! on with Hoods and Scarf! (pursued he, to Lucy.) Then addressing himself again to his Lady; Madam, (said he) we'll wait on you. In less Time than I could have drank a Bottle to my Share, the Coach was got ready, and on they drove to the Play-House. By the way, said Friendly to Val. Your Honour, noble Peer, must be set down at Long's; for only Lucy and I must be seen to his Majesty of Bantam: And now, I doubt not, you understand what you must trust to. To be robb'd of her Majesty's Company, I warrant (return'd the other) for these long three Hours. Why (cry'd Lucy) you don't mean, I hope, to leave me with his Majesty of Bantam? 'Tis for thy Good, Child! 'Tis for thy Good (return'd Friendly.) To the Rose they got then; where Goodland alighted, and expected Sir Philip; who led Lucy into the King's Box, to his new Majesty; where, after the first Scene, he left them together. The over-joy'd fantastick Monarch would fain have said some fine obliging Things to the Knight, as he was going out; but Friendly's Haste prevented 'em, who went directly to Valentine, took one Glass, call'd a Reckoning, mounted his Chariot, and away Home they came: where I believe he was welcome to his Lady; for I never heard any thing to the contrary.

In the mean Time, his Majesty had not the Patience to stay out half the Play, at which he was saluted by above twenty Gentlemen and Ladies by his new and mighty Title: but out he led Miss Majesty ere the third Act was half done; pretending, that it was so damn'd a bawdy Play, that he knew her Modesty had been already but too much offended at it; so into his Coach he got her. When they were seated, she told him she would go to no Place with him, but to the Lodgings her Mother had taken for her, when she first came to Town, and which still she kept. Your Mother, Madam, (cry'd he) why, is Sir Philip's Sister living then? His Brother's Widow is, Sir, (she reply'd.) Is she there? (he ask'd.) No, Sir, (she return'd;) she is in the Country. Oh, then we will go thither to chuse. The Coach-man was then order'd to drive to Jermain-Street; where, when he came in to the Lodgings, he found 'em very rich and modishly furnish'd. He presently call'd one of his Slaves, and whisper'd him to get three or four pretty Dishes for Supper; and then getting a Pen, Ink and Paper, writ a Note to C—d the Goldsmith with Temple-Bar, for five hundred guineas; which Watchful brought him, in less than an Hour's time, when they were just in the Height of Supper; Lucy having invited her Landlady, for the better Colour of the Matter. His Bantamite Majesty took the Gold from his Slave, and threw it by him in the Window, that Lucy might take Notice of it; (which you may assure yourself she did, and after Supper wink'd on the goodly Matron of the House to retire, which she immediately obey'd.) Then his Majesty began his Court very earnestly and hotly, throwing the naked Guineas into her Lap: which she seemed to refuse with much Disdain; but upon his repeated Promises, confirm'd by unheard of Oaths and Imprecations, that he would give her Sister three thousand Guineas to her Portion, she began by Degrees to mollify, and let the Gold lie quietly in her Lap: And the next Night, after he had drawn Notes on two or three of his Bankers, for the Payment of three thousand Guineas to Sir Philip, or Order, and received his own Bond, made for what he had lost at Play, from Friendly, she made no great Difficulty to admit his Majesty to her Bed. Where I think fit to leave 'em for the present; for (perhaps) they had some private Business.

The next Morning before the Titular King was (I won't say up, or stirring, but) out of Bed, young Goodland and Philibella were privately marry'd; the Bills being all accepted and paid in two Days Time. As soon as ever the fantastick Monarch could find in his Heart to divorce himself from the dear and charming Embraces of his beautiful Bedfellow, he came flying to Sir Philip, with all the Haste that Imagination big with Pleasure could inspire him with, to discharge it self to a suppos'd Friend. The Knight told him, that he was really much troubled to find that his Niece had yielded so soon and easily to him; however, he wish'd him Joy: To which the other return'd, that he could never want it, whilst he had the Command of so much Beauty, and that without the ungrateful Obligations of Matrimony, which certainly are the most nauseous, hateful, pernicious and destructive of Love imaginable. Think you so, Sir? (ask'd the Knight;) we shall hear what a Friend of mine will say on such an Occasion, to-morrow about this Time: but I beseech your Majesty to conceal your Sentiments of it to him, lest you make him as uneasy as you seem to be in that Circumstance. Be assur'd I will, (return'd the other:) But when shall I see the sweet, the dear, the blooming, the charming Philibella?

She will be with us at Dinner. Where's her Majesty? (ask'd Sir Philip) Had you enquir'd before, she had been here; for, look, she comes! Friendly seems to regard her with a Kind of Displeasure, and whisper'd Majesty, that he should express no particular Symptoms of Familiarity with Lucy in his House, at any Time, especially when Goodland was there, as then he was above with his Lady and Philibella, who came down presently after to Dinner.

About Four o'Clock, as his Majesty had intrigu'd with her, Lucy took a Hackney-Coach, and went to her Lodgings; whither about an Hour after, he follow'd her, Next Morning, at nine, he came to Friendly's, who carry'd him up to see his new-married Friends. But (O Damnation to Thoughts!) what Torments did he feel, when he saw young Goodland and Philibella in bed together; the last of which return'd him humble and hearty Thanks for her Portion and Husband, as the first did for his Wife. He shook his Head at Sir Philip, and without speaking one Word, left 'em, and hurry'd to Lucy, to lament the ill Treatment he had met with from Friendly. They coo'd and bill'd as long as he was able; she (sweet Hypocrite) seeming to bemoan his Misfortunes; which he took so kindly, that when he left her, which was about three in the Afternoon, he caus'd a Scrivener to draw up an Instrument, wherein he settled a hundred Pounds a Year on Lucy for her Life, and gave her a hundred Guineas more against her Lying-in: (For she told him, and indeed 'twas true, that she was with child, and knew her self to be so from a very good Reason) And indeed she was so—by the Friendly Knight. When he return'd to her, he threw the obliging Instrument into her Lap; (it seems he had a particular Kindness for that Place—) then call'd for Wine, and something to eat; for he had not drank a Pint to his Share all the Day, (tho' he had ply'd it at the Chocolate-House.) The Landlady, who was invited to sup with 'em, bid 'em good-night, about eleven; when they went to bed, and partly slept till about six; when they were entertain'd by some Gentleman of their Acquaintance, who play'd and sung very finely, by way of Epithalamium, these Words and more:

Joy to great Bantam!
Live long, love and wanton!
And thy Royal Consort!
For both are of one Sort, &c.

The rest I have forgot. He took some Offence at the Words; but more at the Visit that Sir Philip, and Goodland, made him, about an Hour after, who found him in Bed with his Royal Consort; and after having wish'd 'em Joy, and thrown their Majesties own Shoes and Stockings at their Head, retir'd. This gave Monarch in Fancy so great a Caution that he took his Royal Consort into the Country, (but above forty Miles off the Place where his own Lady was) where, in less than eight Months, she was deliver'd of a Princely Babe, who was Christen'd by the Heathenish Name of Hayoumorecake Bantam, while her Majesty lay in like a pretty Queen.

NOTES: The King of Bantam.

**Last new Plays, being then in the Year 1683**. The new plays acted at the Theatre Royal in 1682 were: Southerne's The Loyal Brother; or, The Persian Prince; Tate's Ingratitude of a Commonwealth; or, The Fall of Caius Marius Coriolanus; Settle's The Heir of Morocco, with the Death of Gayland; Banks' The Unhappy Favourite; or, the Earl of Essex; D'Urfey's The Injur'd Princess; or, The Fatal Wager. There were also an unusual number of revivals of the older plays at this house. At Dorset Garden the following were produced: Otway's Venice Preserved; or, A Plot Discovered; Mrs. Behn's The City Heiress; or, Sir Timothy Treatall; D'Urfey's The Royalist; Mrs. Behn's The False Count; or, A New Way to Play an Old Game; Banks' Virtue Betray'd; or, Anna Bullen; Mrs. Behn's The Roundheads; or, The Good Old Cause; Ravenscroft's The London Cuckolds; and Romulus and Hersilia; or, The Sabine War, an anonymous tragedy. There were also notable revivals of Randolph's The Jealous Lovers, and

Fletcher's The Maid in the Mill. The two Companies amalgamated in the autumn, opening at the Theatre Royal, 16 November, for which occasion a special Prologue and Epilogue were written by Dryden. 4 December, Dryden and Lee's famous tragedy, The Duke of Guise, had a triumphant first night. It will be remembered that Mrs. Behn is writing of incidents which took place on 6 January, 1683, Twelfth Night, so 'the last new plays' must refer to the productions of 1682. Of course, fresh songs, and probably musical entertainments, would be inserted at the different revivals of the older plays which were so frequent during that year.

**Statira, . . .** Roxana. In allusion to the two rival princesses for Alexander's love as they appear in Nat Lee's famous tragedy, The Rival Queens; or, Alexander the Great, produced at Drury Lane, 1677. It held the stage over a century and a half, longest of his plays, and is indeed an excellent piece. Originally, Hart played Alexander; Mrs. Marshall, the glowing Roxana; and Mrs. Boutell, Statira. Genest chronicles a performance at Drury Lane, 23 June, 1823, with Kean as Alexander; Mrs. W. West, Statira; Mrs. Glover, Roxana.

**Forty the Lurch.** 'Lurch' is a very common old term (now rare) 'used in various games to denote a certain concluding state of the game in which one player is enormously ahead of the other; often a "maiden set" or love-game', N.E.D. cf. Urquhart's Rabelais (1653), II, xii: 'By two of my table-men in the corner point I have gained the lurch.' Gouldman's Latin Dictionary (1674), gives: 'A lurch; duplex palma, facilis victoria.'

**To Locket's, where they din'd.** This fashionable Ordinary stood on the site of Drummond's Bank, Charing Cross. It was named from Adam Locket, the landlord, who died in 1688. In 1702, however, we find an Edward Locket, probably a son, as proprietor. The reputation of the house was on the wane during the latter years of Anne, and in the reign of George I its vogue entirely ceased. There are very frequent references. In The Country Wife (1675), Horner tells Pinchwife: 'Thou art as shy of my kindness as a Lombard-street alderman of a courtier's civility at Locket's' (IV, iii). In Shadwell's The Scowerers (1691), old Tope, replying to a health, cries: 'I'll answer you in a couple of Brimmers of Claret at Locket's at Dinner' (I, i). In Vanbrugh's The Relapse (1696), Lord Foppington, when asked if he dines at home, surmises: ''tis possible I may dine with some of aur House at Lacket's,' which shows that it was then the very rendezvous of fashion and quality.

**A King and no King.** Langbaine testifies to the popularity of Beaumont and Fletcher's play both before and after the Restoration. Pepys saw it 14 March, 1661, and again, 26 September the same year. The 1676 quarto 'as it is now acted at the Theatre Royal by his Majestie's Servants' gives a full cast with Hart as Arbaces; Kynaston, Tigranes; Mohun, Mardonius; Lacy, Bessus; Mrs. Betty Cox, Panthea; Mrs. Marshall, Spaconia. In the earlier production Nell Gwynne had acted Panthea. The two Companies amalgamated in 1682, opening 16 November. Hart 'never Acted more' after this date. Mrs. Marshall had retired in 1677; and in 1683 Betterton was playing Arbaces with quite a new allotment of the other rôles.

**The Rose.** There are repeated references to this celebrated tavern which stood in Russell Street, Covent Garden. vide The Younger Brother, I, ii (Vol. IV), Motteux' Song: 'Thence to the Rose where he takes his three Flasks,' and the note on that passage.

**The London-Cuckolds.** Ravenscroft's rollicking comedy, which had been produced with great success at the Duke's House in 1682 (4to, 1682), long kept the boards with undiminished favour, being very frequently given each season. Genest has the following true and pertinent remark: 'If it be the province of Comedy not to retail morality to a yawning pit but to make the audience laugh and to keep them in good humour this play must be allowed to be one of the best Comedies in the English language.' 29 October (the old Lord Mayor's Day), 1751, Garrick substituted Eastward Hoe at Drury

Lane for the annual performance of The London Cuckolds, a change not approved by the audience, who promptly damned their new fare. Ravenscroft's comedy was given that evening at Covent Garden, and on 9 November, the following year. It was also performed there in 1753. 9 November, 1754, George II ordered The Provoked Husband. It has often been stated (e.g. by Professor A. W. Ward, 'Ravenscroft', Dictionary of National Biography) that this royal command gave The London Cuckolds its final congé, but such was neither the intent nor the case. The play is billed at Covent Garden, 10 November, 1755; in 1757; and 9 November, 1758. Shuter excelled as Dashwell. A two act version was played at Covent Garden, 10 April, 1782, and repeated on the 12th. This was for the benefit of Quick, who acted Doodle.

**Your Honour** . . . must be set down at Long's. Long's was a famous Ordinary in the Haymarket. It was here that in 1678 Lord Pembroke killed Mr. Coney with his fist. He was tried by his Peers and acquitted. There was at the same period a second tavern in Covent Garden kept by Ben Long, Long's brother. In Dryden's Mr. Limberham (1678), Brainsick cries: 'I have won a wager to be spent luxuriously at Long's.' In Etheredge's The Man of Mode (1676), the following conversation occurs:

Bellair. Where do you dine?
Dorimant. At Long's or Locket's.
Medley. At Long's let it be.

**The King's Box.** The seats in the boxes of the Restoration Theatre were let out severally to separate persons, and although the King had, of course, his own private box when he saw a play, yet when he was not present even the royal box was apportioned to individuals as the rest. There are many allusions to this which prove, moreover, that the front row of the King's box was the most conspicuous and highly coveted position in the house. In Etheredge's The Man of Mode (1676), Dorimant, hearing of a young gentlewoman lately come to town and being taken with his own handsome face, wagers that she must be 'some awkward, ill-fashioned, country toad, who, not having above four dozen of black hairs on her head, has adorned her baldness with a large white fruz, that she may look sparkishly in the forefront of the King's box at an old play.' In Tom Brown's Letters from the Dead to the Living [1] we have one from Julian, 'late Secretary to the Muses,' to Will. Pierre of Lincoln's Inn Fields Playhouse, wherein, recalling how in his lampoons whilst he lived characters about town were shown in no very enviable light, he particularizes that 'the antiquated Coquet was told of her age and ugliness, tho' her vanity plac'd her in the first row in the King's box at the playhouse.'

**Jermain-Street.** Jermyn Street runs parallel with Piccadilly from the Haymarket to St. James. It was built circa 1667, and derives its name from Henry Jermyn, Earl of St. Albans. Shadwell spells it Germin Street, and it was in a house here that old Snarl was wont to receive amorous castigation at the hands of Mrs. Figgup. The Virtuoso (1676), III, ii. It was a fashionable quarter. From 1675 to 1681 the Duke of Marlborough, then Colonel Churchill, lived here. La Belle Stuart, Duchess of Richmond, had a house near Eagle Passage, 1681-3, and was succeeded therein by the Countess of Northumberland. Next door dwelt Henry Saville, Rochester's friend, 1681-3. Three doors from the Duchess again was living in 1683 Simon Verelest, the painter. In 1684 Sir William Soames followed him. In after years also there have been a large number of famous residents connected with this favourite street.

**After having** . . . thrown their Majesties own Shoes and Stockings. For this old bridal custom see ante, Vol. III (p. 223), The Lucky Chance, II, ii: 'we'll toss the Stocking'; and the note on that passage.

*[Footnote 1:* This actual letter was written by Boyer, together with the reply which is dated 5 November, 1701. Julian was a well-known journalistic scribbler and ribald ballader of the time.

William Peer [Pierre], a young actor of little account, is only cast for such walk-on rôles as Jasper, a valet, in Shadwell's The Scowerers (1691); the Parson in D'Urfey's Love for Money (1696).]


THE UNFORTUNATE HAPPY LADY: A True History

I cannot omit giving the World an account, of the uncommon Villany of a Gentleman of a good Family in England practis'd upon his Sister, which was attested to me by one who liv'd in the Family, and from whom I had the whole Truth of the Story. I shall conceal the unhappy Gentleman's own, under the borrow'd Names of Sir William Wilding, who succeeded his Father Sir Edward, in an Estate of near 4000l. a Year, inheriting all that belong'd to him, except his Virtues. 'Tis true, he was oblig'd to pay his only Sister a Portion of 6000l. which he might very easily have done out of his Patrimony in a little Time, the Estate being not in the least incumbred. But the Death of his good Father gave a loose to the Extravagancy of his Inclinations, which till then was hardly observable. The first Discovery he made of his Humour, was in the extraordinary rich Equipage he prepar'd for his Journey to London, which was much greater than his fair and plentiful Fortune cou'd maintain, nor were his Expences any way inferior to the Figure he made here in Town; insomuch, that in less than a Twelve-Month, he was forc'd to return to his Seat in the Country, to Mortgage a part of his Estate of a Thousand Pounds a Year, to satisfy the Debts he had already contracted in his profuse Treats, Gaming and Women, which in a few Weeks he effected, to the great Affliction of his Sister Philadelphia, a young Lady of excellent Beauty, Education, and Virtue; who, fore-seeing the utter Ruin of the Estate, if not timely prevented, daily begg'd of him, with Prayers and Tears, that might have mov'd a Scythian or wild Arab, or indeed any thing but him, to pay her her Portion. To which, however, he seemingly consented, and promis'd to take her to Town with him, and there give her all the Satisfaction she cou'd expect: And having dipp'd some paltry Acres of Land, deeper than ever Heaven dipp'd 'em in Rain, he was as good as his Word, and brought her to Town with him, where he told her he would place her with an ancient Lady, with whom he had contracted a Friendship at his first coming to London; adding, that she was a Lady of incomparable Morals, and of a matchless Life and Conversation. Philadelphia took him in the best Sense, and was very desirous to be planted in the same House with her, hoping she might grow to as great a Perfection in such excellent Qualifications, as she imagined 'em. About four Days therefore after they had been in Town, she sollicits her Brother to wait on that Lady with her: He reply'd, that it is absolutely Necessary and Convenient that I should first acquaint her with my Design, and beg that she will be pleas'd to take you into her Care, and this shall be my chief Business to Day: Accordingly, that very Hour he went to the Lady Beldams, his reverend and honourable Acquaintance, whom he prepar'd for the Reception of his Sister, who he told her was a Cast-Mistress of his, and desir'd her Assistance to prevent the Trouble and Charge, which she knew such Cattle would bring upon young Gentlemen of plentiful Estates. To morrow Morning about Eleven, I'll leave her with your Ladyship, who, I doubt not, will give her a wholesome Lesson or two before Night, and your Reward is certain. My Son, (return'd she) I know the Greatness of your Spirit, the Heat of your Temper has both warm'd and inflam'd me! I joy to see you in Town again. Ah! That I could but recal one twenty Years for your Sake! Well, no matter. I won't forget your Instructions, nor my Duty to Morrow: In the mean time, I'll drink your Health in a Bottle of Sherry or two, O! Cry your Mercy, good my Lady Beldam, (said the young Debauchee) I had like to have forfeited my Title to your Care, in not remembring to leave you an Obligation. There are three Guinea's, which, I hope, will plead for me till to Morrow. So - Your Ladyship's Servant humbly kisses your Hand. Your Honours most Obedient Servant, most gratefully Acknowledges your Favours. Your humble Servant, Good Sir William, added she, seeing him leave her in haste.

Never were three Persons better pleas'd for a Time than this unnatural Man, his sweet innocent Sister, and the Lady Beldam; upon his return to Philadelphia, who could not rest that Night, for thinking on the Happiness she was going to enjoy in the Conversation of so virtuous a Lady as her Brother's Acquaintance, to whom she was in Hopes that she might discover her dearest Thoughts, and complain of Sir William's Extravagance and Unkindness, without running the Hazzard of being betray'd; and at the same Time, reasonably expect from so pious a Lady all the Assistance within her Capacity. On the other side, her Brother hugg'd himself in the Prospect he had of getting rid of his own Sister, and the Payment of 6000l. for the Sum of forty or fifty Guineas, by the Help and Discretion of this sage Matron; who, for her part, by this Time, had reckon'd up, and promis'd to herself an Advantage of at least three hundred Pounds, one way or other by this bargain.

About Ten the next Morning, Sir William took Coach with his Sister, for the old Lady's Enchanted Castle, taking only one Trunk of hers with them for the present, promising her to send her other Things to her the next Day. The young Lady was very joyfully and respectfully received by her Brother's venerable Acquaintance, who was mightily charm'd with her Youth and Beauty. A Bottle of the Best was then strait brought in, and not long after a very splendid Entertainment for Breakfast: The Furniture was all very modish and rich, and the Attendance was suitable. Nor was the Lady Beldam's Conversation less obliging and modest, than Sir William's Discourse had given Philadelphia occasion to expect. After they had eaten and drank what they thought Convenient, the reverend old Lady led 'em out of the Parlour to shew 'em the House, every Room of which they found answerably furnish'd to that whence they came. At last she led 'em into a very pleasant Chamber, richly hung, and curiously adorn'd with the Pictures of several beautiful young Ladies, wherein there was a Bed which might have been worthy the Reception of a Dutchess: This, Madam, (said she) is your Apartment, with the Anti-chamber, and little Withdrawing-Room. Alas, Madam! (returned the dear innocent unthinking Lady) you set too great a Value on your Servant; but I rather think your Ladyship designs me this Honour for the sake of Sir William, who has had the Happiness of your Acquaintance for some Months: Something for Sir William, (returned the venerable Lady Beldam) but much more for your Ladyship's own, as you will have Occasion to find hereafter. I shall Study to deserve your Favours and Friendship, Madam, reply'd Philadelphia: I hope you will, Madam, said the barbarous Man. But my Business now calls me hence; to Morrow at Dinner I will return to you, and Order the rest of your Things to be brought with me. In the mean while (pursu'd the Traytor, kissing his Sister, as he thought and hop'd the last time) be as chearful as you can, my Dear! and expect all you can wish from me. A thousand Thanks, my dearest Brother, return'd she, with Tears in her Eyes: And Madam, (said he to his old mischievous Confederate, giving her a very rich Purse which held 50 Guineas) be pleas'd to accept this Trifle, as an humble Acknowledgment of the great Favour you do this Lady, and the Care of her, which you promise; and I'm sure she cannot want. So, once more, (added he) my Dear! and, Madam! I am your humble Servant Jusqu' a Revoir, and went out bowing. Heavens bless my dear Brother! (cry'd Philadelphia) your Honour's most Faithful and obedient Servant, said the venerable Beldam.

No sooner was the treacherous Brother gone, than the old Lady taking Philadelphia by the Hand, led her into the Parlour; where she began to her to this Effect: If I mistake not, Madam, you were pleas'd to call Sir William Brother once or twice of late in Conversation: Pray be pleas'd to satisfy my Curiosity so far as to inform me in the Truth of this Matter? Is it really so or not? Philadelphia reply'd, blushing, your Ladyship strangely surprizes me with this Question: For, I thought it had been past your Doubt that it is so. Did not he let you know so much himself? I humbly beg your Pardon, Madam, (returned the true Offspring of old Mother Eve) that I have so visibly disturb'd you by my Curiosity: But, indeed, Madam, Sir William did not say your Ladyship was his Sister, when he gave me the Charge of you, as of the nearest and dearest Friend he had in the World. Now our Father and Mother are dead, (said the sweet Innocent) who never had more Children than us two, who can be a nearer or dearer Friend unto me, than my Brother Sir William, or than I his Sister to him? None?

Certainly, you'll excuse me, Madam, (answer'd t'other) a Wife or Mistress may. A Wife indeed, (return'd the beautiful Innocent) has the Pre-eminence, and perhaps, a Mistress too, if honourably lov'd and sought for in Marriage: But, (she continu'd) I can assure your Ladyship that he has not a Wife, nor did I ever hear he had a Mistress yet. Love in Youth (said old Venerable) is very fearful of Discovery. I have known, Madam, a great many fine young Gentlemen and Ladies, who have conceal'd their violent Passions and greater Affection, under the Notion and Appellation of Brother and Sister. And your Ladyship imagines, Sir William and I do so? reply'd Philadelphia, by way of Question. 'Twere no imprudence, if you did, Madam, return'd old Lady Beldam, with all the Subtlety she had learn'd from the Serpent. Alas! Madam, (reply'd she) there is nothing like Secrecy in Love: 'Tis the very Life and Soul of it! I have been young myself, and have known it by Experience. But, all this, Madam, (interrupted Philadelphia, something nettl'd at her Discourse) all this can't convince me, that I am not the true and only Sister both by Father and Mother of Sir William Wilding; however, he wou'd impose upon your Ladyship, for what Ends, indeed, I know not, unless (unhappily, which Heaven forbid!) he designs to gain your Ladyship's Assistance in defeating me of the Portion left me by my Father: But, (she continued with Tears) I have too great an Assurance of your Virtue, to Fear that you will consent to so wicked a Practise. You may be confident, Madam, (said t'other) I never will. And, supposing that he were capable of perpetrating so base an Act of himself, yet if your Ladyship will be guided and directed by me, I will shew you the Means of living Happy and Great, without your Portion, or your Brother's Help; so much I am charm'd with your Beauty and Innocence.

But, pray, Madam, (pursu'd she) what is your Portion? And what makes you doubt your Brother's Kindness? Philadelphia then told her, how much her Brother was to pay her, and gave her an Account of his Extravagancies, as far as she knew 'em; to which t'other was no Stranger; and (doubtless) cou'd have put a Period to her Sorrows with her Life, had she given her as perfect a Relation of his riotous and vicious Practices, as she was capable of: But she had farther Business with her Life, and, in short, bid her be of good Comfort, and lay all her Care on her, and then she cou'd not miss of continual Happiness. The sweet Lady took all her Promises for sterling, and kissing her Impious Hand, humbly return'd her Thanks. Not long after they went to Dinner; and in the Afternoon, three or four young Ladies came to visit the Right Reverend the Lady Beldam; who told her new Guest, that these were all her Relations, and no less than her own Sister's Children. The Discourse among 'em was general and very modest, which lasted for some Hours: For, our Sex seldom wants matter of Tattle. But, whether their Tongues were then miraculously wearied, or that they were tir'd with one continued Scene of Place, I won't pretend to determine: But they left the Parlour for the Garden, where after about half an Hour's Walk, there was a very fine Desert of Sweetmeats and Fruits brought into one of the Arbours. Cherbetts, Ros Solis, rich and small Wines, with Tea, Chocolate, &c. compleated the old Lady's Treat; the Pleasure of which was much heighten'd by the Voices of two of her Ladyship's Sham-Nieces, who sung very charmingly. The Dear, sweet Creature, thought she had happily got into the Company of Angels: But (alas!) they were Angels that had fallen more than once. She heard talk of Nunneries, and having never been out of her own Country till within four or five Days, she had certainly concluded she had been in one of those Religious-Houses now, had she but heard a Bell ring, and seen 'em kneel to Prayers, and make use of their Beads, as she had been told those happy people do. However it was, she was extremely pleas'd with the Place and Company. So nearly do's Hell counterfeit Heaven sometimes. At last, said one of the white Devils, wou'd my dear Tommy were here! O Sister! (cry'd another) you won't be long without your wish: For my Husband and he went out together, and both promis'd to be here after the Play. Is my Brother Sir Francis with him there? (ask'd the first) yes, (answer'd the third) Sir Thomas and Sir Francis took Coach from St. James's, about two Hours since: We shall be excellent Company when they come, (said a fourth); I hope they'll bring the Fiddlers with 'em, added the first: Don't you love Musick, Madam? (ask'd the old Lady Beldam) Sometimes, Madam, (reply'd Philadelphia) but now I am out o'tune myself. A little harmless Mirth will chear your drooping Spirits, my dear, (return'd t'other, taking her by the Hand) come! These are all my Relations, as I told you, Madam; and so consequently are their Husbands. Are these Ladies all marry'd, Madam? Philadelphia ask'd. All, all, my dear Soul! (reply'd the insinuating Mother of Iniquity;) and thou shalt have a Husband too, e're long. Alas, Madam! (return'd the fair Innocent) I have no Merit, nor Money: Besides, I never yet could Love so well as to make Choice of one Man before another.

How long have you liv'd then, Madam? (ask'd the Lady Beldam) too long by almost sixteen Years, (reply'd Philadelphia) had Heaven seen good. This Conversation lasted till Word was brought that Sir Francis and Sir Thomas, with Two other Gentlemen were just lighted at the Gate: Which so discompos'd the fair Innocent, that trembling, she begg'd leave to retire to her Chamber. To which, after some Perswasion to the contrary, the venerable Beldam waited on her. For, these were none of the Sparks to whom Philadelphia was design'd to be Sacrific'd. In her Retirement, the Beautiful dear Creature had the Satisfaction of venting her Grief in Tears, and addressing herself to Heaven, on which only she trusted, notwithstanding all the fair Promises of her reverend Hostess; she had not been retir'd above an Hour, e're a She-attendant waited on her, to know if she wanted any thing, and what she wou'd please to have for her Supper; if she wou'd not give her Lady the Honour of her Company below? To which she return'd, that she wou'd not Sup, and that she wanted nothing but Rest, which she wou'd presently seek in Bed. This Answer brought up the Officious old Lady herself; who, by all Means wou'd needs see her undress'd, for other Reasons more than a bare Compliment; which she perform'd with a great deal of Ceremony, and a Diligence that seem'd more than double. For she had then the Opportunity of observing the Delicacy of her Skin, the fine turn of her Limbs, and the richness of her Night-dress, part of the Furniture of her Trunk. As soon as she had cover'd herself, she kiss'd and wish'd her a good Repose. The dear Soul, as Innocent and White as her Linen, return'd her Thanks, and address'd herself to Sleep; out of which she was waken'd by a loud Consort of Musick, in less than two Hours time, which continu'd till long after Midnight. This occasion'd strange and doubtful Thoughts in her, tho' she was altogether so unskill'd in these Mysteries, that she cou'd not guess the right Meaning. She apprehended, that (possibly) her Brother had a Mistress, from the Lady Beldam's Discourse, and that this was their Place of Assignation: Suspecting too, that either Sir Francis, or Sir Thomas, of whom she had heard not long before, was Sir William, her Brother. The Musick and all the Noise in the House ceas'd about four a Clock in the Morning; when she again fell into a Sleep, that took away the Sense of her Sorrows, and Doubts 'till Nine; when she was again visited from her Lady, by the same She-attendant, to know how she had rested, and if she wou'd Please to Command her any Service. Philadelphia reply'd, That she had rested very well most Part of the Morning, and that she wanted nothing, but to know how her Lady had Slept, and whether she were in Health, unless it were the Sight of her Brother. The Servant return'd with this Answer to her Lady, while Philadelphia made shift to rise, and begin to Dress without an Assistant; but she had hardly put on anything more than her Night-gown, e're the Lady Beldam herself came in her Dishabille, to assure her of her Brother's Company with 'em at Dinner, exactly at One a Clock; and finding Philadelphia doing the Office of a Waiting-woman to herself, call'd up the same Servant, and in a great Heat (in which however she took Care to make Use of none of her familiar develish Dialect) ask'd the Reason that she durst leave the Lady when she was Rising. The Wench trembling, reply'd, That indeed the Lady did not let her know that she had any Thoughts of Rising. Well then (said her seeming offended Lady) stir not from her now, I charge you, 'till she shall think fit to dismiss you, and Command your Absence. Dear Madam, Good Morrow to you, (said she to Philadelphia) I'll make haste and Dress too. Good Morrow to your Ladyship (return'd the design'd Victim) when she was Habille, she desir'd the Servant to withdraw; after which she betook herself to her Devotion; at the end of which the Lady Beldam return'd, attended by a Servant, who brought some Bread and Wine for her Breakfast; which might then be seasonable enough to Philadelphia; who cou'd not forbear discovering the Apprehensions she had of her Brother's Unkindness, still entertaining her Reverence, with the Fear she had of his Disappointment that Day at Dinner; which t'other oppos'd with all the seeming Reasons her Art cou'd suggest, 'till the Clock had struck Twelve; when a Servant came to tell the Lady Beldam, that one Sir William Wilding wou'd certainly wait on her precisely at One, and desir'd that he might Dine in the young Lady's Apartment, to avoid being seen by any Visitants that might come; and besides, that he had invited a Gentleman, his particular Friend, to Dinner with him there. This Message being deliver'd aloud by the Servant, was no little Satisfaction to the poor desponding young Lady, who discours'd very chearfully of indifferent Matters, 'till the Clock gave 'em Notice that the Hour was come; within three Minutes after which, Word was brought to the Lady Beldam, that a Gentleman below enquir'd for Sir William Wilding, whom she immediately went down to receive, and led up to Philadelphia. Madam, (cry'd the great Mistress of her Art) this is the Gentleman whom Sir William has invited to Dinner with us; and I am very Happy to see him, for he is my worthy Friend, and of a long Acquaintance. Trust me, Madam, he is a Man of Honour, and has a very large Estate: I doubt not (added she) that you will find his Merits in his Conversation. Here Gracelove, for that was the Gentleman's Name, saluted Philadelphia, and acquitted himself like a Person of good Sense and Education, in his first Address to her; which she return'd with all the Modesty and ingenuous Simplicity that was still proper to her. At last she ask'd him how long he thought it wou'd be e're Sir William came? To which he reply'd, that Sir William told him, unless he were there exactly at half an Hour after One, they shou'd not stay Dinner for him; that he had not parted with him much above a Quarter of an Hour, when he left him engag'd with particular Company, about some weighty Business: But however, that, if he shou'd be so unhappy as to lose their Conversation at Dinner, he wou'd not fail to wait on 'em by Four at farthest. The young Lady seem'd a little uneasie at this; but the Gentleman appearing so very Modest, and speaking it with such an assur'd Gravity, took away all Thoughts of Suspicion. To say Truth, Gracelove was a very honest, modest, worthy and handsome Person; and had the Command, at present, of a many Thousand Pounds, he was by Profession a Turkey Merchant: He had Travell'd much, for his Age, not having then reach'd Thirty, and had seen most of the Courts in Christendom: He was a Man of a sweet Temper, of just Principles, and of inviolable Friendship, where he promis'd; which was no where, but where 'twas merited. The Minute came then at length, but without any Sir William; so Dinner was serv'd up in the Room next to Philadelphia's Bed-chamber. What they had was Nice and Seasonable; and they were all Three as Pleasant as cou'd be expected, without Sir William; to whose Health the Glass went round once or twice. Dinner over, and the Table clear'd, the old Lady Beldam entreated Mr. Gracelove to entertain the young Lady with a Discourse of his Travels, and of the most remarkable Passages and Encounters of 'em, which he perform'd with a Modesty and Gravity peculiar to himself; and in some part of his Discourse mov'd the innocent Passions of the beauteous and compassionate Philadelphia; who was as attentive as she us'd to be in Church at Divine Service. When the old Lady perceiv'd that he had made an end, or at least, that he desir'd to proceed no farther, she took Occasion to leave 'em together, in haste; pretending, that she had forgotten to give Orders to one of her Servants, about a Business of Moment, and that she wou'd return to 'em in a very little Time. The Gentleman, you may believe, was very well pleas'd with her Retreat, since he had a Discourse to make to Philadelphia of a quite contrary Nature to the Preceding, which requir'd Privacy: But how grateful her Absence was to Philadelphia, we may judge by the Sequel. Madam, (said Gracelove) how do you like the Town? Have you yet seen any Man here whom you cou'd Love? Alas, Sir! (she reply'd) I have not seen the Town, only in a Coach, as I pass'd along, nor ever was in any House, except this and another, where my Brother lodg'd: And to your other Question I must Answer, that I Love all Men. That's generous, indeed, Madam! (cry'd he) there is then some hope that I am one of the Number. No doubt, Sir, (she return'd) that I Love you as well as any, except Sir William. Is he the happy Man then, Madam? (said Gracelove.) If to be loved best by me, may make any Man happy, doubtless it must be he, for he is my own Brother. I fancy, Madam, (return'd he) that you may make me as dear a Relation to you, as Sir William. How is that possible, Sir? she ask'd. Thus, Madam, (replied he, drawing closer to her) by our nearer Approaches to one another. O, Heaven defend me! (cried she aloud) what do you mean? Take away your Hand; you uncivil Man! Help! Madam! my Lady! O, (said Gracelove) she's gone purposely out of hearing. Am I betray'd then? She cried. Betray'd! as if your pretty innocent Ladyship did not know where you were lodged. Ah, Lady, (said he) this Faint will never do. Come, Child, (pursued he) here are an hundred Guineas for you; and I promise you Yearly as much, and Two Hundred with every Child that I shall get on thy sweet Body: Faith I love thee, thou pretty Creature. Come! let's be better acquainted! you know my Meaning. Hell does, no doubt of (she return'd!) O Monster a Man! I hate the Sight of you. With that she flung from him, and ran into the Bed-chamber, where she thought to have locked herself in; but the Key was conveyed into his Pocket. Thither, therefore, he pursued her, crying, Ah, Madam, this is the proper Field for our Dispute. Perceiving her Error, and animated by Despair, she rushed between him and the Door, into the outward Room again, he still following, and dodging her from Chair to Chair, she still Shrieking. At last (cried he) a Parley, Madam, with you. Let me ask you one Question, and will you Answer me directly and truly to it? Indeed, I will, (said she) if it be Civil. Don't you know then, that you are in a naughty House, and that old Beldam is a rank Procuress, to whom I am to give Two hundred Guineas for your Maidenhead? O Heaven (cried she, kneeling with Tears gushing out from her dear Eyes) thou Asserter and Guardian of Innocence! protect me from the impious Practices intended against me! Then looking steadfastly on him, Sir, (pursued she) I can but Difficultly guess what you mean: But I find, that unless you prove what at first you seemed to me, I would say, an honest worthy Gentleman, I shall be in danger of eternal Ruin. You, Sir, are the only Person that may yet Preserve me. Therefore I beseech you, Sir, hear my Story, with the Injuries and Afflictions that so dreadfully torment me; of which, I am sure, none of those Barbarians, of which you had Occasion to speak but now, would have been guilty! O hear, and help me! for Heaven's Sake, hear and help me! I will, poor Creature, (return'd he) methinks I now begin to see my Crime and thy Innocence in thy Words and Looks. Here she recounted to him all the Accidents of her Life, since her Father's Decease, to that very Day, e're Gracelove came to Dinner. And now (cry'd she, sobbing and weeping) how dare I trust this naughty Brother again? Can I be safe with him, think you, Sir? O! no; thou dear sweet Creature! by no Means. O infernal Monsters, Brother and Bawd! If you distrust that I am yet his Sister, here, Sir, take this Key, (said she) and open that Trunk within, where you will find Letters from him to me in his own Hand; and from my own dear dead Father too, Sir Edward, that gracious, that good Man! He shew'd us both the Paths of Virtue: which I have not yet forsaken. Pray satisfy me, Sir, and see the Truth! For your Satisfaction I will, Madam, (said he) but I am now fully convinc'd that you have greater Beauties within, than those I admire without. Saying this, he open'd the Trunk, where he read a Line or two from her Father, and as many from her Brother, which having again laid down, return'd to her, with this Advice: I see, Madam, (said he) that you have Money there, and several Things of Value, which I desire you to secure about you this Moment; for I mean to deliver you out of this cursed Place, if you dare put any Confidence in a Stranger, after your own Brother has acted the Part of so great a Villain; if you dare trust a Stranger too, Madam, who had himself a Design upon you; Heaven forgive me for it! but by all Things sacred, I find my Error: I pity you, and I fear I shall love you. Do you fear that, Sir? (said she) Why I love you dearly now, because I see you are going to be good again; that is, you are going to be yourself again. I hope, nay, I resolve I will, tho' it cost me my Life (said he.) Can you submit, Madam, to attend on a young Lady of my Acquaintance here in Town, 'till I can provide better for you? O I can be any Thing; a Chamber-Maid, a Cook-Maid, a Scullion, what you shall think fit, tho' never so mean, that is not naughty. Well, Madam, (said he) compose your self then, and seem a little pleasant when I bring up that old Factoress of Hell. I will endeavour it, Sir, she return'd; and he went down to the Devil's chief Agent, to whom he said, that the poor Thing was at first very uneasy, but that now she had consented to go along with him for an Hour or two to some other Place, doubting your Secrecy; for she would not have her Brother know it, as she calls him, for a thousand Worlds, and more Money. Well, my Son, (reply'd old Beldam) you may take her with you: But you remember your Bargain. O fie, Mother! (cry'd he) did you ever know me false to you? No, no, you smock'd-fac'd Wag, (said she) but be sure you bring her again to Night, for fear Sir William should come. Never doubt it! Come up with me, (cry'd he) you'll see a strange Alteration, I believe. To Philadelphia they came then, whom they found walking about the Room, and looking something more pleasantly than she had ever done since she came thither. After she had taken her Money, and other Things of Value, so, Madam, (said Beldam) how does your Ladiship now? I find, the Sight of a young handsome Gentleman has work'd Wonders with you in a little Time: I understand you are going to take a Walk with my worthy Friend here, and 'tis well done: I dare trust you with him, but with no other Man living, except Sir William. Madam, (return'd the fair afflicted Lady) I am strangely oblig'd to you for your Care of me, and am sure I shall never be able to return your Obligations as I ought, and as I could wish. You won't stay late, Mr. Gracelove? (said the Mother of Mischief.) No, no, (reply'd he) I will only shew the Lady a Play, and return to Supper. What is play'd to Night? (ask'd the old One) The Cheats, Mother, the Cheats. (answer'd Gracelove.) Ha, (said Beldam, laughing) a very pretty Comedy, indeed! Ay, if well play'd, return'd he. At these Words, they went down, where a Coach was call'd; which carry'd 'em to Counsellor Fairlaw's House, in Great Lincolns-Inn-Fields, whom they found accidentally at Home; but his Lady and Daughter were just gone to Chapel, being then turn'd of Five. Gracelove began his Apology to the good old Counsellor, who was his Relation, for bringing a strange Lady thither, with a Design to place her in his Family: But Sir, continu'd he, if you knew her sorrowful Story, you would be as ambitious of entertaining her, as I am earnest to entreat it of you. A very beautiful Lady 'tis, (return'd the Counsellor) and very modest, I believe. That I can witness (reply'd t'other.) Alas, Sir! (said the fair Unfortunate) I have nothing but my Modesty and honest Education to recommend me to your Regard. I am wrong'd and forsaken by my nearest Relation; then she wept extravagantly: That Gentleman can give you an Account of my Misfortunes, if he pleases, with greater Ease and less Trouble than my self. Not with less Trouble, believe me, Madam; (return'd Gracelove) and then began to inform Fairlaw in every Point of her unhappy Circumstances. The good old Gentleman heard 'em with Amazement and Horror; but told her, however, that she need not despond, for he would take Care to right her against her Brother; and, that in the mean Time she should be as welcome to him as any of his nearest Kindred, except his Wife and Daughter. Philadelphia would have knelt to thank him; but he told her, that humble Posture was due to none but Heaven, and the King sometimes. In a little While after, the Lady Fairlaw and her Daughter came Home, who were surpriz'd at the Sight of a Stranger, but more at her Beauty, and most of all at her Story, which the good old Gentleman himself could not forbear relating to 'em: Which ended, the Mother and Daughter both kindly and tenderly embrac'd her, promising her all the Assistance within their Power, and bid her a thousand Welcomes. Gracelove stay'd there 'till after Supper, and left her extremely satisfy'd with her new Station. 'Twas here she fix'd then; and her Deportment was so obliging, that they would not part with her for any Consideration. About three Days after her coming from that lewd Woman's House, Gracelove took a Constable and some other Assistants, and went to Beldam's to demand the Trunk, and what was in it, which at first her Reverence deny'd to return, 'till Mr. Constable produc'd the Emblem of his Authority, upon which it was deliver'd, without so much as re-minding Gracelove of his Bargain; who then pretended he would search the House for Sir William Wilding; but her graceless Reverence swore most devoutly that he had never been there, and that she had neither seen nor heard from him since the Day he left Philadelphia with her. With these Things, and this Account he return'd to Counsellor Fairlaw's, who desir'd Gracelove, if possible, to find out Sir William, and employ'd several others on the same Account. In less than a Month's Time Gracelove had the good Fortune to find him at his Lodgings in Soho-Square, where he discours'd him about his Sister's Portion, and desir'd Sir William to take some speedy Care for the Payment of it; otherwise she had Friends that would oblige him to it, tho' never so contrary to his Intentions. Wilding ask'd where she was? t'other enquir'd where he left her? Sir William reply'd, that he had plac'd her with an old grave Gentlewoman of his Acquaintance, and that he thought she was there still. No, Sir, (return'd Gracelove) I have deliver'd her out of the Jaws of Perdition and Hell. Come, Sir William, (answer'd he) 'twas impiously done, to leave your beautiful, young, and virtuous Sister, to the Management of that pernicious Woman. I found her at old Beldam's, who would have prostituted her to me for two hundred Guineas; but her heavenly Virtues might have secur'd and guarded her from more violent Attempts than mine. Blush, if you can, Sir! and repent of this! It will become you. If not, Sir, you will hear farther from your Servant, added he, and left him staring after him. This Discourse was a great

Mortification to the Knight, whose Conscience, harden'd as it was, felt yet some Pain by it. He found he was not like to continue safe or at Ease there, where he immediately retreated into a Place of Sanctuary, call'd the Savoy, whither his whole Equipage was remov'd as soon as possible, he having left Order with his Servants, to report that he went out of Town that very Afternoon for his own Country. Gracelove in the mean Time return'd to the Counsellor's, with a great deal of Joy, for having discover'd Sir William at his Lodgings, which was likewise no little Satisfaction to Fairlaw, his Lady and Daughter; Philadelphia only was disturb'd when she heard the good old Gentleman threaten to lay her Brother fast enough: But, alas! he was too cunning for 'em; for in a whole Twelvemonth after, all which Time they made Enquiry, and narrowly search'd for him, they could not see him, nor any one that could give an Account of him, for he had chang'd his true Name and Title, for that of 'Squire Sportman. The farther Pursuit of him then seem'd fruitless to 'em, and they were forc'd to be contented with their Wishes to find him.

Gracelove by this Time had entertain'd the sincerest Affections and noblest Passion that Man can be capable of, for Philadelphia; of which he had made her sensible, who had at that Time comply'd with his honourable Demands, had she not entreated him to expect a kind Turn of Providence, which might, (happily) e're long, put her in Possession of her Right; without which, she told him, she could not consent to marry him, who had so plentiful a Fortune, and she nothing but her Person and Innocence. How, Madam! (cry'd he) have you no Love in Store for me! Yes, Sir, (return'd she) as much as you can wish I have in Store for you, and so I beg it may be kept 'till a better Opportunity. Well, Madam, (said he) I must leave you for some Months, perhaps for a whole Year; I have receiv'd Letters of Advice that urge the Necessity of my going to Turkey; I have not a Week's Time to endeavour so dreaded a Separation as I must suffer; therefore, thou beautiful, thou dear, thou virtuous Creature, let me begin now! Here, thou tenderest Part of my Soul! (continu'd he, giving her a rich Diamond Ring) wear this 'till my Return! I hope the Sight of it may sometimes re-call the dying Memory of Gracelove to your better-busy'd Thoughts. Ah, Gracelove! (said she) nothing can so well, nothing I am sure can better employ my Thoughts, than thy dear self: Heaven only excepted. They enlarg'd a great deal more on this Subject at that Time; but the Night before his Departure was entirely spent in Sighs, Vows, and Tears, on both Sides. In the Morning, after he had again entreated his Cousin's, and the Lady's, and her Daughter's Care and Kindness to Philadelphia, the remaining and best Part of his Soul, with one hearty Kiss, accompany'd with Tears, he took a long Farewel of his dear Mistress, who pursu'd him with her Eyes, 'till they could give her no farther Intelligence of him; and they help'd her Kindness to him, and eas'd her Grief for his Absence in weeping for above a Week together, when in private. He never omitted writing to her and his Cousin by every Opportunity, for near nine Months, as he touch'd at any Port; but afterwards they could not hear from him for above half a Year; when, by Accident, the Counsellor met a Gentleman of Gracelove's Acquaintance at a Coffee-House, who gave him an Account, that the Ship and he were both cast away, near five Months since; that most if not all of the Ship's Company perish'd; of which, 'twas fear'd, Gracelove was one, having never since been heard of. That his Loss in that Ship amounted to above twelve thousand Pounds: With this dreadful and amazing News the good old Gentleman returns Home, afflicts his poor sorrowful Lady and Daughter, and almost kills unhappy Philadelphia; who the next Day, by mere Chance, and from a Stranger, who came on Business to the Counsellor, heard, that one Sir William Wilding, an extravagant, mad, young Spark of such a County, who lately went by the borrow'd Name and Title of 'Squire Sportman, had mortgag'd all his Estate, which was near four thousand a Year, and carry'd the Money over with him into France on Saturday last. This, added to the former News, put so great a Check on her Spirits, that she immediately dropp'd down in a Swoon; whence she only recover'd, to fall into what was of a much more dangerous Consequence, a violent Feaver, which held her for near six Weeks, e're she could get Strength enough to go down Stairs: In all which Time, Madam Fairlaw and Eugenia, her Daughter, attended her as carefully and constantly, as if they had been her own Mother and Sister: The good old Counsellor still commending and encouraging their Care. The Roses and Lillies at last took their

Places again; but the Clouds of her Sorrow were still but too visible. Two Years more past, without one Word of Advice from Gracelove or any Account of him from any one else; insomuch, that they all concluded he was certainly dead: And, 'twas true, indeed, that his Ship and he were cast away, much about that Time that the Gentleman gave Fairlaw a Relation: That 'twas certain he had lost above 1200ol. and had like to have lost his Life; but being very expert in Swimming, he got to Shoar upon the Coast of Barbary, the Wreck happening not to be above three Leagues thence; he was in almost as bad a Condition as if he had been drown'd, for here he was made a Prisoner to one of the Natives; in which miserable Circumstance he lanquish'd for above six Years, for Want of a Ransom; which he had often endeavour'd to raise by Letters, that he sent hither to his Friends (in England;) amongst which Counsellor Fairlaw was one of his most particular and assur'd. But however Providence or Accident, if you please, order'd it, not a Line came to the Hands of any of his Friends; so that had not Heaven had yet a future Blessing in Store for him, he had certainly have better perish'd in the Sea, than to have fall'n into the Power of a People less merciful than Seas, Winds, or hungry wild Beasts in Pursuit of their Prey. But this could not be learn'd (it seems) from any Man but himself, upon his Return, after his Redemption.

Two Years more pass'd on; towards the latter of which the old Lady Fairlaw took her Bed, desperately sick, insomuch that she was given over by all her Physicians; she continu'd in great Misery for near two Months; in all which Time Philadelphia was constantly with her all the Day, or all the Night; much about that Time she dy'd; and, dying, told her Husband, that she had observ'd he had a particular Esteem or Kindness for Philadelphia; which was now a great Satisfaction to her; since she was assur'd, that if he marry'd her, she would prove an excellent Nurse to him, and prolong his Life by some Years. As for Eugenia, (added she) you need not be concern'd; I'm sure she will consent to any Thing that you shall propose, having already so plentifully provided for her. The good old Gentleman answer'd, that he would fulfil her Will as far as lay in his Power: And not long after, she departed this Life. Her Burial was very handsome and honourable. Half a Year was now expir'd since her Interment, when the old Counsellor began to plead his own Cause to young Philadelphia, reminding her that now the Death of Gracelove was out of Question; and that therefore she was as much at her Liberty to make her own Choice of an Husband as he was of a Wife; not forgetting, at the same Time, to let her know, that his Widow, (whoever had the good Fortune to be so) would be worth above thirty thousand Pounds in ready Money, besides a thousand a Year. But, above all, he urg'd his dying Lady's last Advice to him, that he would marry her; and hop'd she would see the Will of the Dead satisfy'd. The young Lady being broken in Sorrows, and having mortify'd all her Appetites to the Enjoyments of this World, and not knowing where to meet with so fair an Overture, tho' at first, in Modesty, she seem'd to refuse it as too great an Honour, yet yielded to less than a Quarter of an Hour's Courtship. And the next Sunday marry'd they were, with the Consent, and to the perfect Satisfaction of, his Daughter, Madam Eugenia; who lov'd Philadelphia sincerely. They kept their Wedding very nobly for a Month, at their own House in Great Lincolns-Inn-Fields; but the Memory of the old Lady was still so fresh with the young Lady Fairlaw, that she prevail'd with him to remove to another, more convenient as she fancy'd, in Covent-Garden. They had dwelt there not much more than four Months, e're the good old Gentleman fell sick and dy'd. Whether it were the Change of an old House for a new, or an old Wife for a young, is yet uncertain, tho' his Physicians said, and are still of Opinion, that, doubtless, it was the last. 'Tis past all Doubt, that she did really mourn for and lament his Death; for she lov'd him perfectly, and pay'd him all the dutiful respect of a virtuous Wife, while she liv'd within that State with him; which he rewarded as I have said before. His Funeral was very sumptuous and honourable indeed! and as soon as it was over, Eugenia desir'd her young beautiful Mother-in-Law to retreat a little with her into the Country, to a pleasant House she had, not twenty Miles distant from Town; urging, That she could by no Means enjoy her self under that Roof, where her dear Father dy'd. The obliging Step-mother, who might more properly have been call'd her Sister, being exactly of the same Age with her, readily comply'd, and she pass'd away all that Summer with Eugenia, at their

Country-Seat, and most Part of the Winter too; for Eugenia could by no Means be prevail'd on to lie one Night in her Mother's House; 'twas with some Reluctancy that she consented to dine there sometimes. At length the whole Year of Philadelphia's Widowhood was expir'd; during which, you can't but imagine that she was solicited and address'd to by as many Lovers, or pretended Lovers, as our dear King Charles, whom God grant long to reign, was lately by the Presbyterians, Independants, Anabaptists, and all those canting whiggish Brethren! But she had never lik'd any Man so well as to make him her Husband, by Inclination, unless it was Gracelove, devour'd by the greedy Inhabitants of the Sea.

Whilst her Fortune began to mend thus, her Brother's grew worse; but that was indeed the Effect of his Extravagancy: In less than two Years Time, he had spent eight thousand Pounds in France, whence he return'd to England, and pursuing his old profuse Manner of Living, contracted above 100l. Debts here, in less than four Months Time; which not being able to satisfy, he was arrested, and thrown into a Goal, whence he remov'd himself into the King's Bench, on that very Day that old Fairlaw dy'd. There, at first, for about a Month, he was entertain'd like a Gentleman; but finding no Money coming, nor having a Prospect of any, the Marshal and his Instruments turn'd him to the Common Side, where he learnt the Art of Peg-making, a Mystery to which he had been a Stranger all his Life long 'till then. 'Twas then he wish'd he might see his Sister, hoping that she was in a Condition to relieve him; which he was apt to believe, from the Discourse he had with Gracelove some Years past. Often he wish'd to see her, but in vain; however, the next Easter after the old Counsellor's Death, Philadelphia, according to his Custom, sent her Steward to relieve all the poor Prisoners about Town; among the rest he visited those in the common Side of the King's Bench, where he heard 'em call Sir William Wilding to partake of his Lady's Charity. The poor Prodigal was then feeding on the Relief of the Basket, not being yet able to get his Bread at his new Trade: To him the Steward gave a Crown, whereas the other had but Half a Crown apiece. Then he enquir'd of some of the unhappy Gentlemen, Sir William's Fellow-Collegians, of what Country Sir William was? How long he had been there? And how much his Debts were? All of which he receiv'd a satisfactory Account. Upon his Return to his Lady, he repeated the dismal News of her Brother's Misfortunes to her; who immediately dispatch'd him back again to the Prison, with Orders to give him twenty Shillings more at present, and to get him remov'd to the Master's Side, into a convenient Chamber, for the Rent of which the Steward engag'd to pay; and promis'd him, as she had commanded, twenty Shillings a Week, as long as he stay'd there, on Condition that he would give the Names of all his Creditors, and of all those to whom he had engag'd any Part of his Estate; which the poor Gentleman did most readily and faithfully: After which, the Steward enquir'd for a Taylor, who came and took Measure of Philadelphia's unkind Brother, and was order'd to provide him Linnen, a Hat, Shoes, Stockings, and all such Necessaries, not so much as omitting a Sword: With all which he acquainted his Lady at his Return; who was very much griev'd at her Brother's unhappy Circumstances, and at the same Time extremely well pleas'd to find her self in a Condition to relieve him. The Steward went constantly once a Week to pay him his Money; and Sir William was continually very curious to know to whom he was oblig'd for so many and great Favours; But he was answer'd, That they came from a Lady who desir'd to have her Name conceal'd. In less than a Year, Philadelphia had paid 2500l. and taken off the Mortgages on 2500l. per Annum of her Brother's Estate; and coming to Town from Eugenia's Country-House one Day, to make the last Payment of two thousand Pounds, looking out of her Coach on the Road, near Dartford, she saw a Traveller on Foot, who seem'd to be tir'd with his Journey, whose Face, she thought, she had formerly known: This Thought invited her to look on him so long, that she, at last, perswaded her self it was Gracelove, or his Ghost: For, to say Truth, he was very pale and thin, his Complexion swarthy, and his Cloaths (perhaps) as rotten as if he had been bury'd in 'em. However, unpleasant as it was, she could not forbear gazing after this miserable Spectacle; and the more she beheld it, the more she was confirmed it was Gracelove, or something that had usurp'd his Figure. In short, she could not rest 'till she call'd to one of her Servants, who rode by the Coach, whom she strictly charg'd to go to that poor Traveller, and mount him on his Horse, 'till they came to Dartford; where she order'd him to take him to the same Inn where she baited, and refresh him with any Thing that he would eat or drink; and after that, to hire a Horse for him, to come to Town with them: That then he should be brought Home to her own House, and be carefully look'd after, 'till farther Orders from her. All which was most duly and punctually perform'd.

The next Morning early she sent for the Steward, whom she order'd to take the Stranger to a Sale-shop, and fit him with a Suit of good Cloaths, to buy him Shirts, and other Linnen, and all Necessaries, as he had provided for her Brother; and gave him Charge to use him as her particular Friend, during his Stay there, bidding him, withal, learn his Name and Circumstances, if possible, and to supply him with Money for his Pocket Expences: All which he most faithfully and discreetly perform'd, and brought his Lady an Account of his Sufferings by Sea, and Slavery among the Turks, as I have before related; adding, that his Name was Gracelove. This was the greatest Happiness, certainly, that ever yet the dear beautiful Creature was sensible of. On t'other Side, Gracelove could not but admire and praise his good Fortune, that had so miraculously and bountifully reliev'd him; and one Day having some private Discourse with the Steward, he could not forbear expressing the Sense he had of it; declaring, That he could not have expected such kind Treatment from any Body breathing, but from his Cousin, Counsellor Fairlaw, his Lady, or another young Lady, whom he plac'd and left with his Cousins. Counsellor Fairlaw! (cry'd the Steward) why, Sir, my Lady is the old Counsellor's Widow; she is very beautiful and young too. What was her Name, Sir, before she marry'd the Counsellor? (ask'd Gracelove) That I know not, (reply'd t'other) for the old Steward dy'd presently after the old Lady, which is not a Year and a Half since; in whose Place I succeed; and I have never been so curious or inquisitive, as to pry into former Passages of the Family. Do you know, Sir, (said Gracelove) whereabouts in Town they liv'd before? Yes, Sir, (return'd the Steward, who was taught how to answer) in Great Lincolns-Inn-Fields, I think, Alas! (cry'd Gracelove) 'twas the same Gentleman to whom I design'd to apply my self when I came to England. You need not despair now, Sir, (said t'other) I dare say my Lady will supply your Wants. O wonderful Goodness of a Stranger! (cry'd Gracelove) uncommon and rare amongst Relations and Friends! How have I, or how can I ever merit this? Upon the End of their Conference, the Steward went to Philadelphia, and repeated it almost verbatim to her; who order'd Gracelove should be taken Measure of by the best Taylor in Covent-Garden; that he should have three of the most modish rich Suits made, that might become a private Gentleman of a Thousand Pounds a Year, and Hats, Perukes, Linnen, Swords, and all Things suitable to 'em, all to be got ready in less than a Month; in which Time, she took all the Opportunity she could either find or make to see him, and not to be seen by him: She oblig'd her Steward to invite him to a Play, whither she follow'd 'em, and sate next to Gracelove, and talk'd with him; but all the while masq'd. In this Month's Time she was daily pester'd with the Visits of her Addressors; several there were of 'em; but the chief were only a Lord of a very small Estate, tho' of a pretty great Age; a young blustering Knight, who had a Place of 500l. a Year at Court; and a County Gentleman, of a very plentiful Estate, a Widower, and of a middle Age. These three only of her Lovers she invited to Dinner, on the first Day of the next Month: In the mean while she sent a rich Suit, and Equipage proportionable, to her Brother, with an Invitation to dine with her on the same Day. Then she writ to Eugenia to come and stay in Town, if not in the same House with her, for two or three Days before; which her affectionate Daughter obey'd; to whom Philadelphia related all her Brother's past Extravagancies and what she had done for him in redeeming most Part of his Estate; begging of her, that if she could fancy his Person, she would take him into her Mercy and marry him. Being assur'd, that such a virtuous Wife as she would prove, must necessarily reclaim him, if yet he were not perfectly convinc'd of his Follies; which, she doubted not, his late long Sufferings had done. Eugenia return'd, That she would wholly be directed and advis'd by her in all Things; and that certainly she could not but like the Brother, since she lov'd the Sister so perfectly and truly.

The Day came, and just at Twelve, Gracelove, meeting the Steward on the Stairs coming from his Lady, Gracelove then told him, that he believ'd he might take the Opportunity of that Afternoon to go over to Putney, and take a Game or two at Bowls. The Steward return'd, Very well, Sir, I shall let my Lady know it, if she enquires for you. Philadelphia, who overheard what they said, call'd the Steward in Haste, and bid him call Gracelove back, and tell him, she expected his Company at her Table to Day, and that she desir'd he would appear like himself. The Steward soon overtook him at the Door, just going out as Eugenia came in, who look'd back on Gracelove: The poor Gentleman was strangely surpriz'd at the Sight of her, as she was at his; but the Steward's Message did more amaze and confound him. He went directly to his Chamber, to dress himself in one of those rich Suits lately made for him; but, the Distraction he was in, made him mistake his Coat for his Wastcoat, and put the Coat on first; but, recalling his straggling Thoughts, he made Shift to get ready time enough to make his Appearance without a second Summons. Philadelphia was as pleasant at Dinner, as ever she had been all her Life; she look'd very obligingly on all the Sparks, and drank to every one of 'em particularly, beginning to the Lord, and ending to the Stranger, who durst hardly lift up his Eyes a second Time to her's, to confirm him that he knew her. Her Brother was so confounded, that he bow'd and continu'd his Head down 'till she had done drinking, not daring to encounter her Eyes, that would then have reproach'd him with his Villany to her.

After Dinner the Cloth was taken away; She began thus to her Lovers: My Lord! Sir Thomas! and Mr. Fat-acres! I doubt not, that it will be of some Satisfaction to you, to know whom I have made Choice for my next Husband; which now I am resolv'd no longer to defer.

The Person to whom I shall next drink, must be the Man who shall ever command me and my Fortune, were it ten times greater than it is; which I wish only for his Sake, since he deserves much more. Here, (said she to one that waited) put Wine into two Glasses: Then she took the Diamond Ring from her Finger, and put it into one of 'em. My dear Gracelove, (cry'd she) I drank to thee; and send thee back thy own Ring, with Philadelphia's Heart. He startl'd, blush'd, and looked wildly; whilst all the Company stared on him. Nay, pledge me, (persu'd she) and return me the Ring: for it shall make us both one the next Morning. He bow'd, kiss'd, and return'd it, after he had taken off his Wine. The defeated Lovers knew not how to resent it? The Lord and Knight were for going, but the Country Gentleman oppos'd it, and told 'em, 'twas the greatest Argument of Folly, to be disturb'd at the Caprice of a Woman's Humour. They sate down again therefore, and she invited 'em to her Wedding on the Morrow.

And now, Brother, (said she) I have not quite forgotten you, tho' you have not been pleas'd to take Notice of me: I have a Dish in Reserve for you, which will be more grateful to your Fancy than all you have tasted to Day. Here! (cry'd she to the Steward) Mr. Rightman, do you serve up that Dish your self. Rightman then set a cover'd Dish on the Table. What! more Tricks yet? (cry'd my Lord and Sir Thomas) Come, Sir William! (said his Sister) uncover it! he did so; and cry'd out, O matchless Goodness of a virtuous Sister! here are the Mortgages of the best Part of my Estate! O! what a Villain! what a Monster have I been! no more, dear Brother; (said she, with Tears in her Eyes) I have yet a greater Happiness in Store for you: This Lady, this beautiful virtuous Lady, with twenty thousand Pounds, will make you happy in her Love. Saying this, she join'd their Hands; Sir William eagerly kiss'd Eugenia's, who blush'd, and said, Thus, Madam, I hope to shew how much I love and honour you. My Cousin Eugenia! (cry'd Gracelove!) The same, my dear lost dead Cousin Gracelove! (reply'd she) O! (said he in a Transport) my present Joys are greater than all my past Miseries! my Mistress and my Friend are found, and still are mine. Nay, (faith, said my Lord) this is pleasant enough to me, tho' I have been defeated of the Enjoyment of the Lady. The whole Company in general went away very well that Night, who return'd the next Morning, and saw the two happy Pair firmly united.

**Ros Solis.** A potent and well-liked tipple.
We abandon all ale
And beer that is stale
Rosa-solis and damnable hum,
But we will rack
In the praise of sack
'Gainst Omne quod exit in um.

*Witts Recreation (1654).*

The Accomplished Female Instructor gives the following recipe: 'Rossa Solis; Take of clean spirits, not too strong, two quarts and a quart of spring-water; let them seethe gently over a soft fire till about a pint is evaporated; then put in four spoonfuls of orange-flower-water, and as much of very good cinnamon-water; crush 3 eggs in pieces, and throw them in shell and all; stir it well, and when it boiles up a little take it off.' This drink was so great a favourite with Louis XIV that a particular sort was named Rossolis du Roi.

**The Cheats**, Mother, the Cheats. John Wilson's excellent comedy, The Cheats, which was written and produced in 1662, attained great popularity. It ran into four editions ('imprimatur, 5 November, 1663'); 4to, 1664; 1671; 1684; 1693. Caustically satirizing the Puritans, it became a stock piece, and was acted as late as May, 1721, when Griffin, Harper, Diggs, and Mrs. Gifford sustained the parts which had been created by Lacy, Mohun, Hart, and Mrs. Corey.

## THE FAIR JILT

### INTRODUCTION

Although The Fair Jilt was published in 1688, it is interesting to note that ten years earlier, Michaelmas Term, 1678, there is advertised for R. Tonson The Amorous Convert; being a true Relation of what happened in Holland, which may very well be the first sketch of Mrs. Behn's maturer novel. The fact that she does not 'pretend here to entertain you with a feign'd story,' but on the contrary, 'every circumstance to a tittle is truth', and that she expressly asserts, 'To a great part of the main I myself was an eye-witness', aroused considerable suspicion in Bernbaum as to the veracity of her narration, a suspicion which, when he gravely discovers history to know no such person as her 'Prince Tarpuin of the race of the last Kings of Rome', is resolved into a certainty that she is romancing fully and freely throughout. It is surely obvious that such a point does not so much demonstrate Mrs. Behn's untruthfulness as her consummate art. With all the nice skill of a born novelist she has so mingled fact and fancy, what did occur and what might have been, that any attempt to disentangle the twain would be idle indeed. The passages where she is most insistent upon the due sequence of events, most detailed in observation are not impossibly purely fictional, the incidents related without stress or emphatic assertions are probably enough the plain unvarnished happenings as she witnessed them. That the history is mainly true admits of little question; that Mrs. Behn has heightened and coloured the interest is equally certain.

The Fair Jilt must be allowed to stand in the very first rank amongst her novels. It has been aptly compared to a novella by Bandello, and is indeed more than worthy of the pen of the good

Dominican Bishop of Agen. In all its incidents and motives the story is eternally true. The fateful beauty, playing now the part of Potiphar's wife, and now the yet commoner rôle of an enchantress whose charms drive men to madness and crime, men who adore her even from their prison cell and are glad to go to a shameful death for her sake, appears in all history, in all literature, nay, in the very newspaper scandals and police courts of to-day. As a picture of untrammelled passion, culpable and corrupt, but yet terribly fascinating in her very recklessness and abandon, Miranda is indeed a powerful study. Always guilty, she is always excused, or if punished but sparingly and little, whilst the friar languishes in a foul dungeon, the page-boy is hanged, her husband stands upon the public scaffold. And then in the end, 'very penitent for her life past', she is received with open arms by Tarquin's old father, who looks upon her as a very angel, and retiring to the tranquility of a country-house she passes her days in 'as perfect a state of happiness as this troublesome world can afford'.

To   HENRY PAIN, ESQ;

Sir,

Dedications are like Love, and no Man of Wit or Eminence escapes them; early or late, the Affliction of the Poet's Complement falls upon him; and Men are oblig'd to receive 'em as they do their Wives; For better, for worse; at lest with a feign'd Civility.

It was not Want of Respect, but Fear, that has hitherto made us keep clear of your Judgment, too piercing to be favourable to what is not nicely valuable. We durst not awaken your Criticism; and by begging your Protection in the Front of a Book, give you an Occasion to find nothing to deserve it. Nor can this little History lay a better Claim to that Honour, than those that have not pretended to it; which has but this Merit to recommend it, That it is Truth: Truth, which you so much admire. But 'tis a Truth that entertains you with so many Accidents diverting and moving, that they will need both a Patron, and an Assertor in this incredulous World. For however it may be imagin'd that Poetry (my Talent) has so greatly the Ascendant over me, that all I write must pass for Fiction, I now desire to have it understood that this is Reality, and Matter of Fact, and acted in this our latter Age: And that in the person of Tarquin, I bring a Prince to kiss your Hands, who own'd himself, and was receiv'd, as the last of the Race of the Roman Kings; whom I have often seen, and you have heard of; and whose Story is so well known to your self, and many Hundreds more: Part of which I had from the Mouth of this unhappy great Man, and was an Eye-Witness to the rest.

'Tis true, Sir, I present you with a Prince unfortunate, but still the more noble Object for your Goodness and Pity; who never valu'd a brave Man the less for being unhappy. And whither shou'd the Afflicted flee for Refuge but to the Generous? Amongst all the Race, he cannot find a better Man, or more certain Friend: Nor amongst all his Ancestors, match your greater Soul, and Magnificence of Mind. He will behold in one English Subject, a Spirit as illustrious, a Heart as fearless, a Wit and Eloquence as excellent, as Rome it self cou'd produce. Its Senate scarce boasted of a better States-man, nor Augustus of a more faithful Subject; as your Imprisonment and Sufferings, through all the Course of our late National Distractions, have sufficiently manifested; But nothing cou'd press or deject your great Heart; you were the same Man still, unmov'd in all Turns, easie and innocent; no Persecution being able to abate your constant good Humour, or wonted Gallantry.

If, Sir, you find here a Prince of less Fortitude and Vertue than your self, charge his Miscarriages on Love: a Weakness of that Nature you will easily excuse, (being so great a Friend to the Fair;) though possibly, he gave a Proof of it too Fatal to his Honour. Had I been to have form'd his Character, perhaps I had made him something more worthy of the Honour of your Protection: But I was oblig'd to pursue the Matter of Fact, and give a just Relation of that part of his Life which, possibly, was the only reproachful part of it. If he be so happy, as to entertain a Man of Wit and Business, I shall not fear his Welcome to the rest of the World: And 'tis only with your Passport he can hope to be so.

The particular Obligations I have to your Bounty and Goodness, O Noble Friend, and Patron of the Muses! I do not so much as pretend to acknowledge in this little Present; those being above the Poet's Pay, which is a sort of Coin, not currant in this Age: though perhaps may be esteem'd as Medals in the Cabinets of Men of Wit. If this be so happy to be of that Number, I desire no more lasting a Fame, that it may bear this Inscription, that I am,

SIR,
Your most Obliged, and Most Humble Servant, A. BEHN.

THE FAIR JILT: or, The Amours of Prince Tarquin and Miranda

As Love is the most noble and divine Passion of the Soul, so it is that to which we may justly attribute all the real Satisfactions of Life; and without it Man is unfinish'd and unhappy.

There are a thousand things to be said of the Advantages this generous Passion brings to those, whose Hearts are capable of receiving its soft Impressions; for 'tis not every one that can be sensible of its tender Touches. How many Examples, from History and Observation, could I give of its wondrous Power; nay, even to a Degree of Transmigration! How many Idiots has it made wise! How many Fools eloquent! How many home-bred Squires accomplish'd! How many Cowards brave! And there is no sort of Species of Mankind on whom it cannot work some Change and Miracle, if it be a noble well-grounded Passion, except the Fop in Fashion, the harden'd incorrigible Fop; so often wounded, but never reclaim'd: For still, by a dire Mistake, conducted by vast Opiniatrety, and a greater Portion of Self-love, than the rest of the Race of Man, he believes that Affectation in his Mein and Dress, that Mathematical Movement, that Formality in every Action, that a Face manag'd with Care, and soften'd into Ridicule, the languishing Turn, the Toss, and the Back-shake of the Periwig, is the direct Way to the Heart of the fine Person he adores; and instead of curing Love in his Soul, serves only to advance his Folly; and the more he is enamour'd, the more industriously he assumes (every Hour) the Coxcomb. These are Love's Play-things, a sort of Animals with whom he sports; and whom he never wounds, but when he is in good Humour, and always shoots laughing. 'Tis the Diversion of the little God, to see what a Fluttering and Bustle one of these Sparks, new-wounded, makes; to what fantastick Fooleries he has Recourse: The Glass is every Moment call'd to counsel, the Valet consulted and plagu'd for new Invention of Dress, the Footman and Scrutore perpetually employ'd; Billet-doux and Madrigals take up all his Mornings, till Play-time in dressing, till Night in gazing; still, like a Sun-flower, turn'd towards the Beams of the fair Eyes of his Cælia, adjusting himself in the most amorous Posture he can assume, his Hat under his Arm, while the other Hand is put carelesly into his Bosom, as if laid upon his panting Heart; his Head a little bent to one Side, supported with a World of Cravat-string, which he takes mighty Care not to put into Disorder; as one may guess by a never-failing and horrid Stiffness in his Neck; and if he had any Occasion to look aside, his whole Body turns at the same Time, for Fear the Motion of the Head alone should incommode the Cravat or Periwig: And sometimes the Glove is well manag'd, and the white Hand display'd. Thus, with a thousand other little Motions and Formalities, all in the common Place or Road of Foppery, he takes infinite Pains to shew himself to the Pit and Boxes, a most accomplish'd Ass. This is he, of all human Kind, on whom Love can do no Miracles, and who can nowhere, and upon no Occasion, quit one Grain of his refin'd Foppery, unless in a Duel, or a Battle, if ever his Stars should be so severe and ill-manner'd, to reduce him to the Necessity of either: Fear then would ruffle that fine Form he had so long preserv'd in nicest Order, with Grief considering, that an unlucky Chance-wound in his Face, if such a dire Misfortune should befal him, would spoil the Sale of it forever.

Perhaps it will be urg'd, that since no Metamorphosis can be made in a Fop by Love, you must consider him one of those that only talks of Love, and thinks himself that happy Thing, a Lover; and wanting fine Sense enough for the real Passion, believes what he feels to be it. There are in the Quiver of the God a great many different Darts; some that wound for a Day, and others for a Year; they are all fine, painted, glittering Darts, and shew as well as those made of the noblest Metal; but the Wounds they make reach the Desire only, and are cur'd by possessing, while the short-liv'd Passion betrays the Cheat. But 'tis that refin'd and illustrious Passion of the Soul, whose Aim is Virtue, and whose end is Honour, that has the Power of changing Nature, and is capable of performing all those heroick Things, of which History is full.

How far distant Passions may be from one another, I shall be able to make appear in these following Rules. I'll prove to you the strong Effects of Love in some unguarded and ungovern'd Hearts; where it rages beyond the Inspirations of a God all soft and gentle, and reigns more like a Fury from Hell.

I do not pretend here to entertain you with a feign'd Story, or any Thing piec'd together with romantick Accidents; but every Circumstance, to a Tittle, is Truth. To a great Part of the Main I myself was an Eye-witness; and what I did not see, I was confirm'd of by Actors in the Intrigue, Holy Men, of the Order of St. Francis: But for the Sake of some of her Relations, I shall give my Fair Jilt a feign'd Name, that of Miranda; but my Hero must retain his own, it being too illustrious to be conceal'd.

You are to understand, that in all the Catholick Countries, where Holy Orders are establish'd, there are abundance of differing Kinds of Religious, both of Men and Women. Amongst the Women, there are those we call Nuns, that make solemn Vows of perpetual Chastity; There are others who make but a simple Vow, as for five or ten Years, or more or less; and that time expir'd, they may contract anew for longer time, or marry, or dispose of themselves as they shall see good; and these are ordinarily call'd Galloping Nuns: Of these there are several Orders; as Canonesses, Begines, Quests, Swart-Sisters, and Jesuitesses, with several others I have forgot. Of those of the Begines was our Fair Votress.

These Orders are taken up by the best Persons of the Town, young Maids of Fortune, who live together, not inclos'd, but in Palaces that will hold about fifteen hundred or two thousand of these Filles Devotes; where they have a regulated Government, under a sort of Abbess, or Prioress, or rather a Governante. They are oblig'd to a Method of Devotion, and are under a sort of Obedience. They wear a Habit much like our Widows of Quality in England, only without a Bando; and their Veil is of a thicker Crape than what we have here, thro' which one cannot see the Face; for when they go abroad, they cover themselves all over with it; but they put 'em up in the Churches, and lay 'em by in the Houses. Every one of these have a Confessor, who is to 'em a sort of Steward: For, you must know, they that go into these Places, have the Management of their own Fortunes, and what their Parents design 'em. Without the Advice of this Confessor, they act nothing, nor admit of a Lover that he shall not approve; at least, this Method ought to be taken, and is by almost all of 'em; tho' Miranda thought her Wit above it, as her Spirit was.

But as these Women are, as I said, of the best Quality, and live with the Reputation of being retir'd from the World a little more than ordinary, and because there is a sort of Difficulty to approach 'em, they are the People the most courted, and liable to the greatest Temptations; for as difficult as it seems to be, they receive Visits from all the Men of the best Quality, especially Strangers. All the Men of Wit and Conversation meet at the Apartments of these fair Filles Devotes, where all Manner of Gallantries are perform'd, while all the Study of these Maids is to accomplish themselves for these noble Conversations. They receive Presents, Balls, Serenades, and Billets; All the News, Wit, Verses, Songs, Novels, Musick, Gaming, and all fine Diversion, is in their Apartments, they themselves being of the best Quality and Fortune. So that to manage these Gallantries, there is no sort of Female Arts they are not practis'd in, no Intrigue they are ignorant of, and no Management of which they are not capable.

Of this happy Number was the fair Miranda, whose Parents being dead, and a vast Estate divided between her self and a young Sister, (who liv'd with an unmarry'd old Uncle, whose Estate afterwards was all divided between 'em) she put her self into this uninclos'd religious House; but her Beauty, which had all the Charms that ever Nature gave, became the Envy of the whole Sisterhood. She was tall, and admirably shaped; she had a bright Hair, and Hazle-Eyes, all full of Love and Sweetness: No Art could make a Face so fair as hers by Nature, which every Feature adorn'd with a Grace that Imagination cannot reach: Every Look, every Motion charm'd, and her black Dress shew'd the Lustre of her Face and Neck. She had an Air, though gay as so much Youth could inspire, yet so modest, so nobly reserv'd, without Formality, or Stiffness, that one who look'd on her would have imagin'd her Soul the Twin-Angel of her Body; and both together made her appear something divine. To this she had a great deal of Wit, read much, and retain'd all that serv'd her Purpose. She sung delicately, and danc'd well, and play'd on the Lute to a Miracle. She spoke several Languages naturally; for being Co-heiress to so great a Fortune, she was bred with the nicest Care, in all the finest Manners of Education; and was now arriv'd to her Eighteenth Year.

'Twere needless to tell you how great a Noise the Fame of this young Beauty, with so considerable a Fortune, made in the World: I may say, the World, rather than confine her Fame to the scanty Limits of a Town; it reach'd to many others: And there was not a Man of any Quality that came to Antwerp, or pass'd thro' the City, but made it his Business to see the lovely Miranda, who was universally ador'd: Her Youth and Beauty, her Shape, and Majesty of Mein, and Air of Greatness, charm'd all her Beholders; and thousands of People were dying by her Eyes, while she was vain enough to glory in her Conquests, and make it her Business to wound. She lov'd nothing so much as to behold sighing Slaves at her Feet, of the greatest Quality; and treated them all with an Affability that gave them Hope. Continual Musick, as soon as it was dark, and Songs of dying Lovers, were sung under her Windows; and she might well have made herself a great Fortune (if she had not been so already) by the rich Presents that were hourly made her; and every body daily expected when she would make some one happy, by suffering her self to be conquer'd by Love and Honour, by the Assiduities and Vows of some one of her Adorers. But Miranda accepted their Presents, heard their Vows with Pleasure, and willingly admitted all their soft Addresses; but would not yield her Heart, or give away that lovely Person to the Possession of one, who could please it self with so many. She was naturally amorous, but extremely inconstant: She lov'd one for his Wit, another for his Face, and a third for his Mein; but above all, she admir'd Quality: Quality alone had the Power to attach her entirely; yet not to one Man, but that Virtue was still admir'd by her in all: Where-ever she found that, she lov'd, or at least acted the Lover with such Art, that (deceiving well) she fail'd not to compleat her Conquest; and yet she never durst trust her fickle Humour with Marriage. She knew the Strength of her own Heart, and that it could not suffer itself to be confin'd to one Man, and wisely avoided those Inquietudes, and that Uneasiness of Life she was sure to find in that married State, which would, against her Nature, oblige her to the Embraces of one, whose Humour was, to love all the Young and the Gay. But Love, who had hitherto only play'd with her Heart, and given it nought but pleasing wanton Wounds, such as afforded only soft Joys, and not Pains, resolv'd, either out of Revenge to those Numbers she had abandon'd, and who had sigh'd so long in vain, or to try what Power he had upon so fickle a Heart, to send an Arrow dipp'd in the most tormenting Flames that rage in Hearts most sensible. He struck it home and deep, with all the Malice of an angry God.

There was a Church belonging to the Cordeliers, whither Miranda often repair'd to her Devotion; and being there one Day, accompany'd with a young Sister of the Order, after the Mass was ended, as 'tis the Custom, some one of the Fathers goes about the Church with a Box for Contribution, or Charity-Money: It happen'd that Day, that a young Father, newly initiated, carried the Box about, which, in his Turn, he brought to Miranda. She had no sooner cast her Eyes on this young Friar, but her Face was overspread with Blushes of Surprize: She beheld him stedfastly, and saw in his Face all the Charms of Youth, Wit, and Beauty; he wanted no one Grace that could form him for Love, he appear'd all that is adorable to the Fair Sex, nor could the mis-shapen Habit hide from her the lovely Shape it endeavour'd to cover, nor those delicate Hands that approach'd her too near with the Box. Besides the Beauty of his Face and Shape, he had an Air altogether great, in spite of his profess'd Poverty, it betray'd the Man of Quality; and that Thought weigh'd greatly with Miranda. But Love, who did not design she should now feel any sort of those easy Flames, with which she had heretofore burnt, made her soon lay all those Considerations aside, which us'd to invite her to love, and now lov'd she knew not why.

She gaz'd upon him, while he bow'd before her, and waited for her Charity, till she perceiv'd the lovely Friar to blush, and cast his Eyes to the Ground. This awaken'd her Shame, and she put her Hand into her Pocket, and was a good while in searching for her Purse, as if she thought of nothing less than what she was about; at last she drew it out, and gave him a Pistole; but with so much Deliberation and Leisure, as easily betray'd the Satisfaction she took in looking on him; while the good Man, having receiv'd her Bounty, after a very low Obeysance, proceeded to the rest; and Miranda casting after him a Look all languishing, as long as he remain'd in the Church, departed with a Sigh as soon as she saw him go out, and returned to her Apartment without speaking one Word all the Way to the young Fille Devote, who attended her; so absolutely was her Soul employ'd with this young Holy Man. Cornelia (so was this Maid call'd who was with her) perceiving she was so silent, who us'd to be all Wit and good Humour, and observing her little Disorder at the Sight of the young Father, tho' she was far from imagining it to be Love, took an Occasion, when she was come home, to speak of him. 'Madam, said she, did you not observe that fine young Cordelier, who brought the Box?' At a Question that nam'd that Object of her Thoughts, Miranda blush'd; and she finding she did so, redoubled her Confusion, and she had scarce Courage enough to say, Yes, I did observe him: And then, forcing herself to smile a little, continu'd, 'And I wonder'd to see so jolly a young Friar of an Order so severe and mortify'd. Madam, (reply'd Cornelia) when you know his Story, you will not wonder.' Miranda, who was impatient to know all that concern'd her new Conqueror, oblig'd her to tell his Story; and Cornelia obey'd, and proceeded.

The Story of Prince Henrick.

'You must know, Madam, that this young Holy Man is a Prince of Germany, of the House of —, whose Fate it was, to fall most passionately in Love with a fair young Lady, who lov'd him with an Ardour equal to what he vow'd her. Sure of her Heart, and wanting only the Approbation of her Parents, and his own, which her Quality did not suffer him to despair of, he boasted of his Happiness to a young Prince, his elder Brother, a Youth amorous and fierce, impatient of Joys, and sensible of Beauty, taking Fire with all fair Eyes: He was his Father's Darling, and Delight of his fond Mother; and, by an Ascendant over both their Hearts, rul'd their Wills.

'This young Prince no sooner saw, but lov'd the fair Mistress of his Brother; and with an Authority of a Sovereign, rather than the Advice of a Friend, warn'd his Brother Henrick (this now young Friar) to approach no more this Lady, whom he had seen; and seeing, lov'd.

'In vain the poor surpriz'd Prince pleads his Right of Love, his Exchange of Vows, and Assurance of a Heart that could never be but for himself. In vain he urges his Nearness of Blood, his Friendship, his

Passion, or his Life, which so entirely depended on the Possession of the charming Maid. All his Pleading serv'd but to blow his Brother's Flame; and the more he implores, the more the other burns; and while Henrick follows him, on his Knees, with humble Submissions, the other flies from him in Rages of transported Love; nor could his Tears, that pursu'd his Brother's Steps, move him to Pity: Hot-headed, vain-conceited of his Beauty, and greater Quality as elder Brother, he doubts not of Success, and resolv'd to sacrifice all to the Violence of his new-born Passion.

'In short, he speaks of his Design to his Mother, who promis'd him her Assistance; and accordingly proposing it first to the Prince her Husband, urging the Languishment of her Son, she soon wrought so on him, that a Match being concluded between the Parents of this young Beauty, and Henrick's Brother, the Hour was appointed before she knew of the Sacrifice she was to be made. And while this was in Agitation, Henrick was sent on some great Affairs, up into Germany, far out of the Way; not but his boding Heart, with perpetual Sighs and Throbs, eternally foretold him his Fate.

'All the Letters he wrote were intercepted, as well as those she wrote to him. She finds herself every Day perplex'd with the Addresses of the Prince she hated; he was ever sighing at her Feet. In vain were all her reproaches, and all her Coldness, he was on the surer Side; for what he found Love would not do, Force of Parents would.

'She complains, in her Heart, of young Henrick, from whom she could never receive one Letter; and at last could not forbear bursting into Tears, in spite of all her Force, and feign'd Courage, when, on a Day, the Prince told her, that Henrick was withdrawn to give him Time to court her; to whom he said, he confess'd he had made some Vows, but did repent of 'em, knowing himself too young to make 'em good: That it was for that Reason he brought him first to see her; and for that Reason, that after that, he never saw her more, nor so much as took Leave of her; when, indeed, his Death lay upon the next Visit, his Brother having sworn to murder him; and to that End, put a Guard upon him, till he was sent into Germany.

'All this he utter'd with so many passionate Asseverations, Vows, and seeming Pity for her being so inhumanly abandon'd, that she almost gave Credit to all he had said, and had much ado to keep herself within the Bounds of Moderation, and silent Grief. Her Heart was breaking, her Eyes languish'd, and her Cheeks grew pale, and she had like to have fallen dead into the treacherous Arms of him that had reduc'd her to this Discovery; but she did what she could to assume her Courage, and to shew as little Resentment as possible for a Heart, like hers, oppress'd with Love, and now abandon'd by the dear Subject of its Joys and Pains.

'But, Madam, not to tire you with this Adventure, the Day arriv'd wherein our still weeping Fair Unfortunate was to be sacrific'd to the Capriciousness of Love; and she was carry'd to Court by her Parents, without knowing to what End, where she was even compell'd to marry the Prince.

'Henrick, who all this While knew no more of his Unhappiness, than what his Fears suggested, returns, and passes even to the Presence of his Father, before he knew any Thing of his Fortune; where he beheld his Mistress and his Brother, with his Father, in such a Familiarity, as he no longer doubted his Destiny. 'Tis hard to judge, whether the Lady, or himself, was most surpriz'd; she was all pale and unmoveable in her Chair, and Henrick fix'd like a Statue; at last Grief and Rage took Place of Amazement, and he could not forbear crying out, Ah, Traytor! Is it thus you have treated a Friend and Brother? And you, O perjur'd Charmer! Is it thus you have rewarded all my Vows? He could say no more; but reeling against the Door, had fallen in a Swoon upon the Floor, had not his Page caught him in his Arms, who was entring with him. The good old Prince, the Father, who knew not what all this meant, was soon inform'd by the young weeping Princess; who, in relating the Story of her Amour with Henrick, told her Tale in so moving a Manner, as brought Tears to the Old Man's Eyes, and Rage to those of her Husband; he immediately grew jealous to the last Degree: He finds himself in Possession ('tis true) of the Beauty he ador'd, but the Beauty adoring another; a Prince young and charming as the Light, soft, witty, and raging with an equal Passion. He finds this dreaded Rival in the same House with him, with an Authority equal to his own; and fancies, where two Hearts are so entirely agreed, and have so good an Understanding, it would not be impossible to find Opportunities to satisfy and ease that mutual Flame, that burnt so equally in both; he therefore resolved to send him out of the World, and to establish his own Repose by a Deed, wicked, cruel, and unnatural, to have him assassinated the first Opportunity he could find. This Resolution set him a little at Ease, and he strove to dissemble Kindness to Henrick, with all the Art he was capable of, suffering him to come often to the Apartment of the Princess, and to entertain her oftentimes with Discourse, when he was not near enough to hear what he spoke; but still watching their Eyes, he found those of Henrick full of Tears, ready to flow, but restrain'd, looking all dying, and yet reproaching, while those of the Princess were ever bent to the Earth, and she as much as possible, shunning his Conversation. Yet this did not satisfy the jealous Husband; 'twas not her Complaisance that could appease him; he found her Heart was panting within, whenever Henrick approach'd her, and every Visit more and more confirmed his Death.

'The Father often found the Disorders of the Sons; the Softness and Address of the one gave him as much Fear, as the angry Blushings, the fierce Looks, and broken Replies of the other, whenever he beheld Henrick approach his Wife; so that the Father, fearing some ill Consequence of this, besought Henrick to withdraw to some other Country, or travel into Italy, he being now of an Age that required a View of the World. He told his Father, That he would obey his Commands, tho' he was certain, that Moment he was to be separated from the Sight of the fair Princess, his Sister, would be the last of his Life; and, in fine, made so pitiful a Story of his suffering Love, as almost moved the old Prince to compassionate him so far, as to permit him to stay; but he saw inevitable Danger in that, and therefore bid him prepare for his Journey.

'That which pass'd between the Father and Henrick, being a Secret, none talked of his departing from Court; so that the Design the Brother had went on; and making a Hunting-Match one Day, where most young People of Quality were, he order'd some whom he had hired to follow his Brother, so as if he chanced to go out of the Way, to dispatch him; and accordingly, Fortune gave 'em an Opportunity; for he lagg'd behind the Company, and turn'd aside into a pleasant Thicket of Hazles, where alighting, he walk'd on Foot in the most pleasant Part of it, full of Thought, how to divide his Soul between Love and Obedience. He was sensible that he ought not to stay; that he was but an Affliction to the young Princess, whose Honour could never permit her to ease any Part of his Flame; nor was he so vicious to entertain a Thought that should stain her Virtue. He beheld her now as his Brother's Wife, and that secured his Flame from all loose Desires, if her native Modesty had not been sufficient of itself to have done it, as well as that profound Respect he paid her; and he consider'd, in obeying his Father, he left her at Ease, and his Brother freed of a thousand Fears; he went to seek a Cure, which if he could not find, at last he could but die; and so he must, even at her Feet: However, that it was more noble to seek a Remedy for his Disease, than expect a certain Death by staying. After a thousand Reflections on his hard Fate, and bemoaning himself, and blaming his cruel Stars, that had doom'd him to die so young, after an Infinity of Sighs and Tears, Resolvings and Unresolvings, he, on the sudden, was interrupted by the trampling of some Horses he heard, and their rushing through the Boughs, and saw four Men make towards him: He had not time to mount, being walk'd some Paces from his Horse. One of the Men advanced, and cry'd, Prince, you must die, I do believe thee, (reply'd Henrick) but not by a Hand so base as thine: And at the same Time drawing his Sword, run him into the Groin. When the Fellow found himself so wounded, he wheel'd off and cry'd, Thou art a Prophet, and hast rewarded my Treachery with Death. The rest came up, and one shot at the Prince, and shot him in the Shoulder; the other two hastily laying hold (but too late) on the Hand of the Murderer, cry'd, Hold, Traytor; we relent, and he shall not die. He reply'd,

'Tis too late, he is shot; and see, he lies dead. Let us provide for ourselves, and tell the Prince, we have done the Work; for you are as guilty as I am. At that they all fled, and left the Prince lying under a Tree, weltering in his Blood.

'About the Evening, the Forester going his Walks, saw the Horse, richly caparison'd, without a Rider, at the Entrance of the Wood; and going farther, to see if he could find its Owner, found there the Prince almost dead; he immediately mounts him on the Horse, and himself behind, bore him up, and carry'd him to the Lodge; where he had only one old Man, his Father, well skilled in Surgery, and a Boy. They put him to Bed; and the old Forester, with what Art he had, dress'd his Wounds, and in the Morning sent for an abler Surgeon, to whom the Prince enjoin'd Secrecy, because he knew him. The Man was faithful, and the Prince in Time was recover'd of his Wound; and as soon as he was well, he came to Flanders, in the Habit of a Pilgrim, and after some Time took the Order of St. Francis, none knowing what became of him, till he was profess'd; and then he wrote his own Story to the Prince his Father, to his Mistress, and his ungrateful Brother. The young Princess did not long survive his Loss, she languished from the Moment of his Departure; and he had this to confirm his devout Life, to know she dy'd for him.

'My Brother, Madam, was an Officer under the Prince his Father, and knew his Story perfectly well; from whose Mouth I had it.'

What! (reply'd Miranda then) is Father Henrick a Man of Quality? Yes, Madam, (said Cornelia) and has changed his Name to Francisco. But Miranda, fearing to betray the Sentiments of her Heart, by asking any more Questions about him, turned the Discourse; and some Persons of Quality came in to visit her (for her Apartment was about six o'Clock, like the Presence-Chamber of a Queen, always filled with the greatest People): There meet all the Beaux Esprits, and all the Beauties. But it was visible Miranda was not so gay as she used to be; but pensive, and answering mal a propos to all that was said to her. She was a thousand times going to speak, against her Will, something of the charming Friar, who was never from her Thoughts; and she imagined, if he could inspire Love in a coarse, grey, ill-made Habit, a shorn Crown, a Hair-cord about his Waist, bare-legg'd, in Sandals instead of Shoes; what must he do, when looking back on Time, she beholds him in a Prospect of Glory, with all that Youth, and illustrious Beauty, set off by the Advantage of Dress and Equipage? She frames an Idea of him all gay and splendid, and looks on his present Habit as some Disguise proper for the Stealths of Love; some feigned put-on Shape, with the more Security to approach a Mistress, and make himself happy; and that the Robe laid by, she has the Lover in his proper Beauty, the same he would have been, if any other Habit (though ever so rich) were put off: In the Bed, the silent gloomy Night, and the soft Embraces of her Arms, he loses all the Friar, and assumes all the Prince; and that awful Reverence, due alone to his Holy Habit, he exchanges for a thousand Dalliances, for which his Youth was made; for Love, for tender Embraces, and all the Happiness of Life. Some Moments she fancies him a Lover, and that the fair Object that takes up all his Heart, has left no Room for her there; but that was a Thought that did not long perplex her, and which, almost as soon as born, she turned to her Advantage. She beholds him a Lover, and therefore finds he has a Heart sensible and tender; he had Youth to be fir'd, as well as to inspire; he was far from the loved Object, and totally without Hope; and she reasonably consider'd, that Flame would of itself soon die, that had only Despair to feed on. She beheld her own Charms; and Experience, as well as her Glass, told her, they never failed of Conquest, especially where they designed it: And she believed Henrick would be glad, at least, to quench that Flame in himself, by an Amour with her, which was kindled by the young Princess of — his Sister.

These, and a thousand other Self-flatteries, all vain and indiscreet, took up her waking Nights, and now more retired Days; while Love, to make her truly wretched, suffered her to sooth herself with fond Imaginations; not so much as permitting her Reason to plead one Moment to save her from undoing: She would not suffer it to tell her, he had taken Holy Orders, made sacred and solemn Vows of everlasting Chastity, that it was impossible he could marry her, or lay before her any Argument that might prevent her Ruin; but Love, mad malicious Love, was always called to Counsel, and, like easy Monarchs, she had no Ears, but for Flatterers.

Well then, she is resolv'd to love, without considering to what End, and what must be the Consequence of such an Amour. She now miss'd no Day of being at that little Church, where she had the Happiness, or rather the Misfortune (so Love ordained) to see this Ravisher of her Heart and Soul; and every Day she took new Fire from his lovely Eyes. Unawares, unknown, and unwillingly, he gave her Wounds, and the Difficulty of her Cure made her rage the more: She burnt, she languished, and died for the young Innocent, who knew not he was the Author of so much Mischief.

Now she resolves a thousand Ways in her tortur'd Mind, to let him know her Anguish, and at last pitch'd upon that of writing to him soft Billets, which she had learn'd the Art of doing; or if she had not, she had now Fire enough to inspire her with all that could charm and move. These she deliver'd to a young Wench, who waited on her, and whom she had entirely subdu'd to her Interest, to give to a certain Lay-Brother of the Order, who was a very simple harmless Wretch, and who served in the Kitchen, in the Nature of a Cook, in the Monastery of Cordeliers. She gave him Gold to secure his Faith and Service; and not knowing from whence they came (with so good Credentials) he undertook to deliver the Letters to Father Francisco; which Letters were all afterwards, as you shall hear, produced in open Court. These Letters failed not to come every Day; and the Sense of the first was, to tell him, that a very beautiful young Lady, of a great Fortune, was in love with him, without naming her; but it came as from a third Person, to let him know the Secret, that she desir'd he would let her know whether she might hope any Return from him; assuring him, he needed but only see the fair Languisher, to confess himself her Slave.

This Letter being deliver'd him, he read by himself, and was surpriz'd to receive Words of this Nature, being so great a Stranger in that Place; and could not imagine or would not give himself the Trouble of guessing who this should be, because he never designed to make Returns.

The next Day, Miranda, finding no Advantage from her Messenger of Love, in the Evening sends another (impatient of Delay) confessing that she who suffer'd the Shame of writing and imploring, was the Person herself who ador'd him. 'Twas there her raging Love made her say all Things that discover'd the Nature of its Flame, and propose to flee with him to any Part of the World, if he would quit the Convent; that she had a Fortune considerable enough to make him happy; and that his Youth and Quality were not given him to so unprofitable an End as to lose themselves in a Convent, where Poverty and Ease was all the Business. In fine, she leaves nothing unurg'd that might debauch and invite him; not forgetting to send him her own Character of Beauty, and left him to judge of her Wit and Spirit by her Writing, and her Love by the Extremity of Passion she profess'd. To all which the lovely Friar made no Return, as believing a gentle Capitulation or Exhortation to her would but inflame her the more, and give new Occasions for her continuing to write. All her Reasonings, false and vicious, he despis'd, pity'd the Error of her Love, and was Proof against all she could plead. Yet notwithstanding his Silence, which left her in Doubt, and more tormented her, she ceas'd not to pursue him with her Letters, varying her Style; sometimes all wanton, loose and raving; sometimes feigning a Virgin-Modesty all over, accusing her self, blaming her Conduct, and sighing her Destiny, as one compell'd to the shameful Discovery by the Austerity of his Vow and Habit, asking his Pity and Forgiveness; urging him in Charity to use his Fatherly Care to persuade and reason with her wild Desires, and by his Counsel drive the God from her Heart, whose Tyranny was worse than that of a Fiend; and he did not know what his pious Advice might do. But still she writes in vain, in vain she varies her Style, by a Cunning, peculiar to a Maid possess'd with such a sort of Passion.

This cold Neglect was still Oil to the burning Lamp, and she tries yet more Arts, which for want of right Thinking were as fruitless. She has Recourse to Presents; her Letters came loaded with Rings of great Price, and Jewels, which Fops of Quality had given her. Many of this Sort he receiv'd, before he knew where to return 'em, or how; and on this Occasion alone he sent her a Letter, and restor'd her Trifles, as he call'd them: But his Habit having not made him forget his Quality and Education, he wrote to her with all the profound Respect imaginable; believing by her Presents, and the Liberality with which she parted with 'em, that she was of Quality. But the whole Letter, as he told me afterwards, was to persuade her from the Honour she did him, by loving him; urging a thousand Reasons, solid and pious, and assuring her, he had wholly devoted the rest of his Days to Heaven, and had no Need of those gay Trifles she had sent him, which were only fit to adorn Ladies so fair as herself, and who had Business with this glittering World, which he disdain'd, and had for ever abandon'd. He sent her a thousand Blessings, and told her, she should be ever in his Prayers, tho' not in his Heart, as she desir'd: And abundance of Goodness more he express'd, and Counsel he gave her, which had the same Effect with his Silence; it made her love but the more, and the more impatient she grew. She now had a new Occasion to write, she now is charm'd with his Wit; this was the new Subject. She rallies his Resolution, and endeavours to re-call him to the World, by all the Arguments that human Invention is capable of.

But when she had above four Months languish'd thus in vain, not missing one Day, wherein she went not to see him, without discovering herself to him; she resolv'd, as her last Effort, to shew her Person, and see what that, assisted by her Tears, and soft Words from her Mouth, could do, to prevail upon him.

It happen'd to be on the Eve of that Day when she was to receive the Sacrament, that she, covering herself with her Veil, came to Vespers, purposing to make Choice of the conquering Friar for her Confessor.

She approach'd him; and as she did so, she trembled with Love. At last she cry'd, Father, my Confessor is gone for some Time from the Town, and I am obliged To-morrow to receive, and beg you will be pleas'd to take my Confession.

He could not refuse her; and let her into the Sacristy, where there is a Confession-Chair, in which he seated himself; and on one Side of him she kneel'd down, over-against a little Altar, where the Priests Robes lye, on which were plac'd some lighted Wax-Candles, that made the little Place very light and splendid, which shone full upon Miranda.

After the little Preparation usual in Confession, she turn'd up her Veil, and discover'd to his View the most wondrous Object of Beauty he had ever seen, dress'd in all the Glory of a young Bride; her Hair and Stomacher full of Diamonds, that gave a Lustre all dazling to her brighter Face and Eyes. He was surpriz'd at her amazing Beauty, and question'd whether he saw a Woman, or an Angel at his Feet. Her Hands, which were elevated, as if in Prayer, seem'd to be form'd of polish'd Alabaster; and he confess'd, he had never seen any Thing in Nature so perfect and so admirable.

He had some Pain to compose himself to hear her Confession, and was oblig'd to turn away his Eyes, that his Mind might not be perplex'd with an Object so diverting; when Miranda, opening the finest Mouth in the World, and discovering new Charms, began her Confession.

'Holy Father (said she) amongst the Number of my vile Offences, that which afflicts me to the greatest Degree, is, that I am in love: Not (continued she) that I believe simple and virtuous Love a Sin, when 'tis plac'd on an Object proper and suitable; but, my dear Father, (said she, and wept) I love with a Violence which cannot be contain'd within the Bounds of Reason, Moderation, or Virtue.

I love a Man whom I cannot possess without a Crime, and a Man who cannot make me happy without being perjur'd. Is he marry'd? (reply'd the Father.) No; (answer'd Miranda.) Are you so? (continued he.) Neither, (said she.) Is he too near ally'd to you? (said Francisco:) a Brother, or Relation? Neither of these, (said she.) He is unenjoy'd, unpromis'd; and so am I: Nothing opposes our Happiness, or makes my Love a Vice, but you, 'Tis you deny me Life: 'Tis you that forbid my Flame: 'Tis you will have me die, and seek my Remedy in my Grave, when I complain of Tortures, Wounds, and Flames. O cruel Charmer! 'tis for you I languish; and here, at your Feet, implore that Pity, which all my Addresses have fail'd of procuring me.'

With that, perceiving he was about to rise from his Seat, she held him by his Habit, and vow'd she would in that Posture follow him, where-ever he flew from her. She elevated her Voice so loud, he was afraid she might be heard, and therefore suffer'd her to force him into his Chair again; where being seated, he began, in the most passionate Terms imaginable, to dissuade her; but finding she the more persisted in Eagerness of Passion, he us'd all the tender Assurance that he could force from himself, that he would have for her all the Respect, Esteem and Friendship that he was capable of paying; that he had a real Compassion for her: and at last she prevail'd so far with him, by her Sighs and Tears, as to own he had a Tenderness for her, and that he could not behold so many Charms, without being sensibly touch'd by 'em, and finding all those Effects, that a Maid so fair and young causes in the Souls of Men of Youth and Sense: But that, as he was assured, he could never be so happy to marry her, and as certain he could not grant any Thing but honourable Passion, he humbly besought her not to expect more from him than such. And then began to tell her how short Life was, and transitory its Joys; how soon she would grow weary of Vice, and how often change to find real Repose in it, but never arrive to it. He made an End, by new Assurance of his eternal Friendship, but utterly forbad her to hope.

Behold her now deny'd, refus'd and defeated, with all her pleading Youth, Beauty, Tears, and Knees, imploring, as she lay, holding fast his Scapular, and embracing his Feet. What shall she do? She swells with Pride, Love, Indignation and Desire; her burning Heart is bursting with Despair, her Eyes grow fierce, and from Grief she rises to a Storm; and in her Agony of Passion, with Looks all disdainful, haughty, and full of Rage, she began to revile him, as the poorest of Animals; tells him his Soul was dwindled to the Meanness of his Habit, and his Vows of Poverty were suited to his degenerate Mind. 'And (said she) since all my nobler Ways have fail'd me; and that, for a little Hypocritical Devotion, you resolve to lose the greatest Blessings of Life, and to sacrifice me to your Religious Pride and Vanity, I will either force you to abandon that dull Dissimulation, or you shall die, to prove your Sanctity real. Therefore answer me immediately, answer my Flame, my raging Fire, which your Eyes have kindled; or here, in this very Moment, I will ruin thee; and make no Scruple of revenging the Pains I suffer, by that which shall take away your Life and Honour.'

The trembling young Man, who, all this While, with extreme Anguish of Mind, and Fear of the dire Result, had listen'd to her Ravings, full of Dread, demanded what she would have him do? When she reply'd - 'Do that which thy Youth and Beauty were ordain'd to do: this Place is private, a sacred Silence reigns here, and no one dares to pry into the Secrets of this Holy Place: We are as secure from Fears and Interruption, as in Desarts uninhabited, or Caves forsaken by wild Beasts. The Tapers too shall veil their Lights, and only that glimmering Lamp shall be Witness of our dear Stealths of Love. Come to my Arms, my trembling, longing Arms; and curse the Folly of thy Bigotry, that has made thee so long lose a Blessing, for which so many Princes sigh in vain.'

At these Words she rose from his Feet, and snatching him in her Arms, he could not defend himself from receiving a thousand Kisses from the lovely Mouth of the charming Wanton; after which, she ran herself, and in an Instant put out the Candles. But he cry'd to her, 'In vain, O too indiscreet Fair One, in vain you put out the Light; for Heaven still has Eyes, and will look down upon my broken

Vows. I own your Power, I own I have all the Sense in the World of your charming Touches; I am frail Flesh and Blood, but, yet, yet I can resist; and I prefer my Vows to all your powerful Temptations. I will be deaf and blind, and guard my Heart with Walls of Ice, and make you know, that when the Flames of true Devotion are kindled in a Heart, it puts out all other Fires; which are as ineffectual, as Candles lighted in the Face of the Sun. Go, vain Wanton, and repent, and mortify that Blood which has so shamefully betray'd thee, and which will one Day ruin both thy Soul and Body.'

At these Words Miranda, more enrag'd, the nearer she imagin'd her self to Happiness, made no Reply; but throwing her self, in that Instant, into the Confessing-Chair, and violently pulling the young Friar into her Lap, she elevated her Voice to such a Degree, in crying out, Help, Help! A Rape! Help, Help! that she was heard all over the Church, which was full of People at the Evening's Devotion; who flock'd about the Door of the Sacristy, which was shut with a Spring-Lock on the Inside, but they durst not open the Door.

'Tis easily to be imagin'd, in what Condition our young Friar was, at this last devilish Stratagem of his wicked Mistress. He strove to break from those Arms that held him so fast; and his Bustling to get away, and her's to retain him, disorder'd his Hair and Habit to such a Degree, as gave the more Credit to her false Accusation.

The Fathers had a Door on the other Side, by which they usually enter'd, to dress in this little Room; and at the Report that was in an Instant made 'em, they hasted thither, and found Miranda and the good Father very indecently struggling; which they mis-interpreted, as Miranda desir'd; who, all in Tears, immediately threw her self at the Feet of the Provincial, who was one of those that enter'd; and cry'd, 'O holy Father! revenge an innocent Maid, undone and lost to Fame and Honour, by that vile Monster, born of Goats, nurs'd by Tygers, and bred up on savage Mountains, where Humanity and Religion are Strangers. For, O holy Father, could it have enter'd into the Heart of Man, to have done so barbarous and horrid a Deed, as to attempt the Virgin-Honour of an unspotted Maid, and one of my Degree, even in the Moment of my Confession, in that holy Time, when I was prostrate before him and Heaven, confessing those Sins that press'd my tender Conscience; even then to load my Soul with the blackest of Infamies, to add to my Number a Weight that must sink me to Hell? Alas! under the Security of his innocent Looks, his holy Habit, and his aweful Function, I was led into this Room to make my Confession; where, he locking the Door, I had no sooner began, but he gazing on me, took fire at my fatal Beauty; and starting up, put out the Candles and caught me in his Arms; and raising me from the Pavement, set me in the Confession-Chair; and then, Oh, spare me the rest.'

With that a Shower of Tears burst from her fair dissembling Eyes, and Sobs so naturally acted, and so well manag'd, as left no doubt upon the good Men, but all she had spoken was Truth.

'At first, (proceeded she) I was unwilling to bring so great a Scandal on his Order, to cry out; but struggled as long as I had Breath; pleaded the Heinousness of the Crime, urging my Quality, and the Danger of the Attempt. But he, deaf as the Winds, and ruffling as a Storm, pursu'd his wild Design with so much Force and Insolence, as I at last, unable to resist, was wholly vanquish'd, robb'd of my native Purity. With what Life and Breath I had, I call'd for Assistance, both from Men and Heaven; but oh, alas! your Succours came too late: You find me here a wretched, undone, and ravish'd Maid. Revenge me, Fathers; revenge me on the perfidious Hypocrite, or else give me a Death that may secure your Cruelty and Injustice from ever being proclaim'd over the World; or my Tongue will be eternally reproaching you, and cursing the wicked Author of my Infamy.'

She ended as she began, with a thousand Sighs and Tears; and received from the Provincial all Assurances of Revenge.

The innocent betray'd Victim, all the while she was speaking, heard her with an Astonishment that may easily be imagined; yet shew'd no extravagant Signs of it, as those would do, who feign it, to be thought innocent; but being really so, he bore with an humble, modest, and blushing Countenance, all her Accusations; which silent Shame they mistook for evident Signs of his Guilt.

When the Provincial demanded, with an unwonted Severity in his Eyes and Voice, what he could answer for himself? calling him Profaner of his Sacred Vows, and Infamy to the Holy Order; the injur'd, but innocently accus'd, only reply'd: 'May Heaven forgive that bad Woman, and bring her to Repentance! For his Part, he was not so much in Love with Life, as to use many arguments to justify his Innocence; unless it were to free that Order from a Scandal, of which he had the Honour to be profess'd. But as for himself, Life or Death were Things indifferent to him, who heartily despis'd the World.'

He said no more, and suffer'd himself to be led before the Magistrate; who committed him to Prison, upon the Accusation of this implacable Beauty; who, with so much feign'd Sorrow, prosecuted the Matter, even to his Tryal and Condemnation; where he refus'd to make any great Defence for himself. But being daily visited by all the Religious, both of his own and other Orders, they oblig'd him (some of 'em knowing the Austerity of his Life, others his Cause of Griefs that first brought him into Orders, and others pretending a nearer Knowledge, even of his Soul it self) to stand upon his Justification, and discover what he knew of that wicked Woman; whose Life had not been so exemplary for Virtue, not to have given the World a thousand Suspicions of her Lewdness and Prostitutions.

The daily Importunities of these Fathers made him produce her Letters: But as he had all the Gown-men on his Side, she had all the Hats and Feathers on her's; all the Men of Quality taking her Part, and all the Church-men his. They heard his daily Protestations and Vows, but not a Word of what passed at Confession was yet discover'd: He held that as a Secret sacred on his Part; and what was said in Nature of a Confession, was not to be revealed, though his Life depended on the Discovery. But as to the Letters, they were forc'd from him, and expos'd; however, Matters were carry'd with so high a Hand against him, that they serv'd for no Proof at all of his Innocence, and he was at last condemn'd to be burn'd at the Market-Place.

After his Sentence was pass'd, the whole Body of Priests made their Addresses to the Marquis Castel Roderigo, the then Governor of Flanders, for a Reprieve; which, after much ado, was granted him for some Weeks, but with an absolute Denial of Pardon: So prevailing were the young Cavaliers of his Court, who were all Adorers of this Fair Jilt.

About this time, while the poor innocent young Henrick was thus languishing in Prison, in a dark and dismal Dungeon, and Miranda, cured of her Love, was triumphing in her Revenge, expecting and daily giving new Conquests; and who, by this time, had re-assum'd all her wonted Gaiety; there was a great Noise about the Town, that a Prince of mighty Name, and fam'd for all the Excellencies of his Sex, was arriv'd; a Prince young, and gloriously attended, call'd Prince Tarquin.

We had often heard of this great Man, and that he was making his Travels in France and Germany: And we had also heard, that some Years before, he being about Eighteen Years of Age, in the Time when our King Charles, of blessed Memory, was in Brussels, in the last Year of his Banishment, that all on a sudden, this young Man rose up upon 'em like the Sun, all glorious and dazling, demanding Place of all the Princes in that Court. And when his Pretence was demanded, he own'd himself Prince Tarquin, of the Race of the last Kings of Rome, made good his Title, and took his Place accordingly. After that he travell'd for about six Years up and down the World, and then arriv'd at Antwerp, about the Time of my being sent thither by King Charles.

Perhaps there could be nothing seen so magnificent as this Prince: He was, as I said, extremely handsome, from Head to Foot exactly form'd, and he wanted nothing that might adorn that native Beauty to the best Advantage. His Parts were suitable to the rest: He had an Accomplishment fit for a Prince, an Air haughty, but a Carriage affable, easy in Conversation, and very entertaining, liberal and good-natur'd, brave and inoffensive. I have seen him pass the Streets with twelve Footmen, and four Pages; the Pages all in green Velvet Coats lac'd with Gold, and white Velvet Tunicks; the Men in Cloth, richly lac'd with Gold; his Coaches, and all other Officers, suitable to a great Man.

He was all the Discourse of the Town; some laughing at his Title, others reverencing it: Some cry'd, that he was an Imposter; others, that he had made his Title as plain, as if Tarquin had reign'd but a Year ago. Some made Friendships with him, others would have nothing to say to him: But all wonder'd where his Revenue was, that supported this Grandeur; and believ'd, tho' he could make his Descent from the Roman Kings very well out, that he could not lay so good a Claim to the Roman Land. Thus every body meddled with what they had nothing to do; and, as in other Places, thought themselves on the surer Side, if, in these doubtful Cases, they imagin'd the worst.

But the Men might be of what Opinion they pleas'd concerning him; the Ladies were all agreed that he was a Prince, and a young handsome Prince, and a Prince not to be resisted: He had all their Wishes, all their Eyes, and all their Hearts. They now dress'd only for him; and what Church he grac'd, was sure, that Day, to have the Beauties, and all that thought themselves so.

You may believe, our amorous Miranda was not the least Conquest he made. She no sooner heard of him, which was as soon as he arriv'd, but she fell in love with his very Name. Jesu! A young King of Rome! Oh, it was so novel, that she doated on the Title; and had not car'd whether the rest had been Man or Monkey almost: She was resolved to be the Lucretia that this young Tarquin should ravish.

To this End, she was no sooner up the next Day, but she sent him a Billet Doux, assuring him how much she admired his Fame; and that being a Stranger in the Town, she begged the Honour of introducing him to all the Belle Conversations, &c. which he took for the Invitation of some Coquet, who had Interest in fair Ladies; and civilly return'd her an Answer, that he would wait on her. She had him that Day watched to Church; and impatient to see what she heard so many People flock to see, she went also to the same Church; those sanctified Abodes being too often profaned by such Devotees, whose Business is to ogle and ensnare.

But what a Noise and Humming was heard all over the Church, when Tarquin enter'd! His Grace, his Mein, his Fashion, his Beauty, his Dress, and his Equipage surprized all that were present: And by the good Management and Care of Miranda, she got to kneel at the Side of the Altar, just over against the Prince, so that, if he would, he could not avoid looking full upon her. She had turned up her Veil, and all her Face and Shape appear'd such, and so inchanting, as I have described; and her Beauty heighten'd with Blushes, and her Eyes full of Spirit and Fire, with Joy, to find the young Roman Monarch so charming, she appear'd like something more than mortal, and compelled his Eyes to a fixed gazing on her Face: She never glanc'd that Way, but she met them; and then would feign so modest a Shame, and cast her Eyes downwards with such inviting Art, that he was wholly ravished and charmed, and she over-joy'd to find he was so.

The Ceremony being ended, he sent a Page to follow that Lady Home, himself pursuing her to the Door of the Church, where he took some holy Water, and threw upon her, and made her a profound Reverence. She forc'd an innocent Look, and a modest Gratitude in her Face, and bow'd, and passed forward, half assur'd of her Conquest; leaving her, to go home to his Lodging, and impatiently wait the Return of his Page. And all the Ladies who saw this first Beginning between the Prince and Miranda, began to curse and envy her Charms, who had deprived them of half their Hopes.

After this, I need not tell you, he made Miranda a Visit; and from that Day never left her Apartment, but when he went home at Nights, or unless he had Business; so entirely was he conquer'd by this Fair One. But the Bishop, and several Men of Quality, in Orders, that profess'd Friendship to him, advised him from her Company; and spoke several Things to him, that might (if Love had not made him blind) have reclaimed him from the Pursuit of his Ruin. But whatever they trusted him with, she had the Art to wind herself about his Heart, and make him unravel all his Secrets; and then knew as well, by feign'd Sighs and Tears, to make him disbelieve all; so that he had no Faith but for her; and was wholly inchanted and bewitch'd by her. At last, in spite of all that would have opposed it, he marry'd this famous Woman, possess'd by so many great Men and Strangers before, while all the World was pitying his Shame and Misfortunes.

Being marry'd, they took a great House; and as she was indeed a great Fortune, and now a great Princess, there was nothing wanting that was agreeable to their Quality; all was splendid and magnificent. But all this would not acquire them the World's Esteem; they had an Abhorrence for her former Life, and despised her; and for his espousing a Woman so infamous, they despised him. So that though they admir'd, and gazed upon their Equipage, and glorious Dress, they foresaw the Ruin that attended it, and paid her Quality little Respect.

She was no sooner married, but her Uncle died; and dividing his Fortune between Miranda and her Sister, leaves the young Heiress, and all her Fortune, entirely in the Hands of the Princess.

We will call this Sister Alcidiana; she was about fourteen Years of Age, and now had chosen her Brother, the Prince, for her Guardian. If Alcidiana were not altogether so great a Beauty as her Sister, she had Charms sufficient to procure her a great many Lovers, though her Fortune had not been so considerable as it was; but with that Addition, you may believe, she wanted no Courtships from those of the best Quality; tho' every body deplor'd her being under the Tutorage of a Lady so expert in all the Vices of her Sex, and so cunning a Manager of Sin, as was the Princess; who, on her Part, failed not, by all the Caresses, and obliging Endearments, to engage the Mind of this young Maid, and to subdue her wholly to her Government. All her Senses were eternally regaled with the most bewitching Pleasures they were capable of: She saw nothing but Glory and Magnificence, heard nothing but Musick of the sweetest Sounds; the richest Perfumes employ'd her Smelling; and all she eat and touch'd was delicate and inviting; and being too young to consider how this State and Grandeur was to be continu'd, little imagined her vast Fortune was every Day diminishing, towards its needless Support.

When the Princess went to Church, she had her Gentleman bare before her, carrying a great Velvet Cushion, with great Golden Tassels, for her to kneel on, and her Train borne up a most prodigious Length, led by a Gentleman Usher, bare; follow'd by innumerable Footmen, Pages, and Women. And in this State she would walk in the Streets, as in those Countries it is the Fashion for the great Ladies to do, who are well; and in her Train two or three Coaches, and perhaps a rich Velvet Chair embroider'd, would follow in State.

It was thus for some time they liv'd, and the Princess was daily press'd by young sighing Lovers, for her Consent to marry Alcidiana; but she had still one Art or other to put them off, and so continually broke all the great Matches that were proposed to her, notwithstanding their Kindred and other Friends had industriously endeavour'd to make several great Matches for her; but the Princess was still positive in her Denial, and one Way or other broke all. At last it happened, there was one proposed, yet more advantageous, a young Count, with whom the young Maid grew passionately in

Love, and besought her Sister to consent that she might have him, and got the Prince to speak in her Behalf; but he had no sooner heard the secret Reasons Miranda gave him, but (entirely her Slave) he chang'd his Mind, and suited it to hers, and she, as before, broke off that Amour: Which so extremely incensed Alcidiana, that she, taking an Opportunity, got from her Guard, and ran away, putting her self into the Hands of a wealthy Merchant, her Kinsman, and one who bore the greatest Authority in the City; him she chuses for her Guardian, resolving to be no longer a Slave to the Tyranny of her Sister. And so well she ordered Matters, that she writ this young Cavalier, her last Lover, and retrieved him; who came back to Antwerp again, to renew his Courtship.

Both Parties being agreed, it was no hard Matter to persuade all but the Princess. But though she opposed it, it was resolved on, and the Day appointed for Marriage, and the Portion demanded; demanded only, but never to be paid, the best Part of it being spent. However, she put them off from Day to Day, by a thousand frivolous Delays; and when she saw they would have Recourse to Force, and all that her Magnificence would be at an End, if the Law should prevail against her; and that without this Sister's Fortune, she could not long support her Grandeur; she bethought herself of a Means to make it all her own, by getting her Sister made away; but she being out of her Tuition, she was not able to accomplish so great a Deed of Darkness. But since it was resolved it must be done, she contrives a thousand Stratagems; and at last pitches upon an effectual one.

She had a Page call'd Van Brune, a Youth of great Address and Wit, and one she had long managed for her Purpose. This Youth was about seventeen Years of Age, and extremely beautiful; and in the Time when Alcidiana lived with the Princess, she was a little in Love with this handsome Boy; but it was checked in its Infancy, and never grew up to a Flame: Nevertheless, Alcidiana retained still a sort of Tenderness for him, while he burn'd in good Earnest with Love for the Princess.

The Princess one Day ordering this Page to wait on her in her Closet, she shut the Door; and after a thousand Questions of what he would undertake to serve her, the amorous Boy finding himself alone, and caress'd by the fair Person he ador'd, with joyful Blushes that beautify'd his Face, told her, 'There was nothing upon Earth, he would not do, to obey her least Commands.' She grew more familiar with him, to oblige him; and seeing Love dance in his Eyes, of which she was so good a Judge, she treated him more like a Lover, than a Servant; till at last the ravished Youth, wholly transported out of himself, fell at her Feet, and impatiently implor'd to receive her Commands quickly, that he might fly to execute them; for he was not able to bear her charming Words, Looks, and Touches, and retain his Duty. At this she smil'd, and told him, the Work was of such a Nature, as would mortify all Flames about him; and he would have more Need of Rage, Envy, and Malice, than the Aids of a Passion so soft as what she now found him capable of. He assur'd her, he would stick at nothing, tho' even against his Nature, to recompense for the Boldness he now, through his Indiscretion, had discover'd. She smiling, told him, he had committed no Fault; and that possibly, the Pay he should receive for the Service she required at his Hands, should be, what he most wish'd for in the World. At this he bow'd to the Earth; and kissing her Feet, bad her command: And then she boldly told him, 'Twas to kill her Sister Alcidiana. The Youth, without so much as starting or pausing upon the Matter, told her, It should be done; and bowing low, immediately went out of the Closet. She call'd him back, and would have given him some Instruction; but he refused it, and said, 'The Action and the Contrivance should be all his own.' And offering to go again, she, again recalled him; putting into his Hand a Purse of a hundred Pistoles, which he took, and with a low Bow departed.

He no sooner left her Presence, but he goes directly, and buys a Dose of Poison, and went immediately to the House where Alcidiana lived; where desiring to be brought to her Presence, he fell a weeping; and told her, his Lady had fallen out with him, and dismissed him her Service, and since from a Child he had been brought up in the Family, he humbly besought Alcidiana to receive him into hers, she being in a few Days to be marry'd. There needed not much Intreaty to a Thing that pleased her so well, and she immediately received him to Pension: And he waited some Days on her, before he could get an Opportunity to administer his devilish Potion. But one Night, when she drank Wine with roasted Apples, which was usual with her; instead of Sugar, or with the Sugar, the baneful Drug was mixed, and she drank it down.

About this Time, there was a great Talk of this Page's coming from one Sister, to go to the other. And Prince Tarquin, who was ignorant of the Design from the Beginning to the End, hearing some Men of Quality at his Table speaking of Van Brune's Change of Place (the Princess then keeping her Chamber upon some trifling Indisposition) he answer'd, 'That surely they were mistaken, that he was not dismissed from the Princess's Service:' And calling some of his Servants, he asked for Van Brune; and whether any Thing had happen'd between her Highness and him, that had occasion'd his being turned off. They all seem'd ignorant of this Matter; and those who had spoken of it, began to fancy there was some Juggle in the Case, which Time would bring to Light.

The ensuing Day 'twas all about the Town, that Alcidiana was poison'd; and though not dead, yet very near it; and that the Doctors said, she had taken Mercury. So that there was never so formidable a Sight as this fair young Creature; her Head and Body swoln, her Eyes starting out, her Face black, and all deformed: So that diligent Search was made, who it should be that did this; who gave her Drink and Meat. The Cook and Butler were examined, the Footman called to an Account; but all concluded, she received nothing but from the Hand of her new Page, since he came into her Service. He was examined, and shew'd a thousand guilty Looks: And the Apothecary, then attending among the Doctors, proved he had bought Mercury of him three or four Days before; which he could not deny; and making many Excuses for his buying it, betray'd him the more; so ill he chanced to dissemble. He was immediately sent to be examined by the Margrave or Justice, who made his Mittimus, and sent him to Prison.

'Tis easy to imagine, in what Fears and Confusion the Princess was at this News: She took her Chamber upon it, more to hide her guilty Face, than for any Indisposition. And the Doctors apply'd such Remedies to Alcidiana, such Antidotes against the Poison, that in a short Time she recover'd; but lost the finest Hair in the World, and the Complexion of her Face ever after.

It was not long before the Trials for Criminals came on; and the Day being arrived, Van Brune was try'd the first of all; every Body having already read his Destiny, according as they wished it; and none would believe, but just indeed as it was: So that for the Revenge they hoped to see fall upon the Princess, every one wished he might find no Mercy, that she might share of his Shame and Misery.

The Sessions-House was filled that Day with all the Ladies, and chief of the Town, to hear the Result of his Trial; and the sad Youth was brought, loaded with Chains, and pale as Death; where every Circumstance being sufficiently proved against him, and he making but a weak Defence for himself, he was convicted, and sent back to Prison, to receive his Sentence of Death on the Morrow; where he owned all, and who set him on to do it. He own'd 'twas not Reward of Gain he did it for, but Hope he should command at his Pleasure the Possession of his Mistress, the Princess, who should deny him nothing, after having entrusted him with so great a Secret; and that besides, she had elevated him with the Promise of that glorious Reward, and had dazzled his young Heart with so charming a Prospect, that blind and mad with Joy, he rushed forward to gain the desired Prize, and thought on nothing but his coming Happiness: That he saw too late the Follies of his presumptuous Flame, and cursed the deluding Flatteries of the fair Hypocrite, who had soothed him to his Undoing: That he was a miserable Victim to her Wickedness; and hoped he should warn all young Men, by his Fall, to avoid the Dissimulation of the deceiving Fair: That he hoped they would have Pity on his Youth, and attribute his Crime to the subtle Persuasions alone of his Mistress the Princess: And that since

Alcidiana was not dead, they would grant him Mercy, and permit him to live to repent of his grievous Crime, in some Part of the World, whither they might banish him.

He ended with Tears, that fell in abundance from his Eyes; and immediately the Princess was apprehended, and brought to Prison, to the same Prison where yet the poor young Father Francisco was languishing, he having been from Week to Week repriev'd, by the Intercession of the Fathers; and possibly she there had Time to make some Reflections.

You may imagine Tarquin left no Means unessay'd, to prevent the Imprisonment of the Princess, and the publick Shame and Infamy she was likely to undergo in this Affair: But the whole City being over-joy'd that she should be punished, as an Author of all this Mischief, were generally bent against her, both Priests, Magistrates and People; the whole Force of the Stream running that Way, she found no more Favour than the meanest Criminal. The Prince therefore, when he saw 'twas impossible to rescue her from the Hands of Justice, suffer'd with Grief unspeakable, what he could not prevent, and led her himself to the Prison, follow'd by all his People, in as much State as if he had been going to his Marriage; where, when she came, she was as well attended and served as before, he never stirring one Moment from her.

The next Day, she was tried in open and common Court; where she appeared in Glory, led by Tarquin, and attended according to her Quality: And she could not deny all the Page had alledged against her, who was brought thither also in Chains; and after a great many Circumstances, she was found Guilty, and both received Sentence; the Page to be hanged till he was dead, on a Gibbet in the Market-Place; and the Princess to stand under the Gibbet, with a Rope about her Neck, the other End of which was to be fastned to the Gibbet where the Page was hanging; and to have an Inscription, in large Characters, upon her Back and Breast, of the Cause why; where she was to stand from ten in the Morning to twelve.

This Sentence, the People with one Accord, believed too favourable for so ill a Woman, whose Crimes deserved Death, equal to that of Van Brune. Nevertheless, there were some who said, it was infinitely more severe than Death it self.

The following Friday was the Day of Execution, and one need not tell of the Abundance of People, who were flocked together in the Market-Place: And all the Windows were taken down, and filled with Spectators, and the Tops of Houses; when at the Hour appointed, the fatal Beauty appear'd. She was dress'd in a black Velvet Gown, with a rich Row of Diamonds all down the fore Part of her Breast, and a great Knot of Diamonds at the Peak behind; and a Petticoat of flower'd Gold, very rich, and laced; with all Things else suitable. A Gentleman carry'd her great Velvet Cushion before her, on which her Prayer-Book, embroider'd, was laid; her Train was borne up by a Page, and the Prince led her, bare; followed by his Footmen, Pages, and other Officers of his House.

When they arrived at the Place of Execution, the Cushion was laid on the Ground, upon a Portugal Mat, spread there for that Purpose; and the Princess stood on the Cushion, with her Prayer-Book in her Hand, and a Priest by her Side; and was accordingly tied up to the Gibbet.

She had not stood there ten Minutes, but she had the Mortification (at least one would think it so to her) to see her sad Page, Van Brune, approach, fair as an Angel, but languishing and pale. That Sight moved all the Beholders with as much Pity, as that of the Princess did with Disdain and Pleasure.

He was dressed all in Mourning, and very fine Linen, bare-headed, with his own Hair, the fairest that could be seen, hanging all in Curls on his Back and Shoulders, very long. He had a Prayer-Book of black Velvet in his Hand, and behaved himself with much Penitence and Devotion.

When he came under the Gibbet, he seeing his Mistress in that Condition, shew'd an infinite Concern, and his fair Face was cover'd over with Blushes; and falling at her Feet, he humbly ask'd her Pardon for having been the Occasion of so great an Infamy to her, by a weak Confession, which the Fears of Youth, and Hopes of Life, had obliged him to make, so greatly to her Dishonour; for indeed he wanted that manly Strength, to bear the Efforts of dying, as he ought, in Silence, rather than of commiting so great a Crime against his Duty, and Honour itself; and that he could not die in Peace, unless she would forgive him. The Princess only nodded her Head, and cried, I do.

And after having spoken a little to his Father-Confessor, who was with him, he chearfully mounted the Ladder, and in Sight of the Princess he was turned off, while a loud Cry was heard thro' all the Market-Place, especially from the Fair Sex; he hanged there till the Time the Princess was to depart; and then she was put into a rich embroider'd Chair, and carry'd away, Tarquin going into his, for he had all that Time stood supporting the Princess under the Gallows, and was very weary. She was sent back, till her Releasement came, which was that Night about seven o'Clock; and then she was conducted to her own House in great State, with a Dozen White Wax Flambeaux about her Chair.

If the Guardian of Alcidiana, and her Friends, before were impatient of having the Portion out of the Hands of these Extravagants, it is not to be imagined, but they were now much more so; and the next Day they sent an Officer, according to Law, to demand it, or to summon the Prince to give Reasons why he would not pay it. The Officer received for Answer, That the Money should be call'd in, and paid in such a Time, setting a certain Time, which I have not been so curious as to retain, or put in my Journal-Observations; but I am sure it was not long, as may be easily imagin'd, for they every Moment suspected the Prince would pack up, and be gone, some time or other, on the sudden; and for that Reason they would not trust him without Bail, or two Officers to remain in his House, to watch that nothing should be remov'd or touch'd. As for Bail, or Security, he could give none; every one slunk their Heads out of the Collar, when it came to that: So that he was oblig'd, at his own Expence, to maintain Officers in his House.

The Princess finding her self reduced to the last Extremity, and that she must either produce the Value of a hundred thousand Crowns, or see the Prince her Husband lodged for ever in a Prison, and all their Glory vanish; and that it was impossible to fly, since guarded; she had Recourse to an Extremity, worse than the Affair of Van Brune. And in order to this, she first puts on a world of Sorrow and Concern, for what she feared might arrive to the Prince: And indeed, if ever she shed Tears which she did not dissemble, it was upon this Occasion. But here she almost over-acted: She stirred not from her Bed, and refused to eat, or sleep, or see the Light; so that the Day being shut out of her Chamber, she lived by Wax-lights, and refus'd all Comfort and Consolation.

The Prince, all raving with Love, tender Compassion and Grief, never stirred from her Bed-side, nor ceas'd to implore, that she would suffer herself to live. But she, who was not now so passionately in Love with Tarquin, as she was with the Prince; nor so fond of the Man as his Titles, and of Glory; foresaw the total Ruin of the last, if not prevented by avoiding the Payment of this great Sum; which could not otherwise be, than by the Death of Alcidiana: And therefore, without ceasing, she wept, and cry'd out, 'She could not live, unless Alcidiana died. This Alcidiana (continued she) who has been the Author of my Shame; who has expos'd me under a Gibbet, in the Publick Market-Place. Oh! I am deaf to all Reason, blind to natural Affection. I renounce her, I hate her as my mortal Foe, my Stop to Glory, and the Finisher of my Days, e'er half my Race of Life be run.'

Then throwing her false, but snowy, charming Arms about the Neck her Heart-breaking Lord, and Lover, who lay sighing, and listening by her Side, he was charmed and bewitch'd into saying all Things that appeased her; and lastly, told her, 'Alcidiana should be no longer any Obstacle to her

Repose; but that, if she would look up, and cast her Eyes of Sweetness and Love upon him, as heretofore; forget her Sorrow, and redeem her lost Health; he would take what Measures she should propose to dispatch this fatal Stop to her Happiness, out of the Way.'

These Words failed not to make her caress him in the most endearing Manner that Love and Flattery could invent; and she kiss'd him to an Oath, a solemn Oath, to perform what he had promised; and he vow'd liberally. And she assumed in an Instant her Good-Humour, and suffer'd a Supper to be prepared, and did eat; which in many Days before she had not done: So obstinate and powerful was she in dissembling well.

The next Thing to be consider'd was, which Way this Deed was to be done; for they doubted not, but when it was done, all the World would lay it upon the Princess, as done by her Command: But she urged, Suspicion was no Proof; and that they never put to Death any one, but when they had great and certain Evidence who were the Offenders. She was sure of her own Constancy, that Racks and Tortures should never get the Secret from her Breast; and if he were as confident on his Part, there was no Danger. Yet this Preparation she made towards laying the Fact on others, that she caused several Letters to be wrote from Germany, as from the Relations of Van Brune, who threaten'd Alcidiana with Death, for depriving their Kinsman (who was a Gentleman) of his Life, though he had not taken away hers. And it was the Report of the Town, how this young Maid was threaten'd. And indeed, the Death of the Page had so afflicted a great many, that Alcidiana had procured her self abundance of Enemies upon that Account, because she might have saved him if she had pleased; but, on the contrary, she was a Spectator, and in full Health and Vigour, at his Execution: And People were not so much concerned for her at this Report, as they would have been.

The Prince, who now had, by reasoning the Matter soberly with Miranda, found it absolutely necessary to dispatch Alcidiana, resolved himself, and with his own Hand, to execute it; not daring to trust to any of his most favourite Servants, though he had many, who possibly would have obey'd him; for they loved him as he deserved, and so would all the World, had he not been so purely deluded by this fair Enchantress. He therefore, as I said, resolved to keep this great Secret to himself; and taking a Pistol, charged well with two Bullets, he watch'd an Opportunity to shoot her as she should go out or into her House, or Coach, some Evening.

To this End he waited several Nights near her Lodgings, but still, either she went not out, or when she return'd, she was so guarded with Friends, her Lover, and Flambeaux, that he could not aim at her without endangering the Life of some other. But one Night above the rest, upon a Sunday, when he knew she would be at the Theatre, for she never missed that Day seeing the Play, he waited at the Corner of the Stadt-House, near the Theatre, with his Cloak cast over his Face, and a black Periwig, all alone, with his Pistol ready cock'd; and remain'd not very long but he saw her Kinsman's Coach come along; 'twas almost dark, Day was just shutting up her Beauties, and left such a Light to govern the World, as serv'd only just to distinguish one Object from another, and a convenient Help to Mischief. He saw alight out of the Coach only one young Lady, the Lover, and then the destin'd Victim; which he (drawing near) knew rather by her Tongue than Shape. The Lady ran into the Play-House, and left Alcidiana to be conducted by her Lover into it: Who led her to the Door, and went to give some Order to the Coachman; so that the Lover was about twenty Yards from Alcidiana; when she stood the fairest Mark in the World, on the Threshold of the Entrance of the Theatre, there being many Coaches about the Door, so that hers could not come so near. Tarquin was resolved not to lose so fair an Opportunity, and advanc'd, but went behind the Coaches; and when he came over-against the Door, through a great booted Velvet Coach, that stood between him and her, he shot; and she having the Train of her Gown and Petticoat on her Arm, in great Quantity, he missed her Body, and shot through her Clothes, between her Arm and her Body. She, frighten'd to find something hit her, and to see the Smoke, and hear the Report of the Pistol; running in, cried, I am shot, I am dead.

This Noise quickly alarm'd her Lover; and all the Coachmen and Footmen immediately ran, some one Way, and some another. One of 'em seeing a Man haste away in a Cloak; he being a lusty, bold German, stopped him; and drawing upon him, bad him stand, and deliver his Pistol, or he would run him through.

Tarquin being surprised at the Boldness of this Fellow to demand his Pistol, as if he positively knew him to be the Murderer (for so he thought himself, since he believed Alcidiana dead) had so much Presence of Mind as to consider, if he suffered himself to be taken, he should poorly die a publick Death; and therefore resolv'd upon one Mischief more, to secure himself from the first: And in the Moment that the German bad him deliver his Pistol, he cried, Though I have no Pistol to deliver, I have a Sword to chastise thy Insolence. And throwing off his Cloak, and flinging his Pistol from him, he drew, and wounded, and disarmed the Fellow.

This Noise of Swords brought every body to the Place; and immediately the Bruit ran, The Murderer was taken, the Murderer was taken; Tho' none knew which was he, nor as yet so much as the Cause of the Quarrel between the two fighting Men; for it was now darker than before. But at the Noise of the Murderer being taken, the Lover of Alcidiana, who by this Time found his Lady unhurt, all but the Trains of her Gown and Petticoat, came running to the Place, just as Tarquin had disarm'd the German, and was ready to kill him; when laying hold of his Arm, they arrested the Stroke, and redeemed the Footman.

They then demanded who this Stranger was, at whose Mercy the Fellow lay; but the Prince, who now found himself venturing for his last Stake, made no Reply; but with two Swords in his Hands went to fight his Way through the Rabble; And tho' there were above a hundred Persons, some with Swords, others with long Whips, (as Coachmen) so invincible was the Courage of this poor unfortunate Gentleman at that Time, that all these were not able to seize him; but he made his Way through the Ring that encompassed him, and ran away; but was, however, so closely pursued, the Company still gathering as they ran, that toiled with fighting, oppressed with Guilt, and Fear of being taken, he grew fainter and fainter, and suffered himself, at last, to yield to his Pursuers, who soon found him to be Prince Tarquin in Disguise: And they carry'd him directly to Prison, being Sunday, to wait the coming Day, to go before a Magistrate.

In an Hour's Time the whole fatal Adventure was carried all over the City, and every one knew that Tarquin was the intended Murderer of Alcidiana; and not one but had a real Sorrow and Compassion for him. They heard how bravely he had defended himself, how many he had wounded before he could be taken, and what numbers he had fought through: And even those that saw his Valour and Bravery, and who had assisted at his being seiz'd, now repented from the Bottom of their Hearts their having any Hand in the Ruin of so gallant a Man; especially since they knew the Lady was not hurt. A thousand Addresses were made to her, not to prosecute him; but her Lover, a hot-headed Fellow, more fierce than brave, would by no Means be pacified, but vowed to pursue him to the Scaffold.

The Monday came, and the Prince being examined, confessed the Matter of Fact, since there was no Harm done; believing a generous Confession the best of his Game: But he was sent back to closer Imprisonment, loaded with Irons, to expect the next Sessions. All his Household-Goods were seiz'd, and all they could find, for the Use of Alcidiana. And the Princess, all in Rage, tearing her Hair, was carried to the same Prison, to behold the cruel Effects of her hellish Designs.

One need not tell here how sad and horrid this Meeting appear'd between her Lord and her: Let it suffice, it was the most melancholy and mortifying Object that ever Eyes beheld. On Miranda's Part, 'twas sometimes all Rage and Fire, and sometimes all Tears and Groans; but still 'twas sad Love, and mournful Tenderness on his. Nor could all his Sufferings, and the Prospect of Death itself, drive from his Soul one Spark of that Fire the obstinate God had fatally kindled there: And in the midst of all his Sighs, he would re-call himself, and cry, I have Miranda still.

He was eternally visited by his Friends and Acquaintance; and this last Action of Bravery had got him more than all his former Conduct had lost. The Fathers were perpetually with him; and all join'd with one common Voice in this, That he ought to abandon a Woman so wicked as the Princess; and that however Fate dealt with him, he could not shew himself a true Penitent, while he laid the Author of so much Evil in his Bosom: That Heaven would never bless him, till he had renounced her: And on such Conditions he would find those that would employ their utmost Interest to save his Life, who else would not stir in this Affair. But he was so deaf to all, that he could not so much as dissemble a Repentance for having married her.

He lay a long Time in Prison, and all that Time the poor Father Francisco remained there also: And the good Fathers who daily visited these two amorous Prisoners, the Prince and Princess; and who found, by the Management of Matters, it would go very hard with Tarquin, entertained 'em often with holy Matters relating to the Life to come; from which, before his Trial, he gathered what his Stars had appointed, and that he was destin'd to die.

This gave an unspeakable Torment to the now repenting Beauty, who had reduced him to it; and she began to appear with a more solid Grief: Which being perceived by the good Fathers, they resolved to attack her on the yielding Side; and after some Discourse upon the Judgment for Sin, they came to reflect on the Business of Father Francisco; and told her, she had never thriven since her accusing of that Father, and laid it very home to her Conscience; assuring her that they would do their utmost in her Service, if she would confess that secret Sin to all the World, so that she might atone for the Crime, by the saving that good Man. At first she seemed inclined to yield; but Shame of being her own Detector, in so vile a Matter, recalled her Goodness, and she faintly persisted in it.

At the End of six Months, Prince Tarquin was called to his Tryal; where I will pass over the Circumstances, which are only what is usual in such criminal Cases, and tell you, that he being found guilty of the Intent of killing Alcidiana, was condemned to lose his Head in the Market-Place, and the Princess to be banished her Country.

After Sentence pronounced, to the real Grief of all the Spectators, he was carry'd back to Prison, and now the Fathers attack her anew; and she, whose Griefs daily encreased, with a Languishment that brought her very near her Grave, at last confess'd all her Life, all the Lewdness of her Practices with several Princes and great Men, besides her Lusts with People that served her, and others in mean Capacity: And lastly, the whole Truth of the young Friar; and how she had drawn the Page, and the Prince her Husband, to this design'd Murder of her Sister. This she signed with her Hand, in the Presence of the Prince, her Husband, and several Holy Men who were present. Which being signify'd to the Magistrates, the Friar was immediately deliver'd from his Irons (where he had languished more than two whole Years) in great Triumph, with much Honour, and lives a most exemplary pious Life, as he did before; for he is now living in Antwerp.

After the Condemnation of these two unfortunate Persons, who begot such different Sentiments in the Minds of the People (the Prince, all the Compassion and Pity imaginable; and the Princess, all the Contempt and Despite;) they languished almost six Months longer in Prison; so great an Interest there was made, in order to the saving his Life, by all the Men of the Robe. On the other side, the

Princes, and great Men of all Nations, who were at the Court of Brussels, who bore a secret Revenge in their Hearts against a Man who had, as they pretended, set up a false Title, only to take Place of them; who indeed was but a Merchant's Son of Holland, as they said; so incens'd them against him, that they were too hard at Court for the Church-men. However, this Dispute gave the Prince his Life some Months longer than was expected; which gave him also some Hope, that a Reprieve for ninety Years would have been granted, as was desired. Nay, Father Francisco so interested himself in this Concern, that he writ to his Father, and several Princes of Germany, with whom the Marquis Castel Roderigo was well acquainted, to intercede with him for the saving of Tarquin; since 'twas more by his Persuasions, than those of all who attacked her, that made Miranda confess the Truth of her Affair with him. But at the End of six Months, when all Applications were found fruitless and vain, the Prince receiv'd News, that in two Days he was to die, as his Sentence had been before pronounced, and for which he prepared himself with all Chearfulness.

On the following Friday, as soon as it was light, all People of any Condition came to take their Leaves of him; and none departed with dry Eyes, or Hearts unconcern'd to the last Degree: For Tarquin, when he found his Fate inevitable bore it with a Fortitude that shewed no Signs of Regret; but address'd himself to all about him with the same chearful, modest, and great Air, he was wont to do in his most flourishing Fortune. His Valet was dressing him all the Morning, so many Interruptions they had by Visitors; and he was all in Mourning, and so were all his Followers; for even to the last he kept up his Grandeur, to the Amazement of all People. And indeed, he was so passionately belov'd by them, that those he had dismiss'd, serv'd him voluntarily, and would not be persuaded to abandon him while he liv'd.

The Princess was also dress'd in Mourning, and her two Women; and notwithstanding the unheard-of Lewdness and Villanies she had confess'd of her self, the Prince still ador'd her; for she had still those Charms that made him first do so; nor, to his last Moment, could he be brought to wish, that he had never seen her; but on the contrary, as a Man yet vainly proud of his Fetters, he said, 'All the Satisfaction this short Moment of Life could afford him, was, that he died in endeavouring to serve Miranda, his adorable Princess.'

After he had taken Leave of all, who thought it necessary to leave him to himself for some Time, he retir'd with his Confessor; where they were about an Hour in Prayer, all the Ceremonies of Devotion that were fit to be done, being already past. At last the Bell toll'd, and he was to take Leave of the Princess, as his last Work of Life, and the most hard he had to accomplish. He threw himself at her Feet, and gazing on her as she sat more dead than alive, overwhelm'd with silent Grief, they both remain'd some Moments speechless; and then, as if one rising Tide of Tears had supply'd both their Eyes, it burst out in Streams at the same Instant: and when his Sighs gave Way, he utter'd a thousand Farewels, so soft, so passionate, and moving, that all who were by were extremely touch'd with it, and said, That nothing could be seen more deplorable and melancholy. A thousand Times they bad Farewel, and still some tender Look, or Word, would prevent his going; then embrace, and bid Farewel again. A thousand Times she ask'd his Pardon for being the Occasion of that fatal Separation; a thousand Times assuring him, she would follow him, for she could not live without him. And Heaven knows when their soft and sad Caresses would have ended, had not the Officers assur'd him 'twas Time to mount the Scaffold. At which Words the Princess fell fainting in the Arms of her Woman, and they led Tarquin out of Prison.

When he came to the Market-Place, whither he walked on Foot, follow'd by his own Domesticks, and some bearing a black Velvet Coffin with Silver Hinges; the Head's-man before him with his fatal Scimiter drawn, his Confessor by his Side, and many Gentlemen and Church-men, with Father Francisco attending him, the People showring Millions of Blessings on him, and beholding him with weeping Eyes, he mounted the Scaffold; which was strewed with some Saw-dust, about the Place where he was to kneel, to receive the Blood: For they behead People kneeling, and with the Back-Stroak of a Scimiter; and not lying on a Block, and with an Axe, as we in England. The Scaffold had a low Rail about it, that every body might more conveniently see. This was hung with black, and all that State that such a Death could have, was here in most decent Order.

He did not say much upon the Scaffold: The Sum of what he said to his Friends was, to be kind, and take Care of the poor Penitent his Wife: To others, recommending his honest and generous Servants, whose Fidelity was so well known and commended, that they were soon promised Preferment. He was some time in Prayer, and a very short time in speaking to his Confessor; then he turned to the Head's-man, and desired him to do his Office well, and gave him twenty Louis d'Ors; and undressing himself with the Help of his Valet and Page, he pull'd off his Coat, and had underneath a white Sattin Waistcoat: He took off his Periwig, and put on a white Sattin Cap, with a Holland one done with Point under it, which he pulled over his Eyes; then took a chearful Leave of all, and kneel'd down, and said, 'When he lifted up his Hands the third Time, the Head's-man should do his Office.' Which accordingly was done, and the Head's-man gave him his last Stroke, and the Prince fell on the Scaffold. The People with one common Voice, as if it had been but one entire one, pray'd for his Soul; and Murmurs of Sighs were heard from the whole Multitude, who scrambled for some of the bloody Saw-dust, to keep for his Memory.

The Head's-man going to take up the Head, as the Manner is, to shew it to the People, he found he had not struck it off, and that the Body stirr'd; with that he stepped to an Engine, which they always carry with 'em, to force those who may be refractory; thinking, as he said, to have twisted the Head from the Shoulders, conceiving it to hang but by a small Matter of Flesh. Tho' 'twas an odd Shift of the Fellow's, yet 'twas done, and the best Shift he could suddenly propose. The Margrave, and another Officer, old Men, were on the Scaffold, with some of the Prince's Friends, and Servants; who seeing the Head's-man put the Engine about the Neck of the Prince, began to call out, and the People made a great Noise. The Prince, who found himself yet alive; or rather, who was past thinking but had some Sense of Feeling left, when the Head's-man took him up, and set his Back against the Rail, and clapp'd the Engine about his Neck, got his two Thumbs between the Rope and his Neck, feeling himself press'd there; and struggling between Life and Death, and bending himself over the Rail backward, while the Head's-man pulled forward, he threw himself quite over the Rail, by Chance, and not Design, and fell upon the Heads and Shoulders of the People, who were crying out with amazing Shouts of Joy. The Head's-man leap'd after him, but the Rabble had lik'd to have pull'd him to Pieces: All the City was in an Uproar, but none knew what the Matter was, but those who bore the Body of the Prince, whom they found yet living; but how, or by what strange Miracle preserv'd, they knew not, nor did examine; but with one Accord, as if the whole Crowd had been one Body, and had had but one Motion, they bore the Prince on their Heads about a hundred Yards from the Scaffold, where there is a Monastery of Jesuits; and there they secur'd him. All this was done, his beheading, his falling, and his being secur'd, almost in a Moment's Time; the People rejoiceing, as at some extraordinary Victory won. One of the Officers being, as I said, an old timorous Man, was so frighten'd at the Accident, the Bustle, the Noise, and the Confusion, of which he was wholly ignorant, that he dy'd with Amazement and Fear; and the other was fain to be let blood.

The Officers of Justice went to demand the Prisoner, but they demanded in vain; the Jesuits had now a Right to protect him, and would do so. All his overjoy'd Friends went to see in what Condition he was, and all of Quality found Admittance: They saw him in Bed, going to be dress'd by the most skilful Surgeons, who yet could not assure him of Life. They desired no body should speak to him, or ask him any Questions. They found that the Head's-man had struck him too low, and had cut him into the Shoulder-bone. A very great Wound, you may be sure; for the Sword, in such Executions, carries an extreme Force: However, so great Care was taken on all Sides, and so greatly the Fathers were concern'd for him, that they found an Amendment, and Hopes of a good Effect of their incomparable Charity and Goodness.

At last, when he was permitted to speak, the first News he ask'd was after the Princess. And his Friends were very much afflicted to find, that all his Loss of Blood had not quenched that Flame, not let out that which made him still love that bad Woman. He was sollicited daily to think no more of her: And all her Crimes are laid so open to him, and so shamefully represented; and on the other Side, his Virtues so admir'd; and which, they said, would have been eternally celebrated, but for his Folly with this infamous Creature; that at last, by assuring him of all their Assistance if he abandon'd her; and to renounce him, and deliver him up, if he did not; they wrought so far upon him, as to promise, he would suffer her to go alone into Banishment, and would not follow her, or live with her any more. But alas! this was but his Gratitude that compell'd this Complaisance, for in his Heart he resolv'd never to abandon her; nor was he able to live, and think of doing it: However, his Reason assur'd him, he could not do a Deed more justifiable, and one that would regain his Fame sooner.

His Friends ask'd him some Questions concerning his Escape; and since he was not beheaded, but only wounded, why he did not immediately rise up? But he replied, he was so absolutely prepossessed, that at the third lifting up his Hands he should receive the Stroke of Death, that at the same Instant the Sword touch'd him, he had no Sense; nay, not even of Pain, so absolutely dead he was with Imagination; and knew not that he stirr'd, as the Head's-man found he did; nor did he remember any Thing, from the lifting up of his Hands, to his fall; and then awaken'd, as out of a Dream, or rather a Moment's Sleep without Dream, he found he liv'd, and wonder'd what was arriv'd to him, or how he came to live; having not, as yet, any Sense of his Wound, tho' so terrible an one.

After this, Alcidiana, who was extremely afflicted for having been the Prosecutor of this great Man; who, bating this last Design against her, which she knew was at the Instigation of her Sister, had oblig'd her with all the Civility imaginable; now sought all Means possible of getting his Pardon, and that of her Sister; tho' of an hundred thousand Crowns, which she should have paid her, she could get but ten thousand; which was from the Sale of her rich Beds, and some other Furniture. So that the young Count, who before should have marry'd her, now went off for want of Fortune; and a young Merchant (perhaps the best of the two) was the Man to whom she was destin'd.

At last, by great Intercession, both their Pardons were obtain'd; and the Prince, who would be no more seen in a Place that had prov'd every way so fatal to him, left Flanders, promising never to live with the Fair Hypocrite more; but e'er he departed, he wrote her a Letter, wherein he order'd her, in a little Time, to follow him into Holland; and left a Bill of Exchange with one of his trusty Servants, whom he had left to wait upon her, for Money for her Accommodation; so that she was now reduced to one Woman, one Page, and this Gentleman. The Prince, in this Time of his Imprisonment, had several Bills of great Sums from his Father, who was exceeding rich, and this all the Children he had in the World, and whom he tenderly loved.

As soon as Miranda was come into Holland, she was welcom'd with all imaginable Respect and Endearment by the old Father; who was impos'd upon so, as that he knew not she was the fatal Occasion of all these Disasters to his Son; but rather look'd on her as a Woman, who had brought him an hundred and fifty thousand Crowns, which his Misfortunes had consum'd. But, above all, she was receiv'd by Tarquin with a Joy unspeakable; who, after some Time, to redeem his Credit, and gain himself a new Fame, put himself into the French Army, where he did Wonders; and after three Campaigns, his Father dying, he return'd home, and retir'd to a Country-House; where, with his Princess, he liv'd as a private Gentleman, in all the Tranquillity of a Man of good Fortune. They say Miranda has been very penitent for her Life past, and gives Heaven the Glory for having given her these Afflictions that have reclaim'd her, and brought her to as perfect a State of Happiness, as this troublesome World, can afford.

Since I began this Relation, I heard that Prince Tarquin, dy'd about three Quarters of a Year ago.

NOTES: The Fair Jilt.

**To Henry Pain**, Esq. Henry Neville Payne, politician and author, was a thorough Tory and an ardent partisan of James II. Downes ascribes to him three plays: The Fatal Jealousy, produced at Dorset Garden in the winter of 1672, a good, if somewhat vehement, tragedy (4to, 1673); Morning Ramble; or, Town Humours, produced at the same theatre in 1673 (4to, 1673), which, though lacking in plot and quick incident, is far from a bad comedy; and The Siege of Constantinople, acted by the Duke's company in 1674 (4to, 1675), a tragedy which very sharply lashes Shaftesbury as the Chancellor, especially in Act II, when Lorenzo, upon his patron designing a frolic, says:

My Lord, you know your old house, Mother Somelie's,
You know she always fits you with fresh girls.

Mother Somelie is, of course, the notorious Mother Mosely.

Henry Payne wrote several loyal pamphlets, and after the Revolution he became, according to Burnet, 'the most active and determined of all King James' agents.' He is said to have been the chief instigator of the Montgomery plot in 1690, and whilst in Scotland was arrested. 10 and 11 December of that year he was severely tortured under a special order of William III, but nothing could be extracted from him. This is the last occasion on which torture was applied in Scotland. After being treated with harshest cruelty by William III, Payne was finally released from prison in December, 1700, or January, 1701, as the Duke of Queensbury, recognizing the serious illegalities of the whole business, urgently advised his liberation. Payne died in 1710. As Macaulay consistently confounds him with a certain Edward Neville, S.J., the statements of this historian with reference to Henry Neville Payne must be entirely disregarded.

**The Fair Jilt.** Editio princeps, 'London. Printed by R. Holt for Will. Canning, at his Shop in the Temple-Cloysters' (1688), 'Licensed 17 April, 1688. Ric. Pocock', has as title: The Fair Jilt; or, The History of Prince Tarquin and Miranda. As half-title it prints: The Fair Hypocrite; or, The Amours of Prince Tarquin and Miranda. All subsequent editions, however, give: The Fair Jilt; or, The Amours of Prince Tarquin and Miranda. The Dedication only occurs in the first edition.

**Scrutore.** Escritoire, cf. Sir T. Herbert, Trav. (1677): 'There they sell . . . Scrutores or Cabinets of Mother of Pearl.'

**Canonesses**, Begines, Quests, Swart-Sisters and Jesuitesses. Canonesses are very ancient in history. The most important Congregations are the Sepulchrines or Canonesses of the Holy Sepulchre, and the Lateran Canonesses. There was an old community of French Hospitaller Canonesses of Saint-Esprit. Thomassin tells us that the Béguines were canonesses, and that their name is derived from S. Begghe (ob. 689), who founded the Canonesses of Andenne. There are also Chapters of secular canonesses, nearly all Benedictine in origin. Many of these only admitted ladies of the highest rank. The French Revolution swept away a great number of these institutions, and some were suppressed by Joseph II of Austria. Premonstratensian (white) Canonesses were common in Belgium.

Begines. Either founded by S. Begghe, or their name is derived from Lambert de Bègue, a priest of Liège, in 1177. Some place their foundation at the beginning of the eleventh century in the Netherlands or Germany. After three years women who are enrolled are entitled to a little house. No vows are taken, but they assist in choir thrice daily. There are several hundreds at Ghent, and the Béguinage (ten Wijngaarde) of Bruges is famous.

Quests. Quêteuses. Extern Sisters, Poor Clares and Colettines; Lay Sisters, Dominicanesses, who go out and beg for the community. 'To quest' is to go alms-begging. The Sisters of Charity are of later foundation. cf. Translation, D'Emilliane's Frauds of Romish Monks (1691): 'The Farmer [of Purgatory Money] sends some of his Emissaries into the Fields to carry on the Quest there for the said Souls'; and Earthquake . . . Peru, iii, 303 (1748): 'If the Friars go into the Country a questing for their Monastery.'

Swart-Sisters. Black Nuns. Dominicanesses, a feature of whose dresses is the cappa, a large black cloak and hood, worn from All Saints' Day till the 'Gloria' on Easter Eve, and on all great solemnities.

Jesuitesses. A common misnomer for the original Congregation founded by Mary Ward (ob. 1645), and named by her 'The Institute of Mary'. It was not until 1703 that they were fully approved by Clement XI.

**Cordeliers**. Observant Franciscans, who follow the strict Rule of Poverty and observe all the fasts and austerities of the Order. This name was first given them in France, where later they were known as Recollects.


OROONOKO; OR THE ROYAL SLAVE

INTRODUCTION

The tale of Oroonoko, the Royal Slave is indisputedly Mrs. Behn's masterpiece in prose. Its originality and power have singled it out for a permanence and popularity none of her other works attained. It is vivid, realistic, pregnant with pathos, beauty, and truth, and not only has it so impressed itself upon the readers of more than two centuries, but further, it surely struck a new note in English literature and one which was re-echoed far and wide. It has been said that 'Oroonoko is the first emancipation novel', and there is no little acumen in this remark. Certainly we may absolve Mrs. Behn from having directly written with a purpose such as animated Mrs. Harriet Beecher Stowe's Uncle Tom's Cabin; but none the less her sympathy with the oppressed blacks, her deep emotions of pity for outraged humanity, her anger at the cruelties of the slave-driver aye ready with knout or knife, are manifest in every line. Beyond the intense interest of the pure narrative we have passages of a rhythm that is lyric, exquisitely descriptive of the picturesque tropical scenery and exotic vegetations, fragrant and luxuriant; there are intimate accounts of adventuring and primitive life; there are personal touches which lend a colour only personal touches can, as Aphara tells her prose-epic of her Superman, Cæsar the slave, Oroonoko the prince.

It is not difficult to trace the influence of Oroonoko. We can see it in many an English author; in Bernardin de Saint-Pierre, in Chateaubriand. Her idyllic romance has inspired writers who perhaps but dimly remember even her name and her genius.

It was often reprinted separately from the rest. There is a little 12mo Oroonoko, 'the ninth edition corrected', published at Doncaster, 1759, 'for C. Plummer', which is rarely seen save in a torn and well-thumbed state.[1]

In 1777 the sentimental and highly proper Mrs. Elizabeth Griffith included Oroonoko in her three volume Collection of Novels selected and revised. Oroonoko, 'written originally by Mrs. Behn and revised by Mrs. Griffith'[2], was also issued separately, 'price sixpence'[3], in 1800, frontispieced by a very crude picture of a black-a-moor about to attack a tiger.

As early as 1709 we find Lebens und Liebes-Geschichte des Königlichen Sclaven Oroonoko in West-Indien, a German translation published at Hamburg, with a portrait of 'Die Sinnreiche Engelländerin Mrs. Afra Behn.'

In 1745 Oroonoko was 'traduit de l'Anglois de Madame Behn,' with the motto from Lucan 'Quo fata trahunt virtus secura sequetur.' There is a rhymed dedication 'A Madame La M. P. D'l . . .' (35 lines), signed D. L.—, i.e., Pierre-Antoine de la Place, a fecund but mediocre writer of the eighteenth century (1707-93), who also translated, Venice Preserv'd, The Fatal Marriage, Tom Jones, and other English masterpieces. There is another edition of de la Place's version with fine plates engraved by C. Baron after Marillier, Londres, 1769.

In 1696 Southerne's great tragedy, founded upon Mrs. Behn's novel, was produced at Drury Lane. Oroonoko was created by Verbruggen, Powell acted Aboan, and the beautiful Mrs. Rogers Imoinda. The play has some magnificent passages, and long kept the stage. Southerne had further added an excellent comic underplot, full of humour and the truest vis comica. It is perhaps worth noting that the intrigues of Lucy and Charlotte and the Lackitt ménage were dished up as a short slap-bang farce by themselves with, curiously enough, two or three scenes in extenso from Fletcher's Monsieur Thomas (III, iii, and V, ii). This hotch potch entitled The Sexes Mis-match'd; or, A New Way to get a Husband is printed in The Strollers' Pacquet open'd. (12mo, 1741.) On 1 December, 1759, there was brought out at Drury Lane a most insipid alteration of Oroonoko by Dr. Hawkesworth, who omitted all Southerne's lighter fare and inserted serious nonsense of his own. Garrick was the Oroonoko and Mrs. Cibber Imoinda. Although Hawkesworth's version was not tolerated, the underplot was none the less pruned in later productions to such an extent that it perforce lost nearly all its pristine wit and fun. There is another adaption of Southerne: 'Oroonoko altered from the original play . . . to which the editor has added near six hundred lines in place of the comic scenes, together with an addition of two new characters, intended for one of the theatres.' (8vo, 1760.) The two new characters are Maria, sister to the Lieutenant-Governor and contracted to Blandford, and one Heartwell; both thoroughly tiresome individuals. In the same year Frank Gentleman, a provincial actor, produced his idea of Oroonoko 'as it was acted at Edinburgh.' (12mo, 1760.) There is yet a fourth bastard: The Prince of Angola, by one J. Ferriar, 'a tragedy altered from the play of Oroonoko and adapted to the circumstances of the present times.'[4] (Manchester, 1788.) It must be confessed that all this tinkering with an original, which does not require from any point of view the slightest alteration or omission, is most uncalled for, crude, and unsuccessful.

In 1698 William Walker, a lad nineteen years old, the son of a wealthy Barbadoes planter, wrote in three weeks a tragedy entitled Victorious Love (4to, 1698), which is confessedly a close imitation of Southerne's theme. It was produced at Drury Lane in June, 1698, with the author himself as Dafila, a youth, and young Mrs. Cross as the heroine Zaraida, 'an European Shipwrack'd an Infant at Gualata'. Possibly Verbruggen acted Barnagasso, the captive king who corresponds to Oroonoko. The scene is laid in the Banze, or Palace of Tombut, whose Emperor, Jamoan, is Barnagasso's rival in Zaraida's love. There is a villain, Zanhaga, who after various more or less successful iniquities, poisons the

Emperor; whereon hero and heroine are happily united. Victorious Love is far from being entirely a bad play; it is, however, very reminiscent of the heroic tragedies of two decades before.

Southerne's Oroonoko was (with some alterations) translated into German. This version is prose and probably either the work of W. H. von Dalberg or von Eisenthal. It has little merit, but proved popular and was printed in 1789 with a somewhat grotesque frontispiece of Oroonoko and Imoinda, both of whom are black 'as pitch or as the cole'.

*[**Footnote 1**: There were also many chap-books on similar themes which enjoyed no small popularity, e.g., The Royal African; or, The Memoirs of the Young Prince of Annamaboe (circa 1750), the romantic narrative of a negro prince, who became a slave in Barbadoes, from whence he was redeemed and brought to England.]*

*[**Footnote 2**: Mis-spelt 'Griffiths' in the 1800 edition.]*

*[**Footnote 3**: There was 'a superior edition on a fine wove paper, Hot-pressed, with Proof Impressions of the Plates. Price only Nine-pence.']*

*[**Footnote 4**: The Agitation for the Abolition of the Slave Trade.]*


**Epistle Dedicatory.**

TO THE RIGHT HONOURABLE THE LORD MAITLAND.

My Lord,

Since the World is grown so Nice and Critical upon Dedications, and will Needs be Judging the Book by the Wit of the Patron; we ought, with a great deal of Circumspection to chuse a Person against whom there can be no Exception; and whose Wit and Worth truly Merits all that one is capable of saying upon that Occasion.

The most part of Dedications are charg'd with Flattery; and if the World knows a Man has some Vices, they will not allow one to speak of his Virtues. This, My Lord, is for want of thinking Rightly; if Men wou'd consider with Reason, they wou'd have another sort of Opinion, and Esteem of Dedications; and wou'd believe almost every Great Man has enough to make him Worthy of all that can be said of him there. My Lord, a Picture-drawer, when he intends to make a good Picture, essays the Face many Ways, and in many Lights, before he begins; that he may chuse from the several turns of it, which is most Agreeable and gives it the best Grace; and if there be a Scar, an ungrateful Mole, or any little Defect, they leave it out; and yet make the Picture extreamly like: But he who has the good Fortune to draw a Face that is exactly Charming in all its Parts and Features, what Colours or Agreements can be added to make it Finer? All that he can give is but its due; and Glories in a Piece whose Original alone gives it its Perfection. An ill Hand may diminish, but a good Hand cannot augment its Beauty. A Poet is a Painter in his way; he draws to the Life, but in another kind; we draw the Nobler part, the Soul and Mind; the Pictures of the Pen shall out-last those of the Pencil, and even Worlds themselves. 'Tis a short Chronicle of those Lives that possibly wou'd be forgotten by other Historians, or lye neglected there, however deserving an immortal Fame; for Men of eminent Parts are as Exemplary as even Monarchs themselves; and Virtue is a noble Lesson to be learn'd, and 'tis by Comparison we can Judge and Chuse. 'Tis by such illustrious Presidents as your Lordship the World can be Better'd and Refin'd; when a great part of the lazy Nobility shall, with Shame, behold the admirable Accomplishments of a Man so Great, and so Young.

Your Lordship has Read innumerable Volumes of Men and Books, not Vainly for the gust of Novelty, but Knowledge, excellent Knowledge: Like the industrious Bee, from every Flower you return Laden with the precious Dew, which you are sure to turn to the Publick Good. You hoard no one Reflection, but lay it all out in the Glorious Service of your Religion and Country; to both which you are a useful and necessary Honour: They both want such Supporters; and 'tis only Men of so elevated Parts, and fine Knowledge; such noble Principles of Loyalty and Religion this Nation Sighs for. Where shall we find a Man so Young, like St. Augustine, in the midst of all his Youth and Gaiety, Teaching the World Divine Precepts, true Notions of Faith, and Excellent Morality, and, at the same time be also a perfect Pattern of all that accomplish a Great Man? You have, My Lord, all that refin'd Wit that Charms, and the Affability that Obliges; a Generosity that gives a Lustre to your Nobility; that Hospitality, and Greatness of Mind that ingages the World; and that admirable Conduct, that so well Instructs it. Our Nation ought to regret and bemoan their Misfortunes, for not being able to claim the Honour of the Birth of a Man who is so fit to serve his Majesty, and his Kingdoms in all Great and Publick Affairs; And to the Glory of your Nation, be it spoken, it produces more considerable Men, for all fine Sence, Wit, Wisdom, Breeding and Generosity (for the generality of the Nobility) than all other Nations can Boast; and the Fruitfulness of your Virtues sufficiently make amends for the Barrenness of your Soil: Which however cannot be incommode to your Lordship; since your Quality and the Veneration that the Commonalty naturally pay their Lords creates a flowing Plenty there . . . that makes you Happy. And to compleat your Happiness, my Lord, Heaven has blest you with a Lady, to whom it has given all the Graces, Beauties, and Virtues of her Sex; all the Youth, Sweetness of Nature, of a most illustrious Family; and who is a most rare Example to all Wives of Quality, for her eminent Piety, Easiness, and Condescention; and as absolutely merits Respect from all the World as she does that Passion and Resignation she receives from your Lordship; and which is, on her part, with so much Tenderness return'd. Methinks your tranquil Lives are an Image of the new Made and Beautiful Pair in Paradise: And 'tis the Prayers and Wishes of all, who have the Honour to know you, that it may Eternally so continue with Additions of all the Blessings this World can give you.

My Lord, the Obligations I have to some of the Great Men of your Nation, particularly to your Lordship, gives me an Ambition of making my Acknowledgements by all the Opportunities I can; and such humble Fruits as my Industry produces I lay at your Lordship's Feet. This is a true Story, of a Man Gallant enough to merit your Protection, and, had he always been so Fortunate, he had not made so Inglorious an end: The Royal Slave I had the Honour to know in my Travels to the other World; and though I had none above me in that Country yet I wanted power to preserve this Great Man. If there is anything that seems Romantick I beseech your Lordship to consider these Countries do, in all things, so far differ from ours that they produce unconceivable Wonders, at least, so they appear to us, because New and Strange. What I have mentioned I have taken care shou'd be Truth, let the Critical Reader judge as he pleases. 'Twill be no Commendation to the Book to assure your Lordship I writ it in a few Hours, though it may serve to Excuse some of its Faults of Connexion, for I never rested my Pen a Moment for Thought: 'Tis purely the Merit of my Slave that must render it worthy of the Honour it begs; and the Author of that of Subscribing herself,

My Lord Your Lordship's most oblig'd and obedient Servant A. Behn.

I do not pretend, in giving you the History of this ROYAL SLAVE, to entertain my Reader with the Adventures of a feign'd Hero, whose Life and Fortunes Fancy may manage at the Poet's Pleasure; nor in relating the Truth, design to adorn it with any Accidents, but such as arrived in earnest to him:

And it shall come simply into the World, recommended by its own proper Merits, and natural Intrigues; there being enough of Reality to support it, and to render it diverting, without the Addition of Invention.

I was myself an Eye-witness to a great Part of what you will find here set down; and what I could not be Witness of, I receiv'd from the Mouth of the chief Actor in this History, the Hero himself, who gave us the whole Transactions of his Youth: And I shall omit, for Brevity's Sake, a thousand little Accidents of his Life, which, however pleasant to us, where History was scarce, and Adventures very rare, yet might prove tedious and heavy to my Reader, in a World where he finds Diversions for every Minute, new and strange. But we who were perfectly charm'd with the Character of this great Man, were curious to gather every Circumstance of his Life.

The Scene of the last Part of his Adventures lies in a Colony in America, called Surinam, in the West-Indies.

But before I give you the Story of this Gallant Slave, 'tis fit I tell you the Manner of bringing them to these new Colonies; those they make Use of there, not being Natives of the Place: for those we live with in perfect Amity, without daring to command 'em; but, on the contrary, caress 'em with all the brotherly and friendly Affection in the World; trading with them for their Fish, Venison, Buffaloes Skins, and little Rarities; as Marmosets, a sort of Monkey, as big as a Rat or Weasel, but of a marvellous and delicate Shape, having Face and Hands like a Human Creature; and Cousheries, a little Beast in the Form and Fashion of a Lion, as big as a Kitten, but so exactly made in all Parts like that Noble Beast, that it is it in Miniature: Then for little Paraketoes, great Parrots, Muckaws, and a thousand other Birds and Beasts of wonderful and surprizing Forms, Shapes, and Colours: For Skins of prodigious Snakes, of which there are some three-score Yards in Length; as is the Skin of one that may be seen at his Majesty's Antiquary's; where are also some rare Flies, of amazing Forms and Colours, presented to 'em by myself; some as big as my Fist, some less; and all of various Excellencies, such as Art cannot imitate. Then we trade for Feathers, which they order into all Shapes, make themselves little short Habits of 'em, and glorious Wreaths for their Heads, Necks, Arms and Legs, whose Tinctures are unconceivable. I had a Set of these presented to me, and I gave 'em to the King's Theatre; it was the Dress of the Indian Queen, infinitely admir'd by Persons of Quality; and was inimitable. Besides these, a thousand little Knacks, and Rarities in Nature; and some of Art, as their Baskets, Weapons, Aprons, &c. We dealt with 'em with Beads of all Colours, Knives, Axes, Pins and Needles, which they us'd only as Tools to drill Holes with in their Ears, Noses and Lips, where they hang a great many little Things; as long Beads, Bits of Tin, Brass or Silver beat thin, and any shining Trinket. The Beads they weave into Aprons about a Quarter of an Ell long, and of the same Breadth; working them very prettily in Flowers of several Colours; which Apron they wear just before 'em, as Adam and Eve did the Fig-leaves; the Men wearing a long Stripe of Linen, which they deal with us for. They thread these Beads also on long Cotton-threads, and make Girdles to tie their Aprons to, which come twenty times, or more, about the Waste, and then cross, like a Shoulder-belt, both Ways, and round their Necks, Arms and Legs. This Adornment, with their long black Hair, and the Face painted in little Specks or Flowers here and there, makes 'em a wonderful Figure to behold. Some of the Beauties, which indeed are finely shap'd, as almost all are, and who have pretty Features, are charming and novel; for they have all that is called Beauty, except the Colour, which is a reddish Yellow; or after a new Oiling, which they often use to themselves, they are of the Colour of a new Brick, but smooth, soft and sleek. They are extreme modest and bashful, very shy, and nice of being touch'd. And tho' they are all thus naked, if one lives for ever among 'em, there is not to be seen an indecent Action, or Glance: and being continually us'd to see one another so unadorn'd, so like our first Parents before the Fall, it seems as if they had no Wishes, there being nothing to heighten Curiosity: but all you can see, you see at once, and every Moment see; and where there is no Novelty, there can be no Curiosity. Not but I have seen a handsome young Indian, dying for Love of a very beautiful young Indian Maid; but all his Courtship was, to fold his Arms, pursue her with his Eyes, and Sighs were all his Language: While she, as if no such Lover were present, or rather as if she desired none such, carefully guarded her Eyes from beholding him; and never approach'd him, but she looked down with all the blushing Modesty I have seen in the most Severe and Cautious of our World. And these People represented to me an absolute Idea of the first State of Innocence, before Man knew how to sin: And 'tis most evident and plain, that simple Nature is the most harmless, inoffensive and virtuous Mistress. 'Tis she alone, if she were permitted, that better instructs the World, than all the Inventions of Man: Religion would here but destroy that Tranquillity they possess by Ignorance; and Laws would but teach 'em to know Offences, of which now they have no Notion. They once made Mourning and Fasting for the Death of the English Governor, who had given his Hand to come on such a Day to 'em, and neither came nor sent; believing, when a Man's Word was past, nothing but Death could or should prevent his keeping it: And when they saw he was not dead, they ask'd him what Name they had for a Man who promis'd a Thing he did not do? The Governor told them, Such a Man was a Lyar, which was a Word of Infamy to a Gentleman. Then one of 'em reply'd, Governor, you are a Lyar, and guilty of that Infamy. They have a native Justice, which knows no Fraud; and they understand no Vice, or Cunning, but when they are taught by the White Men. They have Plurality of Wives; which, when they grow old, serve those that succeed 'em, who are young, but with a Servitude easy and respected; and unless they take Slaves in War, they have no other Attendants.

Those on that Continent where I was, had no King; but the oldest War-Captain was obey'd with great Resignation.

A War-Captain is a Man who has led them on to Battle with Conduct and Success; of whom I shall have Occasion to speak more hereafter, and of some other of their Customs and Manners, as they fall in my Way.

With these People, as I said, we live in perfect Tranquillity, and good Understanding, as it behoves us to do; they knowing all the Places where to seek the best Food of the Country, and the Means of getting it; and for very small and unvaluable Trifles, supplying us with what 'tis almost impossible for us to get; for they do not only in the Woods, and over the Sevana's, in Hunting, supply the Parts of Hounds, by swiftly scouring thro' those almost impassable Places, and by the mere Activity of their Feet, run down the nimblest Deer, and other eatable Beasts; but in the Water, one would think they were Gods of the Rivers, or Fellow-Citizens of the Deep; so rare an Art they have in swimming, diving, and almost living in Water; by which they command the less swift Inhabitants of the Floods. And then for shooting, what they cannot take, or reach with their Hands, they do with Arrows; and have so admirable an Aim, that they will split almost an Hair, and at any Distance that an Arrow can reach: they will shoot down Oranges, and other Fruit, and only touch the Stalk with the Dart's Point, that they may not hurt the Fruit. So that they being on all Occasions very useful to us, we find it absolutely necessary to caress 'em as Friends, and not to treat 'em as Slaves; nor dare we do otherwise, their Numbers so far surpassing ours in that Continent.

Those then whom we make use of to work in our Plantations of Sugar, are Negroes, Black-Slaves altogether, who are transported thither in this Manner.

Those who want Slaves, make a Bargain with a Master, or a Captain of a Ship, and contract to pay him so much apiece, a Matter of twenty Pound a Head, for as many as he agrees for, and to pay for 'em when they shall be deliver'd on such a Plantation: So that when there arrives a Ship laden with Slaves, they who have so contracted, go aboard, and receive their Number by Lot; and perhaps in one Lot that may be for ten, there may happen to be three or four Men, the rest Women and Children. Or be there more or less of either Sex, you are obliged to be contented with your Lot.

Coramantien, a Country of Blacks so called, was one of those Places in which they found the most advantageous Trading for these Slaves, and thither most of our great Traders in that Merchandize traffick; for that Nation is very warlike and brave; and having a continual Campaign, being always in Hostility with one neighbouring Prince or other, they had the Fortune to take a great many Captives: for all they took in Battle were sold as Slaves; at least those common Men who could not ransom themselves. Of these Slaves so taken, the General only has all the Profit; and of these Generals our Captains and Masters of Ships buy all their Freights.

The King of Coramantien was of himself a Man of an hundred and odd Years old, and had no Son, tho' he had many beautiful Black Wives: for most certainly there are Beauties that can charm of that Colour. In his younger Years he had had many gallant Men to his Sons, thirteen of whom died in Battle, conquering when they fell; and he had only left him for his Successor, one Grand-child, Son to one of these dead Victors, who, as soon as he could bear a Bow in his Hand, and a Quiver at his Back, was sent into the Field, to be train'd up by one of the oldest Generals to War; where, from his natural Inclination to Arms, and the Occasions given him, with the good Conduct of the old General, he became, at the Age of seventeen, one of the most expert Captains, and bravest Soldiers that ever saw the Field of Mars: so that he was ador'd as the Wonder of all that World, and the Darling of the Soldiers. Besides, he was adorn'd with a native Beauty, so transcending all those of his gloomy Race, that he struck an Awe and Reverence, even into those that knew not his Quality; as he did into me, who beheld him with Surprize and Wonder, when afterwards he arrived in our World.

He had scarce arrived at his seventeenth Year, when, fighting by his Side, the General was kill'd with an Arrow in his Eye, which the Prince Oroonoko (for so was this gallant Moor call'd) very narrowly avoided; nor had he, if the General who saw the Arrow shot, and perceiving it aimed at the Prince, had not bow'd his Head between, on Purpose to receive it in his own Body, rather than it should touch that of the Prince, and so saved him.

'Twas then, afflicted as Oroonoko was, that he was proclaimed General in the old Man's Place: and then it was, at the finishing of that War, which had continu'd for two Years, that the Prince came to Court, where he had hardly been a Month together, from the Time of his fifth Year to that of seventeen: and 'twas amazing to imagine where it was he learn'd so much Humanity; or to give his Accomplishments a juster Name, where 'twas he got that real Greatness of Soul, those refined Notions of true Honour, that absolute Generosity, and that Softness, that was capable of the highest Passions of Love and Gallantry, whose Objects were almost continually fighting Men, or those mangled or dead, who heard no Sounds but those of War and Groans. Some Part of it we may attribute to the Care of a Frenchman of Wit and Learning, who finding it turn to a very good Account to be a sort of Royal Tutor to this young Black, and perceiving him very ready, apt, and quick of Apprehension, took a great Pleasure to teach him Morals, Language and Science; and was for it extremely belov'd and valu'd by him. Another Reason was, he lov'd when he came from War, to see all the English Gentlemen that traded thither; and did not only learn their Language, but that of the Spaniard also, with whom he traded afterwards for Slaves.

I have often seen and conversed with this Great Man, and been a Witness to many of his mighty Actions; and do assure my Reader, the most illustrious Courts could not have produced a braver Man, both for Greatness of Courage and Mind, a Judgment more solid, a Wit more quick, and a Conversation more sweet and diverting. He knew almost as much as if he had read much: He had heard of and admired the Romans: He had heard of the late Civil Wars in England, and the deplorable Death of our great Monarch; and would discourse of it with all the Sense and Abhorrence of the Injustice imaginable. He had an extreme good and graceful Mien, and all the Civility of a well-bred Great Man. He had nothing of Barbarity in his Nature, but in all Points address'd himself as if his Education had been in some European Court.

This great and just Character of Oroonoko gave me an extreme Curiosity to see him, especially when I knew he spoke French and English, and that I could talk with him. But tho' I had heard so much of him, I was as greatly surprized when I saw him, as if I had heard nothing of him; so beyond all Report I found him. He came into the Room, and addressed himself to me, and some other Women, with the best Grace in the World. He was pretty tall, but of a Shape the most exact that can be fancy'd: The most famous Statuary could not form the Figure of a Man more admirably turn'd from Head to Foot. His Face was not of that brown rusty Black which most of that Nation are, but a perfect Ebony, or polished Jet. His Eyes were the most aweful that could be seen, and very piercing; the White of 'em being like Snow, as were his Teeth. His Nose was rising and Roman, instead of African and flat: His Mouth the finest shaped that could be seen; far from those great turn'd Lips, which are so natural to the rest of the Negroes. The whole Proportion and Air of his Face was so nobly and exactly form'd, that bating his Colour, there could be nothing in Nature more beautiful, agreeable and handsome. There was no one Grace wanting, that bears the Standard of true Beauty. His Hair came down to his Shoulders, by the Aids of Art, which was by pulling it out with a Quill, and keeping it comb'd; of which he took particular Care. Nor did the Perfections of his Mind come short of those of his Person; for his Discourse was admirable upon almost any Subject: and whoever had heard him speak, would have been convinced of their Errors, that all fine Wit is confined to the white Men, especially to those of Christendom; and would have confess'd that Oroonoko was as capable even of reigning well, and of governing as wisely, had as great a Soul, as politick Maxims, and was as sensible of Power, as any Prince civiliz'd in the most refined Schools of Humanity and Learning, or the most illustrious Courts.

This Prince, such as I have describ'd him, whose Soul and Body were so admirably adorned, was (while yet he was in the Court of his Grandfather, as I said) as capable of Love, as 'twas possible for a brave and gallant Man to be; and in saying that, I have named the highest Degree of Love: for sure great Souls are most capable of that Passion.

I have already said, the old General was kill'd by the Shot of an Arrow, by the Side of this Prince, in Battle; and that Oroonoko was made General. This old dead Hero had one only Daughter left of his Race, a Beauty, that to describe her truly, one need say only, she was Female to the noble Male; the beautiful Black Venus to our young Mars; as charming in her Person as he, and of delicate Virtues. I have seen a hundred White Men sighing after her, and making a thousand Vows at her Feet, all in vain and unsuccessful. And she was indeed too great for any but a Prince of her own Nation to adore.

Oroonoko coming from the Wars (which were now ended) after he had made his Court to his Grandfather, he thought in Honour he ought to make a Visit to Imoinda, the Daughter of his Foster-father, the dead General; and to make some Excuses to her, because his Preservation was the Occasion of her Father's Death; and to present her with those Slaves that had been taken in this last Battle, as the Trophies of her Father's Victories. When he came, attended by all the young Soldiers of any Merit, he was infinitely surpriz'd at the Beauty of this fair Queen of Night, whose Face and Person were so exceeding all he had ever beheld, that lovely Modesty with which she receiv'd him, that Softness in her Look and Sighs, upon the melancholy Occasion of this Honour that was done by so great a Man as Oroonoko, and a Prince of whom she had heard such admirable Things; the Awfulness wherewith she receiv'd him, and the Sweetness of her Words and Behaviour while he stay'd, gain'd a perfect Conquest over his fierce Heart, and made him feel, the Victor could be subdu'd. So that having made his first Compliments, and presented her an hundred and fifty Slaves in Fetters, he told her with his Eyes, that he was not insensible of her Charms; while Imoinda, who wish'd for nothing more than so glorious a Conquest, was pleas'd to believe, she understood that silent Language of new-born Love; and, from that Moment, put on all her Additions to Beauty.

The Prince return'd to Court with quite another Humour than before; and tho' he did not speak much of the fair Imoinda, he had the Pleasure to hear all his Followers speak of nothing but the Charms of that Maid, insomuch, that, even in the Presence of the old King, they were extolling her, and heightning, if possible, the Beauties they had found in her: so that nothing else was talk'd of, no other Sound was heard in every Corner where there were Whisperers, but Imoinda! Imoinda!

'Twill be imagin'd Oroonoko stay'd not long before he made his second Visit; nor, considering his Quality, not much longer before he told her, he ador'd her. I have often heard him say, that he admir'd by what strange Inspiration he came to talk Things so soft, and so passionate, who never knew Love, nor was us'd to the Conversation of Women; but (to use his own Words) he said, 'Most happily, some new, and, till then, unknown Power instructed his Heart and Tongue in the Language of Love; and at the same Time, in Favour of him, inspir'd Imoinda with a Sense of his Passion.' She was touch'd with what he said, and return'd it all in such Answers as went to his very Heart, with a Pleasure unknown before. Nor did he use those Obligations ill, that Love had done him, but turn'd all his happy Moments to the best Advantage; and as he knew no Vice, his Flame aim'd at nothing but Honour, if such a Distinction may be made in Love; and especially in that Country, where Men take to themselves as many as they can maintain; and where the only Crime and Sin against a Woman, is, to turn her off, to abandon her to Want, Shame and Misery: such ill Morals are only practis'd in Christian Countries, where they prefer the bare Name of Religion; and, without Virtue or Morality, think that sufficient. But Oroonoko was none of those Professors; but as he had right Notions of Honour, so he made her such Propositions as were not only and barely such; but, contrary to the Custom of his Country, he made her Vows, she should be the only Woman he would possess while he liv'd; that no Age or Wrinkles should incline him to change: for her Soul would be always fine, and always young; and he should have an eternal Idea in his Mind of the Charms she now bore; and should look into his Heart for that Idea, when he could find it no longer in her Face.

After a thousand Assurances of his lasting Flame, and her eternal Empire over him, she condescended to receive him for her Husband; or rather, receive him, as the greatest Honour the Gods could do her.

There is a certain Ceremony in these Cases to be observ'd, which I forgot to ask how 'twas perform'd; but 'twas concluded on both Sides, that in Obedience to him, the Grandfather was to be first made acquainted with the Design: For they pay a most absolute Resignation to the Monarch, especially when he is a Parent also.

On the other Side, the old King, who had many Wives, and many Concubines, wanted not Court-Flatterers to insinuate into his Heart a thousand tender Thoughts for this young Beauty; and who represented her to his Fancy, as the most charming he had ever possess'd in all the long Race of his numerous Years. At this Character, his old Heart, like an extinguish'd Brand, most apt to take Fire, felt new Sparks of Love, and began to kindle; and now grown to his second Childhood, long'd with Impatience to behold this gay Thing, with whom, alas! he could but innocently play. But how he should be confirm'd she was this Wonder, before he us'd his Power to call her to Court, (where Maidens never came, unless for the King's private Use) he was next to consider; and while he was so doing, he had Intelligence brought him, that Imoinda was most certainly Mistress to the Prince Oroonoko. This gave him some Chagrine: however, it gave him also an Opportunity, one Day, when the Prince was a hunting, to wait on a Man of Quality, as his Slave and Attendant, who should go and make a Present to Imoinda, as from the Prince; he should then, unknown, see this fair Maid, and have an Opportunity to hear what Message she would return the Prince for his Present, and from thence gather the State of her Heart, and Degree of her Inclination. This was put in Execution, and the old Monarch saw, and burn'd: He found her all he had heard, and would not delay his Happiness, but found he should have some Obstacle to overcome her Heart; for she express'd her Sense of the Present the Prince had sent her, in Terms so sweet, so soft and pretty, with an Air of Love and Joy that could not be dissembled, insomuch that 'twas past Doubt whether she lov'd Oroonoko entirely. This gave the old King some Affliction; but he salv'd it with this, that the Obedience the People pay their King, was not at all inferior to what they paid their Gods; and what Love would not oblige Imoinda to do, Duty would compel her to.

He was therefore no sooner got into his Apartment, but he sent the Royal Veil to Imoinda; that is the Ceremony of Invitation: He sends the Lady he has a Mind to honour with his Bed, a Veil, with which she is covered, and secur'd for the King's Use; and 'tis Death to disobey; besides, held a most impious Disobedience.

'Tis not to be imagin'd the Surprize and Grief that seiz'd the lovely Maid at this News and Sight. However, as Delays in these Cases are dangerous, and Pleading worse than Treason; trembling, and almost fainting, she was oblig'd to suffer herself to be cover'd, and led away.

They brought her thus to Court; and the King, who had caus'd a very rich Bath to be prepar'd, was led into it, where he sat under a Canopy, in State, to receive this long'd-for Virgin; whom he having commanded to be brought to him, they (after disrobing her) led her to the Bath, and making fast the Doors, left her to descend. The King, without more Courtship, bad her throw off her Mantle, and come to his Arms. But Imoinda, all in Tears, threw herself on the Marble, on the Brink of the Bath, and besought him to hear her. She told him, as she was a Maid, how proud of the Divine Glory she should have been, of having it in her Power to oblige her King: but as by the Laws he could not, and from his Royal Goodness would not take from any Man his wedded Wife; so she believ'd she should be the occasion of making him commit a great Sin, if she did not reveal her State and Condition; and tell him she was another's, and could not be so happy to be his.

The King, enrag'd at this Delay, hastily demanded the Name of the bold Man, that had married a Woman of her Degree, without his Consent. Imoinda seeing his Eyes fierce, and his Hands tremble, (whether with Age or Anger, I know not, but she fancy'd the last) almost repented she had said so much, for now she fear'd the Storm would fall on the Prince; she therefore said a thousand Things to appease the raging of his Flame, and to prepare him to hear who it was with Calmness: but before she spoke, he imagin'd who she meant, but would not seem to do so, but commanded her to lay aside her Mantle, and suffer herself to receive his Caresses, or, by his Gods he swore, that happy Man whom she was going to name should die, tho' it was even Oroonoko himself. Therefore (said he) deny this Marriage, and swear thyself a Maid. That (reply'd Imoinda) by all our Powers I do; for I am not yet known to my Husband. 'Tis enough (said the King) 'tis enough both to satisfy my Conscience and my Heart. And rising from his Seat, he went and led her into the Bath; it being in vain for her to resist.

In this Time, the Prince, who was return'd from Hunting, went to visit his Imoinda, but found her gone; and not only so, but heard she had receiv'd the Royal Veil. This rais'd him to a Storm; and in his Madness, they had much ado to save him from laying violent Hands on himself. Force first prevail'd, and then Reason: They urg'd all to him, that might oppose his Rage; but nothing weigh'd so greatly with him as the King's old Age, uncapable of injuring him with Imoinda. He would give Way to that Hope, because it pleas'd him most, and flatter'd best his Heart. Yet this serv'd not altogether to make him cease his different Passions, which sometimes rag'd within him, and soften'd into Showers. 'Twas not enough to appease him, to tell him, his Grandfather was old, and could not that Way injure him, while he retain'd that awful Duty which the young Men are us'd there to pay to their grave Relations. He could not be convinc'd he had no Cause to sigh and mourn for the Loss of a Mistress, he could not with all his Strength and Courage retrieve, and he would often cry, 'Oh, my Friends! were she in wall'd Cities, or confin'd from me in Fortifications of the greatest Strength; did Inchantments or Monsters detain her from me; I would venture thro' any Hazard to free her; But here, in the Arms of a feeble old Man, my Youth, my violent Love, my Trade in Arms, and all my vast Desire of Glory, avail me nothing. Imoinda is as irrecoverably lost to me, as if she were snatch'd by the cold Arms of Death: Oh! she is never to be retrieved. If I would wait tedious Years; till Fate should bow the old King to his Grave, even that would not leave me Imoinda free; but still that Custom that makes it so vile a Crime for a Son to marry his Father's Wives or Mistresses, would hinder my Happiness; unless I would either ignobly set an ill Precedent to my Successors, or abandon my Country, and fly with her to some unknown World who never heard our Story.'

But it was objected to him, That his Case was not the same: for Imoinda being his lawful Wife by solemn Contract, 'twas he was the injur'd Man, and might, if he so pleas'd, take Imoinda back, the Breach of the Law being on his Grandfather's Side; and that if he could circumvent him, and redeem her from the Otan, which is the Palace of the King's Women, a sort of Seraglio, it was both just and lawful for him so to do.

This Reasoning had some Force upon him, and he should have been entirely comforted, but for the Thought that she was possess'd by his Grandfather. However, he lov'd her so well, that he was resolv'd to believe what most favour'd his Hope, and to endeavour to learn from Imoinda's own Mouth, what only she could satisfy him in, whether she was robb'd of that Blessing which was only due to his Faith and Love. But as it was very hard to get a Sight of the Women, (for no Men ever enter'd into the Otan but when the King went to entertain himself with some one of his Wives or Mistresses; and 'twas Death, at any other Time, for any other to go in) so he knew not how to contrive to get a Sight of her.

While Oroonoko felt all the Agonies of Love, and suffer'd under a Torment the most painful in the World, the old King was not exempted from his Share of Affliction. He was troubled, for having been forc'd, by an irresistible Passion, to rob his Son of a Treasure, he knew, could not but be extremely dear to him; since she was the most beautiful that ever had been seen, and had besides, all the Sweetness and Innocence of Youth and Modesty, with a Charm of Wit surpassing all. He found, that however she was forc'd to expose her lovely Person to his wither'd Arms, she could only sigh and weep there, and think of Oroonoko; and oftentimes could not forbear speaking of him, tho' her Life were, by Custom, forfeited by owning her Passion. But she spoke not of a Lover only, but of a Prince dear to him to whom she spoke; and of the Praises of a Man, who, 'till now, fill'd the old Man's Soul with Joy at every Recital of his Bravery, or even his Name. And 'twas this Dotage on our young Hero, that gave Imoinda a thousand Privileges to speak of him without offending; and this Condescension in the old King, that made her take the Satisfaction of speaking of him so very often.

Besides, he many times enquir'd how the Prince bore himself: And those of whom he ask'd, being entirely Slaves to the Merits and Virtues of the Prince, still answer'd what they thought conduc'd best to his Service; which was, to make the old King fancy that the Prince had no more Interest in Imoinda, and had resign'd her willingly to the Pleasure of the King; that he diverted himself with his Mathematicians, his Fortifications, his Officers, and his Hunting.

This pleas'd the old Lover, who fail'd not to report these Things again to Imoinda, that she might, by the Example of her young Lover, withdraw her Heart, and rest better contented in his Arms. But, however she was forc'd to receive this unwelcome News, in all Appearance, with Unconcern and Content; her Heart was bursting within, and she was only happy when she could get alone, to vent her Griefs and Moans with Sighs and Tears.

What Reports of the Prince's Conduct were made to the King, he thought good to justify, as far as possibly he could, by his Actions; and when he appear'd in the Presence of the King, he shew'd a Face not at all betraying his Heart: so that in a little Time, the old Man, being entirely convinc'd that he was no longer a Lover of Imoinda he carry'd him with him in his Train to the Otan, often to banquet with his Mistresses. But as soon as he enter'd, one Day, into the Apartment of Imoinda, with the King, at the first Glance from her Eyes, notwithstanding all his determined Resolution, he was ready to sink in the Place where he stood; and had certainly done so, but for the Support of Aboan, a young Man who was next to him; which, with his Change of Countenance, had betray'd him, had the King chanc'd to look that Way. And I have observ'd, 'tis a very great Error in those who laugh when one says, A Negro can change Colour: for I have seen 'em as frequently blush, and look pale, and that as visibly as ever I saw in the most beautiful White. And 'tis certain, that both these Changes were evident, this Day, in both these Lovers. And Imoinda, who saw with some Joy the Change in the Prince's Face, and found it in her own, strove to divert the King from beholding either, by a forc'd Caress, with which she met him; which was a new Wound in the Heart of the poor dying Prince. But as soon as the King was busy'd in looking on some fine Thing of Imoinda's making, she had Time to tell the Prince, with her angry, but Love-darting Eyes, that she resented his Coldness, and bemoan'd her own miserable Captivity. Nor were his Eyes silent, but answer'd her's again, as much as Eyes could do, instructed by the most tender and most passionate Heart that ever lov'd: And they spoke so well, and so effectually, as Imoinda no longer doubted but she was the only Delight and Darling of that Soul she found pleading in 'em its Right of Love, which none was more willing to resign than she. And 'twas this powerful Language alone that in an Instant convey'd all the Thoughts of their Souls to each other; that they both found there wanted but Opportunity to make them both entirely happy. But when he saw another Door open'd by Onahal (a former old Wife of the King's, who now had Charge of Imoinda) and saw the Prospect of a Bed of State made ready, with Sweets and Flowers for the Dalliance of the King, who immediately led the trembling Victim from his Sight, into that prepar'd Repose; what Rage! what wild Frenzies seiz'd his Heart! which forcing to keep within Bounds, and to suffer without Noise, it became the more insupportable, and rent his Soul with ten thousand Pains. He was forc'd to retire to vent his Groans, where he fell down on a Carpet, and lay struggling a long Time, and only breathing now and then, Oh Imoinda! When Onahal had finished her necessary Affair within, shutting the Door, she came forth, to wait till the King called; and hearing some one sighing in the other Room, she pass'd on, and found the Prince in that deplorable Condition, which she thought needed her Aid. She gave him Cordials, but all in vain; till finding the Nature of his Disease, by his Sighs, and naming Imoinda, she told him he had not so much Cause as he imagined to afflict himself: for if he knew the King so well as she did, he would not lose a Moment in Jealousy; and that she was confident that Imoinda bore, at this Minute, Part in his Affliction. Aboan was of the same Opinion, and both together persuaded him to re-assume his Courage; and all sitting down on the Carpet, the Prince said so many obliging Things to Onahal, that he half-persuaded her to be of his Party: and she promised him, she would thus far comply with his just Desires, that she would let Imoinda know how faithful he was, what he suffer'd, and what he said.

This Discourse lasted till the King called, which gave Oroonoko a certain Satisfaction; and with the Hope Onahal had made him conceive, he assumed a Look as gay as 'twas possible a Man in his Circumstances could do: and presently after, he was call'd in with the rest who waited without. The King commanded Musick to be brought, and several of his young Wives and Mistresses came all together by his Command, to dance before him; where Imoinda perform'd her Part with an Air and Grace so surpassing all the rest, as her Beauty was above 'em, and received the Present ordained as a Prize. The Prince was every Moment more charmed with the new Beauties and Graces he beheld in this Fair-One; and while he gazed, and she danc'd, Onahal was retired to a Window with Aboan.

This Onahal, as I said, was one of the Cast-Mistresses of the old King; and 'twas these (now past their Beauty) that were made Guardians or Governantees to the new and the young ones, and whose Business it was to teach them all those wanton Arts of Love, with which they prevail'd and charm'd heretofore in their Turn; and who now treated the triumphing Happy-ones with all the Severity, as to Liberty and Freedom, that was possible, in Revenge of the Honours they rob them of; envying them those Satisfactions, those Gallantries and Presents, that were once made to themselves, while Youth and Beauty lasted, and which they now saw pass, as it were regardless by, and paid only to the Bloomings. And certainly, nothing is more afflicting to a decay'd Beauty, than to behold in itself declining Charms, that were once ador'd; and to find those Caresses paid to new Beauties, to which once she laid Claim; to hear them whisper, as she passes by, that once was a delicate Woman. Those abandon'd ladies therefore endeavour to revenge all the Despights and Decays of Time, on these flourishing Happy-ones. And 'twas this Severity that gave Oroonoko a thousand Fears he should never prevail with Onahal to see Imoinda. But, as I said, she was now retir'd to a Window with Aboan.

This young Man was not only one of the best Quality, but a Man extremely well made, and beautiful; and coming often to attend the King to the Otan, he had subdu'd the Heart of the antiquated Onahal, which had not forgot how pleasant it was to be in love. And tho' she had some Decays in her Face, she had none in her Sense and Wit; she was there agreeable still, even to Aboan's Youth: so that he took Pleasure in entertaining her with Discourses of Love. He knew also, that to make his Court to these She-favourites, was the Way to be great; these being the Persons that do all Affairs and Business at Court. He had also observed, that she had given him Glances more tender and inviting than she had done to others of his Quality. And now, when he saw that her Favour could so absolutely oblige the Prince, he fail'd not to sigh in her Ear, and look with Eyes all soft upon her, and gave her Hope that she had made some Impressions on his Heart. He found her pleas'd at this, and making a thousand Advances to him: but the Ceremony ending, and the King departing, broke up the Company for that Day, and his Conversation.

Aboan fail'd not that Night to tell the Prince of his Success, and how advantageous the Service of Onahal might be to his Amour with Imoinda. The Prince was overjoy'd with this good News, and besought him, if it were possible, to caress her so, as to engage her entirely, which he could not fail to do, if he comply'd with her Desires: For then (said the Prince) her Life lying at your Mercy, she must grant you the Request you make in my Behalf. Aboan understood him, and assur'd him he would make Love so effectually, that he would defy the most expert Mistress of the Art, to find out whether he dissembled it, or had it really. And 'twas with Impatience they waited the next Opportunity of going to the Otan.

The Wars came on, the Time of taking the Field approached; and 'twas impossible for the Prince to delay his going at the Head of his Army to encounter the Enemy; so that every Day seem'd a tedious Year, till he saw his Imoinda: for he believed he could not live, if he were forced away without being so happy. 'Twas with Impatience therefore that he expected the next Visit the King would make; and, according to his Wish, it was not long.

The Parley of the Eyes of these two Lovers had not pass'd so secretly, but an old jealous Lover could spy it; or rather, he wanted not Flatterers who told him they observ'd it: so that the Prince was hasten'd to the Camp, and this was the last Visit he found he should make to the Otan; he therefore urged Aboan to make the best of this last Effort, and to explain himself so to Onahal, that she deferring her Enjoyment of her young Lover no longer, might make Way for the Prince to speak to Imoinda.

The whole Affair being agreed on between the Prince and Aboan, they attended the King, as the Custom was, to the Otan; where, while the whole Company was taken up in beholding the Dancing, and Antick Postures the Women-Royal made to divert the King, Onahal singled out Aboan, whom she found most pliable to her Wish. When she had him where she believed she could not be heard, she sigh'd to him, and softly cry'd, 'Ah, Aboan! when will you be sensible of my Passion? I confess it with my Mouth, because I would not give my Eyes the Lye; and you have but too much already perceived they have confess'd my Flame: nor would I have you believe, that because I am the abandon'd Mistress of a King, I esteem myself altogether divested of Charms: No, Aboan; I have still a Rest of Beauty enough engaging, and have learn'd to please too well, not to be desirable. I can have Lovers still, but will have none but Aboan. Madam, (reply'd the half-feigning Youth) you have already, by my Eyes, found you can still conquer; and I believe 'tis in pity of me you condescend to this kind Confession. But, Madam, Words are used to be so small a Part of our Country-Courtship, that 'tis rare one can get so happy an Opportunity as to tell one's Heart; and those few Minutes we have, are forced to be snatch'd for more certain Proofs of Love than speaking and sighing: and such I languish for.'

He spoke this with such a Tone, that she hoped it true, and could not forbear believing it; and being wholly transported with Joy for having subdued the finest of all the King's Subjects to her Desires, she took from her Ears two large Pearls, and commanded him to wear 'em in his. He would have refused 'em, crying, Madam these are not the Proofs of our Love that I expect; 'tis Opportunity, 'tis a Lone-Hour only, that can make me happy. But forcing the Pearls into his Hand, she whisper'd softly to him; Oh! do not fear a Woman's Invention, when Love sets her a thinking. And pressing his Hand, she cry'd, This Night you shall be happy. Come to the Gate of the Orange-Grove, behind the Otan, and I will be ready about midnight to receive you. 'Twas thus agreed, and she left him, that no Notice might be taken of their speaking together.

The Ladies were still dancing, and the King, laid on a Carpet, with a great deal of Pleasure was beholding them, especially Imoinda, who that Day appeared more lovely than ever, being enlivened with the good Tidings Onahal had brought her, of the constant Passion the Prince had for her. The Prince was laid on another Carpet at the other End of the Room, with his Eyes fixed on the Object of his Soul; and as she turned or moved, so did they; and she alone gave his Eyes and Soul their Motions. Nor did Imoinda employ her Eyes to any other use, than in beholding with infinite Pleasure the Joy she produced in those of the Prince. But while she was more regarding him than the Steps she took, she chanced to fall, and so near him, as that leaping with extreme Force from the Carpet, he caught her in his Arms as she fell; and 'twas visible to the whole Presence, the Joy wherewith he received her. He clasped her close to his Bosom, and quite forgot that Reverence that was due to the Mistress of a King, and that Punishment that is the Reward of a Boldness of this Nature. And had not the Presence of Mind of Imoinda (fonder of his Safety than her own) befriended him, in making her spring from his Arms, and fall into her Dance again, he had at that Instant met his Death; for the old King, jealous to the last Degree, rose up in Rage, broke all the Diversion, and led Imoinda to her Apartment, and sent out Word to the Prince, to go immediately to the Camp; and that if he were found another Night in Court, he should suffer the Death ordained for disobedient Offenders.

You may imagine how welcome this News was to Oroonoko, whose unseasonable Transport and Caress of Imoinda was blamed by all Men that loved him: and now he perceived his Fault, yet cry'd, That for such another Moment he would be content to die.

All the Otan was in Disorder about this Accident; and Onahal was particularly concern'd, because on the Prince's Stay depended her Happiness; for she could no longer expect that of Aboan: So that e'er they departed, they contrived it so, that the Prince and he should both come that Night to the Grove of the Otan, which was all of Oranges and Citrons, and that there they would wait her Orders.

They parted thus with Grief enough 'till Night, leaving the King in Possession of the lovely Maid. But nothing could appease the Jealousy of the old Lover; he would not be imposed on, but would have it, that Imoinda made a false Step on Purpose to fall into Oroonoko's Bosom, and that all things looked like a Design on both Sides; and 'twas in vain she protested her Innocence: He was old and obstinate, and left her, more than half assur'd that his Fear was true.

The King going to his Apartment, sent to know where the Prince was, and if he intended to obey his Command. The Messenger return'd, and told him, he found the Prince pensive, and altogether unprepar'd for the Campaign; that he lay negligently on the Ground, and answer'd very little. This confirmed the Jealousy of the King, and he commanded that they should very narrowly and privately watch his Motions; and that he should not stir from his Apartment, but one Spy or other should be employ'd to watch him: So that the Hour approaching, wherein he was to go to the Citron-Grove; and taking only Aboan along with him, he leaves his Apartment, and was watched to the very Gate of the Otan; where he was seen to enter, and where they left him, to carry back the Tidings to the King.

Oroonoko and Aboan were no sooner enter'd, but Onahal led the Prince to the Apartment of Imoinda; who, not knowing any thing of her Happiness, was laid in Bed. But Onahal only left him in her Chamber, to make the best of his Opportunity, and took her dear Aboan to her own; where he shewed the Height of Complaisance for his Prince, when, to give him an Opportunity, he suffered himself to be caressed in Bed by Onahal.

The Prince softly waken'd Imoinda, who was not a little surpriz'd with Joy to find him there; and yet she trembled with a thousand Fears. I believe he omitted saying nothing to this young Maid, that might persuade her to suffer him to seize his own, and take the Rights of Love. And I believe she was not long resisting those Arms where she so longed to be; and having Opportunity, Night, and Silence, Youth, Love, and Desire, he soon prevail'd, and ravished in a Moment what his old Grandfather had been endeavouring for so many Months.

'Tis not to be imagined the Satisfaction of these two young Lovers; nor the Vows she made him, that she remained a spotless Maid till that Night, and that what she did with his Grandfather had robb'd him of no Part of her Virgin-Honour; the Gods, in Mercy and Justice, having reserved that for her plighted Lord, to whom of Right it belonged. And 'tis impossible to express the Transports he suffer'd, while he listen'd to a Discourse so charming from her loved Lips; and clasped that Body in his Arms, for whom he had so long languished; and nothing now afflicted him, but his sudden Departure from her; for he told her the Necessity, and his Commands, but should depart satisfy'd in this, That since the old King had hitherto not been able to deprive him of those Enjoyments which only belonged to him, he believed for the future he would be less able to injure him; so that, abating the Scandal of the Veil, which was no otherwise so, than that she was Wife to another, he believed her safe, even in the Arms of the King, and innocent; yet would he have ventur'd at the Conquest of the World, and have given it all to have had her avoided that Honour of receiving the Royal Veil. 'Twas thus, between a thousand Caresses, that both bemoan'd the hard Fate of Youth and Beauty, so liable to that cruel Promotion: 'Twas a Glory that could well have been spared here, tho' desired and aim'd at by all the young Females of that Kingdom.

But while they were thus fondly employ'd, forgetting how Time ran on, and that the Dawn must conduct him far away from his only Happiness, they heard a great Noise in the Otan, and unusual Voices of Men; at which the Prince, starting from the Arms of the frighted Imoinda, ran to a little Battle-Ax he used to wear by his Side; and having not so much Leisure as to put on his Habit, he opposed himself against some who were already opening the Door: which they did with so much

Violence, that Oroonoko was not able to defend it; but was forced to cry out with a commanding Voice, 'Whoever ye are that have the Boldness to attempt to approach this Apartment thus rudely; know, that I, the Prince Oroonoko, will revenge it with the certain Death of him that first enters: Therefore stand back, and know, this Place is sacred to Love and Me this Night; To-morrow 'tis the King's.'

This he spoke with a Voice so resolv'd and assur'd, that they soon retired from the Door; but cry'd, ''Tis by the King's Command we are come; and being satisfy'd by thy Voice, O Prince, as much as if we had enter'd, we can report to the King the Truth of all his Fears, and leave thee to provide for thy own Safety, as thou art advis'd by thy Friends.'

At these Words they departed, and left the Prince to take a short and sad Leave of his Imoinda; who, trusting in the Strength of her Charms, believed she should appease the Fury of a jealous King, by saying, she was surprized, and that it was by Force of Arms he got into her Apartment. All her Concern now was for his Life, and therefore she hasten'd him to the Camp, and with much ado prevail'd on him to go. Nor was it she alone that prevail'd; Aboan and Onahal both pleaded, and both assured him of a Lye that should be well enough contrived to secure Imoinda. So that at last, with a Heart sad as Death, dying Eyes, and sighing Soul, Oroonoko departed, and took his way to the Camp.

It was not long after, the King in Person came to the Otan; where beholding Imoinda, with Rage in his Eyes, he upbraided her Wickedness, and Perfidy; and threatning her Royal Lover, she fell on her Face at his Feet, bedewing the Floor with her Tears, and imploring his Pardon for a Fault which she had not with her Will committed; as Onahal, who was also prostrate with her, could testify: That, unknown to her, he had broke into her Apartment, and ravished her. She spoke this much against her Conscience; but to save her own Life, 'twas absolutely necessary she should feign this Falsity. She knew it could not injure the Prince, he being fled to an Army that would stand by him, against any Injuries that should assault him. However, this last Thought of Imoinda's being ravished, changed the Measures of his Revenge; and whereas before he designed to be himself her Executioner, he now resolved she should not die. But as it is the greatest Crime in Nature amongst them, to touch a Woman after having been possess'd by a Son, a Father, or a Brother, so now he looked on Imoinda as a polluted thing wholly unfit for his Embrace; nor would he resign her to his Grandson, because she had received the Royal Veil: He therefore removes her from the Otan, with Onahal; whom he put into safe Hands, with Order they should be both sold off as Slaves to another Country, either Christian or Heathen, 'twas no Matter where.

This cruel Sentence, worse than Death, they implor'd might be reversed; but their Prayers were vain, and it was put in Execution accordingly, and that with so much Secrecy, that none, either without or within the Otan, knew any thing of their Absence, or their Destiny.

The old King nevertheless executed this with a great deal of Reluctancy; but he believed he had made a very great Conquest over himself, when he had once resolved, and had perform'd what he resolved. He believed now, that his Love had been unjust; and that he could not expect the Gods, or Captain of the Clouds (as they call the unknown Power) would suffer a better Consequence from so ill a Cause. He now begins to hold Oroonoko excused; and to say, he had reason for what he did. And now every body could assure the King how passionately Imoinda was beloved by the Prince; even those confess'd it now, who said the contrary before his Flame was not abated. So that the King being old, and not able to defend himself in War, and having no Sons of all his Race remaining alive, but only this, to maintain him on his Throne; and looking on this as a man disobliged, first by the Rape of his Mistress, or rather Wife, and now by depriving him wholly of her, he fear'd, might make him desperate, and do some cruel thing, either to himself or his old Grandfather the Offender, he began to repent him extremely of the Contempt he had, in his Rage, put on Imoinda. Besides, he consider'd he ought in Honour to have killed her for this Offence, if it had been one. He ought to have had so much Value and Consideration for a Maid of her Quality, as to have nobly put her to Death, and not to have sold her like a common Slave; the greatest Revenge, and the most disgraceful of any, and to which they a thousand times prefer Death, and implore it; as Imoinda did, but could not obtain that Honour. Seeing therefore it was certain that Oroonoko would highly resent this Affront, he thought good to make some Excuse for his Rashness to him; and to that End, he sent a Messenger to the Camp, with Orders to treat with him about the Matter, to gain his Pardon, and endeavour to mitigate his Grief: but that by no Means he should tell him she was sold, but secretly put to Death; for he knew he should never obtain his Pardon for the other.

When the Messenger came, he found the Prince upon the Point of engaging with the Enemy; but as soon as he heard of the Arrival of the Messenger, he commanded him to his Tent, where he embraced him, and received him with Joy; which was soon abated by the down-cast Looks of the Messenger, who was instantly demanded the Cause by Oroonoko; who, impatient of Delay, ask'd a thousand Questions in a Breath, and all concerning Imoinda. But there needed little Return; for he could almost answer himself of all he demanded, from his Sight and Eyes. At last the Messenger casting himself at the Prince's Feet, and kissing them with all the Submission of a Man that had something to implore which he dreaded to utter, besought him to hear with Calmness what he had to deliver to him, and to call up all his noble and heroick Courage, to encounter with his Words, and defend himself against the ungrateful Things he had to relate. Oroonoko reply'd, with a deep Sigh, and a languishing Voice, I am armed against their worst Efforts. For I know they will tell me, Imoinda is no more. And after that, you may spare the rest. Then, commanding him to rise, he laid himself on a Carpet, under a rich Pavilion, and remained a good while silent, and was hardly heard to sigh. When he was come a little to himself, the Messenger asked him Leave to deliver that Part of his Embassy which the Prince had not yet divin'd: And the Prince cry'd, I permit thee. Then he told him the Affliction the old King was in, for the Rashness he had committed in his Cruelty to Imoinda; and how he deign'd to ask Pardon for his Offence, and to implore the Prince would not suffer that Loss to touch his Heart too sensibly, which now all the Gods could not restore him, but might recompense him in Glory, which he begged he would pursue; and that Death, that common Revenger of all Injuries, would soon even the Account between him and a feeble old Man.

Oroonoko bad him return his Duty to his Lord and Master; and to assure him, there was no Account of Revenge to be adjudged between them; If there was, he was the Aggressor, and that Death would be just, and, maugre his Age, would see him righted; and he was contented to leave his Share of Glory to Youths more fortunate and worthy of that Favour from the Gods: That henceforth he would never lift a Weapon, or draw a Bow, but abandon the small Remains of his Life to Sighs and Tears, and the continual Thoughts of what his Lord and Grandfather had thought good to send out of the World, with all that Youth, that Innocence and Beauty.

After having spoken this, whatever his greatest Officers and Men of the best Rank could do, they could not raise him from the Carpet, or persuade him to Action, and Resolutions of Life; but commanding all to retire, he shut himself into his Pavilion all that Day, while the Enemy was ready to engage: and wondring at the Delay, the whole Body of the chief of the Army then address'd themselves to him, and to whom they had much ado to get Admittance. They fell on their Faces at the Foot of his Carpet, where they lay, and besought him with earnest Prayers and Tears to lead them forth to Battle, and not let the Enemy take Advantages of them; and implored him to have Regard to his Glory, and to the World, that depended on his Courage and Conduct. But he made no other Reply to all their Supplications than this, That he had now no more Business for Glory; and for the World, it was a Trifle not worth his Care: Go, (continued he, sighing) and divide it amongst you, and reap with Joy what you so vainly prize, and leave me to my more welcome Destiny.

They then demanded what they should do, and whom he would constitute in his Room, that the Confusion of ambitious Youth and Power might not ruin their Order, and make them a Prey to the Enemy. He reply'd, he would not give himself that Trouble, but wished 'em to chuse the bravest Man amongst 'em, let his Quality or Birth be what it would: 'For, Oh my Friends! (says he) it is not Titles make Men Brave or Good; or Birth that bestows Courage and Generosity, or makes the Owner Happy. Believe this, when you behold Oroonoko the most wretched, and abandoned by Fortune, of all the Creation of the Gods.' So turning himself about, he would make no more Reply to all they could urge or implore.

The Army beholding their Officers return unsuccessful, with sad Faces and ominous Looks, that presaged no good Luck, suffer'd a thousand Fears to take Possession of their Hearts, and the Enemy to come even upon them before they could provide for their Safety by any Defence: and tho' they were assured by some who had a Mind to animate them, that they should be immediately headed by the Prince; and that in the mean time Aboan had Orders to command as General; yet they were so dismay'd for want of that great Example of Bravery, that they could make but a very feeble Resistance; and, at last, down-right fled before the Enemy, who pursued 'em to the very Tents, killing 'em: Nor could all Aboan's Courage, which that Day gained him immortal Glory, shame 'em into a manly Defence of themselves. The Guards that were left behind about the Prince's Tent, seeing the Soldiers flee before the Enemy, and scatter themselves all over the Plain, in great Disorder, made such Out-cries, as rouz'd the Prince from his amorous Slumber, in which he had remained buried for two Days, without permitting any Sustenance to approach him. But, in Spite of all his Resolutions, he had not the Constancy of Grief to that Degree, as to make him insensible of the Danger of his Army; and in that Instant he leaped from his Couch, and cry'd, 'Come, if we must die, let us meet Death the noblest Way; and 'twill be more like Oroonoko to encounter him at an Army's Head, opposing the Torrent of a conquering Foe, than lazily on a Couch, to wait his lingering Pleasure, and die every Moment by a thousand racking Thoughts; or be tamely taken by an Enemy, and led a whining, love-sick Slave to adorn the Triumphs of Jamoan, that young Victor, who already is enter'd beyond the Limits I have prescrib'd him.'

While he was speaking, he suffer'd his People to dress him for the Field; and sallying out of his Pavilion, with more Life and Vigour in his Countenance than ever he shew'd, he appear'd like some Divine Power descended to save his Country from Destruction: And his People had purposely put him on all Things that might make him shine with most Splendor, to strike a reverend Awe into the Beholders. He flew into the thickest of those that were pursuing his Men; and being animated with Despair, he fought as if he came on Purpose to die, and did such Things as will not be believed that human Strength could perform; and such, as soon inspir'd all the rest with new Courage, and new Ardor. And now it was that they began to fight indeed; and so, as if they would not be out-done even by their ador'd Hero; who turning the Tide of the Victory, changing absolutely the Fate of the Day, gain'd an entire Conquest: And Oroonoko having the good Fortune to single out Jamoan, he took him Prisoner with his own Hand, having wounded him almost to Death.

This Jamoan afterwards became very dear to him, being a Man very Gallant, and of excellent Graces, and fine Parts; so that he never put him amongst the Rank of Captives as they used to do, without Distinction, for the common Sale, or Market, but kept him in his own Court, where he retain'd nothing of the Prisoner but the Name, and returned no more into his own Country; so great an Affection he took for Oroonoko, and by a thousand Tales and Adventures of Love and Gallantry, flatter'd his Disease of Melancholy and Languishment; which I have often heard him say, had certainly kill'd him, but for the Conversation of this Prince and Aboan, and the French Governor he had from his Childhood, of whom I have spoken before, and who was a Man of admirable Wit, great Ingenuity and Learning; all which he had infused into his young Pupil. This Frenchman was banished out of his own Country for some Heretical Notions he held; and tho' he was a Man of very little Religion, yet he had admirable Morals, and a brave Soul.

After the total Defeat of Jamoan's Army, which all fled, or were left dead upon the Place, they spent some Time in the Camp; Oroonoko chusing rather to remain a While there in his Tents, than to enter into a Palace, or live in a Court where he had so lately suffer'd so great a Loss, the Officers therefore, who saw and knew his Cause of Discontent, invented all sorts of Diversions and Sports to entertain their Prince: So that what with those Amusements abroad, and others at home, that is, within their Tents, with the Persuasions, Arguments, and Care of his Friends and Servants that he more peculiarly priz'd, he wore off in Time a great Part of that Chagrin, and Torture of Despair, which the first Efforts of Imoinda's Death had given him; insomuch, as having received a thousand kind Embassies from the King, and Invitation to return to Court, he obey'd, tho' with no little Reluctancy; and when he did so, there was a visible Change in him, and for a long Time he was much more melancholy than before. But Time lessens all Extremes, and reduces 'em to Mediums, and Unconcern; but no Motives of Beauties, tho' all endeavour'd it, could engage him in any sort of Amour, tho' he had all the Invitations to it, both from his own Youth, and other Ambitions and Designs.

Oroonoko was no sooner return'd from this last Conquest, and receiv'd at Court with all the Joy and Magnificence that could be express'd to a young Victor, who was not only return'd Triumphant, but belov'd like a Deity, than there arriv'd in the Port an English Ship.

The Master of it had often before been in these Countries, and was very well known to Oroonoko, with whom he had traffick'd for Slaves, and had us'd to do the same with his Predecessors.

This Commander was a Man of a finer sort of Address and Conversation, better bred, and more engaging, than most of that sort of Men are; so that he seem'd rather never to have been bred out of a Court, than almost all his Life at Sea. This Captain therefore was always better receiv'd at Court, than most of the Traders to those Countries were; and especially by Oroonoko, who was more civiliz'd, according to the European Mode, than any other had been, and took more Delight in the White Nations; and, above all, Men of Parts and Wit. To this Captain he sold abundance of his Slaves; and for the Favour and Esteem he had for him, made him many Presents, and oblig'd him to stay at Court as long as possibly he could. Which the Captain seem'd to take as a very great Honour done him, entertaining the Prince every Day with Globes and Maps, and Mathematical Discourses and Instruments; eating, drinking, hunting, and living with him with so much Familiarity, that it was not to be doubted but he had gain'd very greatly upon the Heart of this gallant young Man. And the Captain, in Return of all these mighty Favours, besought the Prince to honour his Vessel with his Presence some Day or other at Dinner, before he should set sail; which he condescended to accept, and appointed his Day. The Captain, on his Part, fail'd not to have all Things in a Readiness, in the most magnificent Order he could possibly: And the Day being come, the Captain, in his Boat, richly adorn'd with Carpets and Velvet Cushions, rowed to the Shore, to receive the Prince; with another Long-boat, where was plac'd all his Musick and Trumpets, with which Oroonoko was extremely delighted; who met him on the Shore, attended by his French Governor, Jamoan, Aboan, and about an Hundred of the noblest of the Youths of the Court: And after they had first carried the Prince on Board, the Boats fetch'd the rest off; where they found a very splendid Treat, with all Sorts of fine Wines; and were as well entertain'd, as 'twas possible in such a Place to be.

The Prince having drank hard of Punch, and several Sorts of Wine, as did all the rest, (for great Care was taken they should want nothing of that Part of the Entertainment) was very merry, and in great Admiration of the Ship, for he had never been in one before; so that he was curious of beholding every Place where he decently might descend. The rest, no less curious, who were not quite overcome with drinking, rambled at their Pleasure Fore and Aft, as their Fancies guided 'em: So that the Captain, who had well laid his Design before, gave the Word, and seiz'd on all his Guests; they clapping great Irons suddenly on the Prince, when he was leap'd down into the Hold, to view that Part of the Vessel; and locking him fast down, secur'd him. The same Treachery was used to all the rest; and all in one Instant, in several Places of the Ship, were lash'd fast in Irons, and betray'd to Slavery. That great Design over, they set all Hands at Work to hoist Sail; and with as treacherous as fair a Wind they made from the Shore with this innocent and glorious Prize, who thought of nothing less than such an Entertainment.

Some have commended this Act, as brave in the Captain; but I will spare my Sense of it, and leave it to my Reader to judge as he pleases. It may be easily guess'd, in what Manner the Prince resented this Indignity, who may be best resembled to a Lion taken in a Toil; so he raged, so he struggled for Liberty, but all in vain: And they had so wisely managed his Fetters, that he could not use a Hand in his Defence, to quit himself of a Life that would by no Means endure Slavery; nor could he move from the Place where he was ty'd, to any solid Part of the Ship, against which he might have beat his Head, and have finish'd his Disgrace that Way. So that being deprived of all other Means, he resolv'd to perish for want of Food; and pleas'd at last with that Thought, and toil'd and tir'd by Rage and Indignation, he laid himself down, and sullenly resolv'd upon dying, and refused all Things that were brought him.

This did not a little vex the Captain, and the more so, because he found almost all of 'em of the same Humour; so that the Loss of so many brave Slaves, so tall and goodly to behold, would have been very considerable: He therefore order'd one to go from him (for he would not be seen himself) to Oroonoko, and to assure him, he was afflicted for having rashly done so unhospitable a Deed, and which could not be now remedied, since they were far from Shore; but since he resented it in so high a Nature, he assur'd him he would revoke his Resolution, and set both him and his Friends ashore on the next Land they should touch at; and of this the Messenger gave him his Oath, provided he would resolve to live. And Oroonoko, whose Honour was such, as he never had violated a Word in his Life himself, much less a solemn Asseveration, believ'd in an Instant what this Man said; but reply'd, He expected, for a Confirmation of this, to have his shameful Fetters dismis'd. This Demand was carried to the Captain; who return'd him Answer, That the Offence had been so great which he had put upon the Prince, that he durst not trust him with Liberty while he remain'd in the Ship, for fear, lest by a Valour natural to him, and a Revenge that would animate that Valour, he might commit some Outrage fatal to himself, and the King his Master, to whom the Vessel did belong. To this Oroonoko reply'd, He would engage his Honour to behave himself in all friendly Order and Manner, and obey the Command of the Captain, as he was Lord of the King's Vessel, and General of those Men under his Command.

This was deliver'd to the still doubting Captain, who could not resolve to trust a Heathen, he said, upon his Parole, a Man that had no Sense or Notion of the God that he worshipp'd. Oroonoko then reply'd, He was very sorry to hear that the Captain pretended to the Knowledge and Worship of any Gods, who had taught him no better Principles, than not to credit as he would be credited. But they told him, the Difference of their Faith occasion'd that Distrust: for the Captain had protested to him upon the Word of a Christian, and sworn in the Name of a great GOD; which if he should violate, he must expect eternal Torments in the World to come. 'Is that all the Obligations he has to be just to his Oath? (reply'd Oroonoko) Let him know, I swear by my Honour; which to violate, would not only render me contemptible and despised by all brave and honest Men, and so give my self perpetual Pain, but it would be eternally offending and displeasing all Mankind; harming, betraying, circumventing, and outraging all Men. But Punishments hereafter are suffer'd by one's self; and the World takes no Cognizance whether this GOD has reveng'd 'em or not, 'tis done so secretly, and deferr'd so long; while the Man of no Honour suffers every Moment the Scorn and Contempt of the honester World, and dies every Day ignominiously in his Fame, which is more valuable than Life. I speak not this to move Belief, but to shew you how you mistake, when you imagine, that he who will violate his Honour, will keep his Word with his Gods.' So, turning from him with a disdainful Smile, he refused to answer him, when he urged him to know what Answer he should carry back to his Captain; so that he departed without saying any more.

The Captain pondering and consulting what to do, it was concluded, that nothing but Oroonoko's Liberty would encourage any of the rest to eat, except the Frenchman, whom the Captain could not pretend to keep Prisoner, but only told him, he was secur'd, because he might act something in Favour of the Prince; but that he should be freed as soon as they came to Land. So that they concluded it wholly necessary to free the Prince from his Irons, that he might shew himself to the rest; that they might have an Eye upon him, and that they could not fear a single Man.

This being resolved, to make the Obligation the greater, the Captain himself went to Oroonoko; where, after many Compliments, and Assurances of what he had already promis'd, he receiving from the Prince his Parole, and his Hand, for his good Behaviour, dismiss'd his Irons, and brought him to his own Cabin; where, after having treated and repos'd him a While, (for he had neither eat nor slept in four Days before) he besought him to visit those obstinate People in Chains, who refused all manner of Sustenance; and intreated him to oblige 'em to eat, and assure 'em of their Liberty the first Opportunity.

Oroonoko, who was too generous not to give Credit to his Words, shew'd himself to his People, who were transported with Excess of Joy at the Sight of their darling Prince; falling at his Feet, and kissing and embracing 'em; believing, as some divine Oracle, all he assur'd 'em. But he besought 'em to bear their Chains with that Bravery that became those whom he had seen act so nobly in Arms; and that they could not give him greater Proofs of their Love and Friendship, since 'twas all the Security the Captain (his Friend) could have against the Revenge, he said, they might possibly justly take for the Injuries sustained by him. And they all, with one Accord, assur'd him, that they could not suffer enough, when it was for his Repose and Safety.

After this, they no longer refus'd to eat, but took what was brought 'em, and were pleas'd with their Captivity, since by it they hoped to redeem the Prince, who, all the rest of the Voyage, was treated with all the Respect due to his Birth, tho' nothing could divert his Melancholy; and he would often sigh for Imoinda, and think this a Punishment due to his Misfortune, in having left that noble Maid behind him, that fatal Night, in the Otan, when he fled to the Camp.

Possess'd with a thousand Thoughts of past Joys with this fair young Person, and a thousand Griefs for her eternal Loss, he endur'd a tedious Voyage, and at last arriv'd at the Mouth of the River of Surinam, a Colony belonging to the King of England, and where they were to deliver some Part of their Slaves. There the Merchants and Gentlemen of the Country going on Board, to demand those Lots of Slaves they had already agreed on; and, amongst those, the Overseers of those Plantations where I then chanc'd to be: The Captain, who had given the Word, order'd his Men to bring up those noble Slaves in Fetters, whom I have spoken of; and having put 'em, some in one, and some in other Lots, with Women and Children, (which they call Pickaninies) they sold 'em off, as Slaves to several Merchants and Gentlemen; not putting any two in one Lot, because they would separate 'em far from each other; nor daring to trust 'em together, lest Rage and Courage should put 'em upon contriving some great Action, to the Ruin of the Colony.

Oroonoko was first seiz'd on, and sold to our Overseer, who had the first Lot, with seventeen more of all Sorts and Sizes, but not one of Quality with him. When he saw this, he found what they meant; for, as I said, he understood English pretty well; and being wholly unarm'd and defenceless, so as it was in vain to make any Resistance, he only beheld the Captain with a Look all fierce and disdainful, upbraiding him with Eyes that forc'd Blushes on his guilty Cheeks, he only cry'd in passing over the Side of the Ship; Farewel, Sir, 'tis worth my Sufferings to gain so true a Knowledge, both of you, and of your Gods, by whom you swear. And desiring those that held him to forbear their Pains, and telling 'em he would make no Resistance, he cry'd, Come, my Fellow-Slaves, let us descend, and see if we can meet with more Honour and Honesty in the next World we shall touch upon. So he nimbly leapt into the Boat, and shewing no more Concern, suffer'd himself to be row'd up the River, with his seventeen Companions.

The Gentleman that bought him, was a young Cornish Gentleman, whose Name was Trefry; a Man of great Wit, and fine Learning, and was carried into those Parts by the Lord — Governor, to manage all his Affairs. He reflecting on the last Words of Oroonoko to the Captain, and beholding the Richness of his Vest, no sooner came into the Boat, but he fix'd his Eyes on him; and finding something so extraordinary in his Face, his Shape and Mein, a Greatness of Look, and Haughtiness in his Air, and finding he spoke English, had a great Mind to be enquiring into his Quality and Fortune; which, though Oroonoko endeavour'd to hide, by only confessing he was above the Rank of common Slaves, Trefry soon found he was yet something greater than he confess'd; and from that Moment began to conceive so vast an Esteem for him, that he ever after lov'd him as his dearest Brother, and shew'd him all the Civilities due to so great a Man.

Trefry was a very good Mathematician, and a Linguist; could speak French and Spanish; and in the three Days they remain'd in the Boat, (for so long were they going from the Ship to the Plantation) he entertain'd Oroonoko so agreeably with his Art and Discourse, that he was no less pleas'd with Trefry, than he was with the Prince; and he thought himself, at least, fortunate in this, that since he was a Slave, as long as he would suffer himself to remain so, he had a Man of so excellent Wit and Parts for a Master. So that before they had finish'd their Voyage up the River, he made no Scruple of declaring to Trefry all his Fortunes, and most Part of what I have here related, and put himself wholly into the Hands of his new Friend, who he found resented all the Injuries were done him, and was charm'd with all the Greatnesses of his Actions; which were recited with that Modesty, and delicate Sense, as wholly vanquish'd him, and subdu'd him to his Interest. And he promis'd him, on his Word and Honour, he would find the Means to re-conduct him to his own Country again; assuring him, he had a perfect Abhorrence of so dishonourable an Action; and that he would sooner have dy'd, than have been the Author of such a Perfidy. He found the Prince was very much concerned to know what became of his Friends, and how they took their Slavery; and Trefry promised to take Care about the enquiring after their Condition, and that he should have an Account of 'em.

Tho', as Oroonoko afterwards said, he had little Reason to credit the Words of a Backearary; yet he knew not why, but he saw a kind of Sincerity, and aweful Truth in the Face of Trefry; he saw Honesty in his Eyes, and he found him wise and witty enough to understand Honour: for it was one of his Maxims, A Man of Wit could not be a Knave or Villain.

In their Passage up the River, they put in at several Houses for Refreshment; and ever when they landed, Numbers of People would flock to behold this Man: not but their Eyes were daily entertain'd with the Sight of Slaves; but the Fame of Oroonoko was gone before him, and all People were in Admiration of his Beauty. Besides, he had a rich Habit on, in which he was taken, so different from the rest, and which the Captain could not strip him of, because he was forc'd to surprize his Person in the Minute he sold him. When he found his Habit made him liable, as he thought, to be gazed at the more, he begged Trefry to give him something more befitting a Slave, which he did, and took off his Robes: Nevertheless, he shone thro' all, and his Osenbrigs (a sort of brown Holland Suit he had on) could not conceal the Graces of his Looks and Mein; and he had no less Admirers than when he had his dazling Habit on: The Royal Youth appear'd in spite of the Slave, and People could not help treating him after a different Manner, without designing it. As soon as they approached him, they venerated and esteemed him; his Eyes insensibly commanded Respect, and his Behaviour insinuated it into every Soul. So that there was nothing talked of but this young and gallant Slave, even by those who yet knew not that he was a Prince.

I ought to tell you, that the Christians never buy any Slaves but they give 'em some Name of their own, their native ones being likely very barbarous, and hard to pronounce; so that Mr. Trefry gave Oroonoko that of Cæsar; which name will live in that Country as long as that (scarce more) glorious one of the great Roman: for 'tis most evident he wanted no Part of the personal Courage of that Cæsar, and acted Things as memorable, had they been done in some Part of the World replenished with People and Historians, that might have given him his Due. But his Misfortune was, to fall in an obscure World, that afforded only a Female Pen to celebrate his Fame; tho' I doubt not but it had lived from others Endeavours, if the Dutch, who immediately after his Time took that Country, had not killed, banished and dispersed all those that were capable of giving the World this great Man's Life, much better than I have done. And Mr. Trefry, who design'd it, died before he began it, and bemoan'd himself for not having undertook it in Time.

For the future therefore I must call Oroonoko Cæsar; since by that Name only he was known in our Western World, and by that Name he was received on Shore at Parham-House, where he was destin'd a Slave. But if the King himself (God bless him) had come ashore, there could not have been greater Expectation by all the whole Plantation, and those neighbouring ones, than was on ours at that Time; and he was received more like a Governor than a Slave: Notwithstanding, as the Custom was, they assigned him his Portion of Land, his House and his Business up in the Plantation. But as it was more for Form, than any Design to put him to his Task, he endured no more of the Slave but the Name, and remain'd some Days in the House, receiving all Visits that were made him, without stirring towards that Part of the Plantation where the Negroes were.

At last, he would needs go view his Land, his House, and the Business assign'd him. But he no sooner came to the Houses of the Slaves, which are like a little Town by itself, the Negroes all having left Work, but they all came forth to behold him, and found he was that Prince who had, at several Times, sold most of 'em to these Parts; and from a Veneration they pay to great Men, especially if they know 'em, and from the Surprize and Awe they had at the Sight of him, they all cast themselves at his Feet, crying out, in their Language, Live, O King! Long live, O King! and kissing his Feet, paid him even Divine Homage.

Several English Gentlemen were with him, and what Mr. Trefry had told 'em was here confirm'd; of which he himself before had no other Witness than Cæsar himself: But he was infinitely glad to find his Grandeur confirmed by the Adoration of all the Slaves.

Cæsar, troubled with their Over-Joy, and Over-Ceremony, besought 'em to rise, and to receive him as their Fellow-Slave; assuring them he was no better. At which they set up with one Accord a most terrible and hideous Mourning and Condoling, which he and the English had much ado to appease: but at last they prevailed with 'em, and they prepared all their barbarous Musick, and every one kill'd and dress'd something of his own Stock (for every Family has their Land apart, on which, at their Leisure-times, they breed all eatable Things) and clubbing it together, made a most magnificent Supper, inviting their Grandee Captain, their Prince, to honour it with his Presence; which he did, and several English with him, where they all waited on him, some playing, others dancing before him all the Time, according to the Manners of their several Nations, and with unwearied Industry endeavouring to please and delight him.

While they sat at Meat, Mr. Trefry told Cæsar, that most of these young Slaves were undone in Love with a fine She-Slave, whom they had had about six Months on their Land; the Prince, who never heard the Name of Love without a Sigh, nor any Mention of it without the Curiosity of examining further into that Tale, which of all Discourses was most agreeable to him, asked, how they came to be so unhappy, as to be all undone for one fair Slave? Trefry, who was naturally amorous, and delighted to talk of Love as well as any Body, proceeded to tell him, they had the most charming Black that ever was beheld on their Plantation, about fifteen or sixteen Years old, as he guess'd; that for his Part he had done nothing but sigh for her ever since she came; and that all the White Beauties he had seen, never charm'd him so absolutely as this fine Creature had done; and that no Man, of any Nation, ever beheld her, that did not fall in love with her; and that she had all the Slaves perpetually at her Feet; and the whole Country resounded with the Fame of Clemene, for so (said he) we have christen'd her: but she denies us all with such a noble Disdain, that 'tis a Miracle to see, that she who can give such eternal Desires, should herself be all Ice and all Unconcern. She is adorn'd with the most graceful Modesty that ever beautify'd Youth; the softest Sigher, that, if she were capable of Love, one would swear she languished for some absent happy Man; and so retired, as if she fear'd a Rape even from the God of Day, or that the Breezes would steal Kisses from her delicate Mouth. Her Task of Work, some sighing Lover every Day makes it his Petition to perform for her; which she accepts blushing, and with Reluctancy, for Fear he will ask her a Look for a Recompence, which he dares not presume to hope; so great an Awe she strikes into the Hearts of her Admirers. 'I do not wonder (reply'd the Prince) that Clemene should refuse Slaves, being, as you say, so beautiful; but wonder how she escapes those that can entertain her as you can do: or why, being your Slave, you do not oblige her to yield?' 'I confess (said Trefry) when I have, against her Will, entertained her with Love so long, as to be transported with my Passion even above Decency, I have been ready to make Use of those Advantages of Strength and Force Nature has given me: But Oh! she disarms me with that Modesty and Weeping, so tender and so moving, that I retire, and thank my Stars she overcame me.' The Company laugh'd at his Civility to a Slave, and Cæsar only applauded the Nobleness of his Passion and Nature, since that Slave might be noble, or, what was better, have true Notions of Honour and Virtue in her. Thus passed they this Night, after having received from the Slaves all imaginable Respect and Obedience.

The next Day, Trefry ask'd Cæsar to walk when the Heat was allay'd, and designedly carried him by the Cottage of the fair Slave; and told him she whom he spoke of last Night lived there retir'd: But (says he) I would not wish you to approach; for I am sure you will be in Love as soon as you behold her. Cæsar assured him, he was Proof against all the Charms of that Sex; and that if he imagined his Heart could be so perfidious to love again after Imoinda, he believed he should tear it from his Bosom. They had no sooner spoke, but a little Shock-Dog, that Clemene had presented her, which she took great Delight in, ran out; and she, not knowing any Body was there, ran to get it in again, and bolted out on those who were just speaking of her: when seeing them, she would have run in again, but Trefry caught her by the Hand, and cry'd, Clemene, however you fly a Lover, you ought to pay some Respect to this Stranger, (pointing to Cæsar.) But she, as if she had resolved never to raise her Eyes to the Face of a Man again, bent 'em the more to the Earth, when he spoke, and gave the Prince the Leisure to look the more at her. There needed no long gazing, or Consideration, to examine who this fair Creature was; he soon saw Imoinda all over her: in a Minute he saw her Face, her Shape, her Air, her Modesty, and all that call'd forth his Soul with Joy at his Eyes, and left his Body destitute of almost Life: it stood without Motion, and for a Minute knew not that it had a Being; and, I believe, he had never come to himself, so oppress'd he was with Over-joy, if he had not met with this Allay, that he perceived Imoinda fall dead in the Hands of Trefry. This awaken'd him, and he ran to her Aid, and caught her in his Arms, where by Degrees she came to her self; and 'tis needless to tell with what Transports, what Extasies of Joy, they both a While beheld each other, without speaking; then snatched each other to their Arms; then gaze again, as if they still doubted whether they possess'd the Blessing they grasped: but when they recover'd their Speech, 'tis not to be imagined what tender Things they express'd to each other; wondring what strange Fate had brought them again together. They soon inform'd each other of their Fortunes, and equally bewail'd their Fate; but at the same Time they mutually protested, that even Fetters and Slavery were soft and easy, and would be supported with Joy and Pleasure, while they could be so happy to possess each other, and to be able to make good their Vows. Cæsar swore he disdained the Empire of the World, while he could behold his Imoinda; and she despised Grandeur and Pomp, those Vanities of her Sex, when she could gaze on Oroonoko. He ador'd the very Cottage where she resided, and said, That little Inch of the World would give him more Happiness than all the Universe could do; and she vow'd it was a Palace, while adorned with the Presence of Oroonoko.

Trefry was infinitely pleased with this Novel, and found this Clemene was the fair Mistress of whom Cæsar had before spoke; and was not a little satisfy'd, that Heaven was so kind to the Prince as to sweeten his Misfortunes by so lucky an Accident; and leaving the Lovers to themselves, was impatient to come down to Parham-House (which was on the same Plantation) to give me an Account of what had happened. I was as impatient to make these Lovers a Visit, having already made a Friendship with Cæsar, and from his own Mouth learned what I have related; which was confirmed by his Frenchman, who was set on shore to seek his Fortune, and of whom they could not make a Slave, because a Christian; and he came daily to Parham-Hill to see and pay his Respects to his Pupil Prince. So that concerning and interesting myself in all that related to Cæsar, whom I had assured of Liberty as soon as the Governour arrived, I hasted presently to the Place where these Lovers were, and was infinitely glad to find this beautiful young Slave (who had already gain'd all our Esteems, for her Modesty and extraordinary Prettiness) to be the same I had heard Cæsar speak so much of. One may imagine then we paid her a treble Respect; and tho' from her being carved in fine Flowers and Birds all over her Body, we took her to be of Quality before, yet when we knew Clemene was Imoinda, we could not enough admire her.

I had forgot to tell you, that those who are nobly born of that Country, are so delicately cut and raised all over the Fore-part of the Trunk of their Bodies, that it looks as if it were japan'd, the Works being raised like high Point round the Edges of the Flowers. Some are only carved with a little Flower, or Bird, at the Sides of the Temples, as was Cæsar; and those who are so carved over the Body, resemble our antient Picts that are figur'd in the Chronicles, but these Carvings are more delicate.

From that happy Day Cæsar took Clemene for his Wife, to the general Joy of all People; and there was as much Magnificence as the Country could afford at the Celebration of this Wedding: And in a very short Time after she conceived with Child, which made Cæsar even adore her, knowing he was the last of his great Race. This new Accident made him more impatient of Liberty, and he was every Day treating with Trefrey for his and Clemene's Liberty, and offer'd either Gold, or a vast Quantity of Slaves, which should be paid before they let him go, provided he could have any Security that he should go when his Ransom was paid. They fed him from Day to Day with Promises, and delay'd him till the Lord-Governor should come; so that he began to suspect them of Falshood, and that they would delay him till the Time of his Wife's Delivery, and make a Slave of the Child too; for all the Breed is theirs to whom the Parents belong. This Thought made him very uneasy, and his Sullenness gave them some Jealousies of him; so that I was obliged, by some Persons who fear'd a Mutiny (which is very fatal sometimes in those Colonies that abound so with Slaves, that they exceed the Whites in vast Numbers) to discourse with Cæsar, and to give him all the Satisfaction I possibly could: They knew he and Clemene were scarce an Hour in a Day from my Lodgings; that they eat with me, and that I oblig'd them in all Things I was capable. I entertained them with the Lives of the Romans, and great Men, which charmed him to my Company; and her, with teaching her all the pretty Works that I was Mistress of, and telling her Stories of Nuns, and endeavouring to bring her to the Knowledge of the true God: But of all Discourses, Cæsar liked that the worst, and would never be reconciled to our Notions of the Trinity, of which he ever made a Jest; it was a Riddle he said would turn his Brain to conceive, and one could not make him understand what Faith was. However, these

Conversations fail'd not altogether so well to divert him, that he liked the Company of us Women much above the Men, for he could not drink, and he is but an ill Companion in that Country that cannot. So that obliging him to love us very well, we had all the Liberty of Speech with him, especially my self, whom he call'd his Great Mistress; and indeed my Word would go a great Way with him. For these Reasons I had Opportunity to take Notice to him, that he was not well pleased of late, as he used to be; was more retired and thoughtful; and told him, I took it ill he should suspect we would break our Words with him, and not permit both him and Clemene to return to his own Kingdom, which was not so long a Way, but when he was once on his Voyage he would quickly arrive there. He made me some Answers that shew'd a Doubt in him, which made me ask, what Advantage it would be to doubt? It would but give us a Fear of him, and possibly compel us to treat him so as I should be very loth to behold; that is, it might occasion his Confinement. Perhaps this was not so luckily spoke of me, for I perceiv'd he resented that Word, which I strove to soften again in vain: However, he assur'd me, that whatsoever Resolutions he should take, he would act nothing upon the White People; and as for myself, and those upon that Plantation where he was, he would sooner forfeit his eternal Liberty, and Life itself, than lift his Hand against his greatest Enemy on that Place. He besought me to suffer no Fears upon his Account, for he could do nothing that Honour should not dictate; but he accused himself for having suffer'd Slavery so long; yet he charg'd that Weakness on Love alone, who was capable of making him neglect even Glory itself; and, for which, now he reproaches himself every Moment of the Day. Much more to this Effect he spoke, with an Air impatient enough to make me know he would not be long in Bondage; and tho' he suffer'd only the Name of a Slave, and had nothing of the Toil and Labour of one, yet that was sufficient to render him uneasy; and he had been too long idle, who us'd to be always in Action, and in Arms. He had a Spirit all rough and fierce, and that could not be tam'd to lazy Rest: And tho' all Endeavours were us'd to exercise himself in such Actions and Sports as this World afforded, as Running, Wrestling, Pitching the Bar, Hunting and Fishing, Chasing and Killing Tygers of a monstrous Size, which this Continent affords in abundance; and wonderful Snakes, such as Alexander is reported to have encounter'd at the River of Amazons, and which Cæsar took great Delight to overcome; yet these were not Actions great enough for his large Soul, which was still panting after more renown'd Actions.

Before I parted that Day with him, I got, with much ado, a Promise from him to rest yet a little longer with Patience, and wait the Coming of the Lord Governour, who was every Day expected on our Shore: He assur'd me he would, and this Promise he desired me to know was given perfectly in Complaisance to me, in whom he had an entire Confidence.

After this, I neither thought it convenient to trust him much out of our View, nor did the Country, who fear'd him; but with one Accord it was advis'd to treat him fairly, and oblige him to remain within such a Compass, and that he should be permitted, as seldom as could be, to go up to the Plantations of the Negroes; or, if he did, to be accompany'd by some that should be rather, in Appearance, Attendants than Spies. This Care was for some time taken, and Cæsar look'd upon it as a Mark of extraordinary Respect, and was glad his Discontent had oblig'd 'em to be more observant to him; he received new Assurance from the Overseer, which was confirmed to him by the Opinion of all the Gentlemen of the Country, who made their Court to him. During this Time that we had his Company more frequently than hitherto we had had, it may not be unpleasant to relate to you the Diversions we entertain'd him with, or rather he us.

My Stay was to be short in that Country; because my Father dy'd at Sea, and never arriv'd to possess the Honour design'd him, (which was Lieutenant-General of six and thirty Islands, besides the Continent of Surinam) nor the Advantages he hop'd to reap by them: So that though we were oblig'd to continue on our Voyage, we did not intend to stay upon the Place. Though, in a Word, I must say thus much of it; That certainly had his late Majesty, of sacred Memory, but seen and known what a vast and charming World he had been Master of in that Continent, he would never have parted so easily with it to the Dutch. 'Tis a Continent, whose vast Extent was never yet known, and may contain more noble Earth than all the Universe beside; for, they say, it reaches from East to West one Way as far as China, and another to Peru: It affords all Things, both for Beauty and Use; 'tis there eternal Spring, always the very Months of April, May, and June; the Shades are perpetual, the Trees bearing at once all Degrees of Leaves, and Fruit, from blooming Buds to ripe Autumn: Groves of Oranges, Lemons, Citrons, Figs, Nutmegs, and noble Aromaticks, continually bearing their Fragrancies: The Trees appearing all like Nosegays, adorn'd with Flowers of different Kinds; some are all White, some Purple, some Scarlet, some Blue, some Yellow; bearing at the same Time ripe Fruit, and blooming young, or producing every Day new. The very Wood of all these Trees has an intrinsic Value, above common Timber; for they are, when cut, of different Colours, glorious to behold, and bear a Price considerable, to inlay withal. Besides this, they yield rich Balm, and Gums; so that we make our Candles of such an aromatic Substance, as does not only give a sufficient Light, but as they burn, they cast their Perfumes all about. Cedar is the common Firing, and all the Houses are built with it. The very Meat we eat, when set on the Table, if it be native, I mean of the Country, perfumes the whole Room; especially a little Beast call'd an Armadillo, a Thing which I can liken to nothing so well as a Rhinoceros; 'tis all in white Armour, so jointed, that it moves as well in it, as if it had nothing on: This Beast is about the Bigness of a Pig of six Weeks old. But it were endless to give an Account of all the divers wonderful and strange Things that Country affords, and which we took a great Delight to go in Search of; tho' those Adventures are oftentimes fatal, and at least dangerous: But while we had Cæsar in our Company on these Designs, we fear'd no Harm, nor suffer'd any.

As soon as I came into the Country, the best House in it was presented me, call'd St. John's Hill: It stood on a vast Rock of white Marble, at the Foot of which, the River ran a vast Depth down, and not to be descended on that Side; the little Waves still dashing and washing the Foot of this Rock, made the softest Murmurs and Purlings in the World; and the opposite Bank was adorn'd with such vast Quantities of different Flowers eternally blowing, and every Day and Hour new, and every Day new 'em with lofty Trees of a thousand rare Forms and Colours, that the Prospect was the most ravishing that Sands can create. On the Edge of this white Rock, towards the River, was a Walk, or Grove, of Orange and Lemon-Trees, about half the Length of the Mall here, whose flowery and Fruit-bearing Branches met at the Top, and hinder'd the Sun, whose Rays are very fierce there, from entring a Beam into the Grove; and the cool Air that came from the River, made it not only fit to entertain People in, at all the hottest Hours of the Day, but refresh the sweet Blossoms, and made it always sweet and charming; and sure, the whole Globe of the World cannot shew so delightful a Place as this Grove was: Not all the Gardens of boasted Italy can produce a Shade to out-vie this, which Nature had join'd with Art to render so exceeding fine; and 'tis a Marvel to see how such vast Trees, as big as English Oaks, could take Footing on so solid a Rock, and in so little Earth as cover'd that Rock: But all Things by Nature there are rare, delightful, and wonderful. But to our Sports.

Sometimes we would go surprising, and in Search of young Tygers in their Dens, watching when the old ones went forth to forage for Prey; and oftentimes we have been in great Danger, and have fled apace for our Lives, when surpriz'd by the Dams. But once, above all other Times, we went on this Design, and Cæsar was with us; who had no sooner stoln a young Tyger from her Nest, but going off, we encounter'd the Dam, bearing a Buttock of a Cow, which she had torn off with her mighty Paw, and going with it towards her Den: We had only four Women, Cæsar, and an English Gentleman, Brother to Harry Martin the great Oliverian; we found there was no escaping this enraged and ravenous Beast. However, we Women fled as fast as we could from it; but our Heels had not saved our Lives, if Cæsar had not laid down her Cub, when he found the Tyger quit her Prey to make the more Speed towards him; and taking Mr. Martin's Sword, desired him to stand aside, or follow the Ladies. He obey'd him; and Cæsar met this monstrous Beast of mighty Size, and vast Limbs, who came with open Jaws upon him; and fixing his aweful stern Eyes full upon those of the Beast, and putting himself into a very steady and good aiming Posture of Defence, ran his Sword quite through his Breast, down to his very Heart, home to the Hilt of the Sword: The dying Beast stretch'd forth her Paw, and going to grasp his Thigh, surpriz'd with Death in that very Moment, did him no other Harm than fixing her long Nails in his Flesh very deep, feebly wounded him, but could not grasp the Flesh to tear off any. When he had done this, he hallow'd to us to return; which, after some Assurance of his Victory, we did, and found him lugging out the Sword from the Bosom of the Tyger, who was laid in her Blood on the Ground. He took up the Cub, and with an Unconcern that had nothing of the Joy or Gladness of Victory, he came and laid the Whelp at my Feet. We all extremely wonder'd at his daring, and at the Bigness of the Beast, which was about the Height of an Heifer, but of mighty great and strong Limbs.

Another time, being in the Woods, he kill'd a Tyger, that had long infested that Part, and borne away abundance of Sheep and Oxen, and other Things, that were for the Support of those to whom they belong'd. Abundance of People assail'd this Beast, some affirming they had shot her with several Bullets quite through the Body at several times; and some swearing they shot her through the very Heart; and they believed she was a Devil, rather than a mortal Thing. Cæsar had often said, he had a Mind to encounter this Monster, and spoke with several Gentlemen who had attempted her; one crying, I shot her with so many poison'd Arrows, another with his Gun in this Part of her, and another in that; so that he remarking all the Places where she was shot, fancy'd still he should overcome her, by giving her another Sort of a Wound than any had yet done; and one Day said (at the Table), 'What Trophies and Garlands, Ladies, will you make me, if I bring you home the Heart of this ravenous Beast, that eats up all your Lambs and Pigs?' We all promis'd he should be rewarded at our Hands. So taking a Bow, which he chose out of a great many, he went up into the Wood, with two Gentlemen, where he imagin'd this Devourer to be. They had not pass'd very far into it, but they heard her Voice, growling and grumbling, as if she were pleas'd with something she was doing. When they came in View, they found her muzzling in the Belly of a new ravish'd Sheep, which she had torn open; and seeing herself approach'd, she took fast hold of her Prey with her fore Paws, and set a very fierce raging Look on Cæsar, without offering to approach him, for Fear at the same Time of loosing what she had in Possession: So that Cæsar remain'd a good while, only taking Aim, and getting an Opportunity to shoot her where he design'd. 'Twas some Time before he could accomplish it; and to wound her, and not kill her, would but have enrag'd her the more, and endanger'd him. He had a Quiver of Arrows at his Side, so that if one fail'd, he could be supply'd: At last, retiring a little, he gave her Opportunity to eat, for he found she was ravenous, and fell to as soon as she saw him retire, being more eager of her Prey, than of doing new Mischiefs; when he going softly to one Side of her, and hiding his Person behind certain Herbage, that grew high and thick, he took so good Aim, that, as he intended, he shot her just into the Eye, and the Arrow was sent with so good a Will, and so sure a Hand, that it stuck in her Brain, and made her caper, and become mad for a Moment or two; but being seconded by another Arrow, she fell dead upon the Prey. Cæsar cut her open with a Knife, to see where those Wounds were that had been reported to him, and why she did not die of 'em. But I shall now relate a Thing that, possibly, will find no Credit among Men; because 'tis a Notion commonly receiv'd with us, That nothing can receive a Wound in the Heart, and live: But when the Heart of this courageous Animal was taken out, there were seven Bullets of Lead in it, the Wound seam'd up with great Scars, and she liv'd with the Bullets a great While, for it was long since they were shot: This Heart the Conqueror brought up to us, and 'twas a very great Curiosity, which all the Country came to see; and which gave Cæsar Occasion of many fine Discourses of Accidents in War, and strange Escapes.

At other times he would go a Fishing; and discoursing on that Diversion, he found we had in that Country a very strange Fish, call'd a Numb-Eel, (an Eel of which I have eaten) that while it is alive, it has a Quality so cold, that those who are angling, tho' with a Line of ever so great a Length, with a Rod at the End of it, it shall in the same Minute the Bait is touch'd by this Eel, seize him or her that holds the Rod with a Numbness, that shall deprive 'em of Sense for a While; and some have fallen into the Water, and others drop'd, as dead, on the Banks of the Rivers where they stood, as soon as this Fish touches the Bait. Cæsar us'd to laugh at this, and believ'd it impossible a Man could lose his Force at the Touch of a Fish; and could not understand that Philosophy, that a cold Quality should be of that Nature; however, he had a great Curiosity to try whether it would have the same Effect on him it had on others, and often try'd, but in vain. At last, the sought-for Fish came to the Bait, as he stood angling on the Bank; and instead of throwing away the Rod, or giving it a sudden Twitch out of the Water, whereby he might have caught both the Eel, and have dismiss'd the Rod, before it could have too much Power over him; for Experiment-sake, he grasp'd it but the harder, and fainting, fell into the River; and being still possess'd of the Rod, the Tide carry'd him, senseless as he was, a great Way, till an Indian Boat took him up; and perceiv'd, when they touch'd him, a Numbness seize them, and by that knew the Rod was in his Hand; which with a Paddle, (that is a short Oar) they struck away, and snatch'd it into the Boat, Eel and all. If Cæsar was almost dead, with the Effect of this Fish, he was more so with that of the Water, where he had remain'd the Space of going a League, and they found they had much ado to bring him back to Life; but at last they did, and brought him home, where he was in a few Hours well recover'd and refresh'd, and not a little asham'd to find he should be overcome by an Eel, and that all the People, who heard his Defiance, would laugh at him. But we chear'd him up; and he being convinc'd, we had the Eel at Supper, which was a quarter of an Ell about, and most delicate Meat; and was of the more Value, since it cost so dear as almost the Life of so gallant a Man.

About this Time we were in many mortal Fears, about some Disputes the English had with the Indians; so that we could scarce trust our selves, without great Numbers, to go to any Indian Towns, or Place where they abode, for fear they should fall upon us, as they did immediately after my coming away; and the Place being in the Possession of the Dutch, they us'd them not so civilly as the English; so that they cut in Pieces all they could take, getting into Houses and hanging up the Mother, and all her Children about her; and cut a Footman, I left behind me, all in Joints, and nail'd him to Trees.

This Feud began while I was there; so that I lost half the Satisfaction I propos'd, in not seeing and visiting the Indian Towns. But one Day, bemoaning of our Misfortunes upon this Account, Cæsar told us, we need not fear, for if we had a Mind to go, he would undertake to be our Guard. Some would, but most would not venture: About eighteen of us resolv'd, and took Barge; and after eight Days, arriv'd near an Indian Town: But approaching it, the Hearts of some of our Company fail'd, and they would not venture on Shore; so we poll'd, who would, and who would not. For my Part, I said, if Cæsar would, I would go. He resolv'd; so did my Brother, and my Woman, a Maid of good Courage. Now none of us speaking the Language of the People, and imagining we should have a half Diversion in gazing only; and not knowing what they said, we took a Fisherman that liv'd at the Mouth of the River, who had been a long Inhabitant there, and oblig'd him to go with us: But because he was known to the Indians, as trading among 'em, and being, by long living there, become a perfect Indian in Colour, we, who had a Mind to surprize 'em, by making them see something they never had seen, (that is, White People) resolv'd only my self, my Brother and Woman should go: So Cæsar, the Fisherman, and the rest, hiding behind some thick Reeds and Flowers that grew in the Banks, let us pass on towards the Town, which was on the Bank of the River all along. A little distant from the Houses, or Huts, we saw some dancing, others busy'd in fetching and carrying of Water from the River. They had no sooner spy'd us, but they set up a loud Cry, that frighted us at first; we thought it had been for those that should kill us, but it seems it was of Wonder and Amazement. They were all naked; and we were dress'd, so as is most commode for the hot Countries, very glittering and rich; so that we appear'd extremely fine; my own Hair was cut short, and I had a Taffety Cap, with black Feathers on my Head; my Brother was in a Stuff-Suit, with Silver Loops and Buttons, and abundance of green Ribbon. This was all infinitely surprising to them; and because we saw them stand still till we approach'd 'em, we took Heart and advanc'd, came up to 'em, and offer'd 'em our Hands; which they took, and look'd on us round about, calling still for more Company; who came swarming out, all wondering, and crying out Tepeeme; taking their Hair up in their Hands, and spreading it wide to those they call'd out to; as if they would say (as indeed it signify'd) Numberless Wonders, or not to be recounted, no more than to number the Hair of their Heads. By Degrees they grew more bold, and from gazing upon us round, they touch'd us, laying their Hands upon all the Features of our Faces, feeling our Breasts, and Arms, taking up one Petticoat, then wondering to see another; admiring our Shoes and Stockings, but more our Garters, which we gave 'em, and they ty'd about their Legs, being lac'd with Silver Lace at the Ends; for they much esteem any shining Things. In fine, we suffer'd 'em to survey us as they pleas'd, and we thought they would never have done admiring us. When Cæsar, and the rest, saw we were receiv'd with such Wonder, they came up to us; and finding the Indian Trader whom they knew, (for 'tis by these Fishermen, call'd Indian Traders, we hold a Commerce with 'em; for they love not to go far from home, and we never go to them) when they saw him therefore, they set up a new Joy, and cry'd in their Language, Oh, here's our Tiguamy, and we shall know whether those Things can speak. So advancing to him, some of 'em gave him their Hands, and cry'd, Amora Tiguamy; which is as much as, How do you do? or, Welcome Friend; and all, with one din, began to gabble to him, and ask'd, if we had Sense and Wit? If we could talk of Affairs of Life and War, as they could do? If we could hunt, swim, and do a thousand Things they use? He answer'd 'em, We could. Then they invited us into their Houses, and dress'd Venison and Buffalo for us; and going out, gather'd a Leaf of a Tree, called a Sarumbo Leaf, of six Yards long, and spread it on the Ground for a Table-Cloth; and cutting another in Pieces, instead of Plates, set us on little low Indian Stools, which they cut out of one entire Piece of Wood, and paint in a sort of Japan-Work. They serve every one their Mess on these Pieces of Leaves; and it was very good, but too high-season'd with Pepper. When we had eat, my Brother and I took out our Flutes, and play'd to 'em, which gave 'em new Wonder; and I soon perceiv'd, by an Admiration that is natural to these People, and by the extreme Ignorance and Simplicity of 'em, it were not difficult to establish any unknown or extravagant Religion among them, and to impose any Notions or Fictions upon 'em. For seeing a Kinsman of mine set some Paper on Fire with a Burning-Glass, a Trick they had never before seen, they were like to have ador'd him for a God, and begg'd he would give 'em the Characters or Figures of his Name, that they might oppose it against Winds and Storms: which he did, and they held it up in those Seasons, and fancy'd it had a Charm to conquer them, and kept it like a holy Relique. They are very superstitious, and call'd him the Great Peeie, that is, Prophet. They shewed us their Indian Peeie, a Youth of about sixteen Years old, as handsome as Nature could make a Man. They consecrate a beautiful Youth from his Infancy, and all Arts are used to compleat him in the finest Manner, both in Beauty and Shape: He is bred to all the little Arts and Cunning they are capable of; to all the legerdemain Tricks, and Slight of Hand, whereby he imposes on the Rabble; and is both a Doctor in Physick and Divinity: And by these Tricks makes the Sick believe he sometimes eases their Pains, by drawing from the afflicted Part little Serpents, or odd Flies, or Worms, or any strange Thing; and though they have besides undoubted good Remedies for almost all their Diseases, they cure the Patient more by Fancy than by Medicines, and make themselves feared, loved, and reverenced. This young Peeie had a very young Wife, who seeing my Brother kiss her, came running and kiss'd me. After this they kiss'd one another, and made it a very great Jest, it being so novel; and new Admiration and Laughing went round the Multitude, that they never will forget that Ceremony, never before us'd or known. Cæsar had a Mind to see and talk with their War-Captains, and we were conducted to one of their Houses, where we beheld several of the great Captains, who had been at Council: But so frightful a Vision it was to see 'em, no Fancy can create; no sad Dreams can represent so dreadful a Spectacle. For my Part, I took 'em for Hobgoblins, or Fiends, rather than Men; But however their Shapes appear'd, their Souls were very humane and noble; but some wanted their Noses, some their Lips, some both Noses and Lips, some their Ears, and others cut through each Cheek, with long Slashes, through which their Teeth appear'd: They had several other formidable Wounds and Scars, or rather Dismembrings. They had Comitias, or little Aprons before them; and Girdles of Cotton, with their Knives naked stuck in it; a Bow at their Back, and a Quiver of Arrows on their Thighs; and most had Feathers on their Heads of divers Colours. They cry'd Amora Tiguamy to us, at our Entrance, and were pleas'd we said as much to them: They seated us, and gave us Drink of the best Sort, and wonder'd as much as the others had done before to see us. Cæsar was marvelling as much at their Faces, wondring how they should be all so wounded in War; he was impatient to know how they all came by those frightful Marks of Rage or Malice, rather than Wounds got in noble Battle: They told us by our Interpreter, That when any War was waging, two Men, chosen out by some old Captain whose fighting was past, and who could only teach the Theory of War, were to stand in Competition for the Generalship, or great War-Captain; and being brought before the old Judges, now past Labour, they are ask'd, What they dare do, to shew they are worthy to lead an Army? When he who is first ask'd, making no Reply, cuts off his Nose, and throws it contemptibly on the Ground; and the other does something to himself that he thinks surpasses him, and perhaps deprives himself of Lips and an Eye: So they slash on 'till one gives out, and many have dy'd in this Debate. And it's by a passive Valour they shew and prove their Activity; a sort of Courage too brutal to be applauded by our Black Hero; nevertheless, he express'd his Esteem of 'em.

In this Voyage Cæsar begat so good an Understanding between the Indians and the English, that there were no more Fears or Heart-burnings during our Stay, but we had a perfect, open, and free Trade with 'em. Many Things remarkable, and worthy reciting, we met with in this short Voyage; because Cæsar made it his Business to search out and provide for our Entertainment, especially to please his dearly ador'd Imoinda, who was a Sharer in all our Adventures; we being resolv'd to make her Chains as easy as we could, and to compliment the Prince in that Manner that most oblig'd him.

As we were coming up again, we met with some Indians of strange Aspects; that is, of a larger Size, and other sort of Features, than those of our Country. Our Indian Slaves, that row'd us, ask'd 'em some Questions; but they could not understand us, but shew'd us a long Cotton String, with several Knots on it, and told us, they had been coming from the Mountains so many Moons as there were Knots: they were habited in Skins of a strange Beast, and brought along with 'em Bags of Gold-Dust; which, as well as they could give as to understand, came streaming in little small Channels down the high Mountains, when the Rains fell; and offer'd to be the Convoy to any Body, or Persons, that would go to the Mountains. We carry'd these Men up to Parham, where they were kept till the Lord-Governor came: And because all the Country was mad to be going on this Golden Adventure, the Governor, by his Letters, commanded (for they sent some of the Gold to him) that a Guard should be set at the Mouth of the River of Amazons (a River so call'd, almost as broad as the River of Thames) and prohibited all People from going up that River, it conducting to those Mountains or Gold. But we going off for England before the Project was further prosecuted, and the Governor being drown'd in a Hurricane, either the Design died, or the Dutch have the Advantage of it: And 'tis to be bemoan'd what his Majesty lost, by losing that Part of America.

Though this Digression is a little from my Story, however, since it contains some Proofs of the Curiosity and Daring of this great Man, I was content to omit nothing of his Character.

It was thus for some Time we diverted him; but now Imoinda began to shew she was with Child, and did nothing but sigh and weep for the Captivity of her Lord, herself, and the Infant yet unborn; and believ'd, if it were so hard to gain the Liberty of two, 'twould be more difficult to get that for three. Her Griefs were so many Darts in the great Heart of Cæsar, and taking his Opportunity, one Sunday, when all the Whites were overtaken in Drink, as there were abundance of several Trades, and Slaves for four Years, that inhabited among the Negro Houses; and Sunday being their Day of Debauch, (otherwise they were a sort of Spies upon Cæsar) he went, pretending out of Goodness to 'em, to feast among 'em, and sent all his Musick, and order'd a great Treat for the whole Gang, about three hundred Negroes, and about an hundred and fifty were able to bear Arms, such as they had, which were sufficient to do Execution, with Spirits accordingly: For the English had none but rusty Swords, that no Strength could draw from a Scabbard; except the People of particular Quality, who took Care to oil 'em, and keep 'em in good Order: The Guns also, unless here and there one, or those newly carried from England, would do no Good or Harm; for 'tis the Nature of that Country to rust and eat up Iron, or any Metals but Gold and Silver. And they are very expert at the Bow, which the Negroes and Indians are perfect Masters of.

Cæsar, having singled out these Men from the Women and Children, made an Harangue to 'em, of the Miseries and Ignominies of Slavery; counting up all their Toils and Sufferings, under such Loads, Burdens and Drudgeries, as were fitter for Beasts than Men; senseless Brutes, than human Souls. He told 'em, it was not for Days, Months or Years, but for Eternity; there was no End to be of their Misfortunes: They suffer'd not like Men, who might find a Glory and Fortitude in Oppression; but like Dogs, that lov'd the Whip and Bell, and fawn'd the more they were beaten: That they had lost the divine Quality of Men, and were become insensible Asses, fit only to bear: Nay, worse; an Ass, or Dog, or Horse, having done his Duty, could lie down in Retreat, and rise to work again, and while he did his Duty, endur'd no Stripes; but Men, villanous, senseless Men, such as they, toil'd on all the tedious Week 'till Black Friday; and then, whether they work'd or not, whether they were faulty or meriting, they, promiscuously, the Innocent with the Guilty, suffer'd the infamous Whip, the sordid Stripes, from their Fellow-Slaves, 'till their Blood trickled from all Parts of their Body; Blood, whose every Drop ought to be revenged with a Life of some of those Tyrants that impose it. 'And why (said he) my dear Friends and Fellow-sufferers, should we be Slaves to an unknown People? Have they vanquished us nobly in Fight? Have they won us in Honourable Battle? And are we by the Chance of War become their Slaves? This would not anger a noble Heart; this would not animate a Soldier's Soul: No, but we are bought and sold like Apes or Monkeys, to be the Sport of Women, Fools and Cowards; and the Support of Rogues and Runagades, that have abandoned their own Countries for Rapine, Murders, Theft and Villanies. Do you not hear every Day how they upbraid each other with Infamy of Life, below the wildest Salvages? And shall we render Obedience to such a degenerate Race, who have no one human Virtue left, to distinguish them from the vilest Creatures? Will you, I say, suffer the Lash from such Hands?' They all reply'd with one Accord, 'No, No, No; Cæsar has spoke like a great Captain, like a great King.'

After this he would have proceeded, but was interrupted by a tall Negro, of some more Quality than the rest, his Name was Tuscan; who bowing at the Feet of Cæsar, cry'd, 'My Lord, we have listen'd with Joy and Attention to what you have said; and, were we only Men, would follow so great a Leader through the World: But O! consider we are Husbands and Parents too, and have Things more dear to us than Life; our Wives and Children, unfit for Travel in those unpassable Woods, Mountains and Bogs. We have not only difficult Lands to overcome, but Rivers to wade, and Mountains to encounter; ravenous Beasts of Prey,' To this Cæsar reply'd, 'That Honour was the first Principle in Nature, that was to be obey'd; but as no Man would pretend to that, without all the Acts of Virtue, Compassion, Charity, Love, Justice and Reason, he found it not inconsistent with that, to take equal Care of their Wives and Children as they would of themselves; and that he did not design, when he led them to Freedom, and glorious Liberty, that they should leave that better Part of themselves to perish by the Hand of the Tyrant's Whip: But if there were a Woman among them so degenerate from Love and Virtue, to chuse Slavery before the Pursuit of her Husband, and with the Hazard of her Life, to share with him in his Fortunes; that such a one ought to be abandoned, and left as a Prey to the common Enemy.'

To which they all agreed, and bowed. After this, he spoke of the impassable Woods and Rivers; and convinced them, the more Danger the more Glory. He told them, that he had heard of one Hannibal, a great Captain, had cut his Way through Mountains of solid Rocks; and should a few Shrubs oppose them, which they could fire before 'em? No, 'twas a trifling Excuse to Men resolved to die, or overcome. As for Bogs, they are with a little Labour filled and harden'd; and the Rivers could be no

Obstacle, since they swam by Nature, at least by Custom, from the first Hour of their Birth: That when the Children were weary, they must carry them by Turns, and the Woods and their own Industry would afford them Food. To this they all assented with Joy.

Tuscan then demanded, what he would do: He said he would travel towards the Sea, plant a new Colony, and defend it by their Valour; and when they could find a Ship, either driven by Stress of Weather, or guided by Providence that Way, they would seize it, and make it a Prize, till it had transported them to their own Countries: at least they should be made free in his Kingdom, and be esteem'd as his Fellow-Sufferers, and Men that had the Courage and the Bravery to attempt, at least, for Liberty; and if they died in the Attempt, it would be more brave, than to live in perpetual Slavery.

They bow'd and kiss'd his Feet at this Resolution, and with one Accord vow'd to follow him to Death; and that Night was appointed to begin their March. They made it known to their Wives, and directed them to tie their Hamocks about their Shoulders, and under their Arms, like a Scarf and to lead their Children that could go, and carry those that could not. The Wives, who pay an entire Obedience to their Husbands, obey'd, and stay'd for 'em where they were appointed: The Men stay'd but to furnish themselves with what defensive Arms they could get; and all met at the Rendezvouz, where Cæsar made a new encouraging Speech to 'em and led 'em out.

But as they could not march far that Night, on Monday early, when the Overseers went to call 'em all together, to go to work, they were extremely surprized, to find not one upon the Place, but all fled with what Baggage they had. You may imagine this News was not only suddenly spread all over the Plantation, but soon reached the neighbouring ones; and we had by Noon about 600 Men, they call the Militia of the Country, that came to assist us in the Pursuit of the Fugitives: But never did one see so comical an Army march forth to War. The Men of any Fashion would not concern themselves, tho' it were almost the Common Cause; for such Revoltings are very ill Examples, and have very fatal Consequences oftentimes, in many Colonies: But they had a Respect for Cæsar, and all Hands were against the Parhamites (as they called those of Parham-Plantation) because they did not in the first Place love the Lord-Governor; and secondly, they would have it that Cæsar was ill used, and baffled with: and 'tis not impossible but some of the best in the Country was of his Council in this Flight, and depriving us of all the Slaves; so that they of the better sort would not meddle in the Matter. The Deputy-Governor, of whom I have had no great Occasion to speak, and who was the most fawning fair-tongu'd Fellow in the World, and one that pretended the most Friendship to Cæsar, was now the only violent Man against him; and though he had nothing, and so need fear nothing, yet talked and looked bigger than any Man. He was a Fellow, whose Character is not fit to be mentioned with the worst of the Slaves: This Fellow would lead his Army forth to meet Cæsar, or rather to pursue him. Most of their Arms were of those Sort of cruel Whips they call Cat with nine Tails; some had rusty useless Guns for Shew; others old Basket Hilts, whose Blades had never seen the Light in this Age; and others had long Staffs and Clubs. Mr. Trefry went along, rather to be a Mediator than a Conqueror in such a Battle; for he foresaw and knew, if by fighting they put the Negroes into Despair, they were a sort of sullen Fellows, that would drown or kill themselves before they would yield; and he advis'd that fair Means was best: But Byam was one that abounded in his own Wit, and would take his own Measures.

It was not hard to find these Fugitives; for as they fled, they were forced to fire and cut the Woods before 'em: So that Night or Day they pursu'd 'em by the Light they made, and by the Path they had cleared. But as soon as Cæsar found that he was pursu'd, he put himself in a Posture of Defence, placing all the Woman and Children in the Rear; and himself, with Tuscan by his Side, or next to him, all promising to die or conquer. Encouraged thus, they never stood to parley, but fell on pell-mell upon the English, and killed some, and wounded a great many; they having Recourse to their Whips, as the best of their Weapons. And as they observed no Order, they perplexed the Enemy so sorely, with lashing 'em in the Eyes; and the Women and Children seeing their Husbands so treated, being of fearful and cowardly Dispositions, and hearing the English cry out, Yield and Live! Yield, and be Pardon'd! they all ran in amongst their Husbands and Fathers, and hung about them, crying out, Yield! Yield, and leave Cæsar to their Revenge; that by Degrees the Slaves abandon'd Cæsar, and left him only Tuscan and his Heroick Imoinda, who grown as big as she was, did nevertheless press near her Lord, having a Bow and a Quiver full of poisoned Arrows, which she managed with such Dexterity, that she wounded several, and shot the Governor into the Shoulder; of which Wound he had like to have died, but that an Indian Woman, his Mistress, sucked the Wound, and cleans'd it from the Venom: But however, he stir'd not from the Place till he had parly'd with Cæsar, who he found was resolved to die fighting, and would not be taken; no more would Tuscan or Imoinda. But he, more thirsting after Revenge of another Sort, than that of depriving him of Life, now made use of all his Art of Talking and Dissembling, and besought Cæsar to yield himself upon Terms which he himself should propose, and should be sacredly assented to, and kept by him. He told him, It was not that he any longer fear'd him, or could believe the Force of two Men, and a young Heroine, could overthrow all them, and with all the Slaves now on their Side also; but it was the vast Esteem he had for his Person, the Desire he had to serve so gallant a Man, and to hinder himself from the Reproach hereafter, of having been the Occasion of the Death of a Prince, whose Valour and Magnanimity deserved the Empire of the World. He protested to him, he looked upon his Action as gallant and brave, however tending to the Prejudice of his Lord and Master, who would by it have lost so considerable a Number of Slaves; that this Flight of his should be look'd on as a Heat of Youth, and a Rashness of a too forward Courage, and an unconsider'd Impatience of Liberty, and no more; and that he labour'd in vain to accomplish that which they would effectually perform as soon as any Ship arrived that would touch on his Coast: 'So that if you will be pleased (continued he) to surrender yourself, all imaginable Respect shall be paid you; and your Self, your Wife and Child, if it be born here, shall depart free out of our Land.' But Cæsar would hear of no Composition; though Byam urged, if he pursued and went on in his Design, he would inevitably perish, either by great Snakes, wild Beasts or Hunger; and he ought to have Regard to his Wife, whose Condition requir'd Ease, and not the Fatigues of tedious Travel, where she could not be secured from being devoured. But Cæsar told him, there was no Faith in the White men, or the Gods they ador'd; who instructed them in Principles so false, that honest Men could not live amongst them; though no People profess'd so much, none perform'd so little: That he knew what he had to do when he dealt with Men of Honour; but with them a Man ought to be eternally on his Guard, and never to eat and drink with Christians, without his Weapon of Defence in his Hand; and, for his own Security, never to credit one Word they spoke. As for the Rashness and Inconsiderateness of his Action, he would confess the Governor is in the right; and that he was ashamed of what he had done in endeavouring to make those free, who were by Nature Slaves, poor wretched Rogues, fit to be used as Christian Tools; Dogs, treacherous and cowardly, fit for such Masters; and they wanted only but to be whipped into the Knowledge of the Christian Gods, to be the vilest of all creeping Things; to learn to worship such Deities as had not Power to make them just, brave, or honest: In fine, after a thousand Things of this Nature, not fit here to be recited, he told Byam, He had rather die, than live upon the same Earth with such Dogs. But Trefry and Byam pleaded and protested together so much, that Trefry believing the Governor to mean what he said, and speaking very cordially himself, generously put himself into Cæsar's Hands, and took him aside, and persuaded him, even with Tears, to live, by surrendring himself, and to name his Conditions. Cæsar was overcome by his Wit and Reasons, and in Consideration of Imoinda; and demanding what he desired, and that it should be ratify'd by their Hands in Writing, because he had perceived that was the common Way of Contract between Man and Man amongst the Whites; all this was performed, and Tuscan's Pardon was put in, and they surrender'd to the Governor, who walked peaceably down into the Plantation with them, after giving Order to bury their Dead. Cæsar was very much toil'd with the Bustle of the Day, for he had fought like a Fury; and what Mischief was done, he and Tuscan performed alone; and gave their Enemies a fatal Proof, that they durst do any Thing, and fear'd no mortal Force.

But they were no sooner arrived at the Place where all the Slaves receive their Punishments of Whipping, but they laid Hands on Cæsar and Tuscan, faint with Heat and Toil; and surprizing them, bound them to two several Stakes, and whipped them in a most deplorable and inhuman Manner, rending the very Flesh from their Bones, especially Cæsar, who was not perceived to make any Moan, or to alter his Face, only to roll his Eyes on the faithless Governor, and those he believed Guilty, with Fierceness and Indignation; and to complete his Rage, he saw every one of those Slaves who but a few Days before ador'd him as something more than Mortal, now had a Whip to give him some Lashes, while he strove not to break his Fetters; tho' if he had, it were impossible: but he pronounced a Woe and Revenge from his Eyes, that darted Fire, which was at once both aweful and terrible to behold.

When they thought they were sufficiently revenged on him, they unty'd him, almost fainting with Loss of Blood, from a thousand Wounds all over his Body; from which they had rent his Clothes, and led him bleeding and naked as he was, and loaded him all over with Irons; and then rubb'd his Wounds, to complete their Cruelty, with Indian Pepper, which had like to have made him raving mad; and, in this Condition made him so fast to the Ground, that he could not stir, if his Pains and Wounds would have given him Leave. They spared Imoinda, and did not let her see this Barbarity committed towards her Lord, but carried her down to Parham, and shut her up; which was not in Kindness to her, but for Fear she should die with the Sight, or miscarry, and then they should lose a young Slave, and perhaps the Mother.

You must know, that when the News was brought on Monday Morning, that Cæsar had betaken himself to the Woods, and carry'd with him all the Negroes, we were possess'd with extreme Fear, which no Persuasions could dissipate, that he would secure himself till Night, and then would come down and cut all our Throats. This Apprehension made all the Females of us fly down the River, to be secured; and while we were away, they acted this Cruelty; for I suppose I had Authority and Interest enough there, had I suspected any such Thing, to have prevented it: but we had not gone many Leagues, but the News overtook us, that Cæsar was taken and whipped liked a common Slave. We met on the River with Colonel Martin, a Man of great Gallantry, Wit, and Goodness, and whom I have celebrated in a Character of my new Comedy, by his own Name, in Memory of so brave a Man: He was wise and eloquent, and, from the Fineness of his Parts, bore a great Sway over the Hearts of all the Colony: He was a Friend to Cæsar, and resented this false Dealing with him very much. We carried him back to Parham, thinking to have made an Accommodation; when he came, the first News we heard, was, That the Governor was dead of a Wound Imoinda had given him; but it was not so well. But it seems, he would have the Pleasure of beholding the Revenge he took on Cæsar; and before the cruel Ceremony was finished, he dropt down; and then they perceived the Wound he had on his Shoulder was by a venom'd Arrow, which, as I said, his Indian Mistress healed by sucking the Wound.

We were no sooner arrived, but we went up to the Plantation to see Cæsar; whom we found in a very miserable and unexpressible Condition; and I have a thousand Times admired how he lived in so much tormenting Pain. We said all Things to him, that Trouble, Pity and Good-Nature could suggest, protesting our Innocency of the Fact, and our Abhorrence of such Cruelties; making a thousand Professions and Services to him, and begging as many Pardons for the Offenders, till we said so much, that he believed we had no Hand in his ill Treatment; but told us, He could never pardon Byam; as for Trefry, he confess'd he saw his Grief and Sorrow for his Suffering, which he could not hinder, but was like to have been beaten down by the very Slaves, for speaking in his Defence: But for Byam, who was their Leader, their Head, and should, by his Justice and Honour, have been an

Example to 'em, for him, he wished to live to take a dire Revenge of him; and said, It had been well for him, if he had sacrificed me, instead of giving me the comtemptible Whip. He refused to talk much; but begging us to give him our Hands, he took them, and protested never to lift up his to do us any Harm. He had a great Respect for Colonel Martin, and always took his Counsel like that of a Parent; and assured him, he would obey him in any Thing but his Revenge on Byam: 'Therefore (said he) for his own Safety, let him speedly dispatch me; for if I could dispatch myself, I would not, till that Justice were done to my injured Person, and the Contempt of a Soldier: No, I would not kill myself, even after a Whipping, but will be content to live with that Infamy, and be pointed at by every grinning Slave, till I have completed my Revenge; and then you shall see, that Oroonoko scorns to live with the Indignity that was put on Cæsar.' All we could do, could get no more Words from him; and we took Care to have him put immediately into a healing Bath, to rid him of his Pepper, and ordered a Chirurgeon to anoint him with healing Balm, which he suffer'd, and in some Time he began to be able to walk and eat. We failed not to visit him every Day, and to that End had him brought to an Apartment at Parham.

The Governor had no sooner recover'd, and had heard of the Menaces of Cæsar, but he called his Council, who (not to disgrace them, or burlesque the Government there) consisted of such notorious Villains as Newgate never transported; and, possibly, originally were such who understood neither the Laws of God or Man, and had no sort of Principles to make them worthy the Name of Men; but at the very Council-Table would contradict and fight with one another, and swear so bloodily, that 'twas terrible to hear and see 'em. (Some of 'em were afterwards hanged, when the Dutch took Possession of the Place, others sent off in Chains.) But calling these special Rulers of the Nation together, and requiring their Counsel in this weighty Affair, they all concluded, that (damn 'em) it might be their own Cases; and that Cæsar ought to be made an Example to all the Negroes, to fright 'em from daring to threaten their Betters, their Lords and Masters; and at this Rate no Man was safe from his own Slaves; and concluded, nemine contradicente, That Cæsar should be hanged.

Trefry then thought it Time to use his Authority, and told Byam, his Command did not extend to his Lord's Plantation; and that Parham was as much exempt from the Law as White-Hall; and that they ought no more to touch the Servants of the Lord (who there represented the King's Person) than they could those about the King himself; and that Parham was a Sanctuary; and tho' his Lord were absent in Person, his Power was still in being there, which he had entrusted with him, as far as the Dominions of his particular Plantations reached, and all that belonged to it; the rest of the Country, as Byam was Lieutenant to his Lord, he might exercise his Tyranny upon. Trefry had others as powerful, or more, that interested themselves in Cæsar's Life, and absolutely said, he should be defended. So turning the Governor, and his wise Council, out of Doors, (for they sat at Parham-House) we set a Guard upon our Lodging-Place, and would admit none but those we called Friends to us and Cæsar.

The Governor having remain'd wounded at Parham, till his Recovery was completed, Cæsar did not know but he was still there, and indeed for the most Part, his Time was spent there: for he was one that loved to live at other Peoples Expence, and if he were a Day absent, he was ten present there; and us'd to play, and walk, and hunt, and fish with Cæsar: So that Cæsar did not at all doubt, if he once recover'd Strength, but he should find an Opportunity of being revenged on him; though, after such a Revenge, he could not hope to live: for if he escaped the Fury of the English Mobile, who perhaps would have been glad of the Occasion to have killed him, he was resolved not to survive his Whipping; yet he had some tender Hours, a repenting Softness, which he called his Fits of Cowardice, wherein he struggled with Love for the Victory of his Heart, which took Part with his charming Imoinda there; but for the most Part, his Time was pass'd in melancholy Thoughts, and black Designs. He consider'd, if he should do this Deed, and die either in the Attempt, or after it, he left his lovely Imoinda a Prey, or at best a Slave to the enraged Multitude; his great Heart could not endure that Thought: Perhaps (said he) she may be first ravish'd by every Brute; expos'd first to their nasty Lusts, and then a shameful Death: No, he could not live a Moment under that Apprehension, too insupportable to be borne. These were his Thoughts, and his silent Arguments with his Heart, as he told us afterwards: So that now resolving not only to kill Byam, but all those he thought had enraged him; pleasing his great Heart with the fancy'd Slaughter he should make over the whole Face of the Plantation; he first resolved on a Deed, (that however horrid it first appear'd to us all) when we had heard his Reasons, we thought it brave and just. Being able to walk, and, as he believed, fit for the Execution of his great Design, he begg'd Trefry to trust him into the Air, believing a Walk would do him good; which was granted him; and taking Imoinda with him, as he used to do in his more happy and calmer Days, he led her up into a Wood, where (after with a thousand Sighs, and long gazing silently on her Face, while Tears gush'd, in spite of him, from his Eyes) he told her his Design, first of killing her, and then his Enemies, and next himself, and the Impossibility of escaping, and therefore he told her the Necessity of dying. He found the heroick Wife faster pleading for Death, than he was to propose it, when she found his fix'd Resolution; and, on her Knees, besought him not to leave her a Prey to his Enemies. He (grieved to Death) yet pleased at her noble Resolution, took her up, and embracing of her with all the Passion and Languishment of a dying Lover, drew his Knife to kill this Treasure of his Soul, this Pleasure of his Eyes; while Tears trickled down his Cheeks, hers were smiling with Joy she should die by so noble a Hand, and be sent into her own Country (for that's their Notion of the next World) by him she so tenderly loved, and so truly ador'd in this: For Wives have a Respect for their Husbands equal to what any other People pay a Deity; and when a Man finds any Occasion to quit his Wife, if he love her, she dies by his Hand; if not, he sells her, or suffers some other to kill her. It being thus, you may believe the Deed was soon resolv'd on; and 'tis not to be doubted, but the parting, the eternal Leave-taking of two such Lovers, so greatly born, so sensible, so beautiful, so young, and so fond, must be very moving, as the Relation of it was to me afterwards.

All that Love could say in such Cases, being ended, and all the intermitting Irresolutions being adjusted, the lovely, young and ador'd Victim lays herself down before the Sacrificer; while he, with a Hand resolved, and a Heart-breaking within, gave the fatal Stroke, first cutting her Throat, and then severing her yet smiling Face from that delicate Body, pregnant as it was with the Fruits of tenderest Love. As soon as he had done, he laid the Body decently on Leaves and Flowers, of which he made a Bed, and conceal'd it under the same Cover-lid of Nature; only her Face he left yet bare to look on: But when he found she was dead, and past all Retrieve, never more to bless him with her Eyes, and soft Language, his Grief swell'd up to Rage; he tore, he rav'd, he roar'd like some Monster of the Wood, calling on the lov'd Name of Imoinda. A thousand Times he turned the fatal Knife that did the Deed towards his own Heart, with a Resolution to go immediately after her; but dire Revenge, which was now a thousand Times more fierce in his Soul than before, prevents him; and he would cry out, 'No, since I have sacrific'd Imoinda to my Revenge, shall I lose that Glory which I have purchased so dear, as at the Price of the fairest, dearest, softest Creature that ever Nature made? No, no!' Then at her Name Grief would get the Ascendant of Rage, and he would lie down by her Side, and water her Face with Showers of Tears, which never were wont to fall from those Eyes; and however bent he was on his intended Slaughter, he had not Power to stir from the Sight of this dear Object, now more beloved, and more ador'd than ever.

He remained in this deplorable Condition for two Days, and never rose from the Ground where he had made her sad Sacrifice; at last rouzing from her Side, and accusing himself with living too long, now Imoinda was dead, and that the Deaths of those barbarous Enemies were deferred too long, he resolved now to finish the great Work: but offering to rise, he found his Strength so decay'd, that he reeled to and fro, like Boughs assailed by contrary Winds; so that he was forced to lie down again, and try to summon all his Courage to his Aid. He found his Brains turned round, and his Eyes were dizzy, and Objects appear'd not the same to him they were wont to do; his Breath was short, and all his Limbs surpriz'd with a Faintness he had never felt before. He had not eat in two Days, which was one Occasion of his Feebleness, but Excess of Grief was the greatest; yet still he hoped he should recover Vigour to act his Design, and lay expecting it yet six Days longer; still mourning over the dead Idol of his Heart, and striving every Day to rise, but could not.

In all this time you may believe we were in no little Affliction for Cæsar and his Wife; some were of Opinion he was escaped, never to return; others thought some Accident had happened to him: But however, we fail'd not to send out a hundred People several Ways, to search for him. A Party of about forty went that Way he took, among whom was Tuscan, who was perfectly reconciled to Byam: They had not gone very far into the Wood, but they smelt an unusual Smell, as of a dead Body; for Stinks must be very noisom, that can be distinguish'd among such a Quantity of natural Sweets, as every Inch of that Land produces: so that they concluded they should find him dead, or some body that was so; they pass'd on towards it, as loathsom as it was, and made such rustling among the Leaves that lie thick on the Ground, by continual falling, that Cæsar heard he was approach'd; and though he had, during the Space of these eight Days, endeavour'd to rise, but found he wanted Strength, yet looking up, and seeing his Pursuers, he rose, and reel'd to a neighbouring Tree, against which he fix'd his Back; and being within a dozen Yards of those that advanc'd and saw him, he call'd out to them, and bid them approach no nearer, if they would be safe. So that they stood still, and hardly believing their Eyes, that would persuade them that it was Cæsar that spoke to them, so much he was alter'd; they ask'd him, what he had done with his Wife, for they smelt a Stink that almost struck them dead? He pointing to the dead Body, sighing, cry'd, Behold her there. They put off the Flowers that cover'd her, with their Sticks, and found she was kill'd, and cry'd out, Oh, Monster! that hast murder'd thy Wife. Then asking him, why he did so cruel a Deed? He reply'd, He had no Leisure to answer impertinent Questions: 'You may go back (continued he) and tell the faithless Governor, he may thank Fortune that I am breathing my last; and that my Arm is too feeble to obey my Heart, in what it had design'd him': But his Tongue faultering, and trembling, he could scarce end what he was saying. The English taking Advantage by his Weakness, cry'd, Let us take him alive by all Means. He heard 'em; and, as if he had reviv'd from a Fainting, or a Dream, he cried out, 'No, Gentlemen, you are deceived; you will find no more Cæsars to be whipt; no more find a Faith in me; Feeble as you think me, I have Strength yet left to secure me from a second Indignity.' They swore all anew; and he only shook his Head, and beheld them with Scorn. Then they cry'd out, Who will venture on this single Man? Will nobody? They stood all silent, while Cæsar replied, Fatal will be the Attempt of the first Adventurer, let him assure himself, (and, at that Word, held up his Knife in a menacing Posture:) Look ye, ye faithless Crew, said he, 'tis not Life I seek, nor am I afraid of dying, (and at that Word, cut a Piece of Flesh from his own Throat, and threw it at 'em) yet still I would live if I could, till I had perfected my Revenge: But, oh! it cannot be; I feel Life gliding from my Eyes and Heart; and if I make not haste, I shall fall a Victim to the shameful Whip. At that, he rip'd up his own Belly, and took his Bowels and pull'd 'em out, with what Strength he could; while some, on their Knees imploring, besought him to hold his Hand. But when they saw him tottering, they cry'd out, Will none venture on him? A bold Englishman cry'd, Yes, if he were the Devil, (taking Courage when he saw him almost dead) and swearing a horrid Oath for his farewel to the World, he rush'd on him. Cæsar with his arm'd Hand, met him so fairly, as stuck him to the Heart, and he Fell dead at his feet. Tuscan seeing that, cry'd out, I love thee, O Cæsar! and therefore will not let thee die, if possible; and running to him, took him in his Arms; but, at the same time, warding a Blow that Cæsar made at his Bosom, he receiv'd it quite through his Arm; and Cæsar having not Strength to pluck the Knife forth, tho' he attempted it, Tuscan neither pull'd it out himself, nor suffer'd it to be pull'd out, but came down with it sticking in his Arm; and the Reason he gave for it, was, because the Air should not get into the Wound. They put their Hands a-cross, and carry'd Cæsar between six of 'em, fainting as he was, and they thought dead, or just dying; and they brought him to Parham, and laid him on a Couch, and had the Chirurgeon immediately to him, who dressed his Wounds, and sow'd up his Belly, and us'd Means to bring him to Life, which they effected. We ran all to see him; and, if before we thought him so beautiful a Sight, he was now so alter'd, that his Face was like a Death's-Head black'd over, nothing but Teeth and Eye-holes: For some Days we suffer'd no Body to speak to him, but caused Cordials to be poured down his Throat; which sustained his Life, and in six or seven Days he recovered his Senses: For, you must know, that Wounds are almost to a Miracle cur'd in the Indies; unless Wounds in the Legs, which they rarely ever cure.

When he was well enough to speak, we talk'd to him, and ask'd him some Questions about his Wife, and the Reasons why he kill'd her; and he then told us what I have related of that Resolution, and of his Parting, and he besought us we would let him die, and was extremely afflicted to think it was possible he might live: He assur'd us, if we did not dispatch him, he would prove very fatal to a great many. We said all we could to make him live, and gave him new Assurances; but he begg'd we would not think so poorly of him, or of his Love to Imoinda, to imagine we could flatter him to Life again: But the Chirurgeon assur'd him he could not live, and therefore he need not fear. We were all (but Cæsar) afflicted at this News, and the Sight was ghastly: His Discourse was sad; and the earthy Smell about him so strong, that I was persuaded to leave the Place for some time, (being my self but sickly, and very apt to fall into Fits of dangerous Illness upon any extraordinary Melancholy.) The Servants, and Trefry, and the Chirurgeons, promis'd all to take what possible Care they could of the Life of Cæsar; and I, taking Boat, went with other Company to Colonel Martin's, about three Days Journey down the River. But I was no sooner gone, than the Governor taking Trefry, about some pretended earnest Business, a Day's Journey up the River, having communicated his Design to one Banister, a wild Irish Man, one of the Council, a Fellow of absolute Barbarity, and fit to execute any Villany, but rich; he came up to Parham, and forcibly took Cæsar, and had him carried to the same Post where he was whipp'd; and causing him to be ty'd to it, and a great Fire made before him, he told him he should die like a Dog, as he was. Cæsar replied, This was the first piece of Bravery that ever Banister did, and he never spoke Sense till he pronounc'd that Word; and if he would keep it, he would declare, in the other World, that he was the only Man, of all the Whites, that ever he heard speak Truth. And turning to the Men that had bound him, he said, My Friends, am I to die, or to be whipt? And they cry'd, Whipt! no, you shall not escape so well. And then he reply'd, smiling, A Blessing on thee; and assur'd them they need not tie him, for he would stand fix'd like a Rock, and endure Death so as should encourage them to die: But if you whip me (said he) be sure you tie me fast.

He had learn'd to take Tobacco; and when he was assur'd he should die, he desir'd they would give him a Pipe in his Mouth, ready lighted; which they did: And the Executioner came, and first cut off his Members, and threw them into the Fire; after that, with an ill-favour'd Knife, they cut off his Ears and his Nose, and burn'd them; he still smoak'd on, as if nothing had touch'd him; then they hack'd off one of his Arms, and still he bore up and held his Pipe; but at the cutting off the other Arm, his Head sunk, and his Pipe dropt, and he gave up the Ghost, without a Groan, or a Reproach. My Mother and Sister were by him all the While, but not suffer'd to save him; so rude and wild were the Rabble, and so inhuman were the Justices who stood by to see the Execution, who after paid dear enough for their Insolence. They cut Cæsar into Quarters, and sent them to several of the chief Plantations: One Quarter was sent to Colonel Martin; who refus'd it, and swore, he had rather see the Quarters of Banister, and the Governor himself, than those of Cæsar, on his Plantations; and that he could govern his Negroes, without terrifying and grieving them with frightful Spectacles of a mangled King.

Thus died this great Man, worthy of a better Fate, and a more sublime Wit than mine to write his Praise: Yet, I hope, the Reputation of my Pen is considerable enough to make his glorious Name to survive to all Ages, with that of the brave, the beautiful and the constant Imoinda.

NOTES: Oroonoko.

**Appendix.** Oronooko: Epistle Dedicatory. Richard Maitland, fourth Earl of Lauderdale (1653-95), eldest son of Charles, third Earl of Lauderdale by Elizabeth, daughter and heiress of Richard Lauder of Halton, was born 20 June, 1653. Before his father succeeded to the Lauderdale title he was styled of Over-Gogar; after that event he was known as Lord Maitland. 9 October, 1678, he was sworn a Privy Councillor, and appointed Joint General of the Mint with his father. In 1681 he was made Lord Justice General, but deprived of that office three years later on account of suspected communications with his father-in-law, Argyll, who had fled to Holland in 1681. Maitland, however, was in truth a strong Jacobite, and refusing to accept the Revolution settlement became an exile with his King. He is said to have been present at the battle of the Boyne, 1 July, 1690. He resided for some time at St. Germains, but fell into disfavour, perhaps owing to the well-known protestant sympathies of his wife, Lady Agnes Campbell (1658-1734), second daughter of the fanatical Archibald, Earl of Argyll. From St. Germains Maitland retired to Paris, where he died in 1695. He had succeeded to the Earldom of Lauderdale 9 June, 1691, but was outlawed by the Court of Justiciary, 23 July, 1694. He left no issue. Lauderdale was the author of a verse translation of Virgil (8vo, 1718 and 2 Vols., 12mo, 1737). Dryden, to whom he sent a MS. copy from Paris, states that whilst working on his own version he consulted this whenever a crux appeared in the Latin text. Lauderdale also wrote A Memorial on the Estate of Scotland (about 1690), printed in Hooke's Correspondence (Roxburghe Club), and there wrongly ascribed to the third Earl, his father.

The Dedication only occurs in the first edition of Oronooko (1688), of which I can trace but one copy. This is in the library of Mr. F. F. Norcross of Chicago, whose brother-in-law, Mr. Harold B. Wrenn, most kindly transcribed and transmitted to me the Epistle Dedicatory. It, unfortunately, arrived too late for insertion at p. 129.

**I gave 'em to the King's Theatre.** Sir Robert Howard and Dryden's heroic tragedy, The Indian Queen, was produced at the Theatre Royal in mid-January, 1663. It is a good play, but the extraordinary success it attained was in no small measure due to the excellence and magnificence of the scenic effects and mounting. 27 January, Pepys noticed that the streets adjacent to the theatre were 'full of coaches at the new play The Indian Queen, which for show, they say, exceeds Henry VIII.' On 1 February he himself found it 'indeed a most pleasant show'. The grandeur of the mise en scène became long proverbial in theatrical history. Zempoalla, the Indian Queen, a fine rôle, was superbly acted by Mrs. Marshall, the leading tragedienne of the day. The feathered ornaments which Mrs. Behn mentions must have formed a quaint but doubtless striking addition to the actress's pseudo-classic attire. Bernbaum pictures 'Nell Gwynn[5] in the true costume of a Carib belle', a quite unfair deduction from Mrs. Behn's words.

**Osenbrigs.** More usually 'osnaburg', so named from Osnabrück in North Germany, a kind of coarse linen made in this town. Narborough's Journal, 1669 (An Account of Several Late Voyages, 1694), speaks of 'Cloth, Osenbrigs, Tobacco'. cf. Pennsylvania Col. Records (1732): 'That to each there be given a couple of Shirts, a Jackett, two pairs of trowsers of Oznabrigs.'

**as soon as the Governour arrived.** The Governor was Francis Willoughby, fifth Baron Willoughby of Parham (1613?-1666). He had arrived at Barbadoes, 29 April, 1650, and was received as Governor 7 May, which same day he caused Charles II to be proclaimed. An ardent royalist, he was dispossessed by an Act of Parliament, 4 March, 1652, and summoned back to England. At the Restoration he was reinstated, and arrived the second time with full powers in Barbadoes, 10 August, 1663. About the end of July, 1666, he was lost at sea on board the good ship Hope.

**my Father** . . . never arriv'd to possess the Honour design'd him. Bernbaum, following the mistaken statement that Mrs. Behn's father, John Amis, was a barber, argues that a man in such a position could hardly have obtained so important a post, and if her 'father was not sent to Surinam, the only reason she gives for being there disappears.' However, since we know her father to have been no barber, but of good family, this line of discussion falls to the ground.

**Brother to Harry Martin** the great Oliverian. Henry, or Harry, and George Marten were the two sons of Sir Henry Marten (ob. 1641) and his first wife, Elizabeth, who died 19 June, 1618. For the elder brother, Henry Marten, (1602-80), see note Vol. I, p. 457.

**The Deputy Governor**. William Byam was 'Lieutenant General of Guiana and Governor of Willoughby Land', 1661-7. Even previously to this he had gained no little influence and power in these colonies. He headed the forces that defended Surinam in 1667 against the Dutch Admiral Crynsens, who, however, proved victorious.

**my new Comedy**. The Younger Brother; or, The Amorous Jilt, posthumously produced under the auspices of, and with some alterations by, Charles Gildon at Drury Lane in 1696. George Marteen, acted by Powell, is the young and gallant hero of the comedy.

**his Council**. In The Widow Ranter Mrs. Behn draws a vivid picture of these deboshed ruffians.

**one Banister**. Sergeant Major James Banister being, after Byam's departure in 1667, 'the only remaining eminent person' became Lieutenant-Governor. It was he who in 1668 made the final surrender of the colony. Later, having quarrelled with the Dutch he was imprisoned by them.

[**Footnote 5**: Nell Gwynne had no part in the play.]


AGNES DE CASTRO

INTRODUCTION

The 'sweet sentimental tragedy' of Agnes de Castro was founded by Mrs. Behn upon a work by Mlle S. B. de Brillac, Agnès de Castro, nouvelle portugaise (1688), and various subsequent editions. In the same year (1688) as Mrs. Behn's Agnes de Castro; or, The Force of Generous Blood was published there appeared 'Two New Novels, i. The Art of Making Love. [1] ii. The Fatal Beauty of Agnes de Castro: Taken out of the History of Portugal. Translated from the French by P. B. G. [2] For R. Bentley' (12mo). Each has a separate title page. Bellon's version does not differ materially from Mrs. Behn, but she far exceeds him in spirit and niceness of style.

So much legend has surrounded the romantic history of the beautiful Ines de Castro that it is impossible fully to elucidate every detail of her life. Born in the early years of the fourteenth century, she was the daughter of Pedro Fernandez de Castro, major domo to Alphonso XI of Castille. She accompanied her relative, Dona Constança Manuel, daughter to the Duke of Peñafiel, to the court of Alphonso IV of Portugal when this lady was to wed the Infante Don Pedro. Here Ines excited the fondest love in Pedro's heart and the passion was reciprocated. She bore him several children, and there can be no doubt that Dona Constança was madly jealous of her husband's amour with her fair friend. 13 November, 1345, Constança died, and Pedro immediately married his mistress at Braganza in the presence of the Bishop of Guarda. Their nuptials were kept secret, and the old King kept pressing his son to take a wife. Before long his spies found out the reason of the Infante's constant refusals; and, beside himself with rage, he watched an opportunity whilst Pedro, on a great hunting expedition, was absent from Coimbra where they resided, and had Ines cruelly assassinated 7

January, 1355. The grief of Pedro was terrible, he plunged the country into civil war, and it was only by the tenderest solicitations of his mother and the authority of several holy monks and bishops that he was restrained from taking a terrible revenge upon his father. Alphonso died, his power curtailed, his end unhappy, May, 1357.

A very literature has grown up around the lovely Ines, and many more than a hundred items of interest could be enumerated. The best authority is J. de Araujo, whose monumental Bibliographia Inesiana was published in 1897. Mrs. Behn's novel was immensely popular and is included, with some unnecessary moral observations as preface, in Mrs. Griffith's A Collection of Novels (1777), Vol. III, which has a plate illustrating the tale. It was turned into French by Marie-Geneviève-Charlotte Tiroux d' Arconville (1720-1805), wife of a councillor of the Parliament, an aimable blue-stocking who devoted her life wholly to literature, and translated freely from English. This work is to be found in Romans (les deux premiers . . . tirés des Lettres Persanes . . . par M. Littleton et le dernier . . . d'un Recueil de Romans . . . de Madame Behn) traduits de l' Anglois, (Amsterdam, 1761.) It occurs again in Mélanges de Litterature (12mo, 1775, etc.), Vol. VI.

A tragedy, Agnes de Castro, written by that philosophical lady, Catherine Trotter (afterwards Cockburn), at the early age of sixteen, and produced at the Theatre Royal, 1696, with Powell, Verbruggen, Mrs. Rogers in the principal parts, is directly founded upon Mrs. Behn. It is a mediocre play, and the same can even more truly be said of Mallet's cold Elvira (1763). This was acted, however, with fair success thirteen times. Garrick played Don Pedro, his last original part, and Mrs. Cibber Elvira. Such dull exercises as C. Symmons, Inez, a tragedy (1796), and Ignez de Castro, a tragedy in verse, intended for Hoad's Magazine call for no comment.

There is a French play by Lamotte on the subject of Ines de Castro, which was first produced 6 April, 1723. Voltaire found the first four acts execrable and laughed consumedly. The fifth was so tender and true that he melted into tears. In Italian we have, from the pen of Bertoletti, Inez de Castro, tragedia, Milano, 1826.

In Spanish and Portuguese there are, of course, innumerable poems, treaties, tragedies, studies, romances. Lope de Vega wrote Dona Inez de Castro, and the beautiful episode of Camoens is deservedly famous. Antonio Ferreira's splendid tragedy is well known. First published in Comedias Famosas dos Doctores de Sa de Mirande (4to, 1622), it can also be read in Poemas lusitanos (2 Vols., 8vo, Lisbon, 1771). Domingo dos Reis Quita wrote a drama, Ignez de Castro, a translation of which, by Benjamin Thompson, was published in 1800. There is also a play Dona Ignez de Castro, by Nicolas Luiz, which was Englished by John Adamson, whose version was printed at Newcastle, 1808.

*[Footnote 1: Mr. Arundell Esdaile in his Bibliography of Fiction (printed before 1740) erroneously identifies this amusing little piece with Mrs. Behn's The Lover's Watch. It is, however, quite another thing, dealing with a pseudo-Turkish language of love.]*

*[Footnote 2: i.e., Peter Bellon, Gent. Bellon was an assiduous hackney writer and translator of the day. He has also left one comedy, The Mock Duellist; or, The French Valet (4to, 1675).]*

THE HISTORY OF AGNES de CASTRO

Tho' Love, all soft and flattering, promises nothing but Pleasures; yet its Consequences are often sad and fatal. It is not enough to be in love, to be happy; since Fortune, who is capricious, and takes delight to trouble the Repose of the most elevated and virtuous, has very little respect for passionate and tender Hearts, when she designs to produce strange Adventures.

Many Examples of past Ages render this Maxim certain; but the Reign of Don Alphonso the IVth, King of Portugal, furnishes us with one, the most extraordinary that History can produce.

He was the Son of that Don Denis, who was so successful in all his Undertakings, that it was said of him, that he was capable of performing whatever he design'd, (and of Isabella, a Princess of eminent Virtue) who when he came to inherit a flourishing and tranquil State, endeavour'd to establish Peace and Plenty in abundance in his Kingdom.

And to advance this his Design, he agreed on a Marriage between his Son Don Pedro (then about eight Years of Age) and Bianca, Daughter of Don Pedro, King of Castile; and whom the young Prince married when he arriv'd to his sixteenth Year.

Bianca brought nothing to Coimbra but Infirmities and very few Charms. Don Pedro, who was full of Sweetness and Generosity, lived nevertheless very well with her; but those Distempers of the Princess degenerating into the Palsy, she made it her request to retire, and at her Intercession the Pope broke the Marriage, and the melancholy Princess conceal'd her Languishment in a solitary Retreat: And Don Pedro, for whom they had provided another Match, married Constantia Manuel, Daughter of Don John Manuel, a Prince of the Blood of Castile, and famous for the Enmity he had to his King.

Constantia was promised to the King of Castile; but the King not keeping his word, they made no Difficulty of bestowing her on a young Prince, who was one Day to reign over a number of fine Provinces. He was but five and twenty years of Age, and the Man of all Spain that had the best Fashion and Grace: and with the most advantageous Qualities of the Body he possest those of the Soul, and shewed himself worthy in all things of the Crown that was destin'd for him.

The Princess Constantia had Beauty, Wit, and Generosity, in as great a measure as 'twas possible for a Woman to be possest with; her Merit alone ought to have attach'd Don Pedro, eternally to her; and certainly he had for her an Esteem, mix'd with so great a Respect, as might very well pass for Love with those that were not of a nice and curious Observation: but alas! his real Care was reserved for another Beauty.

Constantia brought into the World, the first Year after her Marriage, a Son, who was called Don Louis: but it scarce saw the Light, and dy'd almost as soon as born. The loss of this little Prince sensibly touched her, but the Coldness she observ'd in the Prince her Husband, went yet nearer her Heart; for she had given her self absolutely up to her Duty, and had made her Tenderness for him her only Concern: But puissant Glory, which ty'd her so entirely to the Interest of the Prince of Portugal, open'd her Eyes upon his Actions, where she observ'd nothing in his Caresses and Civilities that was natural, or could satisfy her delicate Heart.

At first she fancy'd her self deceiv'd, but time having confirmed her in what she fear'd, she sighed in secret; yet had that Consideration for the Prince, as not to let him see her Disorder: and which nevertheless she could not conceal from Agnes de Castro, who lived with her, rather as a Companion, than a Maid of Honour, and whom her Friendship made her infinitely distinguish from the rest.

This Maid, so dear to the Princess, very well merited the Preference her Mistress gave her; she was beautiful to excess, wise, discreet, witty, and had more Tenderness for Constantia than she had for her self, having quitted her Family, which was illustrious, to give her self wholly to the Service of the Princess, and to follow her into Portugal. It was into the Bosom of this Maid, that the Princess unladed her first Moans; and the charming Agnes forgot nothing that might give ease to her afflicted Heart.

Nor was Constantia the only Person who complained of Don Pedro: Before his Divorce from Bianca, he had expressed some Care and Tenderness for Elvira Gonzales, Sister to Don Alvaro Gonzales, Favourite to the King of Portugal; and this Amusement in the young Years of the Prince, had made a deep Impression on Elvira, who flatter'd her Ambition with the Infirmities of Bianca. She saw, with a secret Rage, Constantia take her place, who was possest with such Charms, that quite divested her of all Hopes.

Her Jealousy left her not idle, she examined all the Actions of the Prince, and easily discover'd the little Regard he had for the Princess; but this brought him not back to her. And it was upon very good grounds that she suspected him to be in love with some other Person, and possessed with a new Passion; and which she promised herself, she would destroy as soon as she could find it out. She had a Spirit altogether proper for bold and hazardous Enterprizes; and the Credit of her Brother gave her so much Vanity, as all the Indifference of the Prince was not capable of humbling.

The Prince languished, and concealed the Cause with so much Care, that 'twas impossible for any to find it out. No publick Pleasures were agreeable to him, and all Conversations were tedious; and it was Solitude alone that was able to give him any ease.

This Change surprized all the World. The King, who loved his Son very tenderly, earnestly pressed him to know the Reason of his Melancholy; but the Prince made no answer, but only this, That it was the effect of his Temper.

But Time ran on, and the Princess was brought to bed of a second Son, who liv'd, and was called Fernando. Don Pedro forc'd himself a little to take part in the publick Joy, so that they believ'd his Humour was changing; but this Appearance of a Calm endur'd not long, and he fell back again into his black Melancholy.

The artful Elvira was incessantly agitated in searching out the Knowledge of this Secret. Chance wrought for her; and, as she was walking, full of Indignation and Anger, in the Garden of the Palace of Coimbra, she found the Prince of Portugal sleeping in an obscure Grotto.

Her Fury could not contain it self at the sight of this loved Object, she roll'd her Eyes upon him, and perceived in spite of Sleep, that some Tears escaped his Eyes; the Flame which burnt yet in her Heart, soon grew soft and tender there: But oh! she heard him sigh, and after that utter these words, Yes, Divine Agnes, I will sooner die than let you know it: Constantia shall have nothing to reproach me with. Elvira was enraged at this Discourse, which represented to her immediately, the same moment, Agnes de Castro with all her Charms; and not at all doubting, but it was she who possest the Heart of Don Pedro, she found in her Soul more Hatred for this fair Rival, than Tenderness for him.

The Grotto was not a fit Place to make Reflections in, or to form Designs. Perhaps her first Transports would have made her waken him, if she had not perceived a Paper lying under his Hand, which she softly seiz'd on; and that she might not be surprized in the reading it, she went out of the Garden with as much haste as confusion.

When she was retired to her Apartment, she open'd the Paper, trembling, and found in it these Verses, writ by the Hand of Don Pedro; and which, in appearance, he had newly then compos'd.

In vain, Oh! Sacred Honour, you debate
The mighty Business in my Heart:
Love! Charming Love! rules all my Fate;
Interest and Glory claim no part.
The God, sure of his Victory, triumphs there,
And will have nothing in his Empire share.

In vain, Oh! Sacred Duty, you oppose;
In vain, your Nuptial Tye you plead:
Those forc'd Devoirs LOVE overthrows,
And breaks the Vows he never made.
Fixing his fatal Arrows every where,
I burn and languish in a soft Despair.

Fair Princess, you to whom my Faith is due;
Pardon the Destiny that drags me on:
'Tis not my fault my Heart's untrue,
I am compell'd to be undone.
My Life is yours, I gave it with my Hand,
But my Fidelity I can't command.

Elvira did not only know the Writing of Don Pedro, but she knew also that he could write Verses. And seeing the sad Part which Constantia had in these which were now fallen into her hands, she made no scruple of resolving to let the Princess see 'em: but that she might not be suspected, she took care not to appear in this Business her self; and since it was not enough for Constantia to know that the Prince did not love her, but that she must know also that he was a Slave to Agnes de Castro, Elvira caused these few Verses to be written in an unknown Hand, under those writ by the Prince.

Sleep betrayed th' unhappy Lover,
While Tears were streaming from his Eyes;
His heedless Tongue without disguise,
The Secret did discover:
The Language of his Heart declare,
That Agnes' Image triumphs there.

Elvira regarded neither Exactness nor Grace in these Lines: And if they had but the effect she design'd, she wished no more.

Her Impatience could not wait till the next day to expose them: she therefore went immediately to the Lodgings of the Princess, who was then walking in the Garden of the Palace; and passing without resistance, even to her Cabinet, she put the Paper into a Book, in which the Princess used to read, and went out again unseen, and satisfy'd with her good Fortune.

As soon as Constantia was return'd, she enter'd into her Cabinet, and saw the Book open, and the Verses lying in it, which were to cost her so dear: She soon knew the Hand of the Prince which was so familiar to her; and besides the Information of what she had always fear'd, she understood it was Agnes de Castro (whose Friendship alone was able to comfort her in her Misfortunes) who was the fatal Cause of it: she read over the Paper an hundred times, desiring to give her Eyes and Reason the

Lye; but finding but too plainly she was not deceiv'd, she found her Soul possest with more Grief than Anger: when she consider'd, as much in love as the Prince was, he had kept his Torment secret. After having made her moan, without condemning him, the Tenderness she had for him, made her shed a Torrent of Tears, and inspir'd her with a Resolution of concealing her Resentment.

She would certainly have done it by a Virtue extraordinary, if the Prince, who missing his Verses when he waked, and fearing they might fall into indiscreet Hands, had not enter'd the Palace, all troubled with his Loss; and hastily going into Constantia's Apartment, saw her fair Eyes all wet with Tears, and at the same instant cast his own on the unhappy Verses that had escaped from his Soul, and now lay before the Princess.

He immediately turned pale at this sight, and appear'd so mov'd, that the generous Princess felt more Pain than he did: 'Madam, said he, (infinitely alarm'd) from whom had you that Paper? It cannot come but from the Hand of some Person, answer'd Constantia, who is an Enemy both to your Repose and mine. It is the Work, Sir, of your own Hand; and doubtless the Sentiment of your Heart. But be not surprized, and do not fear; for if my Tenderness should make it pass for a Crime in you, the same Tenderness which nothing is able to alter, shall hinder me from complaining.'

The Moderation and Calmness of Constantia, served only to render the Prince more asham'd and confus'd. How generous are you, Madam, (pursu'd he) and how unfortunate am I! Some Tears accompany'd his Words, and the Princess, who lov'd him with extreme Ardour, was so sensibly touch'd, that it was a good while before she could utter a word. Constantia then broke silence, and shewing him what Elvira had caus'd to be written: You are betray'd, Sir, (added she) you have been heard speak, and your Secret is known. It was at this very moment that all the Forces of the Prince abandon'd him; and his Condition was really worthy Compassion: He could not pardon himself the involuntary Crime he had committed, in exposing the lovely and the innocent Agnes. And tho' he was convinced of the Virtue and Goodness of Constantia, the Apprehensions that he had, that this modest and prudent Maid might suffer by his Conduct, carry'd him beyond all Consideration.

The Princess, who heedfully survey'd him, saw so many Marks of Despair in his Face and Eyes, that she was afraid of the Consequences; and holding out her Hand, in a very obliging manner to him, she said, 'I promise you, Sir, I will never more complain of you, and that Agnes shall always be very dear to me; you shall never hear me make you any Reproaches: And since I cannot possess your Heart, I will content myself with endeavouring to render myself worthy of it.' Don Pedro, more confus'd and dejected than before he had been, bent one of his Knees at the feet of Constantia, and with respect kiss'd that fair kind Hand she had given him, and perhaps forgot Agnes for a moment.

But Love soon put a stop to all the little Advances of Hymen; the fatal Star that presided over the Destiny of Don Pedro had not yet vented its Malignity; and one moment's sight of Agnes gave new Force to his Passion.

The Wishes and Desires of this charming Maid had no part in this Victory; her Eyes were just, tho' penetrating, and they searched not in those of the Prince, what they had a desire to discover to her.

As she was never far from Constantia, Don Pedro was no sooner gone out of the Closet, but Agnes enter'd; and finding the Princess all pale and languishing in her Chair, she doubted not but there was some sufficient Cause for her Affliction: she put herself in the same Posture the Prince had been in before, and expressing an Inquietude, full of Concern; 'Madam, said she, by all your Goodness, conceal not from me the Cause of your Trouble. Alas, Agnes, reply'd the Princess, what would you know? And what should I tell you? The Prince, the Prince, my dearest Maid, is in love; the Hand that he gave me, was not a Present of his Heart; and for the Advantage of this Alliance, I must become the Victim of it. What! the Prince in Love! (reply'd Agnes, with an Astonishment mix'd with Indignation) What Beauty can dispute the Empire over a Heart so much your due? Alas, Madam, all the Respect I owe him, cannot hinder me from murmuring against him. Accuse him of nothing, (interrupted Constantia) he does what he can; and I am more oblig'd to him for desiring to be faithful, than if I possest his real Tenderness. It is not enough to fight, but to overcome; and the Prince does more in the Condition wherein he is, than I ought reasonably to hope for: In fine, he is my Husband, and an agreeable one; to whom nothing is wanting, but what I cannot inspire; that is, a Passion which would have made me but too happy. Ah! Madam, (cry'd out Agnes, transported with her Tenderness for the Princess) he is a blind and stupid Prince, who knows not the precious Advantages he possesses. He must surely know something, (reply'd the Princess modestly.) But, Madam, (reply'd Agnes) Is there any thing, not only in Portugal, but in all Spain, that can compare with you? And without considering the charming Qualities of your Person, can we enough admire those of your Soul? My dear Agnes, (interrupted Constantia, sighing) she who robs me of my Husband's Heart, has but too many Charms to plead his Excuse; since it is thou, Child, whom Fortune makes use of, to give me the killing Blow. Yes, Agnes, the Prince loves thee; and the Merit I know thou art possest of, puts bounds to my Complaints, without suffering me to have the least Resentment.'

The delicate Agnes little expected to hear what the Princess told her: Thunder would have less surpriz'd, and less oppres'd her. She remain'd a long time without speaking; but at last, fixing her Looks all frightful on Constantia, 'What say you, Madam? (cry'd she) And what Thoughts have you of me? What, that I should betray you? And coming hither only full of Ardor to be the Repose of your Life, do I bring a fatal Poison to afflict it? What Detestation must I have for the Beauty they find in me, without aspiring to make it appear? And how ought I to curse the unfortunate Day, on which I first saw the Prince? But, Madam, it cannot be me whom Heaven has chosen to torment you, and to destroy all your Tranquillity: No, it cannot be so much my Enemy, to put me to so great a Tryal. And if I were that odious Person, there is no Punishment, to which I would not condemn my self. It is Elvira, Madam, the Prince loves, and loved before his Marriage with you, and also before his Divorce from Bianca; and somebody has made an indiscreet Report to you of this Intrigue of his Youth: But, Madam, what was in the time of Bianca, is nothing to you. It is certain that Don Pedro loves you, (answer'd the Princess) and I have Vanity enough to believe, that, none besides your self could have disputed his Heart with me: But the Secret is discover'd, and Don Pedro has not disown'd it. What, (interrupted Agnes, more surpriz'd than ever) is it then from himself you have learned his Weakness?' The Princess then shew'd her the Verses, and there was never any Despair like to hers.

While they were both thus sadly employ'd, both sighing, and both weeping, the impatient Elvira, who was willing to learn the Effect of her Malice, returned to the Apartment of the Princess, where she freely enter'd; even to the Cabinet where these unhappy Persons were: who all afflicted and troubled as they were, blushed at her approach, whose Company they did not desire: She had the Pleasure to see Constantia hide from her the Paper which had been the Cause of all their Trouble, and which the Princess had never seen, but for her Spite and Revenge; and to observe also in the Eyes of the Princess, and those of Agnes, an immoderate Grief: She staid in the Cabinet as long as it was necessary to be assur'd, that she had succeeded in her Design; but the Princess, who did not desire such a Witness of the Disorder in which she then was, pray'd to be left alone. Elvira then went out of the Cabinet, and Agnes de Castro withdrew at the same time.

It was in her own Chamber, that Agnes examining more freely this Adventure, found it as cruel as Death. She loved Constantia sincerely, and had not till then any thing more than an Esteem, mixt with Admiration, for the Prince of Portugal; which indeed, none could refuse to so many fine Qualities. And looking on her self as the most unfortunate of her Sex, as being the Cause of all the Sufferings of the Princess, to whom she was obliged for the greatest Bounties, she spent the whole

Night in Tears and Complaints, sufficient to have reveng'd Constantia for all the Griefs she made her suffer.

The Prince, on his side, was in no great Tranquillity; the Generosity of his Princess increas'd his Remorse, without diminishing his Love: he fear'd, and with reason, that those who were the occasion of Constantia's seeing those Verses, should discover his Passion to the King, from whom he hoped for no Indulgence: and he would most willingly have given his Life, to have been free from this Extremity.

In the mean time the afflicted Princess languished in a most deplorable Sadness; she found nothing in those who were the Cause of her Misfortunes, but things fitter to move her Tenderness than her Anger: It was in vain that Jealousy strove to combat the Inclination she had to love her fair Rival; nor was there any occasion of making the Prince less dear to her: and she felt neither Hatred, nor so much as Indifference for innocent Agnes.

While these three disconsolate Persons abandon'd themselves to their Melancholy, Elvira, not to leave her Vengeance imperfect, study'd in what manner she might bring it to the height of its Effects. Her Brother, on whom she depended, shew'd her a great deal of Friendship, and judging rightly that the Love of Don Pedro to Agnes de Castro would not be approved by the King, she acquainted Don Alvaro her Brother with it, who was not ignorant of the Passion the Prince had once protested to have for his Sister. He found himself very much interested in this News, from a second Passion he had for Agnes; which the Business of his Fortune had hitherto hindred him from discovering: and he expected a great many Favours from the King, that might render the Effort of his Heart the more considerable.

He hid not from his Sister this one thing, which he found difficult to conceal; so that she was now possest with a double Grief, to find Agnes Sovereign of all the Hearts to which she had a pretension.

Don Alvaro was one of those ambitious Men, that are fierce without Moderation, and proud without Generosity; of a melancholy, cloudy Humour, of a cruel Inclination, and to effect his Ends, found nothing difficult or unlawful. Naturally he lov'd not the Prince, who, on all accounts, ought to have held the first Rank in the Heart of the King, which should have set bounds to the Favour of Don Alvaro; who when he knew the Prince was his Rival, his Jealousy increas'd his Hate of him: and he conjured Elvira to employ all her Care, to oppose an Engagement that could not but be destructive to them both; she promised him, and he not very well satisfy'd, rely'd on her Address.

Don Alvaro, who had too lively a Representation within himself, of the Beauties and Grace of the Prince of Portugal, thought of nothing, but how to combat his Merits, he himself not being handsome, or well made: His Fashion was as disagreeable as his Humour, and Don Pedro had all the Advantages that one Man may possibly have over another. In fine, all that Don Alvaro wanted, adorn'd the Prince: but as he was the Husband of Constantia, and depended upon an absolute Father, and that Don Alvaro was free, and Master of a good Fortune, he thought himself more assur'd of Agnes, and fixed his Hopes on that Thought.

He knew very well, that the Passion of Don Pedro could not but inspire a violent Anger in the Soul of the King. Industrious in doing ill, his first Business was to carry this unwelcome News to him. After he had given time to his Grief, and had compos'd himself to his Desire, he then besought the King to interest himself in his amorous Affair, and to be the Protector of his Person.

Tho' Don Alvaro had no other Merit to recommend him to the King, than a continual and blind Obedience to all his Commands; yet he had favour'd him with several Testimonies of his vast Bounty:

and considering the Height to which the King's Liberality had rais'd him, there were few Ladies that would have refused his Alliance. The King assured him of the Continuation of his Friendship and Favour, and promised him, if he had any Authority, he would give him the charming Agnes.

Don Alvaro, perfectly skilful in managing his Master, answer'd the King's last Bounties with a profound Submission. He had yet never told Agnes what he felt for her; but he thought now he might make a publick Declaration of it, and sought all means to do it.

The Gallantry which Coimbra seem'd to have forgotten, began now to be awakened. The King to please Don Alvaro, under pretence of diverting Constantia, order'd some publick Sports, and commanded that every thing should be magnificent.

Since the Adventure of the Verses, Don Pedro endeavour'd to lay a constraint on himself, and to appear less troubled; but in his heart he suffer'd always alike: and it was not but with great uneasiness he prepar'd himself for the Tournament. And since he could not appear with the Colours of Agnes, he took those of his Wife, without Device, or any great Magnificence.

Don Pedro adorn'd himself with the Liveries of Agnes de Castro; and this fair Maid, who had yet found no Consolation from what the Princess had told her, had this new cause of being displeas'd.

Don Pedro appear'd in the List with an admirable Grace; and Don Alvaro, who looked on this Day as his own, appear'd there all shining with Gold, mix'd with Stones of Blue, which were the Colours of Agnes; and there were embroider'd all over his Equipage, flaming Hearts of Gold on blue Velvet, and Nets for the Snares of Love, with abundance of double A's; his Device was a Love coming out of a Cloud, with these Verses written underneath:

Love from a Cloud breaks like the God of Day,   And to the World his Glories does display;   To gaze on charming Eyes, and make 'em know,   What to soft Hearts, and to his Power they owe.

The Pride of Don Alvaro was soon humbled at the feet of the Prince of Portugal, who threw him against the Ground, with twenty others, and carry'd alone the Glory of the Day. There was in the Evening a noble Assembly at Constantia's, where Agnes would not have been, unless expresly commanded by the Princess. She appear'd there all negligent and careless in her Dress, but yet she appear'd all beautiful and charming. She saw, with disdain, her Name, and her Colours, worn by Don Alvaro, at a publick Triumph; and if her Heart was capable of any tender Motions, it was not for such a Man as he for whom her Delicacy destin'd them: She look'd on him with a Contempt, which did not hinder him from pressing so near, that there was a necessity for her to hear what he had to declare to her.

She treated him not uncivilly, but her Coldness would have rebated the Courage of any but Alvaro. 'Madam, said he, (when he could be heard of none but herself) I have hitherto concealed the Passion you have inspired me with, fearing it should displease you; but it has committed a Violence on my Respect; and I could no longer conceal it from you. I never reflected on your Actions (answer'd Agnes with all the Indifference of which she was capable) and if you think you offend me, you are in the wrong to make me perceive it. This Coldness is but an ill Omen for me (reply'd Don Alvaro) and if you have not found me out to be your Lover to-day, I fear you will never approve my Passion.'

'Oh! what a time have you chosen to make it appear to me? (pursued Agnes.) Is it so great an Honour for me, that you must take such care to shew it to the World? And do you think that I am so desirous of Glory, that I must aspire to it by your Actions? If I must, you have very ill maintain'd it in the Tournament; and if it be that Vanity that you depend upon, you will make no great progress on a Soul that is not fond of Shame. If you were possest of all the Advantages, which the Prince has this day carried away, you yet ought to consider what you are going about; and it is not a Maid like me, who is touched with Enterprizes, without respect or permission.'

The Favourite of the King was too proud to hear Agnes, without Indignation: but as he was willing to conceal it, and not offend her, he made not his Resentment appear; and considering the Observation she made on the Triumphs of Don Pedro, (which increased his Jealousies) 'If I have not overcome at the Tournament, reply'd he, I am not the less in love for being vanquish'd, nor less capable of Success on occasion.'

They were interrupted here, but from that day, Don Alvaro, who had open'd the first Difficulties, kept no more his wonted Distance, but perpetually persecuted Agnes; yet, tho' he were protected by the King, that inspir'd in her never the more Consideration for him. Don Pedro was always ignorant by what means the Verses he had lost in the Garden, fell into the hands of Constantia. As the Princess appeared to him indulgent, he was only concerned for Agnes; and the love of Don Alvaro, which was then so well known, increas'd the Pain: and had he been possess'd of the Authority, he would not have suffer'd her to have been expos'd to the Persecutions of so unworthy a Rival. He was also afraid of the King's being advertised of his Passion, but he thought not at all of Elvira, nor apprehended any Malice from her Resentment.

While she burnt with a Desire of destroying Agnes, against whom she vented all her Venom, she was never weary of making new Reports to her Brother, assuring him, that tho' they could not prove that Agnes made any returns to the Tenderness of the Prince, yet that was the Cause of Constantia's Grief: And, that if this Princess should die of it, Don Pedro might marry Agnes. In fine, she so incens'd the jealous Don Alvaro's Jealousy, that he could not hinder himself from running immediately to the King, with the discovery of all he knew, and all he guest, and who, he had the pleasure to find, was infinitely inrag'd at the News. 'My dear Alvaro, said the King, you shall instantly marry this dangerous Beauty: And let Possession assure your Repose and mine. If I have protected you on other Occasions, judge what a Service of so great an Importance for me, would make me undertake; and without any reserve, the Forces of this State are in your power, and almost any thing that I can give shall be assured you, so you render your self Master of the Destiny of Agnes.'

Don Alvaro pleas'd, and vain with his Master's Bounty, made use of all the Authority he gave him: He passionately lov'd Agnes, and would not, on the sudden, make use of Violence; but resolv'd with himself to employ all possible Means to win her fairly; yet if that fail'd, to have recourse to force, if she continued always insensible.

While Agnes de Castro (importun'd by his Assiduities, despairing at the Grief of Constantia, and perhaps made tender by those she had caus'd in the Prince of Portugal) took a Resolution worthy of her Virtue; yet, amiable as Don Pedro was, she found nothing in him, but his being Husband to Constantia, that was dear to her: And, far from encouraging the Power she had got over his Heart, she thought of nothing but of removing from Coimbra. The Passion of Don Alvaro, which she had no inclination to favour, served her as a Pretext; and press'd with the fear of causing, in the end, a cruel Divorce between the Prince and his Princess, she went to find Constantia, with a trouble, which all her Care was not able to hide from her.

The Princess easily found it out; and their common Misfortunes having not chang'd their Friendship, 'What ails you, Agnes? (said the Princess to her, in a soft Tone, and with her ordinary Sweetness) And what new Misfortune causes that sadness in thy Looks? Madam (reply'd Agnes, shedding a Rivulet of Tears) the Obligations and Ties I have to you, put me upon a cruel Tryal; I had bounded the

Felicity of my Life in hope of passing it near your Highness, yet I must carry to some other part of the World this unlucky Face of mine, which renders me nothing but ill Offices: And it is to obtain that Liberty, that I am come to throw my self at your feet; looking upon you as my Sovereign.'

Constantia was so surpriz'd and touch'd with the Proposition of Agnes, that she lost her Speech for some moments; Tears, which were sincere, express'd her first Sentiments: And after having shed abundance, to give a new mark of her Tenderness to the fair afflicted Agnes, she with a sad and melancholy Look, fix'd her Eyes upon her, and holding out her Hand to her, in a most obliging manner, sighing, cry'd - 'You will then, my dear Agnes, leave me; and expose me to the Griefs of seeing you no more? Alas, Madam, (interrupted this lovely Maid) hide from the unhappy Agnes a Bounty which does but increase her Misfortunes: It is not I, Madam, that would leave you; it is my Duty, and my Reason that orders my Fate. And those Days which I shall pass far from you, promise me nothing to oblige me to this Design, if I did not see my self absolutely forc'd to it. I am not ignorant of what passes at Coimbra; and I shall be an Accomplice of the Injustice there committed, if I should stay there any longer. Ah, I know your Virtue, (cry'd Constantia) and you may remain here in all safety, while I am your Protectress; and let what will happen, I will accuse you of nothing. There's no answering for what's to come, (reply'd Agnes, sadly) and I shall be sufficiently guilty, if my Presence cause Sentiments, which cannot be innocent. Besides, Madam, the Importunities of Don Alvaro are insupportable to me; and tho' I find nothing but Aversion to him, since the King protects his Insolence, and he's in a condition of undertaking any thing, my Flight is absolutely necessary. But, Madam, tho' he has nothing but what seems odious to me; I call Heaven to witness, that if I could cure the Prince by marrying Don Alvaro, I would not consider of it a moment; and finding in my Punishment the Consolation of sacrificing my self to my Princess, I would support it without murmuring. But if I were the Wife of Don Alvaro, Don Pedro would always look upon me with the same Eyes: So that I find nothing more reasonable for me, than to hide my self in some Corner of the World; where, tho' I shall most certainly live without Pleasure, yet I shall preserve the Repose of my dearest Mistress. All the Reason you find in this Design, (answered the Princess) cannot oblige me to approve of your Absence: Will it restore me the Heart of Don Pedro? And will he not fly away with you? His Grief is mine, and my Life is ty'd to his; do not make him despair then, if you love me. I know you, I tell you so once more; and let your Power be ever so great over the Heart of the Prince, I will not suffer you to abandon us.'

Tho' Agnes thought she had perfectly known Constantia, yet she did not expect to find so intire a Virtue in her, which made her think her self more happy, and the Prince more criminal. 'Oh, Wisdom! Oh, Bounty without Example! (cry'd she) Why is it, that the cruel Destinies do not give you all you deserve? You are the disposer of my Actions, (continued she in kissing the Hand of Constantia) I'll do nothing but what you'll have me: But consider, and weigh well the Reasons that ought to counsel you in the Measures you oblige me to take.'

Don Pedro, who had not seen the Princess all that day, came in then, and finding 'em both extremely troubled, with a fierce Impatience, demanded the Cause: 'Sir, answered Constantia, Agnes too wise, and too scrupulous, fears the Effects of her Beauty, and will live no longer at Coimbra; and it was on this Subject, (which cannot be agreeable to me) that she ask'd my Advice.' The Prince grew pale at this Discourse, and snatching the Words from her Mouth (with more concern than possest either of them) cry'd with a Voice very feeble, 'Agnes cannot fail if she follow your Counsel, Madam: and I leave you full liberty to give it her.' He then immediately went out, and the Princess, whose Heart he perfectly possest, not being able to hide her Displeasure, said, 'My dear Agnes, if my Satisfaction did not only depend on your Conversation, I should desire it of you, for Don Pedro's sake; it is the only Advantage that his unfortunate Love can hope: And would not the World have reason to call me barbarous, if I contribute to deprive him of that? But the sight of me will prove a Poison to him (reply'd Agnes) And what should I do, my Princess, if after the Reserve he has hitherto kept, his

Mouth should add anything to the Torments I have already felt, by speaking to me of his Flame? You would hear him sure, without causing him to despair, (reply'd Constantia) and I should put this Obligation to the account of the rest you have done. Would you then have me expect those Events which I fear, Madam? (reply'd Agnes) Well, I will obey, but just Heaven (pursued she) if they prove fatal, do not punish an innocent Heart for it.' Thus this Conversation ended. Agnes withdrew into her Chamber, but it was not to be more at ease.

What Don Pedro had learn'd of the Design of Agnes, caus'd a cruel Agitation in his Soul; he wished he had never loved her, and desir'd a thousand times to die: But it was not for him to make Vows against a thing which Fate had design'd him; and whatever Resolutions he made, to bear the Absence of Agnes, his Tenderness had not force enough to consent to it.

After having, for a long time, combated with himself, he determined to do what was impossible for him to let Agnes do. His Courage reproach'd him with the Idleness, in which he past the most youthful and vigorous part of his Days: and making it appear to the King, that his Allies, and even the Prince Don John Emanuel, his Father-in-law, had concerns in the World which demanded his Presence on the Frontiers, he easily obtain'd Liberty to make this Journey, to which the Princess would put no Obstacle.

Agnes saw him part without any Concern, but it was not upon the account of any Aversion she had to him. Don Alvaro began then to make his Importunity an open Persecution; he forgot nothing that might touch the insensible Agnes, and made use, a long time, only of the Arms of Love: But seeing that this Submission and Respect was to no purpose, he form'd strange Designs.

As the King had a deference for all his Counsels, it was not difficult to inspire him with what he had a mind to: He complain'd of the ungrateful Agnes, and forgot nothing that might make him perceive that she was not cruel to him on his account, but from the too much Sensibility she had for the Prince. The King, who was extreme angry at this, reiterated all the Promises he had made him.

The King had not yet spoken to Agnes in favour of Don Alvaro; and not doubting but his Approbation would surmount all Obstacles, he took an occasion to entertain her with it: And removing some distance from those who might hear him, 'I thought Don Alvaro had Merit enough (said he to her) to have obtained a little share in your Esteem; and I could not imagine there would have been any necessity of my solliciting it for him: I know you are very charming, but he has nothing that renders him unworthy of you; and when you shall reflect on the Choice my Friendship has made of him from among all the great Men of my Court, you will do him at the same time Justice. His Fortune is none of the meanest, since he has me for his Protector: He is nobly born, a Man of Honour and Courage: he adores you, and it seems to me that all these Reasons are sufficient to vanquish your Pride.'

The Heart of Agnes was so little disposed to give it self to Don Alvaro, that all the King of Portugal had said had no effect on her in his favour. 'If Don Alvaro, Sir, (answered she) were without Merit, he possesses Advantages enough in the Bounty your Majesty is pleased to honour him with, to make him Master of all things, it is not that I find any Defect in him that I answer not his Desires: But, Sir, by what obstinate Power would you that I should love, if Heaven has not given me a Soul that is tender? And why should you pretend that I should submit to him, when nothing is dearer to me than my liberty? You are not so free, nor so insensible, as you say, (answer'd the King, blushing with Anger;) and if your Heart were exempt from all sorts of Affection, he might expect a more reasonable Return than what he finds. But imprudent Maid, conducted by an ill Fate, (added he in fury) what Pretensions have you to Don Pedro? Hitherto I have hid the Chagrin, which his Weakness, and yours give me; but it was not the less violent for being hid. And since you oblige me to break out, I must tell you, that if my Son were not already married to Constantia, he should never be your Husband; renounce then those vain Ideas, which will cure him, and justify you.'

The courageous Agnes was scarce Mistress of the first Transports, at a Discourse so full of Contempt; but calling her Virtue to the aid of her Anger, she recover'd herself by the assistance of Reason: And considering the Outrage she receiv'd, not as coming from a great King, but a Man blinded and possest by Don Alvaro, she thought him not worthy of her Resentment; her fair Eyes animated themselves with so shining a vivacity, they answer'd for the purity of her Sentiments; and fixing them steadfastly on the King, 'If the Prince Don Pedro have Weaknesses, (reply'd she, with an Air disdainful) he never communicated 'em to me; and I am certain, I never contributed wilfully to 'em: But to let you see how little I regard your Defiance, and to put my Glory in safety, I will live far from you, and all that belongs to you: Yes, Sir, I will quit Coimbra with pleasure; and for this Man, who is so dear to you, (answer'd she with a noble Pride and Fierceness, of which the King felt all the force) for this Favourite, so worthy to possess the most tender Affections of a great Prince, I assure you, that into whatever part of the World Fortune conducts me, I will not carry away the least Remembrance of him.' At these words she made a profound Reverence, and made such haste from his Presence, that he could not oppose her going if he would.

The King was now more strongly convinc'd than ever, that she favour'd the Passion of Don Pedro, and immediately went to Constantia, to inspire her with the same Thought; but she was not capable of receiving such Impressions, and following her own natural Inclinations, she generously defended the Virtue of his Actions. The King, angry to see her so well intentioned to her Rival, whom he would have had her hated, reproached her with the sweetness of her Temper, and went thence to mix his Anger with Don Alvaro's Rage, who was totally confounded when he saw the Negotiation of his Master had taken no effect. The haughty Maid braves me then, Sir, said he to the King, and despises the Honour which your Bounty offered her! Why cannot I resist so fatal a Passion? But I must love her, in spite of my self; and if this Flame consume me, I can find no way to extinguish it. What can I further do for you, replied the King? Alas, Sir, answered Don Alvaro, I must do by force, what I cannot otherwise hope from the proud and cruel Agnes. Well then, added the King, since it is not fit for me to authorize publickly a Violence in the midst of my Kingdom, chuse those of my Subjects whom you think most capable of serving you, and take away by force the Beauty that charms you; and if she do not yield to your Love, put that Power you are Master of in execution, to oblige her to marry you.

Don Alvaro, ravish'd with this Proposition, which at the same time flatter'd both his Love and his Anger, cast himself at the Feet of the King, and renewed his Acknowledgments by fresh Protestations, and thought of nothing but employing his unjust Authority against Agnes.

Don Pedro had been about three Months absent, when Alvaro undertook what the King counselled him to; tho' the Moderation was known to him, yet he feared his Presence, and would not attend the return of a Rival, with whom he would avoid all Disputes.

One Night, when the said Agnes, full of her ordinary Inquietudes, in vain expected the God of Sleep, she heard a Noise, and after saw some Men unknown enter her Chamber, whose Measures being well consulted, they carried her out of the Palace, and putting her in a close Coach, forced her out of Coimbra, without being hinder'd by any Obstacle. She knew not of whom to complain, nor whom to suspect: Don Alvaro seem'd too puissant to seek his Satisfaction this way; and she accus'd not the Prince of this attempt, of whom she had so favourable an Opinion: whatever she could think or say, she could not hinder her ill Fortune: They hurried her on with diligence, and before it was Day, were a considerable way off from the Town.

As soon as Day began to break, she surveyed those that encompassed her, without so much as knowing one of them; and seeing that her Cries and Prayers were all in vain with these deaf Ravishers, she satisfied her self with imploring the Protection of Heaven, and abandon'd herself to its Conduct.

While she sat thus overwhelmed with Grief, uncertain of her Destiny, she saw a Body of Horse advance towards the Troop which conducted her: the Ravishers did not shun them, thinking it to be Don Alvaro: but when he approached more near, they found it was the Prince of Portugal who was at the head of 'em, and who, without foreseeing the occasion that would offer it self of serving Agnes, was returning to Coimbra full of her Idea, after having performed what he ought in this Expedition.

Agnes, who did not expect him, changed now her Opinion, and thought that it was the Prince that had caused her to be stolen away. 'Oh, Sir! (said she to him, having still the same Thought) is it you that have torn me from the Princess? And could so cruel a Blow come from a Hand that is so dear to her? What will you do with an unfortunate Creature, who desires nothing but Death? And why will you obscure the Glory of your Life, by an Artifice unworthy of you?' This Language astonish'd the Prince no less than the sight of Agnes had done; he found by what she had said, that she was taken away by force; and immediately passing to the height of Rage, he made her understand by one only Look, that he was not the base Author of her trouble. 'I tear you from Constantia, whose only Pleasure you are! replied he: What Opinion have you of Don Pedro? No, Madam, tho' you see me here, I am altogether innocent of the Violence that has been done you; and there is nothing I will refuse to hinder it.' He then turned himself to behold the Ravishers, but his Presence had already scatter'd 'em, he order'd some of his Men to pursue 'em, and to seize some of 'em, that he might know what Authority it was that set 'em at work.

During this, Agnes was no less confus'd than before; she admir'd the Conduct of her Destiny, that brought the Prince at a time when he was so necessary to her. Her Inclinations to do him justice, soon repair'd the Offence her Suspicions had caus'd; she was glad to have escap'd a Misfortune, which appear'd certain to her: but this was not a sincere Joy, when she consider'd that her Lover was her Deliverer, and a Lover worthy of all her Acknowledgments, but who owed his Heart to the most amiable Princess in the World.

While the Prince's Men were pursuing the Ravishers of Agnes, he was left almost alone with her; and tho' he had always resolv'd to shun being so, yet his Constancy was not proof against so fair an Occasion: 'Madam, said he to her, is it possible that Men born amongst those that obey us, should be capable of offending you? I never thought my self destin'd to revenge such an Offence; but since Heaven has permitted you to receive it, I will either perish or make them repent it.' 'Sir, replied Agnes, more concern'd at this Discourse than at the Enterprize of Don Alvaro, those who are wanting in their respect to the Princess and you, are not obliged to have any for me. I do not in the least doubt that Don Alvaro was the undertaker of this Enterprize; and I judged what I ought to fear from him, by what his Importunities have already made me suffer. He is sure of the King's Protection, and he will make him an Accomplice in his Crime: but, Sir, Heaven conducted you hither happily for me, and I am indebted to you for the liberty I have of serving the Princess yet longer.' 'You will do for Constantia, replied the Prince, what 'tis impossible not to do for you; your Goodness attaches you to her, and my Destiny engages me to you for ever.'

The modest Agnes, who fear'd this Discourse as much as the Misfortune she had newly shunned, answer'd nothing but by down-cast Eyes; and the Prince, who knew the trouble she was in, left her to go to speak to his Men, who brought back one of those that belong'd to Don Alvaro, by whose

Confession he found the truth: He pardon'd him, thinking not fit to punish him, who obey'd a Man whom the Weakness of his Father had render'd powerful.

Afterwards they conducted Agnes back to Coimbra, where her Adventure began to make a great Noise: the Princess was ready to die with Despair, and at first thought it was only a continuation of the design this fair Maid had of retiring; but some Women that served her having told the Princess, that she was carried away by Violence, Constantia made her Complaint to the King, who regarded her not at all.

'Madam, said he to her, let this fatal Plague remove it self, who takes from you the Heart of your Husband; and without afflicting your self for her absence, bless Heaven and me for it.'

The generous Princess took Agnes's part with a great deal of Courage, and was then disputing her defence with the King, when Don Pedro arrived at Coimbra.

The first Object that met the Prince's Eyes was Don Alvaro, who was passing thro' one of the Courts of the Palace, amidst a Croud of Courtiers, whom his Favour with the King drew after him. This sight made Don Pedro rage; but that of the Princess and Agnes caus'd in Alvaro another sort of Emotion: He easily divin'd, that it was Don Pedro, who had taken her from his Men, and, if his Fury had acted what it would, it might have produc'd very sad effects.

'Don Alvaro, said the Prince to him, is it thus you make use of the Authority which the King my Father hath given you? Have you receiv'd Employments and Power from him, for no other end but to do these base Actions, and to commit Rapes on Ladies? Are you ignorant how the Princess interests her self in all that concerns this Maid? And do you not know the tender and affectionate Esteem she has for her.' No, replied Don Alvaro, (with an Insolence that had like to have put the Prince past all patience) 'I am not ignorant of it, nor of the Interest your Heart takes in her.' 'Base and treacherous as thou art, replied the Prince, neither the Favour which thou hast so much abused, nor the Insolence which makes thee speak this, should hinder me from punishing thee, wert thou worthy of my Sword; but there are other ways to humble thy Pride, and 'tis not fit for such an Arm as mine to seek so base an Employment to punish such a Slave as thou art.'

Don Pedro went away at these Words, and left Alvaro in a Rage, which is not to be express'd; despairing to see himself defeated in an Enterprize he thought so sure; and at the Contempt the Prince shewed him, he promis'd himself to sacrifice all to his Revenge.

Tho' the King lov'd his Son, he was so prepossessed against his Passion, that he could not pardon him what he had done, and condemn'd him as much for this last act of Justice, in delivering Agnes, as if it had been the greatest of Crimes.

Elvira, whom the sweetness of Hope flatter'd some moments, saw the return of Agnes with a sensible Displeasure, which suffer'd her to think of nothing but irritating her Brother.

In fine, the Prince saw the King, but instead of being receiv'd by him with a Joy due to the success of his Journey, he appear'd all sullen and out of humour. After having paid him his first Respects, and given him an exact account of what he had done, he spoke to him about the Violence committed against the Person of Agnes de Castro, and complain'd to him of it in the Name of the Princess, and of his own: 'You ought to be silent in this Affair, replied the King; and the Motive which makes you speak is so shameful for you, that I sigh and blush at it. What is it to you, if this Maid, whose Presence is troublesome to me, be removed hence, since 'tis I that desire it?' 'But, Sir, interrupted the Prince, what necessity is there of employing Force, Artifice, and the Night, when the least of your

Orders had been sufficient? Agnes would willingly have obey'd you; and if she continue at Coimbra, it is perhaps against her Will: but be it as it will, Sir, Constantia is offended, and if were not for fear of displeasing you, (the only thing that retains me) the Ravisher should not have gone unpunished.' 'How happy are you, replied the King, smiling with disdain, in making use of the Name of Constantia to uphold the Interest of your Heart! You think I am ignorant of it, and that this unhappy Princess looks on the Injury you do her with Indifference. Never speak to me more of Agnes, (with a Tone very severe.) Content your self, that I pardon what's past, and think maturely of the Considerations I have for Don Alvaro, when you would design any thing against him.' 'Yes, Sir, replied the Prince with fierceness, I will speak to you no more of Agnes; but Constantia and I will never suffer, that she should be any more expos'd to the Insolence of your Favourite.' The King had like to have broke out into a Rage at this Discourse: but he had yet a rest of Prudence left that hinder'd him. 'Retire (said he to Don Pedro) and go make Reflections on what my Power can do, and what you owe me.'

During this Conversation, Agnes was receiving from the Princess, and from all the Ladies of the Court, great Expressions of Joy and Friendship: Constantia saw again her Husband, with a great deal of satisfaction: and far from being sorry at what he had lately done for Agnes, she privately return'd him thanks for it, and still was the same towards him, notwithstanding all the Jealousy which was endeavour'd to be inspir'd in her.

Don Alvaro, who found in his Sister a Maliciousness worthy of his trust, did not conceal his Fury from her. After she had made vain attempts to moderate it, in blotting Agnes out of his Heart, seeing that his Disease was incurable, she made him understand, that so long as Constantia should not be jealous, there were no hopes: That if Agnes should once be suspected by her, she would not fail of abandoning her, and that then it would be easy to get Satisfaction, the Prince being now so proud of Constantia's Indulgency. In giving this Advice to her Brother, she promis'd to serve him effectually; and having no need of any body but her self to perform ill things, she recommended Don Alvaro to manage well the King.

Four Years were pass'd in that melancholy Station, and the Princess, besides her first dead Child, and Ferdinando, who was still living, had brought two Daughters into the World.

Some days after Don Pedro's return, Elvira, who was most dextrous in the Art of well-governing any wicked Design, did gain one of the Servants who belong'd to Constantia's Chamber. She first spoke her fair, then overwhelm'd her with Presents and Gifts; and finding in her as ill a Disposition as in her self, she readily resolv'd to employ her.

After she was sure of her, she compos'd a Letter, which was after writ over again in an unknown Hand, which she deposited in that Maid's Hands, that she might deliver to Constantia with the first Opportunity, telling her, that Agnes had drop'd it. This was the Substance of it:

I Employ not my own Hand to write to you, for Reasons that I shall   acquaint you with. How happy am I to have overcome all your   Scruples! And what Happiness shall I find in the Progress of our Intrigue! The whole Course of my Life shall continually represent to   you the Sincerity of my Affections; pray think on the secret   Conversation that I require of you: I dare not speak to you in publick, therefore let me conjure you here, by all that I have   suffer'd, to come to-night to the Place appointed, and speak to me   no more of Constantia; for she must be content with my Esteem, since my Heart can be only yours.

The unfaithful Portuguese serv'd Elvira exactly to her Desires; and the very next day seeing Agnes go out from the Princess, she carry'd Constantia the Letter; which she took, and found there what she was far from imagining: Tenderness never produc'd an Effect more full of grief, than what it made her suffer. 'Alas! they are both culpable, (said she, sighing) and in spite of the Defence my Heart would make for 'em, my Reason condemns 'em. Unhappy Princess, the sad subject of the Capriciousness of Fortune! Why dost not thou die, since thou hast not a Heart of Honour to revenge it self? O Don Pedro! why did you give me your Hand, without your Heart? And thou, fair, and ungrateful! wert thou born to be the Misfortune of my Life, and perhaps the only cause of my Death?' After having given some Moments to the Violence of her Grief, she called the Maid, who brought her the Letter, commanding her to speak of it to no body, and to suffer no one to enter into her Chamber.

She consider'd then of that Prince with more liberty, whose Soul she was not able to touch with the least Tenderness; and of the cruel Fair One that had betray'd her: Yet, even while her Soul was upon the Rack, she was willing to excuse 'em, and ready to do all she could for Don Pedro; at least, she made a firm Resolution, not to complain of him.

Elvira was not long without being inform'd of what had pass'd, nor of the Melancholy of the Princess, from whom she hop'd all she desir'd.

Agnes, far from foreseeing this Tempest, return'd to Constantia; and hearing of her Indisposition, pass'd the rest of the Day at her Chamber-door, that she might from time to time learn news of her Health: for she was not suffer'd to come in, at which Agnes was both surpriz'd and troubled. The Prince had the same Destiny, and was astonish'd at an Order which ought to have excepted him.

The next day Constantia appear'd, but so alter'd, that 'twas not difficult to imagine what she had suffer'd. Agnes was the most impatient to approach her, and the Princess could not forbear weeping, They were both silent for some time, and Constantia attributed this silence of Agnes to some Remorse which she felt: and this unhappy Maid being able to hold no longer; 'Is it possible, Madam, (said she) that two Days should have taken from me all the Goodness you had for me? What have I done? And for what do you punish me?' The Princess regarded her with a languishing Look, and return'd her no Answer but Sighs. Agnes, offended with this reserve, went out with very great Dissatisfaction and Anger; which contributed to her being thought criminal. The Prince came in immediately after, and found Constantia more disorder'd than usual, and conjur'd her in a most obliging manner to take care of her Health: The greatest good for me (said she) is not the Continuation of my Life; I should have more care of it if I loved you less: but - She could not proceed; and the Prince, excessively afflicted at her trouble, sigh'd sadly, without making her any answer, which redoubled her Grief. Spite then began to mix it self; and all things persuading the Princess that they made a Sacrifice of her, she would enter into no Explanation with her Husband, but suffered him to go away without saying any thing to him.

Nothing is more capable of troubling our Reason, and consuming our Health, than secret Notions of Jealousy in Solitude.

Constantia, who us'd to open her Heart freely to Agnes, now believing she had deceiv'd her, abandon'd her self so absolutely to Grief, that she was ready to sink under it; she immediately fell sick with the violence of it, and all the Court was concern'd at this Misfortune: Don Pedro was truly afflicted at it, but Agnes more than all the World beside. Constantia's Coldness towards her, made her continually sigh; and her Distemper created merely by fancy, caus'd her to reflect on every thing that offer'd it self to her Memory: so that at last she began even to fear her self, and to reproach her self for what the Princess suffer'd.

But the Distemper began to be such, that they fear'd Constantia's Death, and she her self began to feel the Approaches of it. This Thought did not at all disquiet her: she look'd on Death as the only relief from all her Torments; and regarded the Despair of all that approach'd her without the least concern.

The King, who lov'd her tenderly, and who knew her Virtue, was infinitely mov'd at the Extremity she was in. And Don Alvaro, who lost not the least Occasion of making him understand that it was Jealousy which was the cause of Constantia's Distemper, did but too much incense him against Criminals, worthy of Compassion. The King was not of a Temper to conceal his Anger long: 'You give fine Examples, (said he to the Prince) and such as will render your Memory illustrious! The Death of Constantia (of which you are only to be accus'd) is the unhappy Fruit of your guilty Passion. Fear Heaven after this: and behold your self as a Monster that does not deserve to see the Light. If the Interest you have in my Blood did not plead for you, what ought you not to fear from my just Resentment? But what must not imprudent Agnes, to whom nothing ties me, expect from my hands? If Constantia dies, she, who has the Boldness, in my Court, to cherish a foolish Flame by vain Hopes, and make us lose the most amiable Princess, whom thou art not worthy to possess, shall feel the Effects of her Indiscretion.'

Don Pedro knew very well, that Constantia was not ignorant of his Sentiments for Agnes; but he knew also with what Moderation she receiv'd it: He was very sensible of the King's Reproaches; but as his Fault was not voluntary, and that a commanding Power, a fatal Star, had forc'd him to love in spite of himself, he appear'd afflicted and confus'd: 'You condemn me, Sir, (answer'd he) without having well examin'd me; and if my Intentions were known to you; perhaps you would not find me so criminal: I would take the Princess for my Judge, whom you say I sacrifice, if she were in a condition to be consulted. If I am guilty of any Weakness, her Justice never reproach'd me for it; and my Tongue never inform'd Agnes of it. But suppose I have committed any Fault, why would you punish an innocent Lady, who perhaps condemns me for it as much as you? Ah, Villain! (interrupted the King) she has but too much favour'd you: You would not have lov'd thus long, had she not made you some Returns. Sir, (reply'd the Prince, pierced with Grief for the Outrage that was committed against Agnes) you offend a Virtue, than which nothing can be purer; and those Expressions which break from your Choler, are not worthy of you. Agnes never granted me any Favours; I never asked any of her; and I protest to Heaven, I never thought of any thing contrary to the Duty I owe Constantia.'

As they thus argued, one of the Princess's Women came all in Tears to acquaint Don Pedro, that the Princess was in the last Extremities of Life: 'Go see thy fatal Work, (said the King) and expect from a too-long patient Father the Usage thou deservest.'

The Prince ran to Constantia, whom he found dying, and Agnes in a swoon, in the Arms of some of the Ladies. What caus'd this double Calamity, was, that Agnes, who could suffer no longer the Indifferency of the Princess, had conjur'd her to tell her what was her Crime, and either to take her Life from her, or restore her to her Friendship.

Constantia, who found she must die, could no longer keep her secret Affliction from Agnes; and after some Words, which were a Preparation to the sad Explanation, she shewed her that fatal Billet, which Elvira had caus'd to be written: 'Ah, Madam! (cry'd out the fair Agnes, after having read it) Ah, Madam! how many cruel Inquietudes had you spared me had you open'd your Heart to me with your wonted Bounty! 'Tis easy to see that this Letter is counterfeit, and that I have Enemies without Compassion. Could you believe the Prince so imprudent, to make use of any other Hand but his own, on an occasion like this? And do you believe me so simple to keep about me this Testimony of my Shame, with so little Precaution? You are neither betray'd by your Husband nor me; I attest Heaven, and those Efforts I have made to leave Coimbra. Alas, my dear Princess, how little have you known her, whom you have so much honoured? Do not believe that when I have justify'd my self, I will have any more Communication with the World: No, no; there will be no Retreat far enough from hence for me. I will take care to hide this unlucky Face, where it shall be sure to do no more harm.'

The Princess touched at this Discourse, and the Tears of Agnes, press'd her hand, which she held in hers; and fixing Looks upon her capable of moving Pity in the most insensible Souls, 'If I have committed any Offence, my dear Agnes, (answer'd she) Death, which I expect in a moment, shall revenge it. I ought also to protest to you, That I have not ceas'd loving you, and that I believe every thing you have said, giving you back my most tender Affections.'

'Twas at this time that the Grief, which equally oppress'd 'em, put the Princess into such an Extremity, that they sent for the Prince. He came, and found himself almost without Life or Motion at this sight. And what secret Motive soever might call him to the aid of Agnes, 'twas to Constantia he ran. The Princess, who finding her last Moments drawing on, by a cold Sweat that cover'd her all over; and finding she had no more business with Life, and causing those Persons she most suspected to retire, 'Sir, (said she to Don Pedro) if I abandon Life without regret, it is not without Trouble that I part with you. But, Prince, we must vanquish when we come to die; and I will forget my self wholly, to think of nothing but of you. I have no Reproaches to make against you, knowing that 'tis Inclination that disposes Hearts, and not Reason. Agnes is beautiful enough to inspire the most ardent Passion, and virtuous enough to deserve the first Fortunes in the World. I ask her, once more, pardon for the Injustice I have done her, and recommend her to you, as a Person most dear to me. Promise me, my dear Prince, before I expire, to give her my Place in your Throne: it cannot be better fill'd: you cannot chuse a Princess more perfect for your People, nor a better Mother for our little Children. And you my dear and faithful Agnes (pursu'd she) listen not to a Virtue too scrupulous, that may make any opposition to the Prince of Portugal: Refuse him not a Heart of which he is worthy; and give him that Friendship which you had for me, with that which is due to his Merit. Take care of my little Fernando, and the two young Princesses: let them find me in you, and speak to them sometimes of me. Adieu, live both of you happy, and receive my last Embraces.'

The afflicted Agnes, who had recover'd a little her Forces, lost them again a second time; Her Weakness was follow'd with Convulsions so vehement, that they were afraid of her Life; but Don Pedro never removed from Constantia: 'What, Madam (said he) you will leave me then; and you think 'tis for my Good. Alas, Constantia! if my Heart has committed an Outrage against you, your Virtue has sufficiently revenged you on me in spite of you. Can you think me so barbarous?' As he was going on, he saw Death shut the Eyes of the most generous Princess for ever; and he was within a very little of following her.

But what Loads of Grief did this bring upon Agnes, when she found in that Interval, wherein Life and Death were struggling in her Soul, that Constantia was newly expir'd! She would then have taken away her own Life, and have let her Despair fully appear.

At the noise of the Death of the Princess, the Town and the Palace were all in Tears. Elvira, who saw then Don Pedro free to engage himself, repented of having contributed to the Death of Constantia; and thinking her self the Cause of it, promis'd in her Griefs never to pardon herself.

She had need of being guarded several days together; during which time she fail'd not incessantly to weep. And the Prince gave all those days to deepest Mourning. But when the first Emotions were past, those of his Love made him feel that he was still the same.

He was a long time without seeing Agnes; but this Absence of his served only to make her appear the more charming when he did see her.

Don Alvaro, who was afraid of the Liberty of the Prince, made new Efforts to move Agnes de Castro, who was now become insensible to every thing but Grief. Elvira, who was willing to make the best of the Design she had begun, consulted all her Womens Arts, and the Delicacy of her Wit, to revive the Flames with which the Prince once burnt for her: But his Constancy was bounded, and it was Agnes alone that was to reign over his Heart. She had taken a firm Resolution, since the Death of Constantia, to pass the rest of her Days in a solitary Retreat. In spite of the precaution she took to hide this Design, the Prince was informed of it, and did all he was able to dispose his Constancy and Fortitude to it. He thought himself stronger than he really was; but after he had well consulted his Heart, he found but too well how necessary the Presence of Agnes was to him. 'Madam (said he to her one day, with a Heart big, and his Eyes in Tears) which Action of my Life has made you determine my Death? Tho' I never told you how much I loved you, yet I am persuaded you are not ignorant of it. I was constrained to be silent during some Years for your sake, for Constantia's, and my own; but 'tis not possible for me to put this force upon my Heart for ever: I must once at least tell you how it languishes. Receive then the Assurances of a Passion, full of Respect and Ardour, with an offer of my Fortune, which I wish not better, but for your advantage.'

Agnes answer'd not immediately to these words, but with abundance of Tears; which having wiped away, and beholding Don Pedro with an air which made him easily comprehend she did not agree with his Desires; 'If I were capable of the Weakness with which you'd inspire me, you'd be obliged to punish me for it: What! (said she) Constantia is scarce bury'd, and you would have me offend her! No, my Prince (added she with more Softness) no, no, she whom you have heap'd so many Favours on, will not call down the Anger of Heaven, and the Contempt of Men upon her, by an Action so perfidious. Be not obstinate then in a Design in which I will never shew you Favour. You owe to Constantia, after her Death, a Fidelity that may justify you: and I, to repair the Ills I have made her suffer ought to shun all converse with you.' 'Go, Madam (reply'd the Prince, growing pale) go, and expect the News of my Death; in that part of the World, whither your Cruelty shall lead you, the News shall follow close after; you shall quickly hear of it: and I will go seek it in those Wars which reign among my Neighbours.'

These Words made the fair Agnes de Castro perceive that her Innocency was not so great as she imagined, and that her Heart interested it self in the Preservation of Don Pedro: 'You ought, Sir, to preserve your Life (reply'd Agnes) for the sake of the little Prince and Princesses, which Constantia has left you. Would you abandon their Youth (continued she, with a tender Tone) to the Cruelty of Don Alvaro? Live! Sir, live! and let the unhappy Agnes be the only Sacrifice.' 'Alas, cruel Maid! (interrupted Don Pedro) Why do you command me to live, if I cannot live with you? Is it an effect of your Hatred?' 'No, Sir, (reply'd Agnes) I do not hate you; and I wish to God that I could be able to defend my self against the Weakness with which I find my self possess'd. Oblige me to say no more, Sir: you see my Blushes, interpret them as you please: but consider yet, that the less Aversion I find I have to you, the more culpable I am; and that I ought no more to see, or speak to you. In fine, Sir, if you oppose my Retreat, I declare to you, that Don Alvaro, as odious as he is to me, shall serve for a Defence against you; and that I will sooner consent to marry a Man I abhor, than to favour a Passion that cost Constantia her Life.' 'Well then, Agnes (reply'd the Prince, with Looks all languishing and dying) follow the Motions which barbarous Virtue inspires you with; take these Measures you judge necessary against an unfortunate Lover, and enjoy the Glory of having cruelly refused me.'

At these Words he went away; and troubled as Agnes was, she would not stay him: Her Courage combated with her Grief, and she thought now, more than ever, of departing.

'Twas difficult for her to go out of Coimbra; and not to defer what appear'd to her so necessary, she went immediately to the Apartment of the King, notwithstanding the Interest of Don Alvaro. The King received her with a Countenance severe, not being able to consent to what she demanded: You shall not go hence, (said he) and if you are wise, you shall enjoy here with Don Alvaro both my Friendship and my Favour. I have taken another Resolution (answer'd Agnes) and the World has no part in it. You will accept Don Pedro (reply'd the King) his Fortune is sufficient to satisfy an ambitious Maid: but you will not succeed Constantia, who lov'd you so tenderly; and Spain has Princesses enough to fill up part of the Throne which I shall leave him. Sir, (reply'd Agnes, piqu'd at this Discourse) if I had a Disposition to love, and a Design to marry, perhaps the Prince might be the only Person on whom I would fix it: And you know, if my Ancestors did not possess Crowns, yet they were worthy to wear 'em. But let it be how it will, I am resolved to depart, and to remain no longer a Slave in a Place to which I came free.

This bold Answer, which shew'd the Character of Agnes, anger'd and astonished the King. You shall go when we think fit (reply'd he) and without being a Slave at Coimbra, you shall attend our order.

Agnes saw she must stay, and was so griev'd at it, that she kept her Chamber several days, without daring to inform herself of the Prince; and this Retirement spared her the Affliction of being visited by Don Alvaro.

During this, Don Pedro fell sick, and was in so great danger, that there was a general apprehension of his Death. Agnes did not in the least doubt, but it was an effect of his Discontent: she thought at first she had Strength and Resolution enough to see him die, rather than to favour him; but had she reflected a little, she had soon been convinc'd to the contrary. She found not in her Heart that cruel Constancy she thought there so well established: She felt Pains and Inquietude, shed Tears, made Wishes; and, in fine, discover'd that she lov'd.

'Twas impossible to see the Heir of the Crown, a Prince that deserved so well, even at the point of Death, without a general Affliction. The People who loved him, pass'd whole days at the Palace-gate to hear News of him: The Court was all over-whelm'd with Grief.

Don Alvaro knew very well how to conceal a malicious Joy, under an Appearance of Sadness. Elvira, full of Tenderness, and perhaps of Remorse, suffer'd also on her side. The King, altho' he condemned the Love of his Son, yet still had a Tenderness for him, and could not resolve to lose him. Agnes de Castro, who knew the Cause of his Distemper, expected the End of it with strange Anxieties: In fine, after a Month had pass'd away in Fears, they began to have a little hopes of his Recovery. The Prince and Don Alvaro were the only Persons that were not glad of it: But Agnes rejoic'd enough for all the rest.

Don Pedro, seeing that he must live whether he wou'd or no, thought of nothing but passing his days in melancholy and discontent: As soon as he was in a condition to walk, he sought out the most solitary Places, and gain'd so much upon his own Weakness, to go every where, where Agnes was not; but her Idea followed him always, and his Memory, faithful to represent her to him with all her Charms, render'd her always dangerous.

One day, when they had carry'd him into the Garden, he sought out a Labyrinth which was at the farthest part of it, to hide his Melancholy, during some hours; there he found the sad Agnes, whom Grief, little different from his, had brought thither; the sight of her whom he expected not, made him tremble: She saw by his pale and meagre Face the remains of his Distemper; his Eyes full of Languishment troubled her, and tho' her Desire was so great to have fled from him, an unknown Power stopt her, and 'twas impossible for her to go.

After some Moments of Silence, which many Sighs interrupted, Don Pedro rais'd himself from the Place where his Weakness had forced him to sit; he made Agnes see, as he approach'd her, the sad

Marks of his Sufferings: and not content with the Pity he saw in her Eyes, You have resolved my Death then, cruel Agnes, (said he) my desire was the same with yours; but Heaven has thought fit to reserve me for other Misfortunes, and I see you again, as unhappy, but more in love than ever.

There was no need of these Words to move Agnes to compassion, the Languishment of the Prince spoke enough; and the Heart of this fair Maid was but too much disposed to yield it self: She thought then that Constantia ought to be satisfy'd; Love, which combated for Don Pedro, triumphed over Friendship, and found that happy Moment, for which the Prince of Portugal, had so long sighed.

Do not reproach me, for that which has cost me more than you, Sir, (replied she) and do not accuse a Heart, which is neither ingrateful nor barbarous: and I must tell you, that I love you. But now I have made you that Confession, what is it farther that you require of me? Don Pedro, who expected not a Change so favourable, felt a double Satisfaction; and falling at the Feet of Agnes, he express'd more by the Silence his Passion created, than he could have done by the most eloquent Words.

After having known all his good Fortune, he then consulted with the amiable Agnes, what was to be feared from the King; they concluded that the cruel Billet, which so troubled the last days of Constantia, could come from none but Elvira and Don Alvaro. The Prince, who knew that his Father had searched already an Alliance for him, and was resolv'd on his Favourite's marrying Agnes, conjur'd her so tenderly to prevent these Persecutions, by consenting to a secret Marriage, that, after having a long time consider'd, she at last consented. I will do what you will have me (said she) tho' I presage nothing but fatal Events from it; all my Blood turns to Ice, when I think of this Marriage, and the Image of Constantia seems to hinder me from doing it.

The amorous Prince surmounted all her Scruples, and separated himself from Agnes, with a Satisfaction which soon redoubled his Forces; he saw her afterward with the Pleasure of a Mystery: And the Day of their Union being arrived, Don Gill, Bishop of Guarda, performed the Ceremony of the Marriage, in the Presence of several Witnesses, faithful to Don Pedro, who saw him Possessor of all the Charms of the fair Agnes.

She lived not the more peaceable for belonging to the Prince of Portugal; her Enemies, who continually persecuted her, left her not without Troubles: and the King, whom her Refusal inrag'd, laid his absolute Commands on her to marry Don Alvaro, with Threats to force her to it, if she continu'd rebellious.

The Prince took loudly her part; and this, join'd to the Refusal he made of marrying the Princess of Arragon, caus'd Suspicions of the Truth in the King his Father. He was seconded by those that were too much interested, not to unriddle this Secret. Don Alvaro and his Sister acted with so much care, gave so many Gifts, and made so many Promises, that they discover'd the secret Engagements of Don Pedro and Agnes.

The King wanted but little of breaking out into all the Rage and Fury so great a Disappointment could inspire him with, against the Princess. Don Alvaro, whose Love was changed into the most violent Hatred, appeased the first Transports of the King, by making him comprehend, that if they could break the Marriage of 'em, that would not be a sufficient Revenge; and so poison'd the Soul of the King, to consent to the Death of Agnes.

The barbarous Don Alvaro offered his Arm for this terrible Execution, and his Rage was Security for the Sacrifice.

The King, who thought the Glory of his Family disgraced by this Alliance, and his own in particular in the Procedure of his Son, gave full Power to this Murderer, to make the innocent Agnes a Victim to his Rage.

It was not easy to execute this horrid Design: Tho' the Prince saw Agnes but in secret, yet all his Cares were still awake for her, and he was marry'd to her above a Year, before Don Alvaro could find out an opportunity so long sought for.

The Prince diverted himself but little, and very rarely went far from Coimbra; but on a Day, an unfortunate Day, and marked out by Heaven for an unheard-of and horrid Assassination, he made a Party to hunt at a fine House, which the King of Portugal had near the City.

Agnes lov'd every thing that gave the Prince satisfaction; but a secret Trouble made her apprehend some Misfortune in this unhappy Journey. Sir, (said she to him, alarm'd, without knowing the Reason why) I tremble, seeing you today as it were designed the last of my Life: Preserve your self, my dear Prince; and tho' the Exercise you take be not very dangerous, beware of the least Hazards, and bring me back all that I trust with you. Don Pedro, who had never found her so handsome and so charming before, embraced her several times, and went out of the Palace with his Followers, with a Design not to return till the next Day.

He was no sooner gone, but the cruel Don Alvaro prepared himself for the Execution he had resolv'd on; he thought it of that importance, that it required more Hands than his own, and so chose for his Companions Don Lopez Pacheo, and Pedro Cuello, two Monsters like himself, whose Cruelty he was assur'd of by the Presents he had made 'em.

They waited the coming of the Night, and the lovely Agnes was in her first Sleep, which was the last of her Life, when these Assassins approach'd her Bed. Nothing made resistance to Don Alvaro, who could do every thing, and whom the blackest Furies introduced to Agnes; she waken'd, and opening her Curtains, saw, by the Candle burning in her Chamber, the Ponyard with which Don Alvaro was armed; he having his Face not cover'd, she easily knew him, and forgetting herself, to think of nothing but the Prince: Just Heaven (said she, lifting up her fine Eyes) if you will revenge Constantia, satisfy your self with my Blood only, and spare that of Don Pedro. The barbarous Man that heard her, gave her not time to say more; and finding he could never (by all he could do by Love) touch the Heart of the fair Agnes, he pierc'd it with his Ponyard: his Accomplices gave her several Wounds, tho' there was no necessity of so many to put an end to an innocent Life.

What a sad Spectacle was this for those who approach'd her Bed the next day! And what dismal News was this to the unfortunate Prince of Portugal! He returned to Coimbra at the first report of this Adventure, and saw what had certainly cost him his Life, if Men could die of Grief. After having a thousand times embraced the bloody Body of Agnes, and said all that a just Despair could inspire him with, he ran like a Mad-man into the Palace, demanding the Murderers of his Wife, of things that could not hear him. In fine, he saw the King, and without observing any respect, he gave a loose to his Resentment: after having rail'd a long time, overwhelm'd with Grief, he fell into a Swoon, which continu'd all that day. They carry'd him into his Apartment: and the King, believing that his Misfortune would prove his Cure, repented not of what he had permitted.

Don Alvaro, and the two other Assassins, quitted Coimbra. This Absence of theirs made 'em appear guilty of the Crime; for which the afflicted Prince vow'd a speedy Vengeance to the Ghost of his lovely Agnes, resolving to pursue them to the uttermost part of the Universe; He got a considerable number of Men together, sufficient to have made resistance, even to the King of Portugal himself, if he should yet take the part of the Murderers: with these he ravaged the whole Country, as far as the

Duero Waters, and carry'd on a War, even till the Death of the King, continually mixing Tears with Blood, which he gave to the revenge of his dearest Agnes.

Such was the deplorable End of the unfortunate Love of Don Pedro of Portugal, and of the fair Agnes de Castro, whose Remembrance he faithfully preserv'd in his Heart, even upon the Throne, to which he mounted by the Right of his Birth, after the Death of the King.

APHRA BEHN – A SHORT BIOGRAPHY

Aphra Behn was baptised on December 14th in 1640.

Although she was a prolific and well established writer in her own lifetime facts about her remain scant and difficult to confirm. What can safely be said though is that Aphra Behn is now regarded as a key English playwright and a major figure in Restoration theatre

In fact even where and to whom she was born are subject to discussion.

According to which account you read – and there are many – Aphra was born in Harbledown, near Canterbury. Another that she was born to a barber, John Amis and his wife Amy. Or again she was born to a couple named Cooper.

In the "The Histories And Novels of the Late Ingenious Mrs. Behn" (1696) it is written that Aphra was born to Bartholomew Johnson, a barber, and Elizabeth Denham, a wet-nurse. However a claim by Colonel Thomas Colepeper, who states he knew her as a child, wrote in Adversaria that she was born at "Sturry or Canterbury" to a Mr Johnson and that she had a sister named Frances. Anne Kingsmill Finch, Countess of Winchilsea, a poetic contemporary, says that Aphra was born in Wye in Kent, and was the 'Daughter to a Barber.'

None of these accounts can be relied upon and it follows that with so few facts the early part of her life cannot be clearly illustrated.

However what can be accurately suggested is that Aphra was born in the rising tensions to the English Civil War. Obviously a time of much division and difficulty as the King and Parliament, and their respective forces, came ever closer to conflict.

But still facts do not reveal themselves in any quantity. As a young woman a version exists of Aphra's journeying to Surinam with Bartholomew Johnson. He was said to have died on the journey, leaving his wife and children spending some months in the country. It is during this trip that Aphra claims to have met an African slave leader. These experiences formed the basis for one of her most famous works, "Oroonoko". In "Oroonoko" Behn Aphra gifts herself the position of narrator and her first biographer accepted the proposition that Aphra was indeed the daughter of the lieutenant general of Surinam, as in the story. There is little evidence to support this case, and none of her contemporaries acknowledge this, or any, aristocratic status. There is also no evidence that Oroonoko existed as an actual person or that any such slave revolt, is anything but an invention.

However it is possible that she acted a spy in the colony. Possibilities exist. Perhaps Aphra re-wrote her own history as and when it suited her needs at the time.

The common method of gathering information in these times was Church records and for a few, tax records. Aphra Behn is mentioned in neither. As well as Aphra Behn or Mrs Behn she was, at times, also known as Ann Behn, Mrs Bean, agent 160 and Astrea.

Shortly after her supposed return to England from Surinam in 1664, Aphra may have married Johan Behn (also written as Johann and John Behn). He could have been a merchant of German or Dutch extraction, possibly from Hamburg. He died or the couple separated that same year, however from this point we can be sure Aphra used the title "Mrs Behn" as her professional name.

There is some suggestion that Aphra may have been a Catholic or at least leaned towards this school of faith. She once commented that she was "designed for a nun." Many of those around her were Catholic, such as Henry Neville who was later arrested for his Catholicism, and this would have aroused suspicions during the anti-Catholic fervour of the 1680s. She was a monarchist, and her sympathy for the Stuarts, and particularly for the Catholic Duke of York may be demonstrated by her dedication of her play "The Rover, Part II" to him after he had been exiled for the second time. Aphra was dedicated to the restored King Charles II. As political parties emerged during this time, Aphra became a Tory supporter.

By 1666 Aphra had become attached to the court. Domestically the Plague was sweeping the Nation and the Great Fire was about to erupt through London. In foreign affairs England and the Netherlands had engaged in The Second Anglo-Dutch War from 1665. Aphra was recruited as a political spy in Antwerp on behalf of King Charles II, possibly in league with Thomas Killigrew.

This is probably the beginning of more accurate records on Aphra's life. Her code name is said to have been Astrea (though there are others), a name under which she later published many of her writings. Her chief duty was to establish a relationship with William Scot, son of Thomas Scot, a regicide who had been executed in 1660. Scot was believed to be ready to become a spy in the English service and to report on the activities of the English exiles who were thought to be plotting against the King. Aphra arrived in Bruges in July 1666 with a mission to secure Scot into a double agent, but there is evidence that Scot would betray her to the Dutch.

Aphra however found life as a spy not quite the romantic interlude that many assume would be the case. She arrived unprepared; the cost of living shocked her, and after a month, she had to pawn her jewellery. King Charles was slow in paying, either for her services or for her expenses whilst abroad. She had to borrow money so she could return to London, where she spent a year petitioning King Charles for payment unsuccessfully. A short while later a warrant was issued for her arrest, but little to suggest it was actually served or that she went to prison for her debt.

The death of her husband and her debts seemed to push her towards a more sustainable and substantial career. Aphra began work for the King's Company and the Duke's Company players as a scribe. These were, in fact, the only two licensed theatre groups in London. The theatres had been closed under Cromwell and were now re-opening under Charles II and a more liberal atmosphere. Theatre technology was being imported from Europe and being integrated into the staging of some plays. It was a great moment on which to embark upon a career in theatre.

Aphra who had previously only written poetry now embarked on such a career. Her first, "The Forc'd Marriage", was staged in 1670, followed by "The Amorous Prince" (1671). After her third play, "The Dutch Lover", fails to please Aphra had a three year lull in her writing career. Again it is speculated that she went travelling again, possibly once again as a spy.

After this sojourn her writing moves towards comic works, which prove commercially more successful. Her most popular works included "The Rover" and "Love-Letters Between a Nobleman and His Sister" (1684–87).

With her growing reputation Aphra became friends with many of the most notable writers of the day. This is The Age of Dryden and his literary dominance. As well as his friendship she includes also those of Elizabeth Barry, John Hoyle, Thomas Otway and Edward Ravenscroft, and was also attached to the circle of the Earl of Rochester.

Aphra often used her plays to attack the parliamentary Whigs claiming, "In public spirits call'd, good o' th' Commonwealth... So tho' by different ways the fever seize...in all 'tis one and the same mad disease." This was Aphra's criticism to parliament which had denied the king funds.

From the mid 1680's Aphra's health began to decline. This was exacerbated by her continual state of debt and descent into poverty.

In 1687 she published A Discovery of New Worlds, a translation of a French popularisation of astronomy, Entretiens sur la pluralité des mondes, by Bernard le Bovier de Fontenelle, written as a novel in a form similar to her own work, but with her new, religiously oriented preface.

As her end approached in 1689 it became increasingly hard for her to even hold a pen though her desire to continue to write was unquenchable. In her final days, she wrote the translation of the final book of Abraham Cowley's Six Books of Plants.

Aphra Behn died on April 16th 1689, and is buried in the East Cloister of Westminster Abbey. The inscription on her tombstone reads: "Here lies a Proof that Wit can never be Defence enough against Mortality." She was quoted as stating that she had led a "life dedicated to pleasure and poetry."

Her legacy is broad. Firstly as a woman she broke down many of the barriers which regarded only men as writers, especially in the commercial arena. In all she would write and have performed 19 plays, contribute to more, and become one of the first prolific, high-profile female dramatists in these Isles.

In her own golden age of the 1670s and 1680s she was one of the most productive playwrights in Britain, second only to the immense talents of the Poet Laureate John Dryden.

Much of her work has been criticised for its bawdy tone as well as its masculine form but needs must and she was working to live, to survive, and to widen her spread as an author.

She received widespread support from many other successful writers including Thomas Otway, Nahum Tate (also a Poet Laureate), Jacob Tonson, Nathaniel Lee and Thomas Creech.

Aphra is now rightly seen as a key dramatist of the seventeenth-century theatre. Her prose vitally important to the on-going development of the English novel.

Following Aphra's death new female dramatists such as 'Ariadne', Delarivier Manley, Mary Fix, Susanna Centlivre and Catherine Trotter acknowledged Behn as an inspiration who opened up the public space for women writers to be accepted.

In succeeding centuries her appreciation has been volatile. For instance in the morally reserved Victorian clime both the writer and her works were ignored or dismissed as indecent. The Victorian novelist and critic Julia Kavanagh wrote, "the disgrace of Aphra Behn is that, instead of raising man to woman's moral standard, she sank woman to the level of man's coarseness".

However by the 20th century, however, Aphra's fame was back in fashion. Since then her works have been well appreciated and her place in our literary pantheon assured.


APHRA BEHN – A CONCISE BIBLIOGRAPHY

Plays
The Forced Marriage (1670)
The Amorous Prince (1671)
The Dutch Lover (1673)
Abdelazer (1676)
The Town Fop (1676)
The Rover, Part I (1677)
Sir Patient Fancy (1678)
The Feigned Courtesans (1679)
The Young King (1679)
The False Count (1681)
The Rover, Part II (1681)
The Roundheads (1681)
The City Heiress (1682)
Like Father, Like Son (1682)
Prologue and Epilogue to Romulus and Hersilia, or The Sabine War (November 1682)
The Lucky Chance (1686) with composer John Blow
The Emperor of the Moon (1687)
The Widow Ranter (1689)
The Younger Brother (1696)

Novels
The Fair Jilt
Agnes de Castro
Love-Letters Between a Nobleman and His Sister (1684)
Oroonoko (1688)

Short Stories
The Fair Jilt (1688)
The History of the Nun: or, the Fair Vow-Breaker (1688)
The History of the Servant
The Lover-Boy of Germany
The Girl Who Loved the German Lover-Boy

Poetry Collections
Poems upon Several Occasions, with A Voyage to the Island of Love (1684)
Lycidus; or, The Lover in Fashion (1688)